HAVE
NEED BILLIONAIRE

BY
MAUREEN CHILD

AND

THE BOSS'S
BABY AFFAIR

BY
TESSA RADLEY

"If you can't be nice and at least *pretend* to smile, you'll just have to go away."

"Oh, for God's sake." Simon had had enough of this. He wasn't going to be chastised by anybody, least of all the short, curvy woman giving him a disgusted look.

He stalked across the small kitchen, plucked the baby from Tula's grasp and held Nathan up to eye level. The baby's pout disappeared as if it had never been and the two of them simply stared at each other.

In that instant Simon was lost. He knew even as he stood there, beneath Tula Barrons's less than approving stare, that this was his son and he would do whatever he had to in order to keep him. If this woman stood in his way, he'd roll right over her without a moment's pause. Something in his gaze must have given away his thoughts, because the small blonde lifted her chin, met his eyes in a bold stare and told him silently that she wouldn't give an inch. Fine. She'd learn soon enough that when Simon Bradley entered a contest—he never lost.

Dear Reader,

All writers are different. But for me, when I've finished writing a book, I'm satisfied with the way my characters' story has played out and I'm ready to move on.

Usually. But Tula Barrons was different. Tula first showed up in my story *The Wrong Brother*. Tula was my heroine Annie's best friend. And I loved her so much, I couldn't let her go until she had a story of her own.

So in *Have Baby, Need Billionaire*, Tallulah "Tula" Barrons gets her hero. Tula didn't have a great childhood, but she does have the best attitude ever. She's made her own life and she's happy with it. Until she inherits a baby and falls in love with that little boy's father. Simon Bradley doesn't know what hit him. Finding a son he didn't know about is a surprise, but the baby's guardian is the one who knocks him for a loop.

Simon is a rules guy. Tula has never met a rule she didn't break. Simon likes order and Tula thrives on chaos. Bringing these two very opposite people together was a lot of fun for me. And this time, when the book was finished, I was happy with Tula's story. I hope you are, too!

Follow me on Facebook, visit my website at www. maureenchild.com or write to me at PO Box 1883, Westminster, CA 92684-1883, USA.

Happy reading!

Maureen

HAVE BABY, NEED BILLIONAIRE

BY
MAUREEN CHILD

Published in Great Britain 2012
by Mills & Boon, an imprint of Harlequin (UK) Limited,
Eton House, 18-24 Paradise Road, Richmond, Surrey TW9 1SR

© Maureen Child 2011

ISBN: 978 0 263 89095 2

51-0112

Harlequin (UK) policy is to use papers that are natural, renewable and
recyclable products and made from wood grown in sustainable forests. The
logging and manufacturing processes conform to the legal environmental
regulations of the country of origin.

Printed and bound in Spain
by Blackprint CPI, Barcelona

Maureen Child is a California native who loves to travel. Every chance they get, she and her husband are taking off on another research trip. The author of more than sixty books, Maureen loves a happy ending and still swears that she has the best job in the world. She lives in Southern California with her husband, two children and a golden retriever with delusions of grandeur. Visit Maureen's website at www.maureenchild.com.

For Carter
He's never met the Lonely Bunny
But he loves the Little Critters

<u>One</u>

Simon Bradley didn't like surprises.

In his experience, any time a man let himself be taken unawares, disaster happened.

Order. Rules. He was a man of discipline. Which is why it only took one look at the woman standing in his office to know that *she* wasn't his kind of female.

Pretty though, he told himself, his gaze sweeping her up and down in a brisk, detailed look. She stood about five foot four and looked even shorter because she was so delicately made. She was tiny, really, with short blond hair that clung to her head in chunky layers that framed her face. Big silver hoops dangled from her ears and her wide blue eyes were fixed on him thoughtfully. Her mouth was curved in what appeared to be a permanent half smile and a single dimple winked at him from her right cheek. She wore black jeans, black boots and a bright red sweater that molded itself to her slight but curvy body.

He ignored the flash of purely male interest as he met her gaze and stood up behind his desk. "Ms. Barrons, is it? My assistant tells me you insisted on seeing me about something 'urgent'?"

"Yes, hi. And please, call me Tula," she said, her words tumbling from her delectable-looking mouth in a rush. She walked toward him, right hand extended.

His fingers folded over hers and he felt a sudden, intense surge of heat. Before he could really question it, she shook his hand briskly, then stepped back. Looking past him at the wide window behind him, she said, "Wow, that's quite a view. You can see all of San Francisco from here."

He didn't turn around to share the view. He watched her instead. His fingers were still buzzing and he rubbed them together to dissipate the sensation. No, she wasn't his type at all, but damned if he wasn't enjoying looking at her. "Not all, but a good part of it."

"Why don't you have your desk facing the window?"

"If I did that, I'd have my back to the door, wouldn't I?"

"Right." She nodded then shrugged. "Still, I think it'd be worth it."

Pretty, but disorganized, he thought. He glanced at his wristwatch. "Ms. Barrons—"

"Tula."

"Ms. Barrons," he said deliberately, "if you've come to talk about the view, I don't really have time for this. I've got a board meeting in fifteen minutes and—"

"Right. You're a busy man. I get that. And no, I didn't

come to talk about the view, I got a little distracted, that's all."

Distractions, he thought wryly, *are probably how this woman lives her life.* She was already letting her gaze slide around his office rather than getting to the point of her visit. He watched her as she took in the streamlined office furniture, the framed awards from the city and the professionally done photos of the other Bradley department stores across the country.

Pride rose up inside him as he, too, took a moment to admire those photos. Simon had worked hard for the last ten years to rebuild a family dynasty that his father had brought to the brink of ruin. In one short decade, Simon had not only regained ground lost, thanks to his father's sloppy business sense, he'd taken the Bradley family chain of upscale shopping centers further than anyone else ever had.

And he hadn't accomplished all of that by being distracted. Not even by a pretty woman.

"If you don't mind," he said, coming around his desk to escort her personally to the door, "I am rather busy today…."

She flashed him a full smile and Simon felt his heart take an odd, hard lurch in his chest. Her eyes lit up and that dimple in her cheek deepened and she was suddenly the most beautiful thing he'd ever seen. Shaken, Simon brushed that thought aside and told himself to get a grip.

"Sorry, sorry," Tula said, waving both hands in the air as if to erase her own tendency to get sidetracked. "I really am here to talk to you about something very important."

"All right then, what is it that's so urgent you vowed to

spend a week in my waiting area if you weren't allowed to speak to me immediately?"

She opened her mouth, shut it again, then suggested, "Maybe you should sit down."

"Ms. Barrons…"

"Fine," she said with a shake of her head. "Your call. But don't say I didn't warn you."

Pointedly, he glanced at his watch.

"I get it," she told him. "Busy man. You want it and you want it now. Okay then, here it is. Congratulations, Simon Bradley. You're a father."

He stiffened and any sense of courtesy went out the window along with his sense of bemused tolerance. "Your five minutes are up, Ms. Barrons." He took her elbow in a firm grip and steered her toward the door.

Her much shorter legs were moving fast, trying to either keep up or slow him down, he wasn't sure which. Either way, it didn't make a difference to him. Beautiful or not, whatever game she was playing, it wasn't going to work. Simon was no one's father and he damn well knew it.

"Hey!" She finally dug the heels of her boots into the lush carpet and slowed his progress a bit. "Wait a second! Geez, overreact much?"

"I'm not a father," he ground out tightly. "And trust me when I say that if I had ever slept with you, I would remember."

"I didn't say I was the baby's mother."

He didn't listen. Just kept moving toward the door at a relentless pace.

"I would have worked up to that little declaration slower, you know," she was babbling. "You're the one who wanted it direct and fast."

"I see. This was for my benefit."

"No, it's for your son's benefit, you boob."

He staggered a little in spite of knowing that she had to be lying. A son? Impossible.

She took advantage of the momentary pause in his forced march toward the door to break free of his grip and step back just out of reach. He was unsettled enough to let her go. He didn't know what she was trying to pull, but at the moment, her eyes looked soft but determined as she met his gaze.

"I realize this is coming as a complete shock to you. Heck, it would be for anybody."

Simon shook his head and narrowed his eyes on her. Enough of this. He didn't have a son and he wasn't going to fall for whatever moneygrubbing scheme she'd come up with in her delusional fantasies. Best to lay that on the line right from the start.

"I've never even seen you before, Ms. Barrons, so obviously, we don't have a child together. Next time you want to convince someone to pay for a child that doesn't exist, you might want to try it on someone you've actually slept with."

She blinked up at him in confusion, then a moment later she laughed. "No, no. I told you, I'm not the baby's mother. I'm the baby's aunt. But you're definitely his father. Nathan has your eyes and even that stubborn chin of yours. Which does not bode well, I suppose. But stubbornness can often be a good quality, don't you think?"

Nathan.

The imaginary baby had a name.

But that didn't make any of this situation real.

"This is insane," he told her. "You're obviously

after something, so why not just spill it and get it over with."

She was muttering to herself as she walked back to his desk and Simon was forced to follow her. "I had a speech all prepared, you know. You rushed me and everything's confused now."

"I think you're the only thing confused here," Simon told her, moving to pick up his phone and call security. They could escort her out and he'd be done with this and back to work.

"I'm not confused," she said. She read his expression and added, "I'm not crazy, either. Look, give me five minutes, okay?"

He hung up. Wasn't sure why. Maybe it was the gleam in her blue eyes. Maybe it was that tantalizing dimple that continued to show itself and disappear again. But if there was the slightest chance that what she was saying was true, then he owed it to himself to find out.

"All right," he said, checking his watch. "Five minutes."

"Okay." She took a deep breath and said, "Here we go. Do you remember dating a woman named Sherry Taylor about a year and a half ago?"

A thin thread of apprehension slithered through Simon as he searched his memory. "Yes," he said warily.

"Well…I'm Sherry's cousin, Tula Barrons. Actually, Tallulah, named after my grandmother, but that's such a hideous name that I go by Tula…."

He was hardly listening to her now. Instead his mind was focused on those nebulous memories of a woman in his past. Was it possible?

She took another steadying breath and said, "I know

this is hard to take in, but while you two were together, Sherry got pregnant. She gave birth to your son six months ago, in Long Beach."

"She *what?*"

"I know, I know. She should have told you," the woman said, lifting both hands as if to say it wasn't her fault. "I actually tried to convince her to tell you, but she said she didn't want to intrude on your life or anything, so…"

Intrude on his life.

That was an understatement. God, he could barely remember what the woman looked like. Simon rubbed at the spot between his eyes as if somehow that might clear up the foggy memories. But all he came up with was a vague image of a woman who had been in and out of his life in about two weeks' time.

And while he'd gone on his way without a backward glance, she'd been *pregnant?* With *his* child? And didn't even bother to *tell* him?

"What? Why? How?"

"All very good questions," she said, smiling at him again, this time in a sympathetic fashion. "I'm really sorry this is such a shock, but—"

Simon wasn't interested in her sympathy. He wanted answers. If he really did have a son, then he needed to know everything.

"Why now?" he demanded. "Why did your cousin wait until now to tell me, and why isn't she here herself?"

Her eyes filmed over and he had the horrifying thought that she was going to cry. Damn it. He hated when women cried. Made a man feel completely helpless. Not something he enjoyed at all. But a moment later, the woman had gotten control of her emotions and managed to stem the tide of those tears. Her eyes still glittered with them, but she refused to let them fall and Simon found, unexpectedly, that he admired her for it.

"Sherry died a couple of weeks ago," she said softly.

Another quick jolt of surprise in a morning that felt full of them. "I'm sorry," he said, knowing it sounded lame and clichéd, but what else was there to say?

"Thanks," she said. "It was a car accident. She died instantly."

"Look, Ms. Barrons…"

She sighed. "If I *beg,* will you please call me Tula?"

"Fine. Tula," he amended, thinking it really was the least he could do, considering. For the first time in a very long time, Simon had been caught completely off guard.

He wasn't sure how to react. His instinct, of course, was to find this baby and if it was his son, to claim him. But all he had was this stranger's word, along with memories that were too obscure to trust. Why in the hell would a woman get pregnant and not tell the baby's father? Why wouldn't she have come to him if that child really was his?

He scrubbed one hand across his jaw. "Look, I'm sorry to say, I don't really remember much about your cousin. We weren't together long. I don't see why you're so sure this baby is mine."

"Because Sherry named you on the baby's birth certificate."

"She gave the baby my name and didn't bother to tell me?" He didn't even know what to say to that.

"I know," she said, her tone soothing.

He didn't want to be soothed. Or understood. "She could have put anyone's name down," he pointed out.

"Sherry didn't lie."

Simon laughed at the ridiculousness of that statement. "Is that right?"

Tula winced. "All right, fine. She lied to you, but she wouldn't have lied to her son. She wouldn't have lied about Nathan's name."

"Why should I believe that the boy is mine?"

"You did have sex with her?"

Scowling, Simon admitted, "Well, yes, I did, but—"

"And you do know how babies are made, right?"

"That's very amusing."

"I'm not trying to be funny," she told him. "Just honest. Look, you can do a paternity test, but I can tell you that Sherry would never have named you as Nathan's father in her will if she wasn't sure."

"Her will?" The silent clang of a warning bell went off in his mind.

"Didn't I already tell you that part?"

"No."

She shook her head and dropped into one of the chairs angled in front of his desk. "Sorry. It's been a busy couple of weeks for me, what with Sherry's accident and arranging the funeral and closing up her house and moving the baby up here to my house in Crystal Bay."

Sensing that this was going to go on far longer than the original five minutes he'd allowed her, Simon walked around the edge of his desk and took a seat. At the very least, he was now in the position of power. He watched the pretty blonde and asked, "What about the will?"

Tula reached into the oversize black leather bag she had slung over her shoulder. She pulled out a large manila envelope and dropped it onto his desk. "That's a copy of Sherry's will. If you look, you'll see that I've been named temporary guardian of Nathan. Until I'm sure that you're ready to be the baby's father."

Her voice, her words, were no more than a buzz of sound in his head. He read through the will quickly, scanning until he found the provisions for the child Sherry had named as his. *Custody of minor, Nathan Taylor, goes to the child's father, Simon Bradley.*

He sat back in his chair and kept rereading those words until he was fairly certain they'd been burned into his brain. Was this true? Was he a father?

Lifting his gaze to hers, Simon found Tula Barrons studying him through those wide, brilliant blue eyes. She was waiting for him to say something.

Damned if he knew what it should be.

He'd been careful, always, in his relationships with women. He'd had no desire to be a father. And yet he had a vague memory of being with Sherry Taylor. The woman herself was hardly more than a smudge in his memories—but he did remember the night the condom had broken. A man didn't forget things like that. But she'd never said anything about a baby, so he'd forgotten about the incident.

It was possible.

He might really have a son.

Tula watched as Simon Bradley came to terms with a whole new reality.

She gave him points. Sure, he'd been a little edgy, temperamental…all right, *rude,* at first. But she supposed that was to be expected. After all, it wasn't every day you found out you were a father, for heaven's sake.

Her gaze moved over him while he was reading the

will and Tula had to admit that he wasn't at all what she'd been expecting. She and her cousin Sherry hadn't been close, by any means, but Tula would have bet that she would at least know Sherry's taste in men.

And tall, dark, gorgeous and crabby wasn't it. Normally, Sherry had gone for the quiet, sweet, geeky type. Simon was about as far from that description as a man could get. He practically radiated power, strength. Ever since she had walked into the room, Tula had felt a sizzle of attraction for him that she was still battling. She so didn't need yet one more complication at the moment.

"What exactly is it you want from me?"

His voice shattered her thoughts and she met his gaze. "I should think that would be obvious."

He dropped the sheaf of papers to his desktop. "Well, you would be wrong."

"Okay, how about this? Why don't you come out to my place in Crystal Bay? Meet your son. Then we can talk and figure out our next move together."

He scrubbed one hand across the back of his neck. She'd dumped a lot of information on him all at once, Tula told herself. Of course he was going to need a little time to acclimate.

"Fine," he said at last. "What's your address?"

She told him, then watched as he stood up behind his desk in a clear signal of dismissal. Well, that was all right with her. She had things to do anyway and what more was there to say at the moment? Tula stood up, too, and held her right hand out toward him.

A moment's pause, then his hand engulfed hers. Again, just as it had happened earlier, the instant their palms met a bolt of heat shot up her arm and ricocheted around her chest like a manic Ping-Pong ball. He must have felt the same thing because he dropped her hand and shoved his own into his pocket.

She took a breath, blew it out and forced a smile that felt wobbly. "I'll see you tonight then."

As she left, Tula felt his gaze on her and the heat engendered by his stare stayed with her on the long ride home.

Two

"How'd it go?"

Tula smiled at the sound of her best friend's voice. Anna Cameron Hale was the one human being on the face of the planet that Tula could count on being on her side. So, naturally, the moment she'd returned from San Francisco and facing down Simon Bradley, she dialed Anna's number.

"About as you'd expect."

"Ouch," Anna said. "So he had no idea about the baby?"

"Nope." Tula turned to look at Nathan, sitting in his bouncy seat. The babysitter, Mrs. Klein, had said that the baby was "good as gold" the whole time she was gone. Now, as he bounced and pushed off with his toes, the springs squeaked into motion, jolting him up and down in the small kitchen.

Tula's heart gave a little Nathan-caused twinge that she was starting to get used to. How was it possible to love someone so much in the span of a couple of short weeks?

"In his defense, it must have been a shock for him to be faced with this out of the blue," Anna said.

"True. I mean I knew about Nathan and it was still a stunner when Sherry died and suddenly I'm responsible for him." Although, she thought, it hadn't taken more than five minutes for her to adjust. "But when I told Simon, he looked like he'd been hit with a two-by-four."

"God, honey, I'm sorry it didn't go well. So what do you do now?"

"He's coming here tonight to meet Nathan and then we're going to talk." Tula thought briefly about the little buzz of sensation she'd received when he shook her hand and then pushed that thought right out of her mind. There was already plenty going on at the moment. She *so* didn't need anything else to think about.

But her mind couldn't quite keep from remembering him as he stood over her, all fierce and furious.

"He's going to your house?" Anna asked.

Tula shook her head and paid attention. "Yeah, why?"

"Nothing. But maybe I could come over and help you get ready."

She knew exactly what Anna was thinking and Tula couldn't help laughing. "You are not coming over to clean my house. He's not visiting royalty or something."

Anna laughed, too. "Fine. Just warn him when he walks in to watch where he steps."

Tula stepped away from the kitchen counter and shot

a look into her tiny living room. Toys littered the floor, her laptop was sitting open on the coffee table and her latest manuscript was beside it. She was doing revisions for her editor and when she was working, other things— like picking up clutter—tended to go by the wayside.

Shrugging, she silently admitted that though her house was clean, it did tend to get a little messy. Especially now that she had Nathan living with her. She hadn't had any idea just how much *stuff* came along with a baby.

"Why did I call you again?" Tula asked.

"Because I'm your best friend and you know you need me."

"Right, that was it." Tula smiled and reached out one hand to smooth the wispy hairs on the top of Nathan's head as he scooted past, babbling happily. "It was weird, Anna. Simon was crabby and rude and dismissive and yet…"

"Yet *what?*" Anna prompted.

There was a buzz of interest, Tula thought but didn't say. She hadn't expected it, hadn't wanted it, but hadn't been able to ignore it, either. The suit-and-tie kind of guy was *so* not what she was interested in. And for heaven's sake, the last thing she needed was to be attracted to Nathan's father. This situation was hard enough. Yet she couldn't deny the flash of heat that had flooded her system the moment her hand had met his.

Didn't mean she had to do anything about it though, she assured herself firmly.

"Hello?" Anna said. "Finish what you were saying! What comes after the 'yet'?"

"Nothing," Tula said with sudden determination. One thing she didn't need was to indulge in an attraction for a man she had nothing in common with but a baby they were both responsible for. "Absolutely nothing."

"And you expect me to just accept that?"

"As my friend, I'm asking you to, yeah."

Anna sighed dramatically. "Fine. I will. For *now*."

"Thanks." She'd accept the reprieve, even though she knew that Anna wouldn't let it go forever.

"So what're you going to do tonight?"

"Simon comes here and we talk about Nathan. Set something up so that he can get to know the baby and I can watch them together. I can handle Simon," she said a moment later and wasn't sure whether she was trying to convince Anna or herself. "I grew up around men like him, remember?"

"Tula, not every man who wears a suit is like your dad."

"Not all," she allowed, "but most."

She was in the position to know. Her entire family had practically been born wearing business suits. They lived stuffy, insular lives built around making and keeping money. Tula was half convinced that they didn't even know a world existed beyond their own narrow portion of it.

For example, she knew what Simon Bradley would think of her tiny, cluttered, bayside home because she knew exactly what her father would have thought of it—if he'd ever deigned to visit. He would have thought it too old, too small. He would have hated the bright blue walls and yellow trim in the living room. He'd have loathed the mural of the circus that decorated her bathroom wall. Mostly though, he would have seen her living there as a disgrace.

She had the distinct impression that Simon wouldn't be any different.

"Look, the reality is it doesn't matter what Nathan's father thinks of me or my house. Our only connection is the baby." As she spoke, she told her hormones to listen up. "So I'm not going to put on a show and change my life in any way to try to convince a man I don't even know that I am who I'm not."

A long second passed, then Anna laughed gently. "What does it say about me that I completely understood that?"

"That we've been friends too long?"

"Probably," Anna agreed. "Which is how I know you're making rosemary chicken tonight."

Tula smiled. Anna did know her too well. Rosemary chicken was her go-to meal when she was having company. And unless Simon was a vegetarian, everything would go great. Oh, God—what if he *was* a vegetarian? No, she thought. Men like him did lunch at steak houses with clients. "You've got me there. And once we have dinner, I'll talk to Simon about setting up a schedule for him to get to know Nathan."

"You?" Anna laughed. "A schedule?"

"I can be organized," she argued, though her words didn't carry a lot of confidence. "I just choose to not be."

"Uh-huh. How's the baby?"

Everything in Tula softened. "He's wonderful." Her gaze followed the tiny boy as he continued on his path around the kitchen, laughing and making noises as he explored his world. "Honestly, he's such a good baby. And he's so smart. This morning I asked him where his nose was and he pointed right to it."

Well, he had been waving his stuffed bunny in the air and hit himself in the face with it, but close enough.

"Harvard-bound already."

"I'll sign him up on the waiting list tomorrow," Tula agreed with a laugh. "Look, I gotta go. Get the chicken in the oven, give Nathan a bath and...ooh, maybe myself, too."

"Okay, but call me tomorrow. Let me know how it goes."

"I will." She hung up, leaned against the kitchen counter and let her gaze slide over the bright yellow kitchen. It was small but cheerful, with white cabinets, a bright blue counter and copper-bottomed pans hanging from a rack over the stove.

She loved her house. She loved her life.

And she loved that baby.

Simon Bradley was going to have to work very hard to convince her that he was worthy of being Nathan's father.

The scent of rosemary filled the little house by the bay a few hours later.

Tula danced around the kitchen to the classic rock tunes pouring from the radio on the counter and every few steps, she stopped to steal a kiss from the baby in the high chair. Nathan giggled at her, a deep, full-belly laugh that tickled at the edges of Tula's heart.

"Funny guy," she whispered, planting a kiss on top of his head and inhaling the sweet, clean scent of him. "Laughing at my dance moves isn't usually the way to my heart, you know."

He gave her another grin and kicked his fat legs in excitement.

Tula sighed and smoothed her hand across the baby's wisps of dark hair. Two weeks he'd been a part of her life and already she couldn't imagine her world without him in it. The moment she'd picked him up for the first time, Nathan had carved away a piece of her heart and she knew she'd never get it back.

Now she was supposed to hand him over to a man who would no doubt raise Nathan in the strict, rarified world in which she'd been raised. How could she stand it? How could she sentence this sweet baby to a regimented lifestyle just like the one she'd escaped?

And how could she avoid it?

She couldn't.

Which meant she had only one option. If she couldn't stop Simon from eventually having custody of Nathan—then she'd just have to find a way to loosen Simon up. She'd loosen Simon up, break him out of the world of "suits" so that he wouldn't do to Nathan what her father had tried to do to her.

Looking down into the baby's smiling eyes, she made a promise. "I'll make sure he knows how to have fun, Nathan. Don't you worry. I won't let him make you wear a toddler business suit to preschool."

The baby slapped one hand down onto a pile of dry breakfast cereal on the food tray, sending tiny O's skittering across the kitchen.

"Glad you agree," she said as she bent down, scraped them up into her hand and tossed them into the sink. Then she washed her hands and came back to the baby. "Your daddy's coming here soon, Nathan. He'll probably be crabby and stuffy, so don't let that bother you. It won't last for long. We're going to change him, little man. For his own good. Not to mention *yours*."

He grinned at her.

"Attaboy," she said and bent for another quick kiss just as the doorbell sounded. Her stomach gave a quick spin that had her taking a deep breath to try to steady it. "He's here. You're all strapped in, so you're safe. Just be good for a second and I'll go let him in."

She didn't like leaving Nathan alone in the high chair, even though he was belted in tightly. So Tula hurried across the toy-cluttered floor of her small living room and wondered how it had gotten so messy again. She'd straightened it up earlier. Then she remembered she and the baby playing after she put the chicken in the oven and—too late to worry about it now. She threw open the door and nearly gulped.

Simon was standing there, somehow taller than she remembered. He wasn't wearing a suit, either, which gave her a jolt of surprise. She got another jolt when she realized just how good he looked when he pried himself out of the sleek lines of his business "uniform." Casual in a charcoal-gray sweater, black jeans and cross trainers, he actually looked even more gorgeous, which was just disconcerting. He looked so…different. The only thing familiar about him was the scowl.

When she caught herself just staring at him like a big dummy, she said quickly, "Hi. Come on in. Baby's in the kitchen and I don't want to leave him alone, so close the door, will you, it's cold out there."

Simon opened his mouth to speak, but the damn woman was already gone. She'd left him standing on the porch and raced off before he could so much as say hello. Of course, he'd had the chance to speak, he simply hadn't. He'd been caught up in looking at her. Just as he had earlier that day in his office.

Those big blue eyes of hers were...mesmerizing somehow. Every time he looked into them, he forgot what he was thinking and lost himself for a moment or two. Not something he wanted to admit, even to himself, but there it was. Frowning, he reminded himself that he'd come to her house to set down some rules. To make sure Tula Barrons understood exactly how this bizarre situation was going to progress. Instead, he was standing on the front porch, thinking about just how good a woman could look in a pair of faded blue jeans.

Swallowing the stab of irritation at himself, he followed after her. Tula wasn't his main concern here, after all. He was here because of the child. His son? He was having a hard time believing it was possible, but he couldn't walk away from this until he knew for sure. Because if the baby was his, there was no way he would allow his child to be raised by someone else.

He'd been thinking about little else but this woman and the child she said belonged to him since she'd left his office that morning. With his concentration so unfocused, he'd finally given up on getting any work done and had gone to see his lawyer.

After that illuminating little visit, he'd spent the last couple of hours thinking back to the brief time he'd spent with Sherry Taylor. He still didn't remember much about her, but he had to admit that there was at least the possibility that her child was his.

Which was why he was here. He stepped inside and his foot came down on something that protested with a loud *squeak*. He glanced down at the rubber reindeer and shook his head as he closed the door. His gaze swept the interior of the small house and he shook his head. If more than two people were in the damn living room, they wouldn't be able to breathe at the same time. The house was old and small and…bright, he thought, giving the nearly electric blue walls an astonished glance.

The blue walls boasted dark yellow molding that ran around the circumference of the room at the ceiling. There was a short sofa and one chair drawn up in front of a hearth where a tiny blaze sputtered and spat from behind a wrought-iron screen. Toys were strewn across the floor as if a hurricane had swept through and there was a narrow staircase on the far wall leading to what he assumed was an even tinier second story.

The whole place was a dollhouse. He almost felt like Gulliver. Still frowning, he heard Tula in the kitchen, talking in a singsong voice people invariably tended to use around babies. He told himself to go on in there, but he didn't move. It was as if his feet were nailed to the wood floor. It wasn't that he was afraid of the baby or anything, but Simon knew damn well that the moment he saw the child, his world as he knew it would cease to exist.

If this baby were his son, nothing would ever be the same again.

A child's bubble of laughter erupted in the other room and Simon took a breath and held it. Something inside him tightened and he told himself to move on. To get this first meeting over so that plans could be made, strategies devised.

But he didn't move. Instead, he noticed the framed drawings and paintings on the walls, most of which were of a lop-eared bunny in different poses. Why the woman would choose to display such childish paintings was beyond him, but Tula Barrons, he was discovering, was different from any other woman he'd ever known.

The child laughed again.

Simon nodded to himself and followed the sound and the amazing scents in the air to the kitchen.

It didn't take him long.

Three long strides had him leaving the living room and entering a bright yellow room that was about the size of his walk-in closet at home. Again, he felt as out of place as a beer at a wine tasting. This whole house seemed to have been built for tiny people and a man his size was bound to feel as if he had to hunch his shoulders to keep from rapping his head on the ceiling.

He noted that the kitchen was clean but as cluttered as the living room. Canisters lined up on the counter beside a small microwave and an even smaller TV. Cupboard doors were made of glass, displaying ancient china stacked neatly. A basket with clean baby clothes waiting to be folded was standing on the table for two and the smells pouring from the oven had his mouth watering and his stomach rumbling in response.

Then his gaze dropped on Tula Barrons as she straightened up, holding the baby she'd just taken from a high chair in her arms. She settled the chubby baby on her right hip, gave Simon a brilliant smile and said, "Here he is. Your son."

Simon's gaze locked on the boy who was staring at him out of a pair of eyes too much like his own to deny. His lawyer had advised him to do nothing until a paternity test had been arranged. But Harry had always been too cautious, which was why he made such a great lawyer. Simon tended to go with his gut on big decisions and that instinct had never let him down yet.

So he'd come here mainly to see the baby for himself before arranging for the paternity test his lawyer wanted.

Because Simon had half convinced himself that there was no way this baby was his.

But one look at the boy changed all that. He was stubborn, Simon admitted silently, but he wasn't blind. The baby looked enough like him that no paternity test should be required—though he'd get one anyway. He'd been a businessman too long to do anything but follow the rules and do things in a logical, reasonable manner.

"Nathan," Tula said, glancing from the baby on her hip to Simon, "this is your daddy. Simon, meet your son."

She started toward him and Simon quickly held up one hand to keep her where she was. Tula stopped dead, gave him a quizzical look and tipped her head to one side to watch him. "What's wrong?"

What wasn't? His heart was racing, his stomach was churning. How the hell had this happened? he wondered. How had he made a child and been unaware of the boy's existence? Why had the baby's mother kept him a secret? Damn it, he had had the right to know. To be there for his son's birth. To see him draw his first breath. To watch him as he woke up to the world.

And it had all been stolen from him.

"Just…give me a minute, all right?" Simon stared at the tiny boy, trying to ignore the less-than-pleased expression on Tula Barrons's face. Didn't matter what she thought of him, did it? The important thing here was that Simon's entire world had just taken a sharp right turn.

A father.

He was a father.

Pride and something not unlike sheer panic roared

through him at a matching pace. His gaze locked on the boy, he noticed the dark brown hair, the brown eyes—exact same shade as Simon's own—and, finally, he noticed the baby's lower lip beginning to pout.

"You're making him cry." Tula jiggled the baby while patting him on the back gently.

"I'm not doing anything."

"You look angry and babies are very sensitive to moods around them," she said and soothed the boy by swaying in place and whispering softly. Keeping her voice quiet and singsongy, she snapped, "Honestly, is that scowl a permanent fixture on your face?"

"I'm not—"

"Would it physically kill you to smile at him?"

Frustrated and just a little pissed because he had to admit that she was at least partially right, Simon assumed what he hoped was a reassuring smile.

She rolled her eyes and laughed. "That's the best you've got?"

He kept his voice low, but didn't bother to hide his irritation. "You might want to back off now."

"I don't see why I should," she countered, her voice pleasant despite her words. "Sherry left *me* as guardian for Nathan and I don't like how you're treating him."

"I haven't done anything."

"Exactly," she said with a sharp nod. "You won't even let him get near you. Honestly, haven't you ever seen a child before?"

"Of course I have, I'm just—"

"Shocked? Confused? Worried?" she asked, then continued on before he could speak. "Well, imagine how Nathan must feel. His mother's gone. His home is gone.

He's in a strange place with strangers taking care of him and now there's a big mean bully glaring at him."

He stiffened. "Now just a damn min—"

"Don't swear in front of the baby."

Simon inhaled sharply and shot her a glare he usually reserved for employees he wanted to terrify into improving their work skills, fully expecting her to have the sense to back off. Naturally, she paid no attention to him.

"If you can't be nice and at least *pretend* to smile, you'll just have to go away," she said. Then she spoke to the baby. "Don't you worry, sweetie, Tula won't let the mean man get you."

"I'm not a mean—oh, for God's sake." Simon had had enough of this. He wasn't going to be chastised by anybody, least of all the short, curvy woman giving him a disgusted look.

He stalked across the small kitchen, plucked the baby from her grasp and held Nathan up to eye level. The baby's pout disappeared as if it had never been and the two of them simply stared at each other.

The baby was a solid, warm weight in his hands. Little legs pumped, arms waved and a thin line of drool dripped from his mouth when he gave his father a toothless grin. His chest tight, Simon felt the baby's heartbeat racing beneath his hands and there was a... connection that he'd never felt before. It was basic. Complete. Staggering.

In that instant—that heart-stopping, mind-numbing second—Simon was lost.

He knew it even as he stood there, beneath Tula Barrons's less than approving stare, that this was his son and he would do whatever he had to to keep him.

If this woman stood in his way, he'd roll right over her without a moment's pause. Something in his gaze must have given away his thoughts because the small blonde lifted her chin, met his eyes in a bold stare and told him silently that she wouldn't give an inch.

Fine.

She'd learn soon enough that when Simon Bradley entered a contest—he never lost.

Three

"You're holding him like he's a hand grenade about to explode," the woman said, ending their silent battle.

Despite that swift, sure connection he felt to the child in his arms, Simon wasn't certain at all that the baby wouldn't explode. Or cry. Or expel some gross fluid. "I'm being careful."

"Okay," she said and pulled out a chair to sit down.

He glanced at her, then looked back to the baby. Carefully, Simon eased down onto the other chair pulled up to the postage-stamp-sized table. It looked so narrow and fragile, he almost expected it to shatter under his weight, but it held. He felt clumsy and oversize. As if he were the only grown-up at a little girl's tea party. He had to wonder if the woman had arranged for him to feel out of place. If she was subtly trying to sabotage this first meeting.

Gently, he balanced the baby on his knee and kept one hand on the small boy's back to hold him in place. Only then did he look up at the woman sitting opposite him.

Her big eyes were fixed on him and a half smile tugged at the corner of her mouth, causing that one dimple to flash at him. She'd gone from looking at him as if he were the devil himself to an expression of amused benevolence that he didn't like any better.

"Enjoying yourself?" he asked tightly.

"Actually," she admitted, "I am."

"So happy to entertain you."

"Oh, you're really not happy," she said, her smile quickening briefly again. "But that's okay. You had me worried, I can tell you."

"Worried about what?"

"Well, how you were going to be with Nathan," she told him, leaning against the ladder back of the chair. She crossed her arms over her chest, unconsciously lifting her nicely rounded breasts. "When you first saw him, you looked…"

"Yes?" Simon glanced down when Nathan slapped both chubby fists onto the tabletop.

"…terrified," she finished.

Well, that was humiliating. And untrue, he assured himself. "I wasn't scared."

"Sure you were." She shrugged and apparently was dialing back her mistrust. "And who could blame you? You should have seen me the first time I picked him up. I was so worried about dropping him I had him in a stranglehold."

Nothing in Simon's life had terrified him like that first moment holding a son he didn't know he had. But he wasn't about to admit to that. Not to Tula Barrons at any rate.

He shifted around uncomfortably on the narrow chair. How did an adult sit on one of these things?

"Plus," she added, "you don't look like you want to bite through a brick or something anymore."

Simon sighed. "Are you always so brutally honest?"

"Usually," she said. "Saves a lot of time later, don't you think? Besides, if you lie, then you have to remember what lie you told to who and that just sounds exhausting."

Intriguing woman, he thought while his body was noticing other things about her. Like the way her dark green sweater clung to her breasts. Or how tight her faded jeans were. And the fact that she was barefoot, her toenails were a deep, sexy red and she was wearing a silver toe ring that was somehow incredibly sexy.

She was *nothing* like the kind of woman Simon was used to. The kind Simon preferred, he told himself sternly. Yet, there was something magnetic about her. *Something—*

"Are you just going to stare at me all night or were you going to speak?"

—Irritating.

"Yes, I'm going to speak," he said, annoyed to have been caught watching her so intently. "As a matter of fact, I have a lot to say."

"Good, me too!" She stood up, took the baby from him before he could even begin to protest—not that he would have—and set the small boy back in his high chair. Once she had the safety straps fastened, she shot Simon a quick smile.

"I thought we could talk while we have dinner. I made chicken and I'm a good cook."

"Another truth?"

"Try it for yourself and see."

"All right. Thank you."

"See, we're getting along great already." She moved around the kitchen with an economy of motions. Not surprising, Simon thought, since there wasn't much floor space to maneuver around.

"Tell me about yourself, Simon," she said and reached over to place some sliced bananas on the baby's food tray. Instantly, Nathan chortled, grabbed one of the pieces of fruit and squished it in his fist.

"He's not eating that," Simon pointed out while she walked over to take the roast chicken out of the oven.

"He likes playing with it."

Simon took a whiff of the tantalizing, scented steam wafting from the oven and had to force himself to say, "He shouldn't play with his food though."

She swiveled her head to look at him. "He's a baby."

"Yes, but—"

"Well, all of my cloth napkins are in the laundry and they don't make tuxedos in size six-to-nine months."

He frowned at her. She'd deliberately misinterpreted what he was saying.

"Relax, Simon. He's fine. I promise you he won't smoosh his bananas when he's in college."

She was right, of course, which he didn't really enjoy admitting. But he wasn't used to people arguing with him, either. He was more accustomed to people rushing to please him. To anticipate his every need. He was not used to being corrected and he didn't much like it.

As that thought raced through his head, he winced. God, he sounded like an arrogant prig even in his own mind.

"So, you were saying…"

"Hmm?" he asked. "What?"

"You were telling me about yourself," she prodded as she got down plates, wineglasses and then delved into a drawer for silverware. She had the table set before he gathered his thoughts again.

"What is it you want to know?"

"Well, for instance, how did you meet Nathan's mother? I mean, Sherry was my cousin and I've got to say, you're not her usual type."

"Really?" He turned on the spindly seat and looked at her. "Just what type am I then?"

"Geez, touchy," she said, her smile flashing briefly. "I only meant that you don't look like an accountant or a computer genius."

"Thanks, I think."

"Oh, I'm sure there are attractive accountants and computer wizards, but Sherry never found any." She carried a platter to the counter and began to slice the roast chicken, laying thick wedges of still-steaming meat on the flowered china. "So how did you meet?"

Simon bristled and distracted himself by pulling bits of banana out of the baby's hair. "Does it matter?"

"No," she said. "I was just curious."

"I'd rather not talk about it." He'd made a mistake that hadn't been repeated and it wasn't something he felt like sharing. Especially with *this* woman. No doubt she'd laugh or give him that sad, sympathy-filled smile again and he wasn't in the mood.

"Okay," she said, drawing that one word out into three

or four syllables. "Then how long were the two of you together?"

Irritation was still fresh enough to make his tone sharper than he'd planned. "Are you writing a book?"

She blinked at him in surprise. "No, but Sherry was my cousin, Nathan's my nephew and you're my...well, there's a relationship in there somewhere. I'm just trying to pin it down."

And he was overreacting. It had been a long time since Simon had felt off balance. But since the moment Tula had stepped into his office, nothing in his world had steadied. He watched her as she moved to the stove, scooped mashed potatoes into a bowl and then filled a smaller dish with dark green broccoli. She carried everything to the table and asked him to pour the wine.

He did, pleased at the label on the chardonnay. When they each had full glasses, he tipped his toward her. "I'm not trying to make things harder, but this has been a hell—" he caught himself and glanced at the baby "—heck of a surprise. And I don't much like surprises."

"I'm getting that," she said, reaching out to grab the jar of baby food she'd opened and left on the table. As she spooned what looked like horrific mush into Nathan's open mouth, she asked again, "So how long were you and Sherry together?"

He took a sip of wine. "Not giving up on this, are you?"

"Nope."

He had to admire her persistence, if nothing else.

"Two weeks," he admitted. "She was a nice woman but she—we—didn't work out."

Sighing, Tula nodded. "Sounds like Sherry. She never did stay with any one guy for long." Her voice softened in memory. "She was scared. Scared of making a mistake, picking the wrong man, but scared of being alone, too. She was scared—well, of pretty much everything."

That he remembered very well, too, Simon thought. Images of the woman he'd known in the past were hazy, but recollections of what he'd felt at the time were fairly clear. He remembered feeling trapped by the woman's clinginess, by her need for more than he could offer. By the damp anxiety always shining in her eyes.

Now, he felt…not guilt, precisely, but maybe regret. He'd cut her out of his life neatly, never looking back while she had gone on to carry his child and give birth. It occurred to him that he'd done the same thing with any number of women in his past. Once their time together was at an end, he presented them with a small piece of jewelry as a token and then he moved on. This was the first time that his routine had come back to bite him in the ass.

"I didn't know her well," he said when the silence became too heavy. "And I had no idea she was pregnant."

"I know that," Tula told him with a shake of her head. "Not telling you was Sherry's choice and for what it's worth, I think she was wrong."

"On that, we can agree." He took another sip of the dry white wine.

"Please," she said, motioning to the food on the table, "eat. I will, too, in between feeding the baby these carrots."

"Is that what that is?" The baby seemed to like the stuff, but as far as Simon was concerned, the practically neon orange baby food looked hideous. Didn't smell much better.

She laughed a little at the face he was making. "Yeah, I know. Looks gross, doesn't it? Once I get into the swing of having him around, though, I'm going to go for more organic stuff. Make my own baby food. Get a nice blender and then he won't have to eat this stuff anymore."

"You'll make your own?"

"Why not? I like to cook and then I can fix him fresh vegetables and meat—pretty much whatever I'm having, only mushy." She shrugged as if the extra effort she was talking about meant nothing. "Besides, have you ever read a list of ingredients on baby food jars?"

"Not recently," he said wryly.

"Well, I have. There's too much sodium for one thing. And some of the words I can't even pronounce. That can't be good for tiny babies."

All right, Simon thought, he admired that as well. She had already adapted to the baby being in her life. Something that he was going to have to work at. But he would do it. He'd never failed yet when he went after something he wanted.

He took a bite of chicken and nearly sighed aloud. So she was not only sexy and good with kids, she could cook, too.

"Good?"

Simon looked at her. "Amazing."

"Thanks!" She beamed at him, gave Nathan a few more pieces of banana and then helped herself to her own dinner. After a moment or two of companionable quiet, she asked, "So, what are we going to do about our new 'situation'?"

"I took the will to my lawyer," Simon said.

"Of course you did."

He nodded. "You're temporarily in charge…"

"Which you don't like," she added.

Simon ignored her interruption, preferring to get everything out in the open under his own terms. "Until *you* decide when and if I'm ready to take over care of Nathan."

"That's the bottom line, yes." She angled her head to look at him. "I told you this earlier today."

"The question," he continued, again ignoring her input, "is how do we reach a compromise? I need time with my son. You need the time to *observe* me with him. I live in San Francisco and have to be there for my job. You live here and—where do you work?"

"Here," she said, taking another bite and chasing it with a sip of wine. "I write books. For children."

He glanced at the rabbit-shaped salt and pepper shakers and thought about all of the framed bunnies in her living room. "Something to do with rabbits, I'm guessing."

Tula tensed, suddenly defensive. She'd heard that dismissive tone of his before. As if writing children's books was so easy anybody could do it. As if she was somehow making a living out of a cute little hobby. "As a matter of fact, yes. I write the Lonely Bunny books."

"Lonely Bunny?"

"It's a very successful series for young children." Well, she amended silently, not *very* successful. But she was gaining an audience, growing slowly but surely. And she was proud of what she did. She made children happy. How many other people could say that about their work?

"I'm sure."

"Would you like to see my fan letters? They're scrawled in crayon, so maybe they won't mean much to you. But to me they say that I'm reaching kids. That they enjoy my stories and that I make them happy." She fell back in her chair and snapped her arms across her chest in a clear signal of defense mode. "As far as I'm concerned, that makes my books a success."

One of his eyebrows lifted. "I didn't say they weren't."

No, she thought, but he had been thinking it. Hadn't she heard that tone for years from her own father? Jacob Hawthorne had cut his only daughter off without a dime five years ago, when she finally stood up to him and told him she wasn't going to get an MBA. That she was going to be a writer.

And Simon Bradley was just like her father. He wore suits and lived in a buttoned-down world where whimsy and imagination had no place. Where creativity was scorned and the nonconformist was fired.

She'd escaped that world five years ago and she had no desire to go back. And the thought of having to hand poor little Nathan off to a man who would try to regulate his life just as her father had done to her gave her cold chills. She looked at the happy, smiling baby and wondered how long it would take the suits of the world to suck his little spirit dry. The thought of that was simply appalling.

"Look, we have to work together," Simon said and she realized that he didn't sound any happier about it than she was.

"We do."

"You work at home, right?"

"Yes…"

"Fine, then. You and Nathan can move into my house in San Francisco."

"Excuse me?" Tula actually felt her jaw drop.

"It's the only way," he said simply, decisively. "I have to be in the city for my work. You can work anywhere."

"I'm so happy you think so."

He gave her a patronizing smile that made her grit her teeth to keep from saying something she would probably regret.

"Nathan and I need time together. You have to witness us together. The only reasonable solution is for you and him to move to the city."

"I can't just pick up and leave—"

"Six months," he said. He drained the last of his wine and set the empty goblet onto the table. "It won't take that long, but let's say, for argument's sake, that you move into my house for the next six months. Get Nathan settled. See that I'm going to be fine taking care of my own son, if he is my son, and then you can move back here…" He glanced around the tiny kitchen with a slow shake of his head as if he couldn't understand why anyone would willingly live there. "And we can all get on with our lives."

Damn it, Tula hadn't even considered moving. She loved her house. Loved the life she'd made for herself. Plus, she tended to avoid San Francisco like the plague.

Her father lived in the city.

Ran his empire from the very heart of it.

Heck, for all she knew, Simon Bradley and her father

were the best of friends. Now there was a horrifying thought.

"Well?"

She looked at him. Looked at Nathan. There really wasn't a choice. Tula had promised her cousin that she would be Nathan's guardian and there was no turning back from that obligation now even if she wanted to.

"Look," he said, leaning across the table to meet her eyes as though he knew that she was trying and failing to find a way out of this. "We don't have to get along. We don't even have to like each other. We just have to manage to live together for a few months."

"Wow," she murmured with a half laugh, "doesn't that sound like a good time."

"It's not about a good time, Ms. Barrons..."

"If we're going to be living together, the least you could do is call me Tula."

"Then you agree, *Tula?*"

"Do I get a choice?"

"Not really."

He was right, she told herself. There really wasn't a choice. She had to do what was best for Nathan. That meant moving to the city and finding a way to break Simon out of his rigid world. She blew out a breath and then extended her right hand across the table. "All right then. It's a deal."

"A deal," he agreed.

He took her hand in his and it was as if she'd suddenly clutched a live electrical wire. Tula almost expected to see sparks jumping up from their joined hands. She knew he felt it, too, because he released her instantly and frowned to himself.

She rubbed her fingertips together, still feeling that sizzle on her skin and told herself the next few months were going to be very interesting.

Four

Two days later, Simon swung the bat, connected with the baseball and felt the zing of contact charge up his arms. The ball sailed out into the netting strung across the back of the batting cage and he smiled in satisfaction.

"A triple at least," he announced.

"Right. You flied out to center," Mick Davis called back from the next batting cage.

Simon snorted. He knew a good hit when he saw it. He got the bat high up on his shoulder and waited for the next robotic pitch from the machine.

While he was here, Simon didn't have to think about work or business deals. The batting cages near his home were an outlet for him. He could take out his frustrations by slamming bats into baseballs and that outlet was coming in handy at the moment. While he was concentrating on fastballs, curveballs and sliders, he couldn't think about big blue eyes. A luscious mouth.

Not to mention the child who was—might be—his son.

He swung and missed, the ball crashing into the caged metal door behind him.

"I'm up two now," Mick called out with a laugh.

"Not finished yet," Simon shouted, enjoying the rush of competition. Mick had been his best friend since college. Now he was also Simon's right-hand man at the Bradley company. There was no one he trusted more.

Mick slammed a ball into the far netting and Simon grinned, then punched out one of his own. It felt good to be physical. To blank out his mind and simply enjoy the chance to hit a few balls with his friend. Here, no one cared that he was the CEO of a billion-dollar company. Here, he could just relax. Something he didn't do often. By the time their hour was up, both men were grinning and arguing over which of them had won.

"Give it up." Simon laughed. "You were outclassed."

"In your dreams." Mick handed Simon a bottle of water and after taking a long drink, he asked, "So, you want to tell me why you were swinging with such a vengeance today?"

Simon sat down on the closest bench and watched a handful of kids running to the cages. They were about nine, he guessed, with messy hair, ripped jeans and eager smiles. Something stirred inside him. One day, Nathan would be their age. He had a son. He was a father. In a few years, he'd be bringing his boy to these cages.

Shaking his head, he muttered, "You're not going to believe it."

"Try me." Mick toasted him with his own water and urged him to talk.

So Simon did. While late-afternoon sunshine slipped through the clouds and a cold sea wind whistled past, Simon talked. He told Mick about the visit from Tula. About Nathan. About all of it.

"You have a *son?*"

"Yeah," Simon said with a fast grin. "Probably. I'm getting a paternity test done."

"I'm sure you are," Mick said.

He frowned a little. "It makes sense, but yeah, looking at him, it's hard to ignore. I'm still trying to wrap my head around it myself. Hell, I don't even know what to do first."

"Bring him home?"

"Well, yeah," he said. "That's the plan. I've got crews over at the house right now, fixing up a room for him."

"And this Tula? What's she like?"

Simon pulled at his ice-cold water again, relishing the liquid as it slid down his throat to ease the sudden tightness there. How to explain Tula, he thought. Hell, where would he begin? "She's...different."

Mick laughed. "What the hell does that mean?"

"Good question," Simon muttered. His fingers played with the shrink-wrapped label on the water bottle. "She's fiercely protective of Nathan. And she's as irritating as she is gorgeous—"

"Interesting."

Simon shot him a look. "Don't even go there. I'm not interested."

"You just said she's gorgeous."

"Doesn't mean a thing," he insisted, shooting a look

at the boys as they lined up to take turns at the cages. "She's not my type."

"Good. Your type is boring."

"What?"

Mick leaned both forearms on the picnic table. "Simon, you date the *same* woman, over and over."

"What the hell are you talking about?"

"No matter how their faces change, the inner woman never does. They're all cool, quiet, refined."

Now Simon laughed. "And there's something wrong with that?"

"A little variety wouldn't kill you."

Variety. He didn't need variety. His life was fine just the way it was. If a quick image of Tula Barrons's big blue eyes and flashing dimple rose up in his mind, it was nobody's business but his own.

He'd seen close-up and personal just what happened when a man spent his time looking for *variety* instead of *sensible*. Simon's father had made everyone in the house miserable with his continuing quest for amusement. Simon wasn't interested in repeating any failing patterns.

"All I'm saying is—"

"Don't want to hear it," Simon told him before his friend could get going. "Besides, what the hell do you know about women? You're *married*."

Mick snorted. "Last time I looked, my beautiful wife *is* a woman."

"Katie's different."

"Different from the snooty ice queens you usually date, you mean."

"How did we get onto the subject of my love life?"

"Beats the hell outta me," Mick said with a laugh.

"I just wanted to know what was bugging you and now I do. There's a new woman in your life *and* you're a father."

"Probably," Simon amended.

Mick reached out and slapped Simon's shoulder. "Congratulations, man."

Simon smiled, took another sip of water and let his new reality settle in. He was, most likely, a father. He had a son.

As for Tula Barrons being in his life, that was temporary. Strangely enough, that thought didn't have quite the appeal it should have.

"I don't know what to do about him," Tula said, taking a sip of her latte.

"What *can* you do?" Anna Hale asked from her position on the floor of the bank.

Tula looked down at the baby in his stroller and smiled as Nathan slapped his toy bunny against the tray. "Hey, do you think it's okay for the baby to be in here while you're painting? I mean, the fumes…"

"It's fine. This is just detail work," Anna said, soothing her, then she smiled. "Look at you. You're so mom-like."

"I know." Tula grinned at her. "And I really like it. Didn't think I would, you know? I mean, I always thought I'd like to have kids some day, but I never really had any idea of what it would really be like. It's exhausting. And wonderful. And…" She stopped and frowned thoughtfully. "I have to move to the city."

"It's not forever," Anna told her, pausing in laying down a soft layer of pale yellow that blended with the bottom coat of light blue to make a sun-washed sky.

"Yeah, I know," Tula said on a sigh. She walked to Anna, sat down on the floor and sat cross-legged. "But you know how I hate the idea of going back to San Francisco."

"I do," Anna said, wiping a stray lock of hair off her cheek, leaving a trace of yellow paint in her wake. "But you won't necessarily see your father. It's a big city."

Tula gave her a halfhearted grin. "Not big enough. Jacob Hawthorne throws a huge shadow."

"But you're not in that shadow anymore, remember?" Anna reached out, grabbed her hand, then winced at the yellow paint she transferred to Tula's skin. "Oops, sorry. Tula, you walked away from him. From that life. You don't owe him anything and he doesn't have the power to make you miserable anymore. You're a famous author now!"

Tula laughed, delighted at the image. She was famous in the preschool crowd. Or at least, her Lonely Bunny was a star. She was simply the writer who told his stories and drew his pictures. But, oh, how she loved going to children's bookstores to do signings. To read her books to kids clustered around her with wide eyes and innocent smiles.

Anna was right. Tula had escaped her father's narrow world and his plans for *her* life. She'd made her own way. She had a home she loved and a career she adored. Glancing at the baby boy happily gabbling to himself in his stroller, she told herself silently that she was madly in love with a drooling, nearly bald, one-foot-tall dreamboat.

What she would do when she had to say goodbye to that baby she just didn't know. But for the moment, that time was weeks, maybe months, away.

If ever she'd seen a man who wasn't prepared to be a father, it was Simon Bradley.

Instantly, an image of him popped into her brain and she almost sighed. He really was far too handsome for her peace of mind. But gorgeous or not, he was as stuffy and stern as her own father and she'd had enough of that kind of man. Besides, this wasn't about sexual attraction or the buzzing awareness, this was about Nathan and what was best for him.

So Tula would put aside her own worries and whatever tingly feelings she had for the baby's father and focus instead on taking care of the tiny boy.

She could do this. And just to make herself feel better, she mentally put her adventure into the tone of one of her books. *Lonely Bunny Goes to the City*. She smiled to herself at the thought and realized it wasn't a bad idea for her next book.

"You're absolutely right," Tula said firmly, needing to hear the confident tone in her own voice. "My father can't dictate to me anymore. And besides, it's not as if he's interested in what I'm doing or where I am."

The truth stung a bit, as it always did. Because no matter what, she wished her father were different. But wishing would never make it so.

"I'm not going to worry about running into my father," she said. "I mean, what are the actual odds of that happening anyway?"

"Good for you!" Anna said with an approving grin. Then she added, "Now, would you mind handing me the brush shaped like a fan? I need to get the lacy look on the waves."

"Right." Tula stood, looked through Anna's supplies and found the wide, white sable fan-shaped brush. She handed it over, then watched as her best friend expertly laid down white paint atop the cerulean blue ocean, creating froth on water that looked real enough Tula half expected to hear the sound of the waves.

Anna Cameron Hale was the best faux finish artist in the business. She could lay down a mural on a wall and when she was finished, it was practically alive. Just as, when this painting on the bank wall was complete, it would look like a view of the ocean on a sunny day, as seen through a columned window.

"You're completely amazing, you know that, right?" Tula said.

"Thanks." Anna didn't look back, just continued her painting. "You know, once you're settled into Simon's place, I could come up and do a mural in the baby's room."

"Oooh, great idea."

"And," Anna said coyly, turning her head to look at Tula, "it would be good practice for the nursery Sam and I are setting up."

A second ticked past. Then two. "You're—"

"I am."

"How long?"

"About three months."

"Oh my God, that's huge!" Tula dropped to her knees and swept Anna into a tight hug, then released her. "You're gonna have a baby! How'd Sam take it?"

"Like he's the first man to introduce sperm to egg!" Anna laughed again and the shine in her eyes defined just how happy she really was. "He's really excited. He called Garret in Switzerland to tell him he's going to be an uncle."

"Weird, considering you actually dated Garret for like five minutes."

"Ew." Anna grimaced and shook her head. "I don't like to think about that part," she said, laughing again. "Besides, three dates with Garret or a lifetime with his brother…no contest."

Tula had never seen her friend so happy. So content. As if everything in her world were exactly the way it was supposed to be. For one really awful moment, Tula actually felt envious of that happiness. Of the certainty in Anna's life. Of the love Sam surrounded her with. Then she deliberately put aside her own niggling twist of jealousy and focused on the important thing here. Supporting Anna as she'd always been there for Tula.

"I'm really happy for you, Anna."

"Thanks, sweetie. I know you are." She glanced at the baby boy who was watching them both through interested eyes. "And believe me, I'm glad you're getting so much hands-on experience, Aunt Tula. I don't have a clue how to take care of a baby."

"It's really simple," Tula said, following her friend's gaze to smile at the baby that had so quickly become the center of her world. "All you have to do is love them."

Her heart simply turned over in her chest. Two weeks she'd been a surrogate mom and she could hardly remember a time without Nathan. What on earth had she done with herself before having that little boy to snuggle and care for? How had she gotten through her day without the scent of baby shampoo and the soft warmth of a tiny body to hold?

And how would she ever live without it?

* * *

Simon knew how to get things done.

With Mick's assistant taking care of most of the details, within a week, Simon's house had been readied for Tula and Nathan's arrival.

He had rooms prepared, food delivered and had already lined up several interviews with a popular nanny employment agency. Tula and the baby had been in town only three days and already he had arranged for a paternity test and had pulled a few important strings so that he'd have the results a lot sooner than he normally would have.

Not that he needed legal confirmation. He had known from his first glance at the child that Nathan was his. Had felt it the moment he'd held him. Now he had to deal with the very real fact of parenthood. Though he was definitely going to go slowly in that regard until he had proof.

He'd never planned on being a father. Hell, he didn't know the first thing about parenting. And his own parent had hardly been a sterling role model.

Simon knew he could do it, though. He always found a way.

He opened his front door and accidentally kicked a toy truck. The bright yellow Dumpster was sent zooming across the parquet floor to crash into the opposite wall. He shook his head, walked to the truck and, after picking it up, headed into the living room.

Normally, he got home at five-thirty, had a quiet drink while reading the paper. The silence of the big house was a blessing after a long day filled with clients, board meetings and ringing telephones. His house had been a sanctuary, he thought wryly. But not anymore.

He glanced around the once orderly living room and blew out an exasperated breath. How could one baby have so much…stuff?

"They've only been here three days," he muttered, amazed at what the two of them had done to the dignified old Victorian.

There were diapers, bottles, toys, fresh laundry that had been folded and stacked on the coffee table. There was a walker of some sort in one corner and a discarded bunny with one droopy ear sitting in Simon's favorite chair. He stepped over a baby blanket spread across a hand-stitched throw rug and set his briefcase down beside the chair.

Picking up the bunny, he ran his fingers over the soft, slightly soggy fur. Nathan was teething, Tula had informed him only that morning. Apparently, the bunny was taking the brunt of the punishment. Shaking his head, he laughed a little, amazed anew at just how quickly a man's routine could be completely shattered.

"Simon? Is that you?"

He turned toward the sound of her voice and looked at the hall as if he could see through the walls to the kitchen at the back of the house. Something inside him tightened in expectation at the sound of Tula's voice. His body instantly went on alert, a feeling he was getting used to. In the three days she and the baby had been here, Simon had been in a near-constant state of aching need.

She was really getting to him, and the worst of it was, she wasn't even trying.

Tula was only here as Nathan's guardian. To stay until

she felt Simon was ready to be his son's father. There was nothing more between them and there couldn't be.

So why then, he asked himself, did he spend so damn much time thinking about her? She wasn't the kind of woman who usually caught his eye. But there was something about her. Something alive. Electric.

She smiled and that dimple teased him. She sang to the baby and her voice caressed him. She was here, in his house when he came home from work, and he didn't even miss the normal quiet.

He was in serious trouble.

"Simon?"

Now her voice almost sounded worried because he hadn't answered her. "Yes, it's me."

"That's good. We're in the kitchen!"

He held on to the lop-eared bunny and walked down the long hallway. The rooms were big, the wood gleaming from polish and care and the walls were painted in a warm palate of blues and greens. He knew every creak of the floor, every sigh of the wind against the windows. He'd grown up in this house and had taken it over when his father died a few years ago.

Of course, Simon had put his own stamp on the place. He'd ripped up carpeting that had hidden the tongue-and-groove flooring. He'd had wallpaper removed and had restored crown moldings and the natural wood in the built-in china cabinets and bookcases.

He'd made it his own, determined to wipe out old memories and build new ones.

Now he was sharing it with the son he still could hardly believe was his.

Stepping into the kitchen, he was surrounded by the scented steam lifting off a pot of chili on the stove. At the table, Tula sat cross-legged on a chair while spooning something green and mushy into Nathan's mouth.

"What is that?" he asked.

"Hi! What? Oh, green beans. We went shopping today, didn't we, Nathan?" She gave the boy another spoonful. "We bought a blender and some fresh vegetables and then we came home and cooked them up for dinner, didn't we?"

Simon could have sworn the infant was listening to everything Tula had to say. Maybe it was her way of practically singing her words to him. Or maybe it was the warmth of her tone and the smile on her face that caught the baby's attention.

Much as it had done for the boy's father.

"It's so cold outside, I made chili for us," she said, tossing him a quick grin over her shoulder.

The impact of that smile shook him right down to the bone.

Mick had been right, he thought. Tula was nothing like the cool, controlled beauties he was used to dating.

And he had to wonder if she was as warm in bed as she was out of it.

"Smells good," he managed to say.

"Tastes even better," she promised. "Why don't you come over here and finish feeding Nathan? I'll get dinner for us."

"Okay." He approached her and the baby cautiously and wanted to kick himself for it. Simon Bradley had a reputation for storming into a situation and taking charge. He could feed a baby for God's sake. How difficult could it be?

He took Tula's chair, picked up the bowl of green

bean mush and filled a spoon. Behind him, he could sense Tula's gaze on him, watching. Well, he'd prove not only to himself, but to her, that he was perfectly capable of feeding a baby.

Spooning the green slop into Nathan's mouth, he was completely unprepared when the baby spat it back at him. "What?"

Tula's delighted laughter spilled out around him as Simon wiped green beans from his face. Then she leaned in, kissed him on the cheek and said, "Welcome to fatherhood."

An instant later, her smile died as he looked at her through dark eyes blazing with heat. Her mouth went dry and a sizzle of something dark and dangerous went off inside her.

They stared at each other for what felt like forever until finally Simon said, "That wasn't much of a kiss. We'll have to do better next time."

Next time?

Five

Tula remembered sitting in her own kitchen thinking that this was not a good idea. Now she was convinced.

Yet here she was, living in a Victorian mansion in the city with a man she wasn't sure she liked—but she really did want.

Last night at dinner, Simon had looked so darn cute with green beans on his face that she hadn't been able to stop herself from giving in to the impulse to kiss him. Sure, it was just a quick peck on his cheek. But when he'd turned those dark brown eyes on her and she'd read the barely banked passion there, it had shaken her.

Not like she was some shy, retiring virgin or anything. She wasn't. She'd had a boyfriend in college and another one just a year or so ago. But Simon was nothing like them. In retrospect, they had been boys and Simon was all man.

"Oh God, stop it," she told herself. It wouldn't do any good of course. She'd been indulging in not so idle daydreams centered on Simon Bradley for days now. When she was sleeping, her brain picked up on the subconscious thread and really went to town.

But a woman couldn't be blamed for what she dreamed of when she slept, right?

"It's ridiculous," she said, tugging at her desk to move it into position beneath one of the many mullioned windows. A stray beam of rare January sunlight speared through the clouds and lay across her desktop. She didn't take the time to admire it though, instead, she went back to getting the rest of her temporary office the way she wanted it.

She didn't need much, really. Just her laptop, a drawing table where she could work on the illustrations for her books and a comfy chair where she could sit and think.

"Hmm. If you don't need much stuff, Tula, why is there so much junk in here?" A question for the ages, she thought. She didn't *try* to collect things. It just sort of…happened. And being here in the Victorian where everything had a tidy spot to belong to made her feel like a pack rat.

There were boxes and books and empty shelves waiting to be filled. There were loose manuscript pages and pens and paints and, oh, way too many things to try to organize.

"Settling in?"

She jumped about a foot and spun around, holding one hand to her chest as if trying to keep her heart where it belonged. He stood in the open doorway, a half smile on his handsome face as if he knew darn well that he'd scared about ten years off her life.

Giving Simon a pained glare, she snapped, "Wear a bell or something, okay? I about had a heart attack."

"I do live here," Simon reminded her.

"Yeah, I know." As if she could forget. She'd lain awake in her bed half the night, imagining Simon in his bed just down the hall from her. She never should have kissed him. Never should have breached the tense, polite wall they'd erected between them at their first meeting.

Only that morning, they'd had breakfast together. The three of them sitting cozily in a kitchen three times the size of her own. She had watched Simon feeding a squirming baby oatmeal while dodging the occasional splat of rejected offerings and darned if he hadn't looked...cute doing it.

She groaned inwardly and warned herself again to get a grip. This wasn't about playing house with Simon.

He strolled into her office with a look of stunned amazement on his face. "How do you work in this confusion?"

She'd just been thinking basically the same thing, but she wasn't about to give him the satisfaction of knowing it. "An organized mind is a boring mind."

One dark eyebrow lifted and she noticed he did that a lot when they were talking. Sardonic? Or just irritated?

"You paint, too?" he asked, nodding at the drawing table set up beneath one of the tall windows.

"Draw, really. Just sketches," she said. "I do the illustrations for my books."

"Impressive," he said, moving closer for a better look.

Tula steeled herself against what he might say once he'd had a chance to really study her drawings. Her father had never given her a compliment, she thought. But in the end that hadn't mattered, since she drew her pictures for the children who loved her books. Tula knew she had talent, but she had never fooled herself into believing that she was a great artist.

He thumbed through the sketch papers on the table and she knew what he was seeing. The sketches of Lonely Bunny and the animals who shared his world.

His gaze moving to hers, he said softly, "You're very good. You get a lot of emotion into these drawings."

"Thank you." Surprised but pleased, she smiled at him and felt warmth spill through her when he returned that smile.

"Nathan has a stuffed rabbit. But he needs a new one. The one he has looks a little worse for wear."

She shook her head sadly, because clearly he didn't know how much a worn, beloved toy could mean to a child. "You never read *The Velveteen Rabbit?*" she asked. "Being loved is what makes a toy real. And when you're real, you're a little haggard looking."

"I guess you're right." He laughed quietly and nodded as he looked back at her sketches. "How did you come up with this? The Lonely Bunny, I mean."

Veering away from the personal and back into safe conversation, she thought, oddly disappointed that the brief moment of closeness was already over.

Still, she grinned as she said, "People always ask writers where they get their ideas. I usually say I find my ideas on the bottom shelf of the housewares department in the local market."

One corner of his mouth quirked up. "Clever. But not really an answer, either."

"No," she admitted, wrapping her arms around her middle. "It's not."

He turned around to face her and his warm brown eyes went soft and curious. "Will you tell me?"

She met his gaze and felt the conversation drifting back into the intimate again. But she saw something in his eyes that told her he was actually interested. And until that moment, no one but Anna had ever really cared.

Walking toward him, she picked up one of the sketches off the drawing table and studied her own handiwork. The Lonely Bunny looked back at her with his wide, limpid eyes and sadly hopeful expression. Tula smiled down at the bunny who had come along at just the right time in her life.

"I used to draw him when I was a little girl," she said more to herself than to him. She ran one finger across the pale gray color of his fur and the crooked bend of his ear. "When Mom and I moved to Crystal Bay, there were some wild rabbits living in the park behind our house."

Beside her, she felt him step closer. Felt him watching her. But she was lost in her own memories now and staring back into her past.

"One of the rabbits was different. He had one droopy ear, and he was always by himself," she said, smiling to herself at the image of a young Tula trying to tempt a wild rabbit closer by holding out a carrot. "It looked to me like he didn't have any friends. The other rabbits stayed away from him and I sort of felt that we were two of a kind. I was new in town and didn't have any friends, so I made it my mission to make that bunny like me. But no matter how I tried, I couldn't get him to play with me.

"And believe me, I tried. Every day for a month. Then one day I went to the park and the other rabbits were there, but Lonely Bunny wasn't." She stroked her fingertip across her sketch of that long-ago bunny. "I looked all over for him, but couldn't find him."

She stopped and looked up into eyes filled with understanding and compassion and she felt her own eyes burn with the sting of unexpected tears. The only person she had ever told about that bunny was Anna. She'd always felt just a little silly for caring so much. For missing that rabbit so badly when she couldn't find him.

"I never saw him again. I kept looking, though. For a week, I scoured that park," she mused. "Under every bush, behind every rock. I looked everywhere. Finally, a week later, I was so worried about him, I told my mother and asked her to help me look for him."

"Did she?" His voice was quiet, as if he was trying to keep from shattering whatever spell was spinning out around them.

"No," she said with a sigh. "She told me he had probably been hit by a car."

"What?" Simon sounded horrified. "She said *what?*"

Tula choked out a laugh. "Thanks for the outrage on my behalf, but it was a long time ago. Besides, I didn't believe her. I told myself that he had found a lady bunny and had moved away with her."

She set the drawings down onto the table and turned

to him, tucking her hands into her jeans pockets. "When I decided to write children's books, I brought Lonely Bunny back. He's been good for me."

Nodding, Simon reached out and tapped his finger against one of her earrings, setting it into swing. "I think you were good for him, too. I bet he's still telling his grandbunnies stories about the little girl who loved him."

Her breath caught around a knot of tenderness in the middle of her throat. "You surprise me sometimes, Simon."

"It's only fair," he said. "You surprise me all the damn time."

Seconds ticked past, each of them looking at the other as if for the first time. Simon was the first to speak and when he did, it was clear that the moment they had shared was over. At least for now.

"Do you have everything you need?"

"Yes." She took a breath and an emotional step back. "I just need to move my chair into place and—"

"Where do you want it?"

She looked up at him. He was just home from work, so he was wearing a dark blue suit and the only sign of relaxation was the loosening of the knot in his red silk tie.

"You don't have to—"

He shrugged out of his suit jacket. His tailored, long-sleeved white shirt clung to a truly impressively broad chest. She swallowed hard as she watched him grab hold of the chair and she wondered why simply taking off his suit jacket in front of her seemed such an intimate act.

Maybe, she thought, it was because the suit was who he was. And laying it aside, even momentarily, felt like an important step.

As soon as that thought entered her mind, Tula pushed it away.

Nothing intimate going on here at all, she reminded herself. Just a guy, helping her move a chair. And she'd do well to keep that in mind. Anything else would just be asking for trouble.

"Over there," she said, pointing to the far corner.

"You want to move that box out of the way?"

She did, pushing the heavy box of books with her foot until Simon had a clear path. He muscled the oversize chair across the room, then angled it in a way so that she'd be facing both windows when she sat in it.

"How's that?"

"Perfect, thanks."

He looked around the room again. "Where's the baby?"

"In his room. He took a late nap today."

"Right." He wandered around the room now, peeking into boxes, glancing at the haphazard stacks of papers on her desk. "You know, I've got some colored file folders in my office you could use."

She bristled. "I have my own system."

Simon looked at her and lifted that eyebrow again. "Chaos is a system?"

"It's only chaos if you can't find your way around. I can."

"If you say so." He moved closer. "Is there anything else I can do?"

"Um, no thanks," Tula whispered, feeling the heat of him reach for her. This was her fault, she told herself as tension in the room began to grow. If she hadn't given him that impulsive kiss, they'd still be at odds. If she hadn't opened herself up, causing him to be so darn sweet, they wouldn't be experiencing this closeness now.

So she spoke up fast, before whatever was happening between them could go any further. "Why don't you go check on Nathan while I finish up in here? I've still got a lot of unpacking to do."

She stepped past him and dug into a carton of books, deliberately keeping her back to him. Her heart was pounding and her stomach was spinning with a wild blend of nerves and anticipation. Pulling out a few of the books, she set them on the top shelf and let her fingertips linger on the bindings.

But Simon didn't leave. Instead, he went down on one knee beside her, cupped her chin and turned her face toward him.

"I don't know what's going on between us any more than you do. But you can't avoid me forever, Tula. We're living together, after all."

"We're living in the same house, that's all," she corrected breathlessly. "Not together."

"Semantics," he mused, a half smile tugging at one corner of his mouth.

Oh, she knew what he was thinking because she was thinking the same thing. Well, actually, there was very little *thinking* going on. This was more feeling. Wanting. Needing.

She shook her head. "Simon, you know it would be a bad idea."

"What?" he asked innocently. "A kiss?"

"You're not talking about just a kiss."

"Rather not talk at all," he admitted, his gaze dropping to her mouth.

Tula licked her lips and took a breath that caught in her lungs when she saw his eyes flash. "Simon…"

"You started this," he said, leaning in.

"I know," she answered and tipped her head to one side as she moved to meet him.

"I'll finish it."

"Stop talking," she told him just before his mouth closed over hers.

Heat exploded between them.

Tula had never known anything like it before. His mouth took hers hungrily, his tongue parting her lips, sweeping inside to claim all of her. He pulled her tightly against him until they were both kneeling on the soft, plush carpet. His hands slid up and down her back, dipping to cup the curve of her behind and pull her more tightly against him.

Tula felt the rock-hard proof of just how much Simon wanted her and that need echoed inside her. Her mind blanked out and she gave herself up to the river of sensations he was causing. She tangled her tongue with his, leaning into him, wrapping her arms around his neck and holding on as if she were afraid of sliding off the edge of the world.

He tore his mouth from hers, buried his face in the curve of her neck and whispered, "I've been thinking about doing this, about *you,* ever since you first walked into my office."

"Me, too," she murmured, tipping her head to give him better access. Her body was electrified. Every cell was buzzing, and at the core of her she burned and ached for him.

He dropped his hands to the hem of her sweater and slid his palms beneath the heavy knit material to slide across her skin. She felt the burn of his fingers, the sizzle and pop in her bloodstream as he stoked flames already burning too brightly.

Oh, it had been way too long since anyone had touched her, Tula thought, letting her head fall back on a soft sigh. And she'd *never* been touched like this before.

"Let me," he murmured, drawing her sweater up and off, baring breasts hidden beneath a bra of sheer, pink lace.

Cool air caressed her skin in a counterpoint to the heat Simon was creating. One corner of her mind was shrieking at her to stop this while she still could. But the rest of her was telling that small, insistent voice to shut up and go away.

"Lovely," he said, skimming the backs of his fingers across her nipples.

She shivered when his thumbs moved over the tips of her hardened nipples, the brush of the lace intensifying his touch to an almost excruciating level of excitement. Tula trembled as he unhooked the front clasp of her bra and sucked in a quick breath when he pushed the lacy panel aside and cupped her breasts in his hands.

He bent his head to take first one nipple and then the other into his mouth and Tula swayed in place. Threading her fingers through his thick hair, she held him to her and concentrated solely on the feel of his lips and tongue against her skin.

She wanted him naked, her hands on his body. She wanted to lie back and pull him atop her. She wanted to feel their bodies sliding together, to look up into his eyes as he took her to—

An insistent howl shattered the spell between them.

Simon pulled back from her and whipped his head around to stare at the doorway. "What was that?"

"The baby." Still trembling, Tula grabbed the edges of her bra and hooked it together. Then she reached for her sweater and had it back on in a couple of seconds. "I've got the baby monitor in here so I could hear him while I worked."

She waved one hand at what looked like a space-age communication device and Simon nodded. "Right. The monitor."

Scrambling to her feet, Tula backed away from him quickly.

"Don't do that," Simon said, standing up and reaching for her. "I can see in your eyes that you're already pretending that didn't happen."

"No, I'm not," she assured him, though her voice was as shaky as the rest of her. Pushing one hand through the short, choppy layers of her hair, she blew out a breath and admitted, "But I should."

"Why?" He winced when the baby's cries continued, but didn't let go of her.

Tula shook her head and pulled free of his grasp. "Because this is just one more complication, Simon. One neither one of us should want."

"Yeah," he said, gaze meeting hers. "But we do."

"You can't always have what you want," she countered, taking a step back, closer to the open doorway. "Now I really have to go to the baby."

"Okay. But Tula," he said, stopping her as she started to leave. "You should know that I *always* get what I want."

When Tula carried Nathan into her office half an hour later, she found a stack of colored file folders lying on top of her desk. There was a brief note. "Chaos can be controlled. S."

"As if I didn't know who put them there," she told the baby. "He had to put his initial on the note?"

She set the baby down on a blanket surrounded by toys, then took a seat at her desk. Her fingertips tapped against the file folders until she finally shrugged and opened one.

"I suppose it couldn't hurt to try a little filing, right?"

Nathan didn't have an opinion. He was far too fascinated by the foam truck with bright red headlights he had gripped in his tiny fists.

Tula smiled at him, then set to work straightening up her desk. It went faster than she would have thought and though she hated to admit it, there was something satisfying about filing papers neatly and tucking them away in a cabinet. By the time she was finished, her desktop was cleared off for the first time in...ever.

Her phone rang just as she was getting up to take the baby downstairs for his dinner. "Hello?"

"Tula, hi, this is Tracy."

Her editor's voice was, as always, friendly and businesslike. "Hi, what's up?"

"I just need you to give me the front matter for the next book. Production needs it by tomorrow."

"Right." For one awful moment, Tula couldn't remember where she'd put the letter to her readers that always went in the front of her new books. She liked adding that extra personal touch to the children who read her stories.

The scattered feeling was a familiar one. Despite what she had bragged to Simon about knowing where everything was, she usually experienced a moment of sheer panic when her editor called needing something. Because she knew that she would have to stall her while she located whatever was needed.

"It's okay, Tula," Tracy said as if knowing exactly what she was thinking. "I don't need it this minute and I know it'll take you some time to find it. If you just email the letter to me first thing in the morning, I'll hand it in."

"No, it's okay," Tula said suddenly as she realized that she had just spent hours filing things away neatly. "I actually know right where it is."

"You're kidding."

Laughing, she reached out, opened the once-empty file cabinet and pulled out the blue folder. *Blue for Bunny Letters,* she thought with an inner smile. She even had a system now. Sure, she wasn't certain how long it would last, but the fun of surprising her editor had been worth the extra work.

"Poor Tracy," Tula said with sympathy. "You've been putting up with my disorganization for too long, haven't you?"

"You're organized," Tracy defended her. "Just in your own way."

She appreciated the support, but Tula knew very well that Tracy would have preferred just a touch more organizational effort on her writer's part. "Well, I'm trying something new. I am holding in my hand an actual file folder!"

"Amazing," Tracy said with a chuckle. "An organized writer. I didn't know that was possible. Can you fax the letter to me?"

"I can. You'll have it in a few minutes."

"Well, I don't know what inspired the new outlook, but thanks!"

Once she hung up, Tula faxed in the letter, then filed it again and slipped the folder back into the cabinet with a rush of pride. Wouldn't Simon love to know that he'd been right? As for her, she'd managed to straighten up a mess without losing her identity.

Grinning down at the baby, she asked, "What do you think, Nathan? Can a person have chaos *and* control?"

She was still wondering about that when she carried the baby downstairs to the kitchen.

A few hours later, Tula said sharply, "You have to make sure he doesn't slip."

"Well," Simon assured her, "I actually knew that much on my own."

He was bent over the tub, one hand on Nathan's narrow back while he used his free hand to move a soapy washcloth over the baby's skin. "How is it you're supposed to hold him and wash him at the same time?"

Tula grinned and Simon felt a hard punch to his chest. When she really smiled it was enough to make him want to toss her onto the nearest flat surface and bury himself inside her heat.

The kiss they'd shared only a couple of hours before was still burning through him.

He still had the taste of her in his mouth. Had the feel of her soft, sleek skin on his fingers.

Now, as she leaned over beside him to slide a wet washcloth over Nathan's head, he inhaled and drew her light, floral scent into his lungs. He must have let a groan slip from his throat because she stopped, leaned back and looked up at him.

"Are you okay?"

"Not really," he said tightly, focusing now on the baby who was slapping the water with both hands and chortling over the splashes he made.

"Simon—"

"Forget it, Tula. Let's just concentrate on surviving bath time, okay?"

She sat back on her heels and looked up at him. "Now who's pretending it didn't happen?"

He laughed—a short, sharp sound. "Trust me when I say that's not what I'm doing."

"Then why—"

Giving her a hard look, he said, "Unless you're willing to finish what we started, drop it, Tula."

She snapped her mouth closed and nodded. "Right. Then I'll just go get Nathan's jammies ready while you finish. Are you good on your own?"

Good question.

He always had been.

Before.

Now he wasn't so sure.

"We'll be fine. Just go."

She scooted out of the bathroom a moment later and Nathan drew his first easy breath since bath time had started. He looked down into the baby's eyes and said, "Remember this, Nathan. Women are nothing but trouble."

The tiny boy laughed and slapped the water hard enough to send a small wave into his father's face.

"Traitor," Simon whispered.

Six

A few nights later, Simon had had enough of slipping through his own house like a damn ghost. Ever since the kiss he had shared with Tula, he'd kept his distance, staying away not only from her, but from the baby as well. He wondered where in the hell the paternity test results were and asked himself how he was supposed to keep his mind on anything else when memories of a too brief kiss kept intruding.

Hell, it wasn't just the kiss. It was Tula herself and that was an irritation he hadn't expected. She was in his mind all the time. Moving through his thoughts like a shadow, never really leaving, always haunting.

She walked into the room and he felt a hard slam of desire pulse through him. His body was hard and his hands itched to touch her. But she seemed blissfully unaware of what she was doing to him, so damned if he'd let her know.

"Maybe we should talk about how this is going to work," he said when Tula walked into the living room.

Lamplight shone on her blond hair and glittered in her eyes so that it almost looked as if stars were in their depths, winking at him. She was nothing like the women he was usually drawn to. And she was everything he wanted. God, knowing that she was there, in his house, right down the hall from his own bedroom, was making for some long, sleepless nights.

Oblivious of his thoughts, she smiled at him, crossed the room and dropped into a wingback chair on his right. Curling her feet up beneath her, she said, "Yes, the baby went right to sleep as soon as I laid him down. Thanks for asking."

He frowned to himself and silently admitted that, no, he hadn't been thinking about the baby. Hardly his fault when she was so near. He dared any man to be able to keep his mind off Tula Barrons for long. "I assumed he was sleeping since he's not with you and I can't hear him crying."

She studied him for a thoughtful moment. "Don't you think you should start being a part of the whole putting-Nathan-to-bed routine?"

"When I get the results of the paternity test, I will."

Until then, he was going to hang back. Taking part in bath time a few nights ago had taught him that he was too damn vulnerable where that baby was concerned. He had actually thought of himself as the boy's father.

What if he found out Nathan wasn't his?

No, better to protect himself until he knew for sure.

"Simon, Nathan is your son and pretending he isn't won't change that."

"That's what we need to talk about," he said, standing

to walk to the wet bar across the room. "Do you want a drink?"

"White wine if you've got it."

"I do." He took care of the drinks then sat down again opposite her. Outside, night was crouched at the glass. A fire burned in the hearth and the snap and hiss of the flames was the only sound for a few minutes. Naturally, Tula couldn't keep quiet for long.

"Okay, what did you want to talk about?"

"This," he said, sweeping one hand out as if to encompass the house and everything in it.

"Well, that narrows it down," Tula mused, taking a sip of wine. "Look, I get that you're a little freaked by the whole 'instant parenthood' thing, but we can't change that, right?"

"I didn't say—"

"And I've closed up my house and moved here to help you settle in—"

"Yes, but—"

"You'll get to know the baby. I'll help as much as I can, but a lot of this is going to come down on you. He's your son."

"We don't know that for sure yet and I think—"

She ran right over him again and Simon was beginning to think that he'd never get the chance to have any input in this conversation. Normally, when he spoke, people listened. No one interrupted him. No one talked over him. Except Tula. And as annoying as it was to admit, even to himself, he liked that about her. She wasn't hesitant. Not afraid to stand up for herself or Nathan. And not the least bit concerned about telling him exactly what she thought.

Still, he was forced to grind his teeth and fight for patience as she continued.

She waved her glass of wine and sloshed a bit onto her denim-covered leg. She hardly noticed.

"So basically," she said, "I'm thinking a man like you would feel better with a clear-cut schedule."

That got his attention. "A man like *me?*"

She smiled, damn it and his temperature climbed a bit in response.

"Come on, Simon," she teased. "We both know that you've got a set routine in your life and the baby and I have disrupted it."

This conversation was not going the way he'd planned. He was supposed to be the one taking charge. Telling Tula how things would go from here. Instead, the tiny woman had taken the reins from his hands without him even noticing. Simon took a sip of the aged scotch and let the liquor burn its way down his throat. It sat like a ball of fire in the pit of his stomach and he welcomed the heat. He looked at Tula, watching him with good humor sparkling in her eyes and not a trace of the sexual pull he'd been battling for days.

Irritating as hell that she could so blithely ignore what had been driving him slowly insane. Fresh annoyance spiked at having her so calmly staring him down, pretending to know him and his life and not even once allowing that there was something between them.

Plus, in a few well-chosen words, Tula had managed to both insult and intrigue him.

"I don't have a routine," he grumbled, resenting the hell out of the fact that she had made him sound like a doddering old man concentrating solely on his comfortable rut in life.

She laughed and the sound filled the big room with a warmth it had never known.

"Simon, I've only been in this house a handful of days and I already know your routine as well as you do. Up at six, breakfast at seven," she began, ticking items off on her fingers. "Morning news at seven-thirty, leave for the office at eight. Home by five-thirty..."

He scowled at her, furious that she was reducing his life to a handful of statistics. And even more furious that she was right. How in the hell had that happened? Yes, he preferred order in his life, but there was a distinct difference between a well-laid-out schedule and a monotonous habit.

"A drink and the evening news at six," she went on, still smiling as if she was really enjoying herself, "dinner at six-thirty, work in your study until eight..."

Dear God, he thought in disgust, had he really become so trapped in his own well-worn patterns he hadn't even noticed? If he was this transparent to a woman who had known him little more than a week, what must he look like to those who knew him well? Was he truly that *predictable?* Was he nothing more than an echo of his own habits?

That thought was damned disconcerting.

"Don't stop now," he urged before taking another sip of scotch. "You're on a roll."

"Well, there my tale ends," she admitted. "By eight I'm putting the baby to bed and I have no idea what you do with the rest of your night." She leaned one elbow on the arm of the chair and grinned at him. "Care to enlighten me?"

Oh, he'd like to enlighten her. He'd like to tell her she was wrong about him entirely. Unfortunately, she wasn't. He'd like to take her upstairs and shake up *both* of their routines. But he wasn't going to. Not yet.

"I don't think so," he said tightly, still coming to grips with his own slide into predictability. "Besides, I didn't want to talk about me. We were going to talk about the baby."

"For us to talk about the baby," she countered with a satisfied nod, "you would have to actually spend time with him. Which you manage to avoid with amazing regularity."

"I'm not avoiding him."

"It's a big house, Simon, but it's not that big."

He stood up, suddenly needing to move. Pace. Something. Sitting in a chair while she watched him with barely concealed disappointment was annoying.

Simon knew he shouldn't care what she thought of him, but damned if he wanted her thinking he was some sort of coward, hiding from his responsibilities. *Or* an old man stuck in a routine of his own devising. He walked to the wide bay window with a view of the park directly across the street. Moonlight played on the swing sets and slides, illuminating the playground with a soft light that looked almost otherworldly.

"I haven't gotten the paternity test results back yet," he said, never taking his gaze from the window and the night beyond the glass.

"You know he's yours, Simon. You can feel it."

He looked down at her as she walked up beside him. "What I feel isn't important."

"That's where you're wrong, Simon," she said sadly, looking up at him. "In the end, what you feel is the *only* important thing."

He didn't agree. Feelings got in the way of logical

thought. And logic was the only way to live your life. He had learned that lesson early and well. Hadn't he watched his own father, Jarod Bradley, nearly wipe out the family dynasty by being so chaotic, so disordered and flighty that he neglected everything that was important?

Well, Simon had made a pledge to himself long ago that he was going to be nothing like his father. He ran his world on common sense. On competency. He didn't trust "feelings" to get him through his life. He trusted his mind. His sense of responsibility and order.

Which was how he'd slipped into that rut he was cursing only moments ago. His father hadn't had a routine for anything. He'd greeted each day not knowing what was going to happen next. Simon preferred knowing exactly what his world was doing—and arranging it to suit himself when possible.

Besides, despite what Tula thought, he wasn't so much actively avoiding Nathan as he had been avoiding *her*. Ever since that kiss. Ever since he'd held her breasts cupped in his hands he hadn't been able to think of anything else but getting his hands on her again. And until he figured out exactly what that would mean, he was going to keep right on avoiding her.

Damn it, things used to be simple. He saw an attractive woman, he talked her into his bed. Now, Tula was all wrapped up in a tight knot with the child who was probably his son and Simon was walking a fine line. If he seduced her and then dropped her, couldn't she make it more difficult for him to get custody of Nathan? And what if he had sex with her and didn't *want* to let her go? What then?

There was no room in his life for a woman as flighty

and unorganized as she was. She thrived in chaos. He needed order.

They were a match made in hell.

"Are you even listening to me?"

"Yes," he muttered, though he was actually trying to *not* listen to her.

Which was no more successful than trying not to think about her.

Tula wasn't comfortable in the city.

Ridiculous, of course, since she'd spent so much of her childhood there. Her parents separated when she was only five and her mother, Katherine, had moved them to Crystal Bay. Close enough that Tula could see her father and far enough away that her mother wouldn't have to.

Crystal Bay would always be home to Tula. Right from the first, she'd felt as though she belonged there. Life was simpler, there were no piano lessons and tutors. Instead, there was the local public school where she'd first met Anna Cameron. That friendship had really helped shape who she was. The connection with Anna and her oh-so-normal family had helped her gain the self-confidence to eventually face down her father and refuse to fall in line with his plans for her life.

Now being in San Francisco only reminded her of those long, lonely weekends with her father. Not that Jacob Hawthorne was evil, he simply hadn't been interested in a daughter when he'd wanted a son. And the fact that his daughter didn't care at all about business was another big black mark against her.

Funny, Tula thought, she had long ago gotten past the regrets she had for how her relationship with her father had died away. Apparently though, there was still a tiny spark inside her that wished things had been different.

"It's okay though," she said aloud to the baby who wasn't listening and couldn't have cared less. "I'm doing fine, aren't I, Nathan? And you like me, right?"

If he could speak, she was sure Nathan would have agreed with her and that was good enough for now.

She sighed and pushed the stroller along the sidewalk. Nathan was bundled up as if they were exploring the Arctic Circle, but the wind was cold off the bay and the dark clouds hanging over the city threatened rain.

She and the baby had been in that house for days and it was harder and harder to be there without thoughts of Simon filling her mind. She knew it was pointless, of course. She and Simon had nothing in common except that flash of heat that had practically melded them together during that amazing kiss.

But she couldn't help where her mind went. And lately, her mind kept slipping into wildly inappropriate thoughts of Simon. Which was exactly why she had bundled Nathan up for a walk. She needed to clear her head. Needed to get back to work on the book that was due by the end of the month. It was hard enough eking out the time for illustrations and storyboards while the baby was napping. Forcing herself to work on the Lonely Bunny's antics while daydreaming about Simon made it nearly impossible.

Whenever Tula was having a hard work day, she would take a walk, just to feel the bite of the fresh air, see people, listen to the world outside her own mind. Ideas didn't pop into an idle mind. They had to be fostered, engendered. And that usually meant getting out into the world.

Actually, one of her most popular books had been born at the grocery store in Crystal Bay. She remembered watching a pallet of vegetables being delivered and immediately, she'd felt that magic "click" in her brain that told her an idea was forming. Soon, she'd had the story line for *Lonely Bunny Visits the Market*.

"So see, Nathan, we're actually working!" She chuckled a little and picked up the pace.

There were so many people scurrying along the sidewalks, Tula felt lost. But then she'd been feeling a little lost since settling into Simon Bradley's house. She hadn't written a word in three days and even her illustrations were being ignored. She couldn't keep this up much longer. She had deadlines to meet and editors to appease.

And Simon was taking up so many of her thoughts, she was afraid she wouldn't be able to think of anything else.

The only bright side was that she knew Simon was feeling just as frustrated as she was. That he wanted her as much as she did him. And she couldn't help relishing that sweet rush of completely feminine power that had filled her when he'd practically thrown her out of the bathroom during Nathan's bath time a few days ago. He hadn't trusted himself around her.

Which was just delicious, she thought. Of course it would be crazy to surrender to whatever it was that was simmering between them. She had Nathan to think about, after all. She couldn't just give in to what she was feeling and not think about the consequences.

Don't I sound responsible? she thought with surprise.

Well, she was. Now. Now that she had Nathan in her

life, she had to judge every decision she made along the measurement of what was good for him. And sleeping with his father couldn't be a good idea. Especially knowing that it was up to *her* to decide when Simon was ready for custody.

She stopped short.

Was that why he had kissed her?

Was he trying to seduce her into giving him Nathan?

"Now, that's a horrible thought," she said aloud.

"I beg your pardon?"

"Hmm?" Tula looked at the older woman who had stopped on the sidewalk to look at her. "Oh, sorry. I was actually talking to myself."

"I see." The woman's eyes went wide and she hurried past.

Tula laughed a little, then stepped to the front of the stroller to check on Nathan. "Well, sweetie, I think that nice lady thought I was crazy."

He kicked his legs, waved his arms and grinned at her. All the approval she needed, Tula thought, and stepped around to push him along the sidewalk again.

There were stores, of course. Small boutiques, coffee bars and even a cozy Italian restaurant with tables grouped together on the sidewalk.

But what caught her eye was the bookstore.

"Let's go see, Nathan."

She stepped inside and paused long enough to enjoy the atmosphere. An entire store devoted to books and the people who loved them. Was there anything better? Crossing to the children's section, Tula smiled at the parents indulging their kids by sitting on the brightly colored rugs to pick out books.

When she saw a little girl reading *Lonely Bunny Makes a Friend* Tula's heart swelled with pride.

She wandered over to the shelf where her books were lined up and, taking a pen from her purse, began signing the copies there.

A few minutes later, a voice stopped her mid-scrawl.

"Excuse me."

Tula looked at a woman in her mid-forties with a name tag that read Barbara and smiled. "Hi."

The woman looked her up and down, taking in her faded jeans, blue suede boots and windblown hair before asking, "What are you doing?"

Tula dug into her purse and pulled a roll of gold-and-black autographed copy stickers that she always carried with her. "I'm the author and I thought since I was here I would just sign your stock, if that's all right."

She had never had trouble before. Usually bookstores liked having signed copies of the books on the shelves to help with sales.

"You're Tula Barrons?" Barbara asked with a wide grin. "That's wonderful! My daughter loves your books and I can tell you they sell very well for us here in the store."

"I'm always glad to hear that," Tula said and hurried her signature as Nathan started to fuss.

"You live locally?" Barbara asked.

"Temporarily," Tula told her and felt a slight wince inside at the admission. She didn't know how long she would be staying in the city, but she was already dreading having to leave both Nathan and Simon.

"Would you be interested in doing a signing here at the store?" the woman asked. "We could set it up for you to do a reading at the same time. I think the kids would love it."

"Uh," Tula hedged, not sure if she should agree or not. Normally, she would have, of course. But now that she had Nathan to worry about…

"Please consider it," Barbara urged, looking around the children's area at the brightly colored floor rugs, the tiny tables and chairs. "I know most authors hate doing signings, but I can promise you a success! Your books are very popular here and I know the children would get a big kick out of meeting the woman who writes the Lonely Bunny stories."

Tula followed her gaze and looked at the dozen or so kids sprinkled around the area, each of them lost in the wonders of a book. Yes, her life was a little up in the air at the moment, but a couple hours of her time wasn't that much of a sacrifice, was it?

"I'd love to," she finally said.

"That's *great*," Barbara replied. "If you'll just give me a number where I can reach you, we'll set something up. How does three weeks sound?"

"It's fine," Tula told her. While Barbara went to get a pad and pen to take down her information, Tula told herself that in three weeks, she might be back living in Crystal Bay. Alone. That would mean a drive into the city for the signing, but if she was gone from Simon's life, she would at least be able to stop in and see Nathan while she was here.

Her heart ached at the thought. That baby had become so much a part of her life and world already, she couldn't even imagine being nothing more than a casual visitor to him. She put the signed book back on the shelf, walked to the front of the stroller and went down to her knees.

Running her fingers across the baby's soft cheek, she looked into brown eyes so much like his father's it was eerie and said, "What will I do without you, Nathan? If I lose you now, you won't even remember me, will you?"

He laughed and kicked his legs, turning his head this way and that, taking in all the primary colors and the bright lights.

Her already aching heart began to tear into pieces as she realized that Nathan would never know how much she loved him. Or how much it hurt to think of not being a part of his life.

She'd agreed to be the baby's guardian for her cousin Sherry's sake. But Tula had had no idea then that doing the right thing was going to one day destroy her.

Simon got home early the following day and no one was there to appreciate it.

Damned if he'd be so boring that Tula could set her watch—if she had the organizational skills to wear one—by him. He was still fuming over her monologue the night before, ticking off his daily routine and making him sound as exciting as a moldy rock.

In response, Simon had been shaking up his routine all day long. He had gone through the flagship of the Bradley department stores, stopping to chat with clerks. He'd personally talked to the managers of the departments, instead of sending Mick to do it. He had even helped out in the stockroom, walking a new employee through the inventory process.

His employees had been surprised at his personal

interest in what was happening with the store. But he had also noted that everyone he talked with that day was pleased that he'd taken the extra time to listen to them. To really pay attention to what was happening.

Simon couldn't imagine why he hadn't done it years ago. He was so accustomed to running his empire from the sanctity of his office, he'd nearly forgotten about the thousands of employees who depended on him.

Of course, Mick had ribbed him about his sudden aversion to routine.

"This new outlook on life wouldn't have anything to do with a certain children's book author, would it?"

Simon glared at him. "Butt out."

"Ha! It does." Mick followed him out the door and down the hall to the elevator. "What did she say that got to you?"

He was just aggravated enough by what Tula had had to say the night before that he told Mick everything. He finished by saying, "She ticked off my day hour by hour, on her fingers, damn it."

Mick laughed as the elevator doors swept closed and Simon stabbed the button for the ground floor of the department store. "Wish I'd seen your face."

"Thanks for the support."

"Well come on, Simon," Mick said, still chuckling. "You've got to admit you've dug yourself a pretty deep rut over the years."

"There's nothing wrong with a tight schedule."

Mick leaned against the wall. "As long as you allow yourself some room to breathe."

"You're on her side?"

Grinning, Mick said, "Absolutely."

Grumbling under his breath at the memory, Simon

stalked up the stairs, haunted by the now unnatural silence. For years, he'd come home to the quiet and had relished it. Now after only a few days of having Tula and the baby in residence...the silence was claustrophobic. Made him feel as if the walls were closing in on him.

"Ridiculous. Just enjoy the quiet while you've got it," he muttered. At the head of the stairs, he headed down the hall toward his room, but paused in front of the nursery. The baby wasn't there, but the echo of him remained in the smell of powder and some indefinable scent that was pure baby.

He stepped inside and let his gaze slide across the stacked shelves filled with neatly arranged diapers, toys and stuffed animals. He smiled to himself and inspected the closet as well. Inside hung shirts and jackets, clustered by color. Tiny shoes were lined up like toy soldiers on the floor below.

In the dresser, he knew he would find pajamas, shorts, pants, socks and extra bedding. A colorful quilt lay across the end of the crib and a small set of bookshelves boasted alphabetically arranged children's books.

Tula might thrive in chaos herself, he mused, but here in the baby's room, peace reigned. Everything was tidy. Everything was calm and safe and...perfect. He'd had a crew in to paint the room a neutral beige with cream-colored trim, but Tula had pronounced it too boring to spark the baby's inner creativity. It hadn't taken her long to have pictures of unicorns and rainbows on the walls, or to hang a mobile of primary-colored stars and planets over the crib.

Shaking his head, Simon sat down in the cushioned rocker and idly reached to pull one of the books off the shelves. *Lonely Bunny Finds a Garden.*

"Lonely Bunny," he read aloud with a sigh. Now that he'd heard her story, he could imagine Tula as a lonely little girl with wide blue eyes, trying to make friends with a solitary rabbit. He frowned, thinking about how her mother had so callously treated her daughter's fears.

He was feeling for Tula. Too much.

Opening the book, Simon read the copyright page and stopped. Her name was listed as Tula Barrons Hawthorne.

He frowned as his memory clicked into high gear, shuffling back to when he was dating Nathan's mother, Sherry. He remembered now. She had been living here in the city then and she'd told him that her uncle was in the same business as Simon.

"Jacob Hawthorne." Simon inhaled slowly, deeply, and felt old anger churn in the pit of his stomach.

Jacob Hawthorne had been a thorn in his side for years. The man's chain of discount department stores was forever vying for space that Simon wanted for his own company. Just three years ago, Jacob had cheated Simon out of a piece of prime property in the city that Simon had planned to use for expansion of his flagship store.

That maneuver had cost Simon months in terms of finding another suitable property for expansion.

Not to mention the fact that Jacob had bought up several of the Bradley department stores when Simon's father was busily running the company into the ground. The old man had taken advantage of a bad situation and made it worse. Hell, he'd nearly succeeded in getting his hands on the Bradley *home*.

By the time Simon had taken over the family business, it was in such bad shape he'd spent years rebuilding.

Jacob Hawthorne was ruthless. The old pirate ran his company like a feudal lord and didn't care who he had to steamroll to get his own way.

At the time Simon had briefly dated Sherry, he'd enjoyed the thought of romancing a member of Hawthorne's family, knowing the old coot would have been furious if he'd known. But Sherry's own clingy instability had ended the relationship quickly. Now, though, he had a son with the woman—which made his child a relative of Jacob Hawthorne.

There was a bitter pill to choke down. And he figured it would be even harder for the old pirate to swallow it. But there was more, too. If Sherry and Tula were cousins, then Tula was also a relative of Jacob Hawthorne. Interesting. But before his thoughts could go any further, his cell phone rang.

"Bradley."

"Simon, it's Dave over at the lab."

He tensed. This was the call he'd been waiting for for days. The results of the paternity test were in. He would finally know for sure, one way or the other.

"And?" he asked, not wanting to waste a moment on small talk when something momentous was about to happen.

"Congratulations," his old friend said, a smile in his tone. "You're a father."

Everything in Simon went still.

There was a sense of rightness settling over him even as an unexpected set of nerves shook through him. He was a father. Nathan was really his.

"You're sure?" he asked, moving his gaze around the

room, seeing it now with fresh eyes. His *son* lived here. "No mistakes?"

"Trust me on this. I ran the test twice myself. Just to be sure. The baby's yours."

"Thanks, Dave," he said, tossing the book onto the nearby tabletop and standing up. "I appreciate it."

"No problem."

When his friend hung up, Simon just stared down at his phone. *No problem?*

Oh, he could think of a few.

Such as what to do about the woman who was making him insane. The very woman who stood between him and custody of *his* son.

Seven

Tula knew something was different, she just couldn't put her finger on what it was exactly. Ever since she and Nathan had returned from their walk, Simon had been…watching her. Not that he hadn't looked at her before, but there was something more in his gaze now. Something hungry, yet wary.

There was a strained sense of anticipation hanging over the beautiful house that only added to the anxiety she had been feeling for days. She was on edge. As though there were tightened wires inside her getting ready to snap.

Just being around Simon was difficult now. As it had been ever since that kiss. He made her want too much. Need too much. And now, with those dark eyes locked on her and heat practically rolling off of him in waves, she could hardly draw a breath.

She made it through dinner and through Nathan's bath time and was about to read the baby his nightly story. Oh, she knew the baby didn't understand the words or what the stories meant, but she enjoyed the quiet time with him and felt that Nathan liked hearing the soft soothing tones of her voice as he fell asleep. Before she could begin, Simon walked into the nursery.

Tula smiled in spite of the coiled, unspoken strain between them. For the first time, he was inviting himself to Nathan's nightly ritual. "Hi."

"I thought I'd join you tonight." Simon looked at her for a long moment, then shifted his gaze to the tiny boy in the crib. Slowly, he walked across the floor and Tula sensed that she was witnessing something profound. Simon's features were taut, his eyes unreadable. There was a careful solicitude in his attitude she'd never seen before.

Leaning over the crib, Simon looked down at the boy in the pale blue footed jammies as if really seeing him for the first time.

"Simon?" she asked quietly, as if hesitant to break whatever spell was spinning out into the room. "What is it? You've been weird all night. Is something wrong?"

He shifted a quick look at her before turning his gaze back on Nathan. The baby stared up at him, then rubbed his eyes and sighed sleepily.

"Wrong?" Simon echoed in a thick hush of sound. "No. Nothing's wrong. Everything's right. I got the paternity test results this afternoon."

She sucked in a breath of air. Of course, from the beginning, she had known that Simon was Nathan's father. Sherry wouldn't have lied about something like that. But Tula could understand that Simon, a demon for rules and order and logic, would have to wait to be convinced.

"And?" she prompted.

"He's my son." Three words, spoken with a sort of dazed wonder that sent a flutter of something warm racing along her spine.

He reached into the crib and cupped one side of Nathan's face in the palm of his hand. The baby smiled up at him and Simon's eyes went soft, molten with emotions too deep to speak. Tula watched it all and felt her own heart melt as a man recognized his son for the very first time.

Seconds ticked past and still it was as if the world had taken a breath and held it. As if the planet had stopped spinning and the population of the earth had been reduced to just the three of them.

This small moment was somehow so intense, so important, that the longer it went on the more Tula felt like an outsider. An intruder on a private scene. That thought hurt far more than she would have thought it could.

For weeks now, she alone had been the baby's entire universe. When she was forced to share Nathan with Simon, she was still the central figure because Nathan's father was, if nothing else, a stubborn man. Determined to hold himself emotionally apart even while making room in his life for the boy. Now she saw that Simon had accepted the truth. He knew Nathan was his and he would be determined to have his son for himself.

As it should be, Tula reminded herself, despite the pain ratcheting up in the center of her chest. This was what Sherry had wanted—that Nathan would know his father. That Simon and his son would make a family.

A family, she told herself sadly, of *two*.

With that thought echoing over and over through her mind, Tula stepped back from the crib, intending to leave the two of them alone. But Simon reached out and grabbed her arm, pulling her to a stop.

"Don't go."

She looked up at him. The room was dark but for the night-light that projected constellations of stars onto the ceiling. In the dim glow of those stars, she watched his eyes and shook her head. "Simon, you should have a minute alone with Nathan. It's okay."

"Stay, Tula." His voice was low, hardly more than a dark rumble of sound.

"Simon…"

He pulled her closer until he could wrap one arm around her shoulders. Then he turned her toward the crib and they both looked down at the boy who had fallen asleep. There would be no story tonight. Nathan's tiny features were perfect, the picture of innocence. His small hands were flung up over his head, his fingers curling and relaxing as if in his dreams he was playing catch with the angels.

"He's beautiful," Simon whispered.

Tula's throat tightened even further. It was a miracle, she thought, that she could even breathe past the hard knot of emotion clogging her throat. "Yes, he is."

"I knew he was mine, right from the first," he admitted. "But I had to be sure."

"I know."

He turned his head to look down at her. Emotions charged his eyes with sparks that dazzled her. "I want my son, Tula."

"Of course you do." Her heart cracked a little further.

He would have Nathan and she would have…Lonely Bunny.

"I want you, too," he admitted.

"What?" Jolted out of her private misery, she could only stare up into brown eyes that shimmered with banked heat. This she hadn't seen coming. She hadn't expected. Something inside her woke up and shivered. Was he saying…

"Now," he said, drawing her from the room into the hall, leaving the sleeping infant laying beneath his night-light of floating stars.

"Simon—"

"I want you now, Tula," he repeated, drawing her close, framing her face with his hands.

Ah, she thought. He wanted Nathan forever. He wanted her *now*. That was the difference. She chided herself silently for even considering that he might have meant something different. A twist of regret grabbed at her but she relentlessly pushed it aside.

She'd been in his home for nearly a week. She knew Simon Bradley was a cool, calm man who didn't make decisions lightly. He liked to think he responded to his gut instincts, but the truth was, he looked at a situation from every angle before making a decision.

He wasn't the kind of man who would take some sexual heat and a shared love for a child and build it into some crazy happily-ever-after scenario. That was all in her mind.

And her heart.

She should have known better. *How silly,* she told herself, staring up into his eyes. How foolish she'd been to allow herself to care for him. To idly spin daydreams that had never had a chance to come true.

The three of them weren't a family. They were a temporary unit. Until Simon and Nathan had found their way together. Then good old "Aunt Tula" would go home and maybe come to the city once in a while for a visit.

As Nathan got older, he would no doubt resent time spent with her as simply time lost with his friends. He would be awkward with her, she thought, her heart breaking at the realization. Kind to a distant relative when his father forced him to be polite.

The little boy she loved so much wouldn't remember her love or the comfort he had derived from it. How she had sung to him at night and played peekaboo in the mornings. He wouldn't know that she would have done anything for him. Wouldn't recall that they had once been as close as mother and son.

He would have no memories of these days and nights, but they would haunt *her* forever.

She would be alone again. But this time, it would be so much worse. Because this time, she would know exactly what she was missing.

"Tula," Simon whispered, drawing her back from thoughts that were threatening to drown her in misery. He tipped her face up until their gazes were locked, his searching, hers glittering with a sheen of tears she refused to shed for the death of a dream that should never have been born.

So very foolish, she thought now, looking up at Simon Bradley. Until this very moment, Tula hadn't had any idea that she was more than halfway in love with a man she would never have.

"What is it?" he demanded. "Are you crying?"

"No," she said quickly because she couldn't let him

know that she had just said goodbye to a fantasy of her own making. "Of course not."

He accepted her word for that as his thumbs traced over her cheekbones.

"Come to my room with me, Tula," he said softly, his voice an erotic invitation she knew she couldn't resist. More, she knew she didn't want to resist it. She'd let the fantasy go but she would be a fool to turn her back on the reality, however brief it might be.

Reaching up, she covered his hands with her own and gave him the answer they both needed. "Yes, Simon. I'll come with you. I want you, too. Very much."

"Thank God." He bent and kissed her, hard and fast.

"Just let me turn the monitor on first," she said, walking back into the nursery, shooting a quick look at the baby as he sighed and smiled through his dreams. She flipped the switch on the monitor, knowing the receivers in hers and Simon's rooms would pick up every breath the baby made during the night.

She stared down at Nathan for a long moment, then turned her gaze on the doorway. There Simon stood, dark eyes burning with a fire that thrummed inside her just as hotly. Her body ached, her core went damp with need. She moved toward him and as she stepped into the hallway, he pulled her in close, then swung her up into his arms.

"I can walk, you know," she said wryly, the last of her sorrow draining away against a tide of rising passion. In spite of her protest, she secretly delighted in being carried against his hard, strong body.

"But why walk when you can ride?" One of his eyebrows lifted into the arch that she knew so well and she had to admit that being snuggled against Simon's broad chest was much preferable to a long walk down a silent hall.

The house sighed like a tired old woman settling down for a good night's rest. The creaks and groans of the wood were familiar to her now and Tula felt as though she were wrapped in warmth.

Warmth that suddenly enveloped her in heat as Simon dipped his head to claim another brief, fierce kiss. When he broke the kiss, his dark eyes were flashing with something that sent a quick chill racing along Tula's spine. Passion and just a hint of something more dangerous shone down at her and Tula's stomach erupted with a swarm of what felt like bees.

Head spinning, heart pounding, she linked her arms around his neck as he strode into his bedroom and headed for the wide, quilt-covered bed. She had never been in his room before and she glanced around at the huge space. Wildly masculine, the room was done in brown and dark blue. Deep brown leather chairs were drawn up in front of a blazing tiled fireplace. Twin bay windows overlooked the street, the park beyond and the distant ocean. The bed was big enough, she thought wryly, to sleep four comfortably and moonlight poured through the windows to lay in a silver path along the mattress. As if someone, somewhere, had drawn them a road map to where they both wanted to go.

"Gotta have you. Now," he muttered thickly, dropping her to the bed and following after.

"Yes, Simon," she answered, reaching for the buttons on his shirt, tearing at them when they refused to give.

Simon was half-crazed with wanting her. Everything

he had planned to say to her tonight dried up in the face of the overwhelming need clutching at him. Pulling at the hem of her bloodred sweater, he dragged it up and over her head to display the silky pink camisole she wore beneath. His gaze locked on her pebbled nipples. No bra. That was good. Less time wasted.

Simon hadn't been able to keep his mind on anything but Tula for hours. The question of his son's parentage had been answered and any other damn questions could just wait their turn. This was what he needed. What he had to have. Her.

Just her.

He pulled the camisole up, exposing her breasts to his hungry gaze and his mouth watered for a taste of her. He shrugged out of his shirt as she pushed the material down his arms, but beyond that, he couldn't be bothered.

Clothes would come off when they needed to. For now…he bent his head to her breasts and took first one nipple, then the other into his mouth. She gasped and arched off the bed, pushing herself into him, silently begging for more.

He gave her what she wanted.

Lips, tongue, teeth ran across the pink, sensitized tips of her breasts. Her taste filled him, her sighs inflamed him. Her fingers threaded through his hair, holding him to her breast as she squirmed under him, desperate for more. For everything.

He knew that feeling and shared it. His body ached. He was so hard for her he felt as though he might combust if he didn't get inside her. Tearing his mouth from her breasts, he worked his way down her incredibly lush body.

"So small, so perfect," he whispered, his breath hot against her skin.

"I'm not small," she countered, then gasped when his tongue traced a line around her belly button. "You're just abnormally tall."

He grinned and glanced up at her.

She shrugged. "Fine. I'm short."

"And curvy," he added, flicking the snap of her jeans and drawing down the zipper in one smooth move. His fingertips slid across her skin and she whimpered.

Simon smiled again and tugged at the jeans keeping him from her. They slid off her legs and fell to the floor. He paused then to admire the scrap of pink lace that made up the thong she wore. "If I'd known those jeans were hiding something like this, we'd have made it here long before now."

She ran her tongue across her bottom lip and everything in Simon fisted.

"Now that you know," she teased, "what are you planning on doing about it?"

In answer, he tugged the lace down her legs and off, shifted position and pulled her to the edge of the bed.

"Thought I'd start with this," he said and ran his tongue across the most sensitive spot on her body.

She jolted and instinctively squirmed beneath his strong hands holding her in place. But Simon wasn't letting her go anywhere. Instead, he pulled her closer to him, draped her legs across his shoulders and took her core with his mouth.

Tula groaned helplessly against the onslaught of emotions, sensations rampaging through her system. She looked down the length of her own body to watch him as he kissed her more intimately than anyone ever had before.

It was erotic. Sensuality personified, to see him licking her, tasting her and at the same time to feel what he was making her feel. Spirals of need and want clung together inside her and twisted into a frantic knot that seemed to pulse along with the beat of her heart.

And as her heartbeat quickened so did the tension coiling inside her. Tighter, faster, she felt herself nearing a precipice that swept higher with every passing moment. She raced toward it, surrendering to the incredible sensations coursing through her. She held nothing back—sighing, groaning, whispering his name as he pushed her further along the twisting road to completion.

Her breath was strangled in her lungs. She reached for the explosion she knew was coming and when the end came, her hands clenched the quilt beneath her and Tula held on as if for her life. The world rocked and her mind simply shut down under the onslaught of too many tiny shuddering ripples of pleasure.

Even before the last rolling sigh of satisfaction had settled inside her, Simon was there, moving her on the mattress, levering himself over her.

Staring down into her eyes, he entered her and Tula gasped at yet one more sensation. One more amazing invasion of her heart and mind and body. She held on to his shoulders and looked into dark brown eyes that were shadowed with secrets and shining with the same overpowering passion that held her in its grip. Again and again, his body claimed hers in the most intimate way possible. Again and again, she gave herself up to him, holding nothing back. Again and again, he pushed her higher and faster than she'd ever gone before.

The mind-numbing, soul-shattering climax, when it rushed through her, was enough to steal what little breath she had left. Moments later, she felt his release pound through him and heard him groaning her name. Then he collapsed atop her, his breath wheezing from his lungs, his heartbeat hammering in his chest.

Tula wrapped her arms around him and held him close, not wanting him to move yet. Not wanting to let go of the closeness that was somehow even more intimate than what they had just shared.

What could have been minutes or hours passed in a sensual haze of completion. Finally, he lifted his head, met her gaze and gave her a smile that at once made him look sexy and playful. That one smile slipped inside her and gave her the last nudge she needed to take the slippery slide into something she feared was probably, heaven help her, *love*.

"What is it?" he asked, voice quiet. "You look worried."

She was. Worried for her own sanity. Her own well-being. Falling in love with Simon would be a huge mistake, Tula thought grimly, so she just wouldn't do it. She would refuse to take that last step. It wouldn't be easy, she knew, but protecting herself was too important. Instinctively she realized she needed protection, too. Because loving and *losing* Simon would be enough to devastate her.

"Worried?" she echoed lamely, scrambling for something to say.

"I used protection," he assured her. "You weren't really paying attention, but I did."

"Oh. Thanks," she said, though a part of her wondered if it might not have been better if he hadn't. Then she would have had a chance at having a baby of her own. A child that would help fill the hole that losing Nathan was going to dig in her heart.

"Tula—" He pushed himself up on his elbows, took a breath and said, "We should talk about what just happened."

"Do we have to?" she asked, hating for this time to end with what couldn't possibly be good news. Whenever a man told a woman they had to talk, it was rarely to say, "Boy, that was great, I'm really happy."

He rolled to one side, and the chill in the room settled over her skin the moment he left her. He stacked pillows against the headboard and leaned back, his gaze on her. "Yeah. We do. Look, this was…inevitable, I think."

"Like death and taxes you mean?" she muttered, already hating how this conversation was going.

"You know what I'm talking about."

"Yeah, I do. And you're right," she sighed in agreement and sat up beside him on the bed.

He was sprawled naked, completely at ease. But Tula was suddenly feeling a little fragile. A little exposed. So she grabbed the edge of the quilt and tossed it over her, covering herself from breasts to knees. "Simon, you don't have to feel guilty or make a speech. I wanted this, too. You didn't seduce me into anything."

"I know."

"Well," she said with a small, self-conscious laugh. "Thanks for noticing."

"Not the point, Tula," he said. "The point is, we're still involved over Nathan and I want to make sure we understand each other."

She turned her head to look at him. "What are you talking about?"

Frowning, he pushed one hand through his hair. "Just that, you hold the strings when it comes to Nathan's custody."

She nodded, unable to look away from his eyes, once so warm and now looking as cold as the damp winter night outside. Somehow, he had taken a step away from her without actually leaving her side. Amazing that he could pull that off naked, but he managed.

"I don't want this," he continued, voice hard and flat, "what just happened here between us, to affect that."

Stunned, Tula could only stare at him, dumbfounded. This was not what she had been expecting. She'd thought that he was about to deliver the old, that-was-a-mistake-that-won't-be-repeated speech. Instead, he was intimating… *"What?"*

His mouth flattened into a grim line and that one eyebrow lifted. Surprisingly, she found it far less charming this time.

"Are you serious?" she demanded, indignant fury driving her words. "You really think I'm the kind of person who would use *this* against you somehow?"

"I didn't say that."

"Oh, yes you did," she told him, tossing the quilt aside and scooting off the bed. She grabbed her jeans and pulled them on over bare skin when she couldn't spot her lace thong. "I can't believe this. After what we just did, you could think that I, how could you think that? Amazing. And I'm so stupid. I should have seen this coming."

"Just wait a damn minute—"

She glanced at him over her shoulder. "That is about the most insulting thing anyone's ever said to me."

"I wasn't trying to insult you."

"So it's just a bonus then."

He climbed off the bed and went to grab his own jeans. Tugging them on, he said in a patient, calm tone that made her want to throw something, "Tula, you're overreacting. We're two adults, we should be able to talk about this without getting emotional."

"Emotional? Oh, could I show you emotional. Right now I want to throw something at that swelled head of yours."

"Not helpful," he pointed out, then looked around as if judging what she might grab and hurl at him.

"There's one of the differences between us, Simon," she snapped, whipping her head around to glare at him as she grabbed up her sweater. "Throwing things sounds very helpful to me right now. See, I'm not *afraid* to get emotional."

"What the hell are you talking about?" Now it was his turn to look insulted. "Who said I was afraid? This isn't even about fear."

"Really? Looks that way to me. My God, Simon." She cocked her head and narrowed her eyes on him. Shaking her head, she said, "You relaxed for like what? Twenty minutes? Was I on your schedule? Did you pencil me in—*Sex with Tula*—then back to business?"

"Don't be ridiculous," he muttered.

"Oh, now I'm ridiculous," she echoed, tossing both hands high then letting them fall. "You're the one making this into something it never was. This little speech you're making isn't about Nathan at all. It's about you backing away from allowing yourself to feel something genuine."

"Please." He scoffed at her and that one eyebrow winged up. "This isn't about feelings, Tula. We both had an itch and we scratched it. That's all."

She hissed in a breath and her eyes narrowed even farther until the slits were so tiny it was practically a miracle she could see him at all. "An *itch?* That's what you call what just happened?"

"What do you call it?" he asked.

Good question. She wasn't about to call it anything nice *now*. She wouldn't give him the satisfaction. So instead, she ignored the subject entirely. "Honestly, Simon, the very minute you felt close to me at all, you pulled back and hid behind that stiff, businessman persona you wear as if it were just another three-piece suit."

"Excuse me?"

"Oh," she said, warming to her theme and riding on bruised feelings and insult, "I'm just getting started. You're worried that now that I've been in the fabulous Simon Bradley's bed I might try to use that in deciding Nathan's future? Well, trust me when I say that sex with you won't sway my decision about you taking custody…"

He folded his arms over his chest. "Was there an insult in there?"

"Quite possibly, but I wasn't finished."

"Finish then. I knew there was more coming."

"You haven't proved to me yet that you're anywhere near ready to take care of a baby. Heck, until you were absolutely sure he was your son, you hardly went near him."

"And that's bad?"

"It is when you're too busy protecting yourself to give a child a chance."

"That's not what I was doing."

They stared at each other, gazes simmering with passions that had nothing to do with sex.

"This was clearly a mistake," Tula said a moment later, when she thought she could speak without shrieking. "But thankfully it's one that doesn't have to be repeated."

"Right. Probably best." Simon shoved one hand through his hair and said, "I still want you."

Tula looked at him for a long moment before admitting, "Yeah. Me, too. Good night, Simon."

She left the room and he didn't stop her. But she couldn't help turning back for one last look as she walked out. He looked powerful. Sexy.

Very alone.

And even after everything that had just happened, something inside her urged Tula to go back to him. Wrap her arms around him and hold on.

She had to remind herself that he had *chosen* solitude.

Eight

"I handled it badly, I know that."

"Yeah," Mick agreed cheerfully the following day. "That about covers it. Were you *trying* to piss her off?"

"No," Simon said, shaking his head as he thought about the night before. Hell, he couldn't remember much besides the urgent need he had felt to get her under him. Although the fight afterward was etched clearly enough in his mind. He still wasn't sure how it had happened. He hadn't meant to alert her to the fact that he was aware of the power she held in the situation. Hadn't meant to throw down a gauntlet just so that she could hit him over the head with it.

All he had really wanted to do was let her know that he wasn't going to be led around by his groin. That he was more than his passions. That sex with her, no matter how astounding, wasn't going to change him.

Simon made the rules.

Always.

But somehow, when he was around Tula, rational thought went out the window. Today, here in his office, away from the woman who was making him crazed, he was able to think more clearly. Now what he needed to know was what exactly Mick had found out about Tula Barrons Hawthorne.

"Never fight with a woman after sex," Mick was telling him. "They're feeling all warm and cozy and whatever. Men want to sleep. So hell, even *talking* after sex can be dangerous—if you ever want sex again."

Oh, he did, Simon thought. He wanted her the moment she left his room. He had wanted her all night and had awakened that morning aching for her. *Want* wasn't the issue.

"Just skip the advice and tell me what information you turned up."

Mick frowned at him and Simon thought that this was the downside of having your best friend work for you. He was less likely to take orders well and more likely to deliver his opinion whether Simon wanted it or not. "What did you find out? I know she's related to Jacob Hawthorne, but how? Niece?"

"A lot closer than that, as it turns out. She's his daughter."

"His what?" Simon went on alert. "His *daughter?*"

His mind raced as he listened to Mick give him more details.

"Hawthorne and his ex split when Tula was a kid. Mom moved with her to Crystal Bay. Tula visited her father often, but several years ago, she appears to have cut all ties with people here completely—including her father. My source didn't know much about it, just that Tula's a sore spot with the old man."

He had already known about her moving to that little town with her mother, Simon thought. But why would she cut all ties with everyone here, including her father? And why had he never heard about a daughter before? Was the old bastard protecting his child? Simon wouldn't have thought Jacob Hawthorne capable of familial loyalty.

"And," Mick added, "seems that when she started publishing children's books, she began using her middle name, Barrons. It's a family name, after her maternal grandmother. That grandmother left a will that provided a trust for Tula so that she—"

He straightened up in his desk chair and leaned both forearms on the neatly stacked files on his desk. "How big a trust?"

Mick thumbed through the papers he held. "To you, fairly small. To most of the world, very nice. It at least allowed her to buy her house and support herself while writing."

"Her books don't earn much?"

Mick shook his head. "She has a small, but growing readership for her Lonely Bunny series. The money will probably improve, but between her writing and the trust, she gets along and lives well within her limited means."

"Interesting." Her father was rich and she lived in a tiny house nearly an hour away from the city. What was the story behind that? he wondered.

"She hasn't seen her father in a few years that I can

find," Mick continued. "But then, the old man almost never leaves the city, either."

Hell, Simon thought, Jacob hardly left the Hawthorne building. He had a penthouse suite at the top of the structure that was his company's headquarters. He ruled his world from the top of his tower and rarely interacted with the "little people."

But as he thought that, Simon had to wince. Until the other day when he had deliberately gone through the store chatting with his employees, people could have said the same thing about him. There were some very uncomfortable similarities between Simon and his enemy.

"Is there anything else?" he asked, mainly to get his mind off that realization.

"No," Mick said, laying the sheaf of papers on his lap. "I can probably get more if you want me to dig deeper."

He thought about that for a moment. If he turned Mick loose and told him to dig, he'd have every piece of information available on Tula Barrons within a couple of days. But did he need more? He now knew who she was. He knew that she was the daughter of his enemy.

That was plenty.

While Mick talked, offering advice that he wasn't listening to, Simon tried to consider the situation objectively. He was attracted to Tula, obviously. The passions she stirred in him were like nothing he'd ever known. But now he knew who she was and damned if he could bring himself to trust a Hawthorne. So where did that leave him?

"What're you planning?"

He glanced at Mick. "I don't know what you're talking about."

"Right. I've seen that look before," his friend said, settling into the chair in front of Simon's desk. "Usually just before you're plotting some major takeover of an unsuspecting CEO."

Simon laughed and missed his point deliberately. "No CEO is ever unsuspecting."

"Damn it, Simon, what're you up to?"

"The less you know, the better off you are," he said, knowing that his friend would try to argue him out of the plan quickly forming in his mind.

"You mean the less you have to listen to my objections."

"That, too."

Mick slapped one hand down hard on the arm of his chair. "You're crazy, you know that? So what if she's a Hawthorne? Her father's a miserable old goat. She's got nothing to do with him."

"Doesn't matter."

"Damn it, Simon," Mick continued. "She split with him years ago. Doesn't even use her real name for God's sake."

"She's still his daughter," Simon insisted. "Don't you get it? The daughter of the man who tried to destroy my family is now in *charge* of when I get custody of my own son. How the hell am I supposed to take that, Mick? What if she just decides to never approve my custody of Nathan?"

"You really think she'd do that?"

"She's a Hawthorne." As far as he was concerned, that explained everything. God, he was an idiot. He had actually begun to trust Tula. He'd *felt* for her. More than he had anyone else in his life. Now he finds out this? For all he knew, Jacob had manufactured Nathan's mother's will. Maybe he and his daughter were in this together. Conspiring to dangle his son in front of him only to snatch him back.

He sprang to his feet as if the thought of sitting still another moment was going to kill him. Turning his back on his friend, he stared out the wide window at the view of San Francisco that Tula had admired so the first day he met her.

But instead of the high-rises and the glittering bay beyond the city, he saw *her*.

Her eyes. Her smile. That damn dimple in her cheek. He heard her sigh, felt the ripples of satisfaction rolling through her body as they took each other.

It had been one night since he had been with her and he wanted her again so badly, it was gnawing at him. Had she planned that, too? Had she deliberately set out to seduce him just so she could crush him later and sit with her father to enjoy the show?

His guts tightened and a cold, hard edge wrapped itself around his heart. The nebulous plan still forming in his mind was looking better and better by the moment.

"If you screw this up, you could be risking your son," Mick reminded him unnecessarily.

"No," Simon said, glancing back over his shoulder at his friend. "Don't you get it? A *Hawthorne* is in charge of whether or not I'm fit to care for my son. How could I possibly make that any worse?"

"Let me count the ways," Mick muttered darkly.

"You'll see," Simon told him, warming to his plan even as it took final shape in his mind. "I'm going to seduce Tula—" *again,* he added silently "—until she can't think straight. By the time I'm finished, she'll support me getting custody of Nathan. And when I'm sure of that, I'll go to her father and tell him that I've been sleeping with his daughter. If that doesn't give the old man a stroke, nothing will."

"What'll it do to her?" Mick asked quietly.

For one brief second, Simon considered that. Considered how it would be when she found out that she'd been used by him. But he let that thought go as soon as he remembered that she was a Hawthorne and that her family was more than accustomed to using and being used.

"Doesn't matter," he ground out.

"Whatever you say." Mick stood up and shook his head. "I'm heading home now, but before I go, one more piece of advice."

"I'm not going to like it, am I?"

Mick shrugged. "Whoever likes unsolicited advice?"

"Good point. Okay, let's have it."

"Don't do it."

"Do what?"

"Whatever it is you're planning, Simon." Mick locked his gaze with his friend's and said in all seriousness, "Just let this go."

Simon shook his head. "Hawthorne cheated me."

"His daughter didn't."

"She lied to me. About who she was. Maybe about why she's in my damn house."

"You don't know that. You could just ask her."

Sending a warning glare at his friend, Simon said, "You don't understand."

"You're right," Mick told him, turning for the door.

"I don't. For the last week or so, you've been almost… happy. I'd hate to see you screw that up for yourself, Simon."

He didn't say anything as Mick left. Hell, what was there to say? There was an opportunity here. A chance to get back at Jacob Hawthorne while at the same time indulging himself in a woman he wanted more than he was comfortable admitting.

An image of Tula filled his mind and his body went hard and heavy almost instantly. Remembering how responsive she was in bed had him wanting her so desperately, he'd have done anything to have her that minute. Even that damned fight they'd had hadn't cooled him off any. Instead, it had stoked the fires already inside him. He'd never enjoyed a fight more.

Didn't mean anything though, he told himself. Yes, he'd admitted to liking her. But that was before he knew who she really was. Now he didn't know if he could believe the person she'd shown herself to be. Maybe it was all an act. Maybe everything she had done since arriving at his house had all been part of an elaborate show.

If it was, he would have the last laugh. If it wasn't… he shook his head. He wouldn't consider that. Tula *Hawthorne* was a grown woman. She could make her own decisions. And if she decided to join him in his bed—and she would, *again*—that would be her choice.

She'd be fine.

He'd have his revenge.

And his son.

* * *

"He was a complete jerk," Tula said into her cell phone, then caught the baby watching her warily. She didn't care what some people thought about children and their awareness to the world around them. She knew that Nathan was sensitive to tone and her moods, so she instantly forced a smile, despite the sheen of ice that felt as though it was coating her insides.

"Honey," Anna's sympathetic voice came over the phone. "You're the one who always reminded me that most men are jerks at one point or another."

"Yes, but at *that* point?" Tula said in a hiss, still smiling for Nathan's sake. "Seriously, Anna the glow hadn't even begun to fade and he turned on me like a rabid dog."

"Well, I hope you gave it right back to him."

"I did," she said, remembering their fight last night. It had completely colored everything that went before it and that was saying something.

Sex with Simon had been even more amazing than she had imagined it could be. But to have it all ruined because Simon had donned his metaphorical suit right after was just infuriating.

"Nothing I said got through to him though, so it hardly matters that I fought back," she mused, plucking a windblown brown leaf from the blanket and tossing it into the air. "He was so cold. So..."

"Believe me I know," Anna assured her. "Remember how awful Sam was in the beginning?"

"That's different."

"Really, how?"

Tula laughed halfheartedly. "Because this is about *me*."

"Ah, well sure. Now I see."

Another laugh shot from Tula's throat helplessly. "Fine, fine. You suffered, all women suffer. But *my* suffering is happening now."

"Okay, there you've got me."

"Thanks. So. Advice?"

"Plenty, but advice isn't what you need, Tula. You already know how to handle this."

"Really, how's that?"

"Get Simon ready for Nathan and then come home. Where you belong."

Where she belonged.

For so many years, the tiny house in Crystal Bay had been just that. Tula's haven. The one spot in the world where she felt as if she'd carved out a place for herself. But now, thinking about going back to her old life of work and friends sounded somehow…empty.

Her gaze turned on the baby laying on a blanket spread over the grass of Simon's backyard. She didn't know if she *could* go back home. Her small house would now be crowded with memories of a baby that had brightened it so briefly. She would hear Nathan's cries in the night, find his toys tucked under the couch. She would wonder, always, how he was, what he was doing.

Just as she would wonder about Simon.

The bastard.

How dare he make her care for him and then become just…a *man?* How could he have experienced what they had shared and then turn his back on it all so mechanically? How could he simply flip a mental switch and shut off his emotions as easily as turning off a lightbulb?

Or maybe she was reading too much into him.

Giving him too much credit. Maybe he didn't *have* any emotions. Maybe that suit that so defined him had stunted any natural human feelings. Hadn't she warned herself the very first day she had met him that he was too much like her father? Too caught up in the world of corporate finances for her to be interested in him?

She should have listened to herself.

Then she remembered the look on his face as he had stared down at Nathan, knowing the baby was his son. His features had been easy enough to read. The man was capable of love. He simply wasn't interested in it.

At least, not with her.

"Yoo-hoo?"

"Huh? What?" Tula shook her head and said, "Sorry, sorry. Wasn't listening."

"Yeah, I got that," Anna said wryly. "You're not ready to come home yet, are you?"

"I can't. The baby and—"

"No." Anna's voice was soft and filled with understanding sympathy. "I mean, you're not ready to walk away from Simon yet, are you?"

Tula's shoulders slumped in resignation, though her friend couldn't see it. "No, guess I'm not. That makes me some kind of grand idiot, doesn't it?" Then, without waiting for her friend's response, she answered her own question. "Of course it does. Why would I think I could have feelings for a man so much like my father? Why didn't I stop myself?"

"Because sometimes you just can't, honey." Anna laughed. "Look at me! I took that mural job Sam offered me because I needed the money. I even told him to his face that I couldn't stand him! Now look where I am...

married and pregnant. Sometimes, the heart just wants what it wants and you can't do anything to change it."

"Well, that's not fair at all."

"And so little is," Anna commiserated. "Now, back to my original question with this phone call…do you still want me to come to the city this weekend? Do the mural on Nathan's wall?"

Tula thought about that. Knew Simon would probably hate it—he of the beige-with-cream-trim designing skills. Then Tula looked at the baby, waving his little arms at the naked tree branches high overhead. And she knew that if she couldn't be with him, then at least she could leave behind a physical reminder of her presence. One that both Nathan and Simon would see every day.

"Yeah, I do," Tula told her friend. "Nathan's room needs some brightening up."

"Great! I've already got some fabulous ideas."

"I trust you," Tula said, then added, "I've only got one request."

"What's that?"

"Paint in the Lonely Bunny somewhere, will you?" She reached out and smoothed her fingertips along Nathan's cheek. "That way it will almost be like I'm still here, watching over him. Even after I'm gone."

"Oh, sweetie…"

She heard the sympathy in her friend's voice and steeled herself against it. Tula didn't want pity. In fact, she wasn't sure what exactly she *did* want. Beyond Simon, of course, and that was never going to happen.

It would have been easier to seduce Tula if they hadn't already been to bed only to have the fight that had left both of them furious.

But Simon was nothing if not determined.

He dismissed Mick's warnings that seemed to repeat over and over again in his mind. After all, Mick was married. He and Katie had been together since college. They fit together so well, it was hard to believe they hadn't started out life joined at the hip. So how could his best friend understand the tension, the stubborn refusal to back down once a position was taken? How could he know anything about the sexual heat that flared during an argument?

How could he ever understand the enmity Simon felt for the Hawthorne family?

Simon knew exactly what he was doing—as he always did. And the fact that Mick disagreed wasn't going to stop him.

This plan of his was going to kill two birds with one impressive stone, he told himself. Not only would he be able to indulge himself with Tula—something he hadn't been able to stop thinking of—but he'd also have the revenge on her father that he had been dreaming of for three years. It would absolutely fry that old man when he found out that his daughter had been in Simon's bed.

But first things first. Before his plan could get into motion, Simon had to start making arrangements for when he had custody of Nathan. He wouldn't have Tula to care for the baby while he was at work, so he would need someone responsible for the job.

He didn't let himself think about the fact that when that day came, Tula would be out of their lives.

Nine

An hour later, he was home early again and didn't even stop to admit that since Tula had come into his life, he'd found less and less reason for hanging around the company. Instead, he seemed to be drawn to this old house and the woman inside it.

Simon found Tula in the backyard, watching Nathan squirm on a blanket beneath the winter sun. She turned to look at him and he could actually *see* her freeze up. A part of him regretted being the cause of that. He was too accustomed to her easy smile and ready laugh. Seeing her so wary, so cold, gave him a pause that none of Mick's not so subtle warnings had managed to do.

But he reminded himself that she was a Hawthorne and had never bothered to mention it. How much did he owe her anyway? Besides, he had a plan now and once Simon picked a direction, he didn't deviate. That would indicate that he doubted himself and he never did that.

Stuffing his hands into the pockets of his slacks, he walked down the flagstone steps that led to the landscaped yard. Each step was slow, deliberately careless, letting her know that though she might be angry, he was just fine.

Liar.

His brain shouted out that single word and he recognized the truth in it. But damned if he'd let her know.

"Isn't it a little cold out here for him?" Simon asked, nodding at the boy who was wearing a shoulder-to-toes zip-up blanket sleeper.

"Fresh air's good for him," she said stiffly. She countered, "You're home early."

He grinned, pleased that she'd noticed. "I am. I wanted to talk to you."

"Oh, can't wait," she said, sarcasm coloring her tone. "Our last conversation went so well."

Good, he told himself. She was still bothered. He liked knowing that what they'd shared had hit her as hard as it had him. And more, he wanted to share it all again. A lot.

He took a seat beside her on the blanket and hid a smile when she scooted away a bit. As if she didn't trust herself too near him. He knew just how she felt.

At the moment, all he really wanted to do was grab her and hold her and—

"What can you possibly have left to say that you didn't say last night?"

"Plenty," he admitted, drawing one knee up and resting his forearm on it.

"Let me guess," she said, her blue eyes snapping with banked fury. "You've found a way to blame me for global warming? Or am I a spy of some kind, sent to ferret out all of your secrets and feed them to your enemies?"

He just stared at her. Was that last statement for show or was she actually trying to tell him why she was really there? "Is that a confession?"

"Oh, for heaven's sake, Simon," she snapped in a whispered hiss. "You know darn well it's not. I'm just trying to guess how you'll insult me next."

He wondered, but let it go for now. "As a matter of fact, I don't want to talk about you at all," he said. "Now that we're committed to getting me ready to take over custody of Nathan, we have to find a competent nanny."

"A *nanny?*" she asked in the same tone she might have used to ask, *You want to hire an axe murderer?*

He nodded, pleased with her reaction. Even if he was confused about her motivation for being there, with him, he knew for a fact that she loved Nathan.

"I'll still have to work, so when you leave, I'll need someone here with the baby. I think a live-in nanny would be the best way to go, don't you?"

"I don't know," she said, glancing down at the babbling baby. "I hadn't really thought about someone else caring for him on a day-to-day basis."

Actually, Simon didn't much care for the idea of a stranger in his house taking care of his son while he wasn't there. But he couldn't see any way around it, either. No matter how his plan ended up working out, Tula wouldn't be here for him and Nathan to count on.

He really didn't like the thought of that, but refused to explore the reasons why.

"He can't go to work with me," Simon said abruptly, watching her reaction.

"No, I suppose not."

"Is there a problem?"

Her gaze flicked to his, fired for an instant, then cooled off again until those beautiful blue eyes of hers shone like the surface of a frozen lake. "No. No problem."

"Good," he said. "So I'll call the employment agency and have them send people over. Are you interested in interviewing them or would you prefer I do it?"

She looked torn and he was forced to admit silently that he felt the same way. Funny, this conversation about hiring a nanny didn't have anything to do with his plan. It had only seemed like a reasonable way for him to open communications with Tula again. Besides, theoretically, a caretaker for Nathan had sounded acceptable enough.

In practice though…looking down at his son— innocent, helpless, at the mercy of whoever his father hired to look after him…it felt wrong, somehow. Instantly, half-forgotten news reports flashed through his mind, stories about nannies and babysitters and pre-schools, all of whom were supposedly devoted caregivers. And how the children in their charge had paid the price for their negligence or apathy.

Frowning, Simon told himself this situation would be different. He would have the nanny he hired screened completely. He wouldn't trust just anyone with his son's safety.

But the scowl on his face deepened as he realized

that the only person he really trusted with Nathan's well-being was the woman beside him. The very woman who he already knew to be a liar. She hadn't told him the truth about who she was, so why should he trust her?

But he did. Instinctively, he knew he could trust Tula with his son. But she was also the woman who would be leaving someday soon.

The woman he was planning on using for his own taste of revenge.

Tula thanked the woman for coming and once she'd seen her out, closed the door and leaned back against it. A sigh of defeat slid from her throat.

That was the third prospective nanny she had interviewed in the last two days and she hadn't liked any of them.

"What was wrong with that one?"

Startled, she looked up at Simon, leaning against the newel post of the banister. His eyes were amused and his mouth was curved at one end as if he were trying to hide a smile that hadn't quite made it to his features.

"What're you doing here?" He had the most disconcerting habit of sneaking up on a person. And this new habit of his, splintering the routine he had clung to when she first came to the city, was even more disquieting. He was up to something, she figured. She just didn't know what. Which just put her that much more on guard.

He tossed his suit jacket over the newel post and loosened his red silk tie. "I live here, as I've pointed out before."

"Yes, but it's the middle of the afternoon. On a workday. Are you sick?"

He chuckled. "No, I'm not sick. I just left the office early. No big deal. Now, what was wrong with the woman you just sent packing?"

Still wary, she asked, "Didn't you see the bun she was wearing?"

"Bun?"

She saw the confusion on his face and explained. "Her hair. It was pulled into a taut little knot at the back of her head."

"So? An unattractive hairstyle makes for a bad nanny?"

It sounded silly when he said it, but Tula was going with her instincts. Nathan was too important to take any chances with his safety and happiness. She would find the *right* nanny for him or she just wouldn't leave.

Unless, she thought, that's exactly what she was subconsciously hoping for. That she could stay. That she could be the one raising Nathan, loving him. A worry for another day, she supposed.

"The woman's hair was scraped so tightly, her eyelids were tilted back. Anyone that rigid shouldn't be in charge of a child."

"Ah," he said as though he understood, but she knew he didn't. He was patronizing her.

"So the one yesterday afternoon, with her hair long and loose and curling…?"

She scowled at him. "Too careless. If she doesn't care what her hair looks like, she won't care enough about Nathan."

"And the first one?"

"She had mean eyes," Tula said with no apologies. She just knew that woman was the kind who made children sit in dark closets or go to bed without dinner. She would never leave Nathan with a cold-eyed woman.

Simon's eyebrow lifted again. She was getting to the point where she could judge his moods by the tilt of that eyebrow alone. Right now, she told herself with an inner grumble, he was entertained. By *her*.

Perhaps he had a point. Tula knew what she was doing wasn't fair to the women who had come looking for a job. Except for the mean-eyed one, they seemed nice enough. Certainly qualified. The agency Simon was dealing with was the top one in the city, known for representing the absolute best in nannies.

But how could she be expected to turn over a little boy she loved to a stranger?

He was still watching her with just the barest hint of amusement on his face. An expression she found way too attractive for her own well-being.

"All right," she conceded grudgingly, "maybe I'm being a little too careful in the selection process."

"Maybe?"

She ignored that. Because even if she was being overprotective, it wouldn't hurt that baby any. It would only help ensure that the best possible person would be in charge of him. And if anything, as the baby's father, Simon should appreciate that.

"This is important, Simon. No one knows better than I do just how much the people in a child's life can impact their character. The way they look at the world. The way they think of themselves."

She caught herself when she realized that she was headed in a verbal direction she had had no intention of going.

"Speaking from experience," he mused and she knew

he was remembering the story she'd told him about the bunny she had once tried to befriend. And about her mother's less than maternal attitude toward her.

"Is that so surprising?" she countered. "Doesn't everyone have some sort of issue with their parents? Even the best of them make mistakes, right?"

"True," he acknowledged, but his gaze never left hers. She felt as if he were trying to see inside her mind. To read her thoughts and display all of her secrets.

As if to prove her right, he spoke again.

"Who had that impact on you, Tula?" he asked, voice quiet. "Was it just your mom?"

"This isn't about me," she told him, refusing to be drawn into the very discussion she had unwittingly initiated.

"Isn't it?" he asked, pushing away from the banister to walk toward her.

"No," she insisted with a shake of her head. She felt the intensity of his gaze and flinched from it. Tula didn't need sympathy and wasn't interested in sharing her childhood miseries with a man who had already made it clear just how he felt about her. "This is about Nathan and what's best for him."

He kept coming and was close enough now that she had to hold her breath to keep from inhaling the scent of him. A blend of his aftershave and soap, it was a scent that called to her, made her remember lying beneath him, staring up into his eyes as they flashed with passion. Eyes that were, at the moment, studying her.

"You said it yourself," he told her, "we're all affected by who raised us. And whoever raised you will affect who you choose to care for Nathan."

Instantly, her back went up. He'd somehow touched on the one thing that had given her a lot of misgivings over the years. She had thought about how she was raised and about her parents and had wondered if she should even have a child of her own. But the truth was, Tula's heart yearned for family. Hungered for the kind of love and warmth she used to dream about. And she had always known she would be a good parent because she knew just what a child wanted. Craved.

So she was completely prepared and ready to argue this point with Simon.

"No, Simon. You're wrong about that. The initial input a child is given is important, I agree. And when we're kids and growing up, it pushes us in one direction or another. But at some point, responsible adults make choices. *We* decide who we are. Who we want to be."

He frowned as he thought about what she said. "Do we? I wonder. Seems to me that we are always who we started out to be."

Uncomfortable with being so close to him and unable to touch, she walked into the living room. She wished Nathan were awake right now because then she could claim that she didn't have time to talk. That she had to take care of the baby. But it was nap time and that baby really enjoyed his naps. Ordinarily, she loved that about him because she could get a lot of her own work done. Today, when she could have used Nathan's presence, she had to admit there would be no help coming from that quarter.

She kept walking farther into the huge room and didn't stop until she was standing in front of the bay window. Naturally, Simon followed her, his footsteps sure and slow, sounding out easily against the wood floor.

"So," he said, "you're saying your parents had nothing to do with who you are today?"

Tula laughed to herself but kept the sound quiet, so he wouldn't know just how funny that statement really was. Of course her parents had shaped her. Her mom was a lovely woman who was simply never meant to be a mother. Katherine was more at home with champagne brunches than PTA meetings. Impatient with clumsiness or loud noises, Katherine preferred a more formal atmosphere—one without the clamor of children.

Being responsible for a child had cut into Katherine's lifestyle, though it had significantly increased her alimony when she and Jacob divorced.

But when her stint at motherhood was complete, Katherine left. She moved out of Crystal Bay the morning of her daughter's eighteenth birthday.

Tula still remembered that last hug and brief conversation.

The airport was crowded, of course, with people coming and going. Excitement simmered in the air alongside sorrow as lovers kissed goodbye and family members waved and promised to write.

"You'll be fine, Tula," her mother said as she moved toward her gate. "You're all grown up now, I've done my job and you're entirely capable of taking care of yourself."

Tula wanted to ask her mother to stay. She wanted to tell Katherine that she so wasn't ready to be alone. That she was a little scared about college and the future. But it would have been pointless and she knew that, too. A part of her mother was already gone. Her mind and heart were fixed in Italy, just waiting for her body to catch up.

Katherine was renting a villa outside Florence for the summer, then she would be moving on—to where, Tula had no idea. The only thing she was absolutely sure of was that her mother wouldn't be back.

"Now, I can't miss boarding, so give me a kiss."

Tula did, and fought the urge to hug her mom and hold on. Sure, her mother had never been very maternal, but she had been there. Every day. In the house that would now be empty. That would echo with her own thoughts rattling around in the suffocating silence.

Her father was in the city and Tula wouldn't be seeing him anytime soon, so she was truly on her own for the first time ever. And though she could admit to a certain amount of anticipation, the inherent scariness of the situation was enough to swamp everything else.

Thank God, Tula thought, she still had Anna Cameron and her family. They would be there for her when she needed them. They always had been. That knowledge made saying goodbye to her mother a bit easier, though no less sad.

She'd often dreamed that she and her mother could be closer. She had wished she had the sense of family that Anna had. Though Anna's mom had died when she was a girl, her father and stepmother had supported and loved her. But wishes changed nothing, she told herself firmly, then pasted a bright smile on her face.

"Enjoy Italy, Mom. I'll be fine."

"I know you will, Tula. You're a good girl."

Then she was gone, not even bothering to glance back to see if her daughter was still watching.

Which Tula was.

She stood alone and watched until the plane pulled away from the gate. Until it taxied to the runway. Until it took off and became nothing more than a sun-splashed dot in the sky.

Finally, Tula went home to an empty house and promised herself that one day she would build a family. She would have what she had always longed for.

Simon was watching her, waiting for her to answer his question. She scrubbed her hands up and down her arms and said, "Of course they influenced me. But not in the way you might think. I didn't want to be who they were. I didn't want what they wanted. I made a conscious decision to be myself. *Me.* Not just a twig on the family tree."

A flash of surprise lit his eyes and she wondered why.

"How's that working out for you?"

"Until today," she admitted, "pretty good."

He walked closer and Tula backed up. She was feeling a little vulnerable at the moment and the last thing she needed was to be too near Simon. She kept moving until the backs of her knees hit the ledge of the cushioned window seat. Abruptly, she sat down and her surprise must have shown on her face.

He chuckled and asked, "Am I making you nervous, Tula?"

"Of course not," she replied, while her mind was screaming, *Yes!* Everything about him was suddenly making her nervous and she wasn't sure how to handle it. Since she'd met him, he'd irritated her, intrigued her. But this anxiousness was a new sensation.

Tula knew everyone thought of her as flaky. The crazy artist. But she wasn't really. She had always known what she wanted. She lived the way she liked and made no apologies for it. She always knew who was in her life and what they meant to her.

At least, she had until Simon. But he was a whole different ball game. He went from insulting her to seducing her. He made her furious one moment and hot and achy the next. For a man who had so loved his routine, he was becoming entirely too unpredictable.

She couldn't seem to pin him down. Or guess what he was going to do or say. She had thought him just another staid businessman, but he was more than that. She simply wasn't sure what that meant for her. Which made her a little nervous, though she'd never admit to it. So to keep herself steady, she started talking again.

"You've heard my story, so tell me, how did wearing a three-piece suit by the age of two affect you?"

He gave her a half smile and sat down beside her on the window seat. Turning his head, he stared through the glass at the winter afternoon behind them.

A storm was piling up on the horizon, Tula saw as she followed his gaze. Thunderclouds huddled together in a dark gray mass that promised rain by evening. Already, the wind was picking up, sending the naked branches of the trees in the park into a frenzied dance. Mothers gathered up their children as the sky darkened further and soon the park was as empty as Tula felt.

When Simon finally spoke, his voice was so soft, she nearly missed it. "You think you've got me figured out, do you?"

She studied him, trying to read his eyes. But it was as if he'd drawn a shutter over them, locking himself away from her.

"I thought so," she admitted and her confusion must

have been evident in her tone. "When I first met you, you reminded me of...someone I used to know," she said, picturing her father, fierce gaze locked on some hapless employee. "But the more I got to know you, the more I realized that I didn't know you at all. Well, that made no sense," she ended with a laugh.

"Yeah, it did," Simon said, shifting to look at her again, closing off the outside world with the intensity of his gaze. Making her feel as if she were the only thing in the world that mattered at the moment.

"Simon..."

"Nobody is what they look like on the surface," he murmured, features carefully blank and unreadable as he studied her. "I'm just really realizing that."

Ten

He was looking at her as if he had never seen her before. As if he were trying to see into her heart and mind again, searching out her secrets. Her desires.

"I don't know what you mean," Tula said.

"Maybe I don't, either." He took a breath, blew it out and after a long, thoughtful moment, changed the subject abruptly. "You know, I grew up here, in this house. My great-grandfather built it originally."

"It's a lovely house," she said, briefly allowing her gaze to sweep the confines of the room. "It feels *warm*."

"Yeah, it does." His gaze was still locked on her. "Now, more than ever."

Why was he telling her this? Why was he being… nice? Weren't they at odds? Didn't their argument still hang in the air between them? Only a few minutes ago, he had looked at her with cool detachment and now everything felt different. She just didn't understand *why*.

"Several years ago, my father almost lost the house," he said, forcing an offhand attitude that didn't mesh with the sudden stiffness of his shoulders or the tightness in his jaw. "Bad investments, trusting the wrong people. My dad didn't have a head for business."

"I can sympathize," she muttered, remembering how many times her own father had made her feel small and ignorant because she hadn't cared to learn the intricacies of keeping ledgers and accounts receivable.

He kept talking, as if she hadn't spoken at all. "He was too unorganized. Couldn't keep anything straight." Shaking his head, he once more stared out at the gathering storm and focused on the windowpane as the first drops of rain plopped against it. But Tula knew he wasn't looking at the outside world so much as he was staring into his own past. Just as she had moments ago.

"My dad entered a deal once with a man who was so unscrupulous he damn near succeeded in taking this house out from under us. This man cheated and lied and did whatever he had to in his effort to bury my father and the Bradley family in general." Simon shook his head again. "My father never saw it coming, either. It was sheer luck that kept this house in the family. Luck that saved what was left of our business."

She heard the old anger in his voice and wondered who it was that had almost cost his family so much. Whoever it was, Simon was still furious with the man and she wished she could say something that would ease that feeling. Tula knew all too well that hanging on to anger didn't hurt the one it was focused on. It only made *you* miserable.

"I'm glad it worked out that way," she said simply. "I can't imagine how hard it must have been for your father. And you."

He looked at her as if judging what she'd said, trying to decide if she had meant it. Finally though, he accepted her words with a nod. "In a way, I guess it wasn't my dad's fault. He went into the family business because his father wanted it that way. My dad hated his life, knew he wasn't any good at it and that must have been hard, living with a sense of failure every day."

"I know what that's like."

He tipped his head to one side and narrowed his eyes. "Do you?"

She smiled, actually enjoying this quiet time with him. The talking, the sharing of old pains and secrets. She had never really talked about her father with anyone but Anna. But somehow, it seemed right now, to let Simon know that he wasn't alone in his feelings about the past.

"My father had plans for me, too," she said sadly. "And they didn't have anything to do with what I wanted."

He nodded again thoughtfully. "For me, I watched what happened with my dad and I learned."

"What?" she prompted, her voice soft and low. "You learned what?"

His eyes narrowed as he watched her and Tula felt the heat of his stare slide into her bones.

"I learned to pay attention. To make rules and follow them. To never let anyone get the best of me. There's no room in my life for chaos, Tula," he said.

There was no subtext there and she knew it. He was saying flat out that there was no room in his life for *her*. She had figured that out for herself, of course. But somehow hearing him say it out loud left a hollow feeling in the pit of her stomach.

"I saw exactly what happens when a man loses focus," Simon added. "My dad couldn't concentrate on work he hated, so he didn't pay attention. I never lose focus. I guess I did the same thing you did. Made my own choices in spite of the early training by my father."

And those choices would keep them apart. He couldn't have been any clearer. So why, she wondered, was he looking at her as if he wanted nothing more than to grab her and carry her up to his bed? Heat filled his eyes even as a chill colored his words. The man was a walking contradiction and Tula really wished she didn't find that so darned attractive.

She shook her head as if to rid herself of that thought and asked, "What about your mother? Didn't she have some impact on you, too?"

"No," he said abruptly. "She died in a car wreck when I was four. Don't remember her at all."

"'I'm sorry' doesn't sound like much," she told him, "but I am."

"Thanks." He looked at her again and this time there was emotion glittering in his eyes. She just wished she could decipher it. Simon Bradley touched her in ways she had never experienced before. Even knowing that nothing was going to come of what was simmering between them couldn't stop her from wishing things were different.

Wishing that just once in her life, someone would see her for who she was and want her.

"Tell me more about your father," Simon said suddenly. "What's he like?"

"Like you," she blurted without thinking.

"Excuse me?"

Tula thought it a little weird that he could look so insulted without even knowing who her father was. "What I mean is, he's a businessman, too. He practically lives in his office and can't see anything in his life if it's not on his profit-loss statements. He's a workaholic and he likes it that way."

He leaned back against a pillow tucked up to the wall. "And that's how you see me?"

"Well, yeah." Grateful to be off the subject of her own family, Tula said, "You're a lot like him. Go to work early, come home late—"

"I'm home early today. Have been for the last few days."

"True and I don't know what to make of that."

"I intrigue you?"

"You confuse me."

"Even better."

"No," she said, inching back on the window seat to keep plenty of room between them. "It's really not, Simon. I don't need more confusion in my life and you've already made it pretty clear what you think about me."

"That fight we had, you mean?"

"Yes."

"Didn't mean a thing," he told her and leaned forward.

"That's not how you felt *then*," she reminded him, trying not to notice that he was just within reach of her.

"As I remember it, you had plenty to say, too."

"Okay, yes. I did. You made me mad."

"Oh, trust me, you made that perfectly clear."

"Good then. We both remember that argument."

"That's not all we remember," he said, voice low, thick. He reached for her hand before she could pull back and rubbed his thumb across her palm.

Tula shivered. It wasn't her fault, she thought frantically. It's not like she *chose* to be this attracted to him. It was simple chemistry. A biological imperative. Simon touched her and she went up in flames.

But she could choose to step back from the fire.

"Simon…"

"Tula, we were good together."

"In bed, sure, but—"

"Let's just concentrate on the bed for right now, huh?"

Oh, that sounded really good, she silently admitted. That featherlight touch on her palm was already firing up every nerve ending in her body. She took a breath, held it, then released it on a sigh.

Oh, Tula, she thought wildly, *you're going to do it, aren't you?*

Even as that disappointed-in-herself sigh wound through her mind, Tula was leaning in toward Simon.

It was inevitable.

Her gaze locked with his as his mouth touched hers. A whispered groan slid from her throat at that first, gentle contact. And she realized just how much she'd missed him. Missed *this*. It didn't seem to matter that they were constantly butting heads. He was right. For now, all she had to concentrate on was what she felt when she was with him. When she surrendered herself to the magic of his touch, his kiss.

No doubt, there would be plenty of time for regrets in the coming weeks and months. For right now there was only *him*.

As if a floodgate had been opened somewhere inside her, emotions churned, fast and furious throughout her system. She leaned in closer, allowing him to deepen the kiss. His arms closed around her, holding her tightly to his chest and suddenly, the wide window seat seemed too narrow. Too public.

He tumbled her to the floor, assuring that he landed on the hardwood and she was cushioned against his chest.

Her breath left her in a whoosh of sound. She lifted her head, looked down into his eyes and grinned. "You okay?"

He winced, then smiled back. "I'm fine. And I'm about to be better."

"Promises, promises..."

A wide smile dazzled his eyes and made her heartbeat jump into a gallop. His hands swept up and down her spine and paused long enough to give her behind a quick squeeze.

"I know a challenge when I hear one," he said and lifted his head from the floor to kiss her again. Harder, deeper, his tongue swept past her defenses and tangled with hers in a sensual dance that stole her breath.

She cupped his face in her palms, loving the feel of his whiskers against her skin. She shivered as his arms tightened around her, holding her so closely she could feel the pounding of his heartbeat shuddering through her.

He rolled over, cradling her in his arms until she was on her back and his heavy weight pressed down on her. Tula sighed, loving the feel of him on top of her. She didn't mind the hardness of the floor beneath her, because he was too busy making sure she felt nothing but pleasure.

He tore his mouth from hers, buried his face in the curve of her neck and nibbled at her throat, sending tiny jolts of sensation across her skin. Tula fought for breath and ran her hands up and down his broad back. His heavy muscles tensed and flexed beneath her fingertips and she smiled at the knowledge of how much her touch affected him.

Staring up at the beamed ceiling overhead, Tula lost herself in the flash of heat swamping her. His hands moved over her body with finesse and determination. He left trails of fire in his wake. She felt as though she were burning up from the inside and all she could think of was the need for even more flames.

His mouth moved over her skin, her throat, her jaw and up again to her mouth where he kissed her until she couldn't breathe, couldn't think. Only sensation was left to her.

Then passion crashed down on them both in the same searing instant. Hands moved quickly, freeing buttons, undoing snaps and zippers and in seconds, they were naked, entwined tightly together on the living room floor.

Rain beat a counterpoint to the gasps and moans sounding out in the dimly lit room. From outside came the muffled heartbeat of the world. Cars whizzing past, wheels on wet streets sounding like steaks sizzling on a grill. Wind rattled the windowpanes and sighed beneath the eaves. From the nearby monitor came the quiet, steady breathing of the child upstairs in his bed.

And none of those sounds were enough to intrude on this moment. Around them, the world continued. But in that room, time stood still. There was only the two of them, Tula thought. Just she and Simon and for this one amazing instant she was going to forget about everything else. Stop trying to read the future, or hide from the past, long enough to enjoy the present.

Instead, she would lose herself in a pair of chocolate-brown eyes that saw too much and revealed too little.

"You're thinking," he accused, one corner of his mouth lifting into a half smile.

"Sorry," she said, smoothing her fingertips across his jaw. "Don't know how that happened."

"Let's just see what I can do about shutting down that busy brain of yours."

"Think you're up to the challenge?" she teased.

"Baby," he assured her, "I'm *very* up for it."

A surprised laugh shot from her throat and Tula sighed with happiness. Having a lover who could make her laugh at the most astonishing times, was really a gift. And maybe, she thought, there were even *more* layers to Simon Bradley than she had assumed. Maybe—

Then he began his quest to shut off her thoughts and he was more than successful. Tula groaned when his mouth came down on her breast. He licked and nibbled and she twisted beneath him, trying to take more of what he offered. Needing to feel all she could of him. Needing—just *needing*.

He suckled her and she gasped, arching into him, holding his head to her breast, as his mouth pulled at her breast. Her fingers speared through his thick, soft hair. She loved the feel of his mouth on her and thought frantically that she could happily spend the rest of her life like this.

He smiled against her skin. She felt the curve of his mouth against her breast and she knew he was aware of the effect he had on her. But she wasn't interested in hiding it from him anyway. Why shouldn't he know that he could splinter her body and shatter her soul with a kiss? A touch?

The wood floor beneath her bare back was cool, but the heat he built within her was more than a match for it. He lay between her thighs and she felt the tip of him prodding at her center. She wanted that invasion of body into body. Wanted to feel the slick slide of his heat into hers.

She lifted her hips in silent welcome, but he didn't respond to her invitation. Instead, he rolled over, taking her with him until she was splayed atop him, staring down into those eyes that fascinated her so.

"The floor's not real comfortable," he told her, reaching up to cup her breasts in the palms of his hands. "Thought we'd just change position for awhile."

"Change is good," she said, straddling him, keeping her gaze fixed on his. Her hands moved over his sculpted chest. At her touch, he hissed in a breath.

Simon looked up at her and felt his mind blur. He'd been planning this seduction for days and now that it was here, his plans meant nothing. The only thing that mattered was her. The feel of her. The taste of her. The soft sighs that drifted from her throat at his touch.

Shadowy light played on her choppy blond hair and winked off the silver hoops in her ears. Her big blue eyes were glazed with the same passion claiming him.

He kneaded her breasts with a firm, gentle touch and tweaked her hardened nipples between his thumbs and forefingers. He loved watching the play of emotion on her face as she hid nothing from him.

Her eager response to lovemaking only fed the fires inside him, pushing at him to take more, to give more. Her hips were rocking instinctively and his own body was hard and tight.

He set his hands at her hips and lifted her high enough off him that he could position himself to slide inside her. She closed her eyes, tipped her head back and, taking control of the situation, slowly, inch by inch, took him inside. She settled herself over him with a deliberately slow slide that was both tantalizing and exasperating. He tried to hurry her, to push himself into her harder, deeper, but the tiny, curvy woman was in control now, whether he liked it or not.

"You're just going to have to lay there and take it," she said, a sly, purely female smile on her lips.

His eyes crossed as she finally settled on top of him, with his body sheathed completely inside hers. She was tight and damp and so damn hot he couldn't think of anything but the sensations crashing down on him.

She moved, just a slight wiggle of her hips, but that small action shot through him with the force of a nine-point earthquake. He felt the world tremble. Or at least his corner of it. And he wanted more.

Didn't matter *why* he'd seduced her, he assured himself. All that mattered now was what they created together. The impossible heat. The incredible friction of two bodies moving as one toward a climax that would be, he knew, richer and more all-encompassing than anything else he'd ever known.

He didn't care who Tula was. Didn't want to remember that he was, in effect, setting her up to be used as a weapon against her own father. What he wanted to concentrate on now was how well they meshed. How their bodies joined so easily it was as if they were two pieces in the same puzzle.

She moved on him again, her hips rocking, taking him in and releasing him in a slow rhythm that built steadily into a pace that stole his breath and the last of his thoughts.

She arched her back, pushing her breasts higher. Her hands were on his chest, bracing herself as she rode him with a frenzied, honest passion that shook him to the core. Hands at her hips, he stared up into her eyes as she moved, and he was caught by the light glittering in those blue depths.

He felt swept up by both passion and emotion and just for that one, staggering moment, Simon forgot about everything else but Tula. She cried out his name as her release claimed her and a single heartbeat later, his body joined hers.

Blindly, Simon reached for her, pulling her down to his chest where he could cradle her close. Where, for a few brief seconds, he could forget that he had maneuvered her into this and instead pretend that what they had just shared was real.

Eleven

It had changed nothing.

And everything.

Two days later, Tula was still trying to understand the shift in her and Simon's relationship. If she could even call it that. Connected by a child, they were two people currently sharing a bed. Did that actually constitute a "relationship"?

Simon was kind and funny and warm and so attentive in bed, she'd hardly had any sleep at all the last two nights. Which, of course, she wasn't exactly complaining about. But was there anything else in his heart for her? Was it just desire? Was it expediency, since she was right there in his house and would be until she decided to hand over custody of Nathan?

She'd given herself to the man she loved with no assurances at all that he would care for her in return. Yes, she loved him. And it was too late now to change that.

How could she have let this happen? Hadn't she made a vow to herself not to take that last slippery step into love? But how could she possibly have avoided it? she asked herself. Simon was so much more than she had originally thought him to be. She had seen glimpses of his caring nature that he fought to bury so deeply. She had watched him with his son and been touched by the gentleness he showed Nathan. She had laughed with Simon, fought with him and made love with him in every possible way.

She couldn't avoid the simple truth any longer. She was in love with a man who was only in lust.

"This can't end well."

"That's the spirit," Anna cheered sarcastically.

Tula just looked at her friend and shook her head. "How you can expect me to be optimistic about this is beyond me. Anna, he doesn't love me."

"You don't know that."

A snort of laughter shot from her throat. "He hasn't said it. Hasn't shown any signs of admitting it. I think that's a good clue."

"All that means is that he's a man," Anna said, her gaze locked on the mural she was painting. "Sweetie, none of them ever want to admit to being in love. For some bizarre reason, the male brain deliberately will jump in the opposite direction the first time the word 'love' is used. They're just naturally skittish."

Tula laughed out loud. The baby on her hip enjoyed the sound and gurgled happily. She planted a quick kiss on his forehead before answering her friend.

"Simon? Skittish?" Shaking her head, she imagined the man in her mind and the idea of him being nervous about anything seemed even more ludicrous. "He's a force of nature, Anna. He sets down rules and expects everyone else to abide by them. And they *do*."

"You don't," she pointed out.

"No, but I'm different."

"He doesn't even expect you to do what he says, does he?"

"Not anymore," Tula assured her. "He knows better."

"Uh-huh." Anna maneuvered her paintbrush across the wall and still kept the conversation going. "So he's broken his own rule when it comes to you."

She thought about that for a second. "I suppose, but only because I made fun of his stupid schedule."

"How did he react?"

"He was all insulted," Tula told her with a laugh. Then she remembered. "But he started changing up his schedule. Coming home early, skipping meetings…"

"Hmm," Anna mused.

"That doesn't mean anything," Tula protested, but her mind was working.

"Only that Mr. I-have-a-schedule-set-in-stone is changing himself because of you."

"But—"

"Men don't do that if they don't care, Tula. Why would they?"

"No," Tula said, shaking her head, "you're wrong. Simon doesn't care about me. Beyond the obvious pluses about having me in his bed and here, taking care of Nathan."

"I don't know…"

"I do," Tula insisted, closing her mind to thoughts of Simon for a minute as she stared at the baby settled at her hip. She wasn't going to pretend everything was great. It wasn't. And it wasn't only the question of Simon's feelings that had her wrapped up so tightly.

Every day that passed she was that much closer to having to say goodbye to Nathan. She was going to lose the child that felt like her own. She was going to lose his father and the illusion of family she'd been living in for weeks. She was going to lose everything that mattered to her and that knowledge was tearing a hole in her heart.

"I'm going to have to leave soon, Anna. I'll have to walk away from Nathan *and* Simon. And the thought of it is just killing me."

Sitting back on her heels, Anna looked up at her. "Who are you and what have you done with Tula?"

"What's that supposed to mean?"

"It means that you are the world's biggest optimist," Anna told her, turning back to the mural she had been working on since the day before. "Even when you had no reason for it, you always maintained the upbeat attitude. Heck, Tula. Even your dad didn't rock your boat. If you wanted something, you went after it, no matter how many people tried to tell you it couldn't be done. So what's happening?"

Tula sat down, balancing Nathan in the circle of her crossed legs. "He did," she said, dropping a kiss onto the baby's head. "This little guy changed everything for me, Anna. I can't just go my own way anymore. Not when I have him to think about."

"Ah," her friend said, "so this isn't about Simon at all? You've been kidding yourself and me? You're just worried about Nathan, huh? Not pining away for the baby's father?"

Eyes narrowed, Tula warned, "No one likes a know-it-all."

"Oooh. Scored a point!" Smiling, Anna swept paint over the forest on the wall, wielding her paintbrush as expertly as a surgeon used his scalpel. "Come on, honey. This sudden case of the poor me's is about more than Nathan. More even than Simon. This is about you finally finding the place you want to be and thinking you have to leave it."

Tula cringed inside because Anna was exactly right.

"You found the home you've been looking for since you were a kid, sweetie." Anna looked at her, understanding and sympathy shining in her eyes. "You love Simon and Nathan both. But it's what they are to you together that's making this so hard. They're the family you always dreamed about. Your heart took them both in, made them yours and now you believe you have to let the dream die."

Nathan babbled and slapped playfully at Tula's hands on his legs. The scent of paint hung in the air despite the two opened windows. Anna's mural was almost complete. Once the woman got started on a painting, she was a whirlwind of activity. Tula looked at the realistic scene of a forest, with a flower-strewn meadow stretching out into the distance. And she smiled at Lonely Bunny, right up front, sitting under a tree and smiling out at the room.

From the house next door, the sound of wind chimes played like a distant symphony. As time passed in a lazy, unhurried way, Tula thought about what her friend had said and admitted silently that Anna was right. She did love Simon and Nathan both. She did love the family the three of them had become, however temporarily. She hated knowing that she was the one who didn't fit. The one who didn't belong. And knowing that she would have to walk away from what might have been was desolating.

"You're right," she finally said.

"The one time I wish I weren't," Anna told her.

"But what can I do? I can't stall Simon forever. He has a right to be his son's father. And I can't stay once I sign over custody."

"It's a problem," Anna agreed. "But there's always a solution. Somewhere."

Tula sighed. "You know, it was a lot easier on me when *you* were the one with man problems."

"I bet," Anna said on a laugh. "But it's your turn now, girl. The question is, what are you going to do about it?"

"What can I do?"

The last few days had been wonderful. And confusing. She had Nathan to care for and work of her own to accomplish during the day. But every night, she and Simon found each other. They shared taking care of Nathan, and once the baby was in bed it was their time.

The sex was incredible. It only got better each time they came together. But for Tula, it was bittersweet. She loved being with him—the problem was, she *loved* him. More than she had ever thought it possible to love someone. Every day here dragged her deeper and deeper into what was going to become a pit of despair one day soon.

Though even as she thought it, she realized that neither of them had so much as hinted about that situation lately.

It might still be the eight-hundred-pound gorilla in the middle of the room, but if no one was talking about it, did it matter?

Nathan babbled happily and Tula sighed.

"Honey, if you want him, why don't you go for it?"

"Oh, I am," she assured her friend.

Laughing, Anna said, "I'm not talking about sex, Tula. I'm talking about love. I know you love Simon. Heck, I can see it. Chances are he can, too."

"Oh, God," she said with a groan. "I hope not."

"Why?" Anna turned to look at her. "Why should you hide what you feel? Didn't you tell me to go for what I wanted?"

"Yes, but—"

"If he doesn't love you back, that's different." She rubbed her nose and transferred a streak of green paint. "Although, I'm willing to bet he does love you. I mean, how could he not? What's not to love? Besides, I saw you two together yesterday and again this morning. The way he looks at you…"

"What?" Hope rose up in Tula's chest.

"As if you're the only thing in the room," Anna said with a smile. "But Tula, you'll never know for sure what he feels if you don't try to get him to admit it."

"How am I supposed to do that?"

Anna grinned. "The best opportunity for getting a man to talk and lower his defenses at the same time? Right after sex. They're happy, they're relaxed and *very* open to suggestion."

Sometimes, she thought. Other times, they were too crabby entirely. Still it was worth a shot. Tula shook her head in admiration. "Does Sam know how truly devious you can be?"

"Sure he does," Anna replied, still grinning devilishly. "But by the time he figures out that I'm sneaking up on him, it's too late."

"I don't know..."

"Who was it who said all's fair in love and war?"

"I don't know that, either," Tula admitted. "But I'll bet it was a man."

"So," Anna said softly, "if it's okay for a man to be sneaky, why can't we try it? Look," she added, "while you're here, don't hold anything back. You can't tell him you love him, but you can show him. Make him want what you could have together. That's all I'm saying."

While her friend turned her attention back to the mural, and Nathan studied his toes with fierce concentration, Tula started thinking.

"You're going to do it, aren't you?"

"Do what?" Simon didn't take his gaze off the pitching machine. Getting hit by a ninety-mile-an-hour fastball didn't sound like a good time.

"Tula. You're going to mess it all up and toss it aside, aren't you?"

Simon hit the pitch high and left. Only then did he glance at Mick in the next cage over. "I don't know what you're talking about."

"Oh, forget it, Simon. I've known you too long to be fooled."

"Have you known me long enough to butt out?"

"Apparently not," Mick said good-naturedly. "Besides, you can always fire me if you don't like what I'm saying."

Simon snorted. "Sure. I fire you, then your wife comes over to kick my butt."

"There is that," Mick said, a pleased note in his voice. "So. About Tula."

"Let it go, Mick. I'm doing what I have to do."

"No," his friend insisted, "you're doing what your damn pride is telling you to do. There's a difference."

Simon hit a curveball dead center, line drive. "This isn't about my pride," he muttered darkly, irritated that his best friend wasn't on his side in this.

Mick was normally an excellent barometer for Simon. If the two of them agreed on something, it turned out to be a good idea. The times when Simon hadn't listened to Mick's advice were a different story. But this time, Mick was wrong. Simon knew it. He felt it.

Ever since her friend left last weekend, after painting a mural of a forest glade, complete with Lonely Bunny sitting beneath a tree, things had been...different.

Actually, the last few days with Tula had been great. Better than great. Amazing even. But it wasn't real. It had all been staged by him. They'd laughed and talked and gone for picnics and out to dinner. They took Nathan for walks and set him in a swing for the first time, making them both nervous. He had felt closer to her than he had to anyone else in his life, he thought darkly.

But none of Tula's responses to him were real because he had seduced her back into his bed for a deliberate reason. So if what he had done wasn't on the up-and-up, how could her reactions be genuine?

If he felt the occasional twinge of guilt over tricking her into being a weapon to use against her father...Simon dismissed the feeling. He didn't do guilt. Plus there was the fact that Tula was an adult, he assured himself, able to make her own choices. And she had *chosen* to be in his bed.

Yet, even as he told himself that, a voice in the back of his mind whispered the question, *Would she still have chosen to be with you if she knew what you were really doing? If she knew she was nothing more to you than a sword to wield against her father?*

Uncomfortable with what the answer to that might have been, he dismissed the mental question. Besides, he argued with himself, Tula wasn't *only* a weapon he'd waited years to find against Jacob Hawthorne. She was more, damn it. He actually…cared about her. Hadn't meant to, but he did.

Which was why he was standing at the batting cages arguing with himself while his best friend ragged on him. But the bottom line was, just because what he and Tula had together was mutually enjoyable, it didn't mean it was necessarily more than that, did it?

Besides, this wasn't even about Tula.

It was about her father.

After hearing what little she'd told him about her parents, she might even be grateful that he had found a way to take a slap at Jacob Hawthorne.

He snorted to himself and hit the next pitch, a slider, into right field. Sure. She'd *thank* him for using her. God, what universe was he living in anyway?

"This is all about your pride, Simon. You got cheated by a guy with no principles."

"Damn right I did," he snapped, turning his head to glare briefly at Mick. "And it wasn't just me, remember. Jacob maneuvered my father, too. That miserable old thief almost cost us our house, damn it."

He hated knowing that Jacob Hawthorne was out there, still chortling over getting the best of two generations of Bradleys. The need for revenge had been gnawing on him for years. Was he expected to now just put it aside because he had feelings for a woman? *Could* he put it aside?

"And your answer to that is to become as unprincipled as the old pirate himself?"

"What the hell are you talking about?"

Mick shook his head, clearly disgusted. "If you do this. If you use Tula to get at her old man, then you're as big a louse as he is."

Simon chewed on those words for a minute or two, then shook them off, determined to stay his course. He'd made a plan, damn it. Now he had to follow through. That was how he lived his life and he wasn't about to change now. Wasn't even sure he could change if he wanted to.

"It's not who you are, Simon," Mick told him. "I hope you remember that before it's too late."

A few days later, Tula was happy.

Anna had been right, she thought. Though she hadn't actually confessed her love for Simon, she had tried to show him over the last several days just how important he had become to her. She was sure she was getting through to him. She felt it. In his easy smile. His touch. The whispered words in the night and the gentle strength in his arms when he held her as she slept.

He hadn't mentioned again the subject of hiring a nanny. They hadn't talked about him taking full custody of Nathan. Instead, the three of them were in a sort of limbo. Locked into a paralyzing state where they didn't move forward and didn't go back. It was as if they were caught in the present, while Tula and Simon tried to decide what might be waiting for them in the still hazy future.

She didn't like waiting. She never had been a patient person, Tula admitted silently. But she was trying to fight her natural inclination—which would be grabbing Simon and shaking him until he admitted he loved her—so she could have the time to show Simon exactly how good they were together.

"Maybe this will work out, Nathan," she told the baby as she zipped up his tiny sweatshirt for their walk to the bookstore. "Maybe we will become a *real* family."

The baby laughed at the idea and clapped his hands together as if applauding her.

"That's my boy." She kissed him, then picked up the baby she thought of as her son and settled him into his stroller. "Now, Nathan, what do you say we go see the nice lady at the bookstore and talk about the signing this weekend?"

For days Simon had been living in two different worlds.

In one, he experienced a kind of happiness that he had never known before. In the other, there was a black cloud of misery hanging over his head, making him feel as though he was about to make the biggest mistake of his life.

He walked down the crowded sidewalk in the heart of downtown San Francisco and hardly noticed the bustle around him. His gaze fixed dead ahead, the expression on his face was ferocious enough to convince other pedestrians to give him a wide berth.

His mind raced with too many thoughts to process at once. Something he wasn't accustomed to at all. His concentration skills were nearly legendary. But even the inner workings of the Bradley department store chain couldn't keep him fixated for long anymore. That acknowledgment shook him to his bones. The Bradley chain had always been his focus. The one mainstay of his life. Rebuilding what the family had lost. Growing the company until it was the biggest of its kind in the country.

Those were tangible goals.

His entire life for the last ten years had been dedicated to making those dreams a reality. But lately, they weren't his only goals.

Tula.

Everything came back to her, he thought and waited impatiently for the light to change and the Walk symbol to flash green. Around him, a teenager danced along to whatever music he had plugged into his ears. A young mother swayed, keeping the baby in her arms happy. Taxis honked, someone shouted and the world, in general, kept spinning.

For everyone but him.

Simon knew he didn't have to go through with this. Didn't have to walk into the exclusive restaurant precisely at twelve-thirty and "accidentally" meet the man he'd waited years to take down. He knew he still had a chance to turn away from his plan. From the decision he had made before Tula became so damned important to him.

Tula.

She was there again. Front and center in his thoughts. Her short, soft hair. Her quick grin. That dimple that continued to devastate him every time he saw it flash in her cheek. She was there with her stories about lonely children befriending rabbits. She was there, rocking Nathan in the middle of the night. She was in the kitchen, dancing to the radio as she cooked. He saw her in her tiny house in Crystal Bay. So small, yet so full of life. Of love.

Tula had waltzed into his life and turned everything he had ever known upside down.

The light changed and he walked with the crowd, a part of them, yet separate.

For days now, he and Tula and Nathan had been what he had never thought to have…a family. Laughing with the baby in the evening, holding Tula all through the night and then waking up with her curled up against him every morning. It was enough to drive a man out of his mind.

This wasn't how Simon had planned for his life to go.

Never before had he made room in his thoughts for babies and bunnies and smart-mouthed women who kissed him as if he contained the last breath on earth. Now he couldn't imagine his life without any of them.

And he didn't damn well know what to do about it.

The wind off the ocean was icy, chilling the blood in his veins until he felt as cold and grim as his thoughts. Outside the restaurant, Simon actually paused and considered the situation.

If Mick was right, then going inside to face down Jacob would ruin whatever he might have with Tula. On the other hand, if he *didn't* go inside and nothing came of whatever was happening between him and Tula, then he had wasted his one opportunity to get back at a man he'd spent too many years hating.

Scrubbing one hand across the back of his neck,

Simon stood in the sea of constantly moving pedestrians like a boulder in the middle of a rushing stream. For the first time in his life, he wasn't sure what his next move should be.

For the first time ever, he wondered if he shouldn't be putting someone else ahead of his own needs.

"Make up your damn mind," he muttered, shifting his gaze to take in the wide windows and the diners seated in leather booths affording a view of downtown.

That's when he saw Jacob Hawthorne.

Everything in Simon went still as ice. The old man was lording it over a group of businessmen at his table. Seated like a king before supplicants, the old thief was clearly holding court. And who knew what he was up to? Who knew which company Jacob was trying to destroy now?

Thoughts of Tula rose up in Simon's mind as if his subconscious was combating what he was seeing. Reminding him of what he could have. What he might lose.

Tula. The daughter of his enemy. Simon shouldn't have been able to trust her. But he did. He shouldn't have cared about her. But he did.

Still, it wasn't enough, he told himself, already reaching for the door handle and tugging it open.

He owed it to his father. Hell, he owed it to *himself* to give Jacob the set down the man had practically been begging to receive for years.

And nothing was going to stop him.

Twelve

There were posters of her latest book cover standing on easels at the front entrance of the bookstore. Management had even put her picture on the sign announcing the author reading and signing that weekend. Cringing a little, Tula tried not to look at her own image.

"Ms. Barrons!"

She turned to smile as Barbara, the employee responsible for all of this, hurried over. "Hi, nice to see you again."

Barbara shook the hand Tula offered and then waved at the sign. "Do you approve?"

"It's very nice," she said, idly noting that she really needed a new publicity picture taken. "Thank you."

"Oh, it's no bother, believe me," Barbara told her. "We've sold so many of your books already, you'll be signing for hours this weekend."

"Now that *is* good news," Tula replied, reaching down to lift Nathan from his stroller when he started to complain. "It's okay, sweetie, we won't be long, then we'll go to the park," she promised.

"You have a beautiful son," Barbara cooed, reaching in to take one of Nathan's tiny hands in hers.

Pleased, Tula didn't correct her. Instead, she felt her own heart swell with longing, pride and love. She looked at the tiny boy in her arms and smiled when he gave her a toothless grin. Kissing him tenderly, she looked at Barbara and said simply, "Thank you."

Simon walked to Jacob's table, dismissing the hostess who tried to intercept him. His gaze locked on the old man; he paid no attention to the other diners or even to the three older men at Jacob's table.

All he could see was the man he'd waited years to get even with. The man who had destroyed Simon's father and nearly cost him the business his family had built over generations.

He stopped beside the table and looked down at the man who was his enemy. Tula had gotten her blue eyes from her father, but the difference was there was no warmth in Jacob's eyes. No silent sense of humor winking out at him. She was nothing like her father at all, Simon thought, wondering how someone as warm as Tula could have sprung from a man with ice in his veins.

"Bradley," the older man said, glancing at him with a sniff of distaste. "What are you doing here?"

"Thought we could have a chat, Jacob," Simon said, not bothering to acknowledge the other men at the table.

"I'm busy. Another time." Jacob turned to the man on his right.

"Actually, now works best for me," Simon said, keeping his voice low enough that only those at the table were privy to what he had to say.

The older man sighed dramatically, turned to face him and said, "Fine. What is it?"

For the first time, Simon glanced at the other men. "Maybe we should do this in private."

"I don't see any need for that," Jacob argued. "This is a scheduled business meeting. You're the intruder here."

Right again. It was only thanks to Mick's reluctantly given information that Simon had known where to find the old goat. Now he didn't argue, he merely turned his flat, no-negotiation stare on the other men at the table. It didn't take them long to excuse themselves and stand up.

"Five minutes," Jacob told them.

"I don't need even that long," Simon assured him as the three men left, heading for the bar.

The steak house was old, moneyed and exclusive. The walls were paneled in dark oak, the carpet was bloodred and the booths and chairs were overstuffed black leather. Candles flickered on every table and wall sconces burned with low-wattage bulbs, making the place seem like a well-decorated cave.

Simon took a seat opposite the old man and met that hard stare with one of his own. This was the moment he had waited for and he wanted to savor it. Jacob had taken something from him. Had tried to destroy Simon's father and almost had. Now Simon had taken something from Jacob.

Payback, the old man was about to learn, really was a bitch.

"What's this about?" Hawthorne leaned back in the seat and draped one arm negligently along the back of the booth. "Come to complain about my getting the property you wanted again? Because if that's it, I'm not interested. Ancient history."

"I'm not here to talk about your dubious business practices, Jacob," Simon told him.

"What you call dubious, I call smart. Efficient." The old man snorted. "Then if that's not what's chewing on you, what is it, boy? I'm a busy man. No time to waste."

"Fine. I'll get right to it then," Simon said, even while that voice in the back of his mind urged him to shut up, stand up and leave before it was too late. But looking into Jacob's eyes, seeing the barely concealed sneer of superiority on his face, made it impossible for Simon to listen.

"Well?" Impatience stained Jacob's tone.

"Just wanted you to know that while you were out stealing that property from me, I stole something from you."

"And what's that?"

"Your daughter." Simon hated himself for doing it, but he watched and waited for the old man's reaction. When it came, it wasn't what he had expected.

Those icy blue eyes frosted over and emptied in the space of a single heartbeat. "I have no daughter."

"You do," Simon argued, leaning forward, lowering his voice. "Tula. She's at my house right now."

Jacob speared him with a hard look. "Tallulah Barrons is not my daughter. Not anymore. If that's what you came for, we're finished."

"You'd deny your own flesh and blood?" Shocked in spite of how badly he had always thought of Jacob Hawthorne, Simon could only stare at him.

Jacob looked away and signaled for the hostess. When she arrived, he said, "Please tell my guests I'm ready to continue our meeting. You'll find them in the bar."

"Yes, sir," she said and hurried off.

"You really don't give a damn about Tula, do you?" Simon hadn't moved. Couldn't force himself to look away from the old man's eyes.

"Why the hell should I?" Jacob countered. "She made her choice. Now what she does—or," he added snidely, "*who* she does it with—is nothing to me. We're done here, Bradley."

Stunned to his bones, Simon realized he actually felt dirty.

Just sitting at the same table with the man. Strange, but he had always pictured the moment of his revenge as tasting sweet. Being satisfying in a soul-deep way. He'd imagined that he would be vindicated. That he would walk away from Hawthorne, head held high, secure in the knowledge that he had bested the old thief. That he had *won*.

Finally.

Instead, years of anticipation fell flat. He felt as though he'd climbed down into the gutter to wrestle a rat for a bone. Mick had been right, of course. Simon had lowered himself to Jacob Hawthorne's level and now he was left with a bitter taste in his mouth and what felt like an oil spill on his soul.

Thoughts of Tula ran through his mind like a soft,

cool breeze on a miserable day. She was the openhearted person he had never been. She was all of the smiles and warmth and joy that he had never known. Everything about her was the opposite of everything he was. Everything her parents had been. Somehow, she was the very heart that he hadn't even realized was missing from his life.

And he'd betrayed her.

He had used her for leverage against a man who didn't even see what an amazing woman his daughter was. But if Jacob Hawthorne was blind, then so had Simon been. Now, though, he could see. Now that it was too late.

Standing up slowly, Simon looked down at the man. Shaking his head, he had the last word as he told Jacob, "You know, I've wasted a lot of years hating your guts. Turns out, you just weren't worth it."

Simon found Tula in the living room, curled up on the window seat reading. She looked up when he walked into the room and the smile she gave him, complete with dimple, tore at his insides. He had made up his mind to tell her the truth. All of it. But he knew the moment he did, everything would be ruined. Over. And he would have to live with the knowledge that he had hurt the one person in the world he shouldn't have.

"Simon? What's wrong?" She came up off the window seat and walked to him, concern in her eyes.

He held up one hand to hold her off, not trusting himself to go through with this confession if she came into his arms. Once he had the feel of her against him again, he might not be able to force himself to let her go. And that's what he had to do.

"I saw your father today," he blurted, knowing there was no easy way to say any of this.

Her jaw dropped and her blue eyes suddenly looked wary. "I didn't realize you knew him."

"Oh, yeah," Simon said tightly. "Remember when I told you about the man who nearly stole this house from my father? The man who stole a piece of property out from under my nose?"

"My father."

"Yeah." Simon walked past her and headed to the wet bar. There he poured himself a short scotch and tossed it down his throat like a gulp of medicine designed to take the inner chill away.

"See, when I found out who you were," he mused aloud, staring down at the crystal glass in his hand before shifting his gaze to hers, "I had the bright idea of somehow using you to get back at your father."

She actually winced. He saw the tiny reaction and, even from across the room, he felt her pain and hated himself for causing it. But he couldn't stop now. Had to tell her everything. Didn't someone say that confession was good for the soul? He didn't think so. It was more like ripping your soul out, piece by piece.

"I told him today that we were together." He waited for a reaction. The only sign she had heard him was the expression of resigned sorrow on her face.

"I could have told you," she finally said into the strained silence, "that he wouldn't care. My father disowned me when I chose to, as he put it, 'waste my brain writing books for sniveling brats.'"

"Tula…" He heard the old pain in her voice and saw her misery shining in her eyes. Everything in him pushed at him to go to her. To hold her. To…love her as she deserved to be loved. But he knew she wouldn't welcome his touch any longer and that brought a whole new world of pain crashing through him.

"He's an idiot," Simon muttered, then added, "and so was I. I didn't want to tell you any of this, but you had the right to know."

"Oh," she said sadly, "*now* I had the right to know."

He gritted his teeth and still managed to say, "I didn't mean to hurt you."

"No," she agreed, "probably not. It was just a by-product of you going after what you wanted. In a way, I'm not surprised. I knew when I first met you that you were like him. Like my father. Both of you only know about business and using people."

He took a step toward her, but stopped when she moved back, instinctively. How could he argue with that simple truth? Maybe, he told himself, he was even worse than her father. He had actually *seen* Tula for who she really was and had lied to her, used her, anyway.

Simon thought back to his meeting with Jacob Hawthorne. He had seen firsthand just what kind of man the old pirate was. And unless he made some changes in his own life, Simon knew he would end up just as cold and ruthless and empty as Jacob was.

Choosing his words carefully, he said, "I know you have no reason to believe me, but I'm not the man I was when you first came here. More, I don't want to be that man."

"Simon," she said softly, shaking her head.

"Let me finish." He took a breath, and said, "There are a lot of things I should say to you, but maybe I don't have the right anymore. So instead, I think the only way to prove to you that I'm not who you think I am, is to let you go."

"What?"

"Hell," he laughed shortly, shoving one hand through his hair with enough strength to yank it all out. "It's the only decent thing to do." He looked into her eyes. "We both know I'm ready to take care of Nathan. I'll hire the best nanny in the country to help me out. And you can go home. Get away from here. From me. It's the right thing to do."

Tula felt the world tip out from under her feet. She swayed under the blow of the unexpected slap. Bad enough to hear that the man she loved had only been pretending to care so that he could use her against the father that didn't give a damn about her anyway. Bad enough to know that her hopes and dreams had just been shattered at her feet.

Now, she was being sent away. From the baby. From Simon.

For her own good.

Pain was a living, breathing entity, and it roared from inside her as it settled in, making a permanent home in the black emptiness where her heart used to be. Hurt, humiliated and just plain tired of being used by the very people in her life she should have been able to count on, Tula sighed.

"Don't you see, Simon?" she whispered sadly. "Even in this, you're still acting like my father."

"No," he argued, but she cut him off because she just didn't want to hear anything else he had to say.

"Letting me go isn't about *me*. It's about *you*. About how you feel about what you did. About assuaging some sense of honor you believe you've lost."

"Tula, that's not—"

"What if I didn't want to go?" she asked, watching him. "What then?"

Naturally, he didn't have an answer for her. But then, it didn't matter, because Tula wasn't waiting for one. It was too late for them and she knew it. She had to go, whether leaving would rip her heart to pieces or not.

Softly, she said, "Nathan's asleep upstairs. If it's all the same to you, I'll leave now, before he wakes up. I don't think I can say goodbye to him."

"Tula, damn it, at least let me—"

"You've done enough, Simon," she told him, turning for the stairs. "Have your lawyer contact me. I'll sign whatever papers are necessary to turn over custody of Nathan to you. And Simon," she added, "promise me you'll love him enough for both of us."

Over the next few days, Simon and Nathan were miserable together.

Nothing was the same. Simon couldn't work—he didn't give a damn about mergers or acquisitions or the price of the company stock. He hated having Mick telling him *I told you so* every five minutes. The memory of Tula in his house was so strong that her absence made the whole place seem cavernous and as empty as a black hole.

He and his son were lost without the only woman either of them wanted.

Nathan cried continuously for the only mother he remembered. Simon comforted him, but it was a hollow effort since he knew exactly how the baby felt. And there was no comfort for either of them as long as Tula wasn't there.

Simon hadn't even hired a nanny. He didn't want some other woman holding Nathan. He wanted Tula back home. With them. Where she belonged. Every day without her was emptier than the one before. His dreams were filled with images of her and his arms ached to hold her.

He had fallen in love with the one woman who probably couldn't stand the sight of him. He had had a family, damn it, and he wanted it back. Yes, he had been a first-class idiot. A prize moron. But Tula had a heart big enough, he hoped, to forgive even him.

If she hadn't promised to do this signing, Tula didn't know if she would have had the nerve to return to the city. Used to be she avoided San Francisco because there were memories of her father here. Now it was so much more.

Nathan and Simon were only blocks from this bookstore. They were in that Victorian that she'd come to love and think of as her own. They were no doubt settling into life with a nanny and she wondered if either of them missed her as desperately as she missed them.

She sat cross-legged in the middle of the "reading rug" at the bookstore and looked at the shining, expectant faces surrounding her. Parents stood on the periphery, watching their children, enjoying their excitement. And Tula knew that she couldn't simply walk away from Simon and Nathan.

Yes, Simon had hurt her. Desperately. But he had told her everything, hadn't he? It couldn't have been easy for him to admit to what he had done. It said something that he'd eventually been honest with her.

Through her pain, through her misery, one truth

had rung clear over the last few days. Despite what had happened, she still loved Simon. And when the book signing was over, she was going to see him. She would just show up at the house and tell Simon Bradley that she loved him. Maybe he wouldn't care. And maybe, if she took a chance, they could start fresh and rebuild their family.

With that thought in mind, she smiled at the kids and asked, "Are you ready to hear about the Lonely Bunny and how he found a friend?"

"Yes!" A dozen childish voices shouting in unison made her laugh and she felt lighter in her soul than she had since walking out of Simon's life.

Opening the book, Tula began to read and for the next half hour gave her young audience her complete attention. When the story of the Lonely Bunny and a white kitten ended, children applauded and parents picked up copies of her books.

Tula smiled to herself as she signed her books and spent a minute or two with each of the children, giving them Lonely Bunny stickers to fix to their shirts. She was enjoying herself even while a corner of her mind worried over going to see Simon.

Through the noise and confusion, Tula felt someone watching her. Her skin prickled and her heartbeat quickened in reaction even before she looked up— directly into Simon's dark brown eyes. Instead of one of his sharply cut business suits, he was wearing jeans and a T-shirt with the Lonely Bunny logo. He held Nathan in his arms and she noticed that the baby wore a matching T-shirt.

Tula laughed and held her breath, afraid to read too much into this surprising visit. Maybe he had simply come to give her the chance to say goodbye to Nathan. Maybe the emotions she read in Simon's eyes were only regret and fondness. And maybe she would make herself nuts if she didn't find out.

She stood up slowly, never taking her gaze from his. Her heart doing somersaults in her chest, Tula tried to speak, but her mouth was dry. When Nathan reached out pudgy arms to her, she took him, grateful to feel his warm, solid weight as he snuggled in with a happy sigh.

Simon shrugged and said, "I, uh, saw the sign out front advertising that you would be here today."

"And you came," she whispered, running one hand up and down the baby's back.

"Of course I came," Simon said, gaze locked with hers, silently telling her everything she had ever wanted to hear. It was all there for her to read. He wasn't hiding anything anymore. So neither would she.

"I was going to come and see you after the signing."

He smiled and moved closer. "You were?"

"I had something to tell you," she said.

He must have seen what he needed to see written on her face because he spoke quickly. "Let me go first. I have so much I want to say to you, Tula."

She laughed a little and glanced around at the kids and their parents, all of them watching with interest. "Now?"

He looked at their audience, then shrugged them off as inconsequential. "Right here, right now."

To her amazement, he went down on one knee in front of her and looked up into her eyes. "Simon…"

"Me first," he said with a smile and shake of his head.

"Tula, I can't live without you. I tried and I just can't do it. You're the air I breathe. You're the heart of me. You're everything I need and can't do without."

Someone in the audience sighed but neither of them paid any attention.

"Oh, Simon—" Tears filled her eyes. She blinked them away because she didn't want to miss a moment of this.

He took her hand and slowly stood up to face her. "I love you. I should have told you that first. But I'll make up for that by saying it often. I love you. I love you."

Tula laughed a little, then harder when Nathan gurgled and laughed along with her. "I love you, too," she told Simon, her heart feeling as though it could pop out of her chest and fly around the room. "That's what I was coming to tell you. I love you, Simon."

"Marry me," he said quickly as if half-afraid she would change her mind. "Marry me. Be my wife and Nathan's mother. Be with me so neither of us ever has to be like your Lonely Bunny again."

"Yes, Simon," Tula said, moving into the circle of his arms. "Oh, yes."

As he stood in the bookstore, with his entire world held close to him, Simon listened to the cheers from the watching crowd. Staring down into Tula's blue eyes, he bent to kiss her and knew that like the Velveteen Rabbit she had told him about, it hurt to become real.

But it was worth it.

Epilogue

A year and a half later, Simon urged, "Push, Tula! Don't stop now, you're almost there!"

"You push for awhile, okay?" she asked, letting her head drop to the pillow. "I'm taking a break."

"Hey," the doctor called out from the foot of the bed, "nobody gets a coffee break yet!"

Simon laughed, planted a hard, fast kiss on Tula's forehead and said, "As soon as this is over, we're *both* taking a break. And, I swear, we'll never do this again."

"Oh, yes, we will," she told him with a sudden gasp. "I want at least six kids."

"You're killin' me," Simon said with a groan. He added, "Come on, honey, one more push."

Tula grinned up at him despite the pain he could see shining in her eyes. "Nag, nag, nag..." Then her features stiffened and she took a breath. "Here it comes again."

Simon had never been so terrified and so excited at once in his life. His gorgeous wife was the bravest, strongest, most miraculous human being in the world. He was humbled by her and so damn grateful to have her in his life.

"You're a warrior, Tula. You can do this. I'm right here, honey, just get it done." And *please* do it fast, he added in a silent prayer.

Mick had warned him that labor was hard on a husband. But Simon had had no idea what it would be like to stand beside the woman he loved and watch her suffer. But typically Tula, she had insisted on going through with this naturally.

Silently, Simon promised that if they ever did this again, God help him, he was going to demand that she take drugs. Or he would.

"Here we go," Doctor Liz Haney called out in encouragement. "Just a little more, Tula!"

She bore down, gritted her teeth and took Simon's hand in a crushing grip that he swore later had pulverized his bones. But then a thin, wailing cry split the air. Tula laughed, delighted, and Simon took his first relieved breath in what felt like months.

"It's a boy!" Doctor Liz reached out and laid the red-faced, squalling, beautiful child across Tula's chest.

"He's amazing," Simon said, "just like his mother."

"Hello, little Gavin," Tula said with a tired sigh as she stroked her newborn son's back. "We've been waiting for you. Your big brother is going to be so excited to meet you."

Simon's heart was so full it was a wonder he could

draw a breath. His world was perfect. Tula was safe and they had another beautiful son.

His exhausted wife looked up at him. "You should call Mick and Katie to check on Nathan—and to tell them our little Gavin is here."

"I will," Simon said, bending down to kiss her reverently. "Have I mentioned lately that I love you?"

"Only every day," she whispered back, her eyes tired but bright with happiness and satisfaction at a job well done.

"We'll just take the baby and clean him up," one of the nurses said, scooping Gavin into her arms.

Tula watched them go, then smiled at Simon when his cell phone chirped, alerting him to an incoming email. "I thought you were turning that off," she said.

"I meant to but I got distracted," he said, grinning as he read the email. "Hey, this isn't about me," he told her. "Your agent emailed to say your latest book just hit the *New York Times* list! Congratulations, honey."

Tula grinned. As exciting as that news was, it couldn't compare to what she felt every day of her life. Taking Simon's hand, she said, "I knew this book would do well. How could it miss with that title?"

He grinned and leaned over her for another kiss. *"Lonely Bunny Finds a Family,"* he whispered, then added, "I hope he's as happy as I am with mine."

* * * * *

"You and I need to talk."

Her expression told him she wasn't looking forward to it.

Dismissively he said, "I'm not trying to change the footing of our relationship to anything more personal—you don't need to worry about that."

Nick knew he was lying through his teeth. Despite his promise that there would be no more kisses, he hungered to kiss Candace again, to see if she tasted as good as he remembered.

But she was good for Jennie…and he needed her for Jennie's sake. He couldn't afford to screw it all up and have her leave.

Nick gritted his teeth. All he could think about was repeating the "mistake" they'd made the night before.

Except Nick couldn't view that kiss as a mistake. Unprofessional, hell yes. But a mistake? No way.

Nick had always gone after what he wanted. And right now he wanted Candace.

He wanted Jennie's nanny.

Dear Reader,

Back in 2009, I wrote my first BILLIONAIRES AND BABIES story, *Billion-Dollar Baby Bargain*, so it's great to be back this month with *The Boss's Baby Affair*.

I love this series, and for me the joy of this series lies in seeing how a so-tough, so-strong hero can show a more tender, protective side when faced with a baby. That big-male-meets-vulnerable-baby moment strikes a chord deep inside me. And, like the heroine, I simply fall more in love…

Jennie is the baby who plays havoc with Nick Valentine's ordered life in *The Boss's Baby Affair*. While Candace is the woman who helps steer him through the maze of confusion. I hope you enjoy Nick and Candace's story.

Check out my website at www.tessaradley.com to find out more about my books.

Happy reading!

Tessa Radley

THE BOSS'S
BABY AFFAIR

BY
TESSA RADLEY

All the characters in this book have no existence outside the imagination of
the author, and have no relation whatsoever to anyone bearing the same name
or names. They are not even distantly inspired by any individual known or
unknown to the author, and all the incidents are pure invention.

Published in Great Britain 2012
by Mills & Boon, an imprint of Harlequin (UK) Limited,
Eton House, 18-24 Paradise Road, Richmond, Surrey TW9 1SR

© Tessa Radley 2011

ISBN: 978 0 263 89095 2

51-0112

Harlequin (UK) policy is to use papers that are natural, renewable and
recyclable products and made from wood grown in sustainable forests. The
logging and manufacturing processes conform to the legal environmental
regulations of the country of origin.

Printed and bound in Spain
by Blackprint CPI, Barcelona

Tessa Radley loves traveling, reading and watching the world around her. As a teen Tessa wanted to be an intrepid foreign correspondent. But after completing a bachelor of arts degree and marrying her sweetheart, she became fascinated by law and ended up studying further and practicing as an attorney in a city firm.

A six-month break spent traveling through Australia with her family reawoke the yen to write. And life as a writer suits her perfectly—traveling and reading count as research, and as for analyzing the world…well, she can think "what if?" all day long. When she's not reading, traveling or thinking about writing, she's spending time with her husband, her two sons or her zany and wonderful friends. You can contact Tessa through her website, www.tessaradley.com.

For Karen Solem
Fantastic agent and fabulous friend

One

Home meant…Jennie.

Nicholas Valentine stared at the glossy black front door and drew a deep breath. The imposing lion-head brass knocker had been one of the few touches he'd selected for the modern three-story Auckland house.

Ignoring the lion's ferocious expression, he keyed a security code into the access pad concealed in the doorframe. The heavy door swung inward.

Pocketing the keys to his Ferrari, Nick stepped forward. Carrara marble gleamed under spotlights that illuminated a triptych of tangled forms painted on three canvases facing the front entrance. He should've been pleased to be home. He should've been elated following a week of success after several months of living on the lip of a volcano.

Instead, he was too jet-lagged to care. He wanted a shower and a bed…but first he had to see Jennie.

It wasn't going to be a comfortable moment, but it had to

be done, regardless of the feelings her existence aroused in him.

Nick stopped at the foot of the white-marble stairs that ascended halfway up the two-story lobby. Resisting the urge to flee into the safety of the living room, where he could take refuge in the television remote, he placed a foot on the first stair.

He hadn't seen Jennie for almost a month.

Nick couldn't identify whether his overwhelming response was guilt—or relief. How was it possible that he could deal with a multimillion-dollar company, several hundred employees and a barrage of reporters without missing a beat, yet Jennie scared him witless? Not that he'd ever admit that to another living soul. Or even a dead one...

At the top of the stairs, a landing ran the length of the house. To the right lay two king suites, to the left four bedrooms with en suites, one of which had been converted into a nursery. In front of the four bedrooms the landing widened into a sitting area decorated in black, gray and white, and highlighted with colors that Jilly had referred to as pistachio and chartreuse yellow.

Nick paused. The usual clutter-free look of the designer-decorated space had given way to bright yellow and pink storage bins he didn't recognize. The glass coffee table had been pushed to one side, and foam squares patterned with numbers covered the area between two white love seats.

Someone—his sister?—clearly had high aspirations for Jennie's mathematical abilities. Nick was positive he hadn't been away long enough for Jennie to learn to count—after all, she was only six months old. A little farther along, some sort of contraption was rigged up on the white wool carpet.

What—?

The door to Jennie's nursery stood ajar. Nick pushed it open and entered.

One sweeping glance revealed that the room was empty.

Three strides took him past a tea party of teddy bears sitting on the floor, to the wall of windows overlooking the pool deck. There was no sign of the child or her motherly nanny—Nick couldn't remember the woman's name—by the pool, or on the expanse of manicured lawn rolling down to the edge of the cliffs overlooking the Pacific Ocean.

He glanced at his watch. Five o'clock. He knew from the schedule he'd memorized that it was Jennie's dinnertime. The baby should be home. Mrs. Busby, his housekeeper, would have an answer.

Downstairs, Mrs. Busby was not in the high-tech chrome-and-black kitchen. Where had all his staff gone? Impatient now, Nick rang the bell.

Long minutes later, Mrs. Busby appeared through the swing doors that led to the basement suites where the staff lived. At the sight of him, the housekeeper tugged at her dress collar. "I'm sorry, Mr. Valentine. I didn't know you were home yet."

Nick didn't bother to tell her that he'd gotten an earlier connection; instead, he got to the crux of what he wanted to know. "Where is Jennie?"

"Candace took her to the park—you can reach her on her cell phone." The housekeeper headed for the kitchen island with its bank of drawers. "I'll get the number—"

"Wait!" Nick's brows jerked together. The nanny's name wasn't Candace. He would've remembered that. "Who is Candace?"

Mrs. Busby hesitated, clearly flustered. "The new nanny. Didn't Mrs. Timmings let you know?"

New nanny? His sister hadn't said a word about any such thing. "What happened to...?" He searched his memory for the woman's name and came up blank.

"When Jennie got sick, Margaret resigned," Mrs. Busby explained hurriedly.

Nick tensed. "Jennie's sick?" He hadn't been notified. "What's wrong with her?"

Mrs. Busby looked increasingly uncomfortable. "She's much better now—Candace has been looking after her. Mrs. Timmings didn't want me worrying you about it." For a moment the housekeeper looked as if she wanted to say something more. Then she added, "She thought it best to wait for you to come back."

Nick's mouth compressed as he bit back his rising impatience. Mrs. Busby looked like she was about to faint with apprehension. But it wasn't her fault he hadn't been told. "I'll speak to my sister."

Relief softened Mrs. Busby's round features. "That would be best. What can I make you to eat, Mr. Valentine?"

Nick waved a dismissive hand as he headed for the double doors leading to the lobby. "I ate on the plane." At her crestfallen expression, he relented. "Maybe one of your special omelets, Mrs. Busby. But first get me the nanny's number. I'll be in the sitting room."

The nanny's cell phone must be off, Nick decided after reaching a crisp, recorded message for the second time. Impatiently, he scrolled through his phone's contacts list for his sister's number.

"Why didn't you let me know Jennie was ill? What happened?" Nick demanded as soon as Alison answered. He paused his pacing in front of the tall glass doors that folded back to reveal the pool deck, and stared unseeingly out over the expanse of water.

Silence hummed across the telephone line. "How about 'Good evening. How are you, Alison?'"

He ignored the sarcasm and started to pace again. "What's wrong with her?"

"An ear infection. I took her to the doctor, we watched it

very carefully—I didn't want to disturb you…" Her voice trailed away.

"She's my daughter." He said it with more conviction than he felt. "You should've given *me* the choice."

"Nicky, she's fine."

"So Mrs. Busby told me." He switched the phone to his other ear. "Do you know how it made me feel to hear from my housekeeper that Jennie had been ill and I didn't know anything about it?"

"I'm sorry, Nicky." His sister sounded subdued. "I should've let you know. Even Richard said so. But I thought you had your hands full—"

He cut her off. "Richard was right." Sometimes Nick pitied his long-suffering brother-in-law.

"I heard on the news that the unrest is over in Indonesia. I've been so worried—you might have let *me* know."

"Your Valentine's stock is safe. And I've managed to source the eco-friendly furniture and statuettes we need for the garden centers."

"That's not what I've been worried about. Though I should tell you we've had an offer on our stock."

"An offer?"

Nick was too tired to follow as his sister leapfrogged from one topic to the next. Yet that one phrase stuck out.

He knew how desperately Alison and Richard needed to liquidate their Valentine's stock to shore up the losses their chain of appliance stores had taken during the recent recession. Out of loyalty to Nick, they'd held off selling to give him an opportunity to buy their Valentine's stock—an impossibility until his usurious debt to his father-in-law, Desmond Perry, had been settled. And now the end was in sight. Tomorrow he would pay Perry every last cent that he owed—it would give Nick more satisfaction than anything in his life to throw the final check down on his former father-in-law's desk.

Of course, that would leave him with no liquid funds, but

if Alison and Richard could hang on for a few months more, he'd be able to acquire their Valentine's stock outright.

With people going out less and spending more time at home, his business was expanding aggressively. To Nick's satisfaction every sizable town in New Zealand's North Island now boasted a Valentine's Garden Center—just as he'd dreamed of when he first started out. People were flocking to his centers in ever-increasing droves, seeking the leisurely family lifestyle that the red heart of the Valentine's logo had come to promise.

Landscaping advice. Tranquil water features. Outdoor furnishings and art. Every plant under the sun. Customers could find it all at a Valentine's Garden Center. He had plans to carry the expansion into South Island and then farther afield into Australia. While the land the centers stood on and the business assets were worth millions, making Nick wealthy beyond his wildest dreams, the rapid expansion had left him short of cash. The repayments to his father-in-law had only made the situation tougher.

Nick knew the end was in sight. But Alison's mention of an offer for their stock had caused a frisson of unease.

"When was the offer made?" he asked.

"A few days ago." His sister sounded suspiciously vague.

"Alison…" he said warningly.

"Nicky, I was much more worried about Jennie's ear…and you." After recent riots in the capital, Alison hadn't been too keen on his trip to Indonesia. "Tell me *you* are okay."

Nick wasn't in the mood to talk about his roller-coaster month away from home. He was focused on Desmond Perry's calling in the final installment of the multimillion-dollar loan three months early. It had—much against his will—forced Nick to consider selling one of the more successful of the garden centers. He'd held off, and now he was relieved that he had.

In the long run, liquidating a center would cost them all. Him. Alison and Richard—and the other stockholders. Each center had been carefully selected for its position; in time every center was going to be a crown jewel. But future profits didn't help his sister; she needed help now.

"I'm okay. I've told you before, you fuss too much," he stalled.

"That's right. Shut me out, Nicky—as you always do. I suppose I should be grateful you at least speak to Richard... although that's only about business, I suppose. Not about your marriage, about what it's been like waiting for the sword of Damocles to drop."

Nick sighed. "Alison—"

"Don't worry, I know! Your marriage is none of my business. I should know by now that you never give an inch... never talk about what matters. One day you'll need to learn to let someone inside that hard shell you've grown."

He rubbed his hand over his eyes—God, he was tired—and resisted the urge to tell his sister that she was overreacting, that the hard shell she harped on was all in her imagination. Whatever he said, she'd only argue.

Instead, he crossed over to the white leather sofa and sank into its cushioned depths. Propping his feet onto one of the four mirrored cubes that together acted as a coffee table, he said, "Well, I want to talk now. Why didn't you let me know the nanny had walked out? That you'd seen fit to hire someone else?"

"Candace isn't really a nanny—she's a nurse."

At once fear flooded him. His hand clenched around the phone. "A *nurse?* Is there something you haven't told me?" Was Jennie a lot sicker than his sister had led him to believe? "Alison—"

"Jennie is fine! And Candace is a godsend—she's very capable. I met her at the hospital. We hit it off instantly and when she heard that Margaret had left—"

"Why *did* Margaret leave?"

"Her blood pressure had risen and when Jennie got ill she said it was too much for her."

Nick closed his eyes and suppressed the urge to swear.

He hadn't known the woman had high blood pressure or he might have had second thoughts when Jilly had hired her. Which was probably why she hadn't mentioned it on her resume. Margaret had seemed so perfect. An older, maternal-looking woman from a reputable agency with impeccable references. He'd been pleased with Jilly's choice. Now it appeared that she hadn't been quite so perfect.

"What do you know about this other woman?"

"She's a pediatric surgery nurse by training. She's been away from the hospital for a little while—traveling or something. But she has fabulous references and the hospital snapped her up to do overflow shifts in the emergency room as soon as she came back." His sister paused to draw a breath, but rushed on before Nick could get a word in edgewise. "Surely even you can see the benefit of Jennie having a nanny who can take care of her if she gets ill, as babies so often do? It certainly sets my mind at ease. I'm sure it's what Jilly would've wanted."

"Let's leave aside what Jilly would've wanted."

Nick wasn't about to let his sister change the focus of the conversation to his mixed-up emotions about his late wife... and Jennie.

"Once you meet Candace, you'll see that she's absolutely perfect." His sister changed direction, one of those frog-leaps Nick was finding more difficult than usual to follow. "I don't know what we'll do when she decides to go back to full-time nursing."

"Hire a real nanny?" suggested Nick, closing his eyes. "So that when I come home from being away for weeks on end Jennie is at least here to greet me?"

A scarlet Ferrari occupied the space that had been empty since Candace had arrived to take care of Jennie.

Candace's mouth set into a firm line as she eased the station wagon that had come with the job in between the sleek sports car and a silver Daimler. So Nick Valentine was home. About time. The electronically activated garage door lowered with a hum behind her. But her ire toward her neglectful employer didn't extend to his daughter. Opening the rear door, Candace crooned to the baby as she lifted her out of the car seat and she was rewarded with a happy smile.

Jennie was the sweetest baby in the world. In her job as a pediatric surgery nurse, Candace had seen many, but this one was special.

Her face softened and she tightened her arms. Jennie made a snuffling sound of contentment against her T-shirt and Candace's heart melted like honey in summer sunshine. Poor little motherless thing. The first time she'd held the baby she'd felt the inexplicable bond. This wasn't her child, she had to remind herself—Jennie belonged to someone else. Yet she couldn't help being smitten…and more than a little envious of the gift that Nick Valentine treated with such cavalier disregard.

Pushing the door leading into the house open, Candace tiptoed into the glossy marble-and-silver perfection of the foyer that made her feel like she'd stumbled into the pages of an architectural design magazine every time she entered the house. No plants softened the hard edges; no flowers spilling out of vases broke the palette of black, silver, icy lemon and white.

The baby in her arms was the only real thing there.

She glanced through to the black-and-chrome kitchen. It was empty. Across the lobby she could hear the blare of the television. Her pulse quickened and her stomach tied itself up in knots. She resisted the urge to flee upstairs. No point putting this meeting off. The sooner she met her boss the better.

Hoisting Jennie higher into her arms, she halted in the

doorway to the sitting room. A tremor of shock quaked through her.

Nick Valentine lay sprawled across a white leather sofa in front of a wide-screen television. His dark-as-midnight hair was rumpled as though he'd raked his fingers through the strands. His suit jacket had been abandoned over the back of the couch and the top two buttons of his striped business shirt had been undone to reveal a patch of bare, tanned skin. He was so much more than she'd bargained for—Candace hadn't expected his sheer physical presence.

Thankfully, the man was asleep.

Candace swallowed. Hurriedly, she forced her delinquent gaze away. A fluffy omelet lay untouched on a tray next to his highly shined shoes, which were propped up on the outsize glass cube serving as a coffee table. A half-empty tumbler of amber liquid sat beside him on the couch.

What had she expected?

A father who couldn't wait to see his baby? Nick Valentine was a businessman—first and always. Jilly Valentine had told her that. Her gaze flicked to the mirror table cube. The kind of man who drank Scotch rather than eating a carefully prepared meal, and fell asleep in front of a sports channel rather than seeking out his daughter after a month's absence.

The hope that perhaps she'd misjudged the man flickered out. Turning away, Candace hugged Jennie closer, suddenly desperate to get away from the baby's uncaring father.

Upstairs it was time to bathe the baby. Afterward, with Jennie changed and ready for bed, Candace headed for the fridge set under the counter in the corner of the nursery where the bottles she'd sterilized earlier waited. In fact, every modern convenience a baby could possibly need was at Candace's fingertips.

There were certainly uses for Nick Valentine's millions. But what did they help a baby whose father showed so little interest in her?

Candace grimaced on discovering that the formula was finished and she'd forgotten to bring another container up. Now she'd have to go fetch it from the well-stocked pantry in the kitchen downstairs.

Putting Jennie in the crib, she shut her ears to the wails of complaint as she made for the door. "I'll only be a moment, Jennie."

A profound sense of disorientation shook Nick.

The bright screen flickering out into the darkness confused him, and he blinked to escape the drowsiness that pressed down on him like smog.

Jennie.

Guilt knifed him. The hectic rush of the past few weeks was no excuse for his reluctance to see the baby. If he'd stayed away much longer, she wouldn't have recognized him.

Nick staggered to his feet. This time the stairs seemed to take forever to climb. And this time the nursery door was firmly closed—not open as he'd left it earlier. Relief flooded him. Jennie might already be sleeping, then he'd be off the hook.

He advanced into the nursery.

A snuffling noise told him the baby was still awake. Swallowing, he took another step. A pool of muted light surrounded the crib where Jennie lay. A quick glance around revealed that the party of teddy bears had been put away...and the rocker that Jilly had insisted on ordering for the nursery was empty. Jennie was alone.

Where the hell was that fancy nurse his sister had raved about?

Three strides took him to the side of the crib.

Once there, he hesitated, fighting his reluctance to pick up the baby. At last he managed to master the fears little Jennie would never know about.

"Hello, Jennie."

The baby fell silent. Her head turned, and wide-spaced eyes gazed up at him. Their color had lightened from the navy blue they'd been the last time he'd seen her. Jilly's eyes had been sapphire blue while his own were a much darker indigo shade. Neither hue was apparent in the cloudy gray depths of Jennie's eyes.

The unspoken dread deepened.

There was a moment of stillness when neither of them moved as they examined each other. Then Jennie gave a coo and stretched out a hand. Nick stilled. What did the past matter? This was a baby…innocent of it all.

He touched her hand with one finger.

Jennie's hand clutched his forefinger. They gazed at each other. Nick held his breath. The silence in the nursery was absolute, the moment powerful and intense.

He cleared his throat, told himself he was being fanciful. Yet something had changed—even as Jennie's fingers wrapped more tightly around his.

It was too much. And too soon. Nick gently shook the baby's fingers loose and turned blindly for the door, head down, desperate to escape, his hand groping for the door handle.

Before he'd found it, the door swung open.

Nick caught sight of a blur of movement and the next instant a hard object thudded against the side of his head.

"Ow! What the—?"

He glared down into the most angelic face he'd ever seen. Wide-spaced silver-gray eyes, an upturned nose, a sweetly curved pink mouth and cascading golden curls.

Nick was in no mood to be converted.

Yet the sudden pull of attraction unsettled him. Fingering the tender spot above his ear, he straightened to his full height, and snarled. "Do you always rush in without looking where you're going?"

* * *

Candace stared up in horror at the man blocking her way to the nursery.

Nick Valentine.

She must've said it out loud, because his glare intensified. "Who else were you expecting?"

"Uh…" She scanned the hard features. The strong, square jaw. The bladed nose, and an ancient scar that cut through one black eyebrow, giving him a dangerous air. Eyes so dark a blue as to appear black. He was much bigger than newspaper photos had suggested, at least six foot three.

Awake and up close, the handsome features were even more forbidding—not helped by that piratical scar and the almost-black eyes. Her heartbeat grew faster.

"I thought you were still downstairs, sleeping." Damn. Damn. Damn. "I'm so sorry."

"I'm going to have a lump like an egg," he accused, rubbing his head.

She stared at his fingers, cursing herself for being in such a hurry. "We should get some ice on it."

"Get some ice on it? That's all you're going to say about assaulting me?"

He was furious. Her pounding heart sank into the comfortable Ugg boots she'd taken to wearing inside to protect her feet from the acres of shiny marble. Her first meeting with her new boss couldn't have gone any worse.

Candace became conscious of how close he was standing. The warm, tangy scent of him swirled around her. "It was an accident," she protested halfheartedly. The force of the contact had jarred her elbow. It must hurt him like blazes. She started to apologize again.

"You need to watch where you're going," he said.

The unfairness of the accusation caused her to flush. "You ran into me," she defended herself.

His fingers probed along his hairline above his ear. "What the hell was the weapon?"

"A tin of formula."

The other hand released her arm, and his gaze followed hers to the floor. "A tin of baby formula?"

The disbelief in his voice compounded the realization that she'd hurt her boss, and her knees went weak. Was he going to think she was totally incompetent?

She sagged against him and mumbled, "I'm truly sorry."

Thankfully, this time he didn't say anything.

And this close to him it was even more difficult to think clearly. Nick's body was taut and unexpectedly muscled under the crumpled, striped business shirt, and much warmer than she'd expected. Much firmer, too. It wasn't the body of a man who sat behind a desk all day.

What was she doing thinking about Nick Valentine's taut and admittedly well-honed body? It struck her that she wasn't giving him a very good impression of her professionalism. Candace jerked upright as a quiver of fear feathered across her heart. If Nick Valentine doubted her ability to look after his daughter, he'd dismiss her without a second thought.

She searched for something to restore normality and asked a little breathlessly, "What did you come upstairs for?"

He didn't answer. Instead, he studied her. Candace shifted nervously. In the dimness of the doorway she couldn't clearly make out his expression. Of course, every emotion on her face would be visible to him under the overhead light. Could he see her apprehension? Was he really going to fire her for her clumsiness?

"You're Candace."

She flinched, and waited a heartbeat. Yet there was no dawning recognition in the narrowed gaze.

"Yes, I'm Candace," she conceded at last. "And you're Nick Valentine."

He inclined his head. "You have the advantage on me. I don't know your last name."

"Morrison." She gave it with reluctance, tensing as she waited warily for his reaction.

Nothing changed in the enigmatic navy-blue eyes. *Her name meant nothing to him.* Only by sheer willpower did she prevent herself from closing her eyes in relief. The longer he remained in ignorance, the better for her. Candace suppressed the notion that he deserved to know, then dismissed the momentary scruple and told herself he wouldn't care. If he'd been the kind of man to care, everything would've played out differently.

Even as she grappled with what to do next, Jennie let out a howl of protest in the room behind them.

Two

Candace could've kissed the baby for the timely distraction.

Nick spun around and hurried into the nursery, and she followed quickly in his wake.

He peered into the crib. "What's wrong with her?"

"She's tired and she wants her bottle." Candace scooped the baby into her arms and handed her to Nick.

He hesitated.

"Hold her while I get the bottle ready," she said hurriedly. "Otherwise, she's going to howl the place down."

On cue, Jennie's protests grew louder. Nick clumsily reached for the baby. Candace hovered, worried that he might drop her. He made some grunting noises, apparently intended to comfort the baby, but they only made Jennie scream more loudly.

"If you hold her a little more firmly, she'd settle."

Watching him, Candace was visited by the insane notion that Nick had never held the baby before. It wasn't possible. Yet he didn't appear familiar with the baby at all.

Her heart ached for Jennie. Poor motherless tyke. Nick was an ambitious businessman who spent more time chasing deals than with his child. Of course, having a full-time nanny made it all too easy for Nick to avoid his parenting responsibilities.

Candace wasn't ready to analyze the surge of emotions that flooded her. Instead, she grabbed his wrist. "Put one hand here…" she placed it behind Jennie's bottom "…and the other here."

"She's *my* daughter. I know how to hold her."

Who was he trying to fool? Yet the warmth of his skin beneath her fingertips drew her attention back to Nick, making Candace aware that her hand still gripped his wrist.

She released him as if she'd been scorched and stepped back, out of his force field, and ordered, "Walk with her."

He gave her a brooding look, then complied.

Jennie's bitter complaints forced Candace to hurriedly retrieve the tin of formula off the floor, open it and mix up a bottle. The howls turned to querulous grumbles that finally abated. Candace didn't pause to see what had caused the change; she kept focused on what she was doing. By the time the bottle was ready, she turned to find Nick holding a bunch of keys in front of the baby, flaunting the famous Ferrari tag with its rearing horse.

Jennie was enthralled. Her plump fingers clutched the keys as she tried to shove them into her mouth. Nick was looking confounded, struggling to keep the keys a safe distance from little madam's face. Every time Jennie opened her mouth, he flinched. What was he expecting—the baby to devour the keys or holler with frustration?

At the sight of Candace, relief darkened his indigo eyes to the shade of midnight. "Take her."

Normally she would've jumped at the invitation. She loved feeding the baby, and the last bottle of the day had become a special shared ritual for them both. The quiet of the nursery, the old-fashioned tick-tock of the antique grandfather clock in the corner, the warmth of the baby's body cuddled up against her. Moments to treasure forever.

Yet his terse command, the way he was ready to rid himself of the baby at the first opportunity, all caused the aching sympathy for the baby to deepen. He was Jennie's father, after all.

Even though he appeared to have forgotten all about her for the past month.

Candace had to try to get through to him, show him what he was missing. No one knew better than she how it felt to yearn for a child…

"Sit in the chair."

He gave her an oddly panic-stricken look. "The rocking chair?"

From his expression she might as well have said electric chair. Not as comfortable with his daughter as he'd like her to believe.

"Yes." She nodded to underscore her answer. Grim humor sparked through her as the millionaire businessman dropped into the purple-painted rocker that was plumped up with lime cushions. If his board of directors could see him now…

She suppressed her mirth and passed him the bottle. "Normally, you'd test the heat against the inside of your wrist but we won't bother this time. I've already done it and Jennie has reached the end of her patience."

The baby was flapping her hands furiously.

As Nick gave her the bottle, she latched desperately on to it, her hands clutched around his. The sight of her little plump fingers against Nick's large, tanned hands caused a strange sensation to flutter in Candace's chest.

His head was bent, his focus on Jennie absolute. In that moment Candace felt unaccountably excluded. For weeks the baby had been her responsibility—these secret moments had been hers alone to treasure.

Now he'd usurped them. She fought the riot of emotions that his presence here in the nursery aroused.

Then Nick raised his head.

The look on his face caused Candace's breath to catch. It held an intensity—pain mingled with something more elusive. For weeks she'd been furious at Nick Valentine's desertion of his daughter. She'd never expected to feel empathy for him—to see the darkness of hell in his eyes.

For the first time, she became aware of Nick Valentine as someone other than a busy, enterprising millionaire—someone other than Jennie's father. He was a man. A man tormented by the loss of his wife…a man who had been saddled with the lonely responsibility of raising their daughter.

A pang pierced her. It couldn't be easy.

The least she could do was grant him a few moments of privacy to deal with whatever demons plagued him. Candace edged to the door. "I'll go and fetch some ice for your head."

The baby had fallen asleep.

Nick studied the bundle in his arms. She radiated heat against his heart and the warmth of her body had spread through him, almost sending him to sleep, too. No doubt the long flight hadn't helped.

Shaking off the drowsiness that threatened to overtake him, Nick rose slowly to his feet. He carried the baby across to the crib and carefully settled her down before covering her with a fleecy blanket. To his relief, she didn't stir. Yawning, Nick turned out the light and let himself out the nursery.

The nanny—Candace, he amended—was coming toward him, her tread soundless on the thick pile of the pale carpet.

"Sorry I took so long. I couldn't find the ice trays." She held up a plastic bag filled with ice.

"It doesn't matter." Nick was so drugged with tiredness he'd forgotten that she'd gone to fetch ice. "Jennie's sleeping," he said to fill the sudden, awkward silence that stretched between them. "She went out like a light."

Candace smiled, and it transformed her face. The serious eyes sparkled with silver glints. "Yes, it's amazing how quickly that happens."

"I'm about to do the same." Resisting the urge to gawk like a teenager, Nick started to walk past her, but her hand came out and rested lightly on his shirtsleeve. "Let me ice your head."

A jolt of electricity buzzed under where her fingers rested. She was barely touching him. Gazing down at her, he found himself falling into wide, gray eyes as clear as a mountain lake. Nick shook his head roughly to rid himself of the illusion.

Jet lag was definitely setting in with a vengeance, he decided.

"I'll be fine," he said brusquely.

Her smile vanished and she blinked, shattering the unwelcome spell that bound him.

"Even ten minutes will make a difference to any possible bruise marks," she wheedled.

"Okay." To make amends for his terseness, Nick gave her a wry smile. "Then I won't have to explain how I came to have a bruise."

Her eyes clouded over. She was about to start apologizing again. Nick hadn't intended that. She'd relaxed a little since leaving him with Jennie. He didn't want to see her looking wretched—he wanted to see her smile. The generous, spontaneous smile that lit up her whole face…and made him feel like a ray of sunlight had stolen into the night.

"Don't worry—it will take more than a bump in the night to keep me down." Reluctantly he moved away from her toward the sitting area off the upstairs lobby and slumped down into the closest sofa, his head falling back against the pile of cushions as he closed his eyes. Man, he was tired.

The sudden cold of the ice pack against his skull made him flinch.

"Try not to move." Candace spoke from behind him. "I'll hold it here for a few minutes."

Despite the pressure of the freezing pack, a bit of peace seeped into him. It was the first time in weeks that he'd done nothing at all.

Candace leaned forward. "Not too cold?"

"At least it's keeping me from falling asleep."

She laughed, a joyous peal of sound. Nick forgot the coldness of the ice pack against his head and became aware of the wholesome scent of baby powder, soap and the hint of something more spicy and sexy that enveloped her.

The surge of desire that thrummed through his blood startled him. How long had it been since he'd allowed himself to feel that heady heat? And now it had happened with a woman he didn't know—his daughter's nanny, for God's sake.

He must be desperate.

Jeez, he *was* desperate.

How long had it been...?

"Relax. Your shoulders are all bunched up. Do you want me to rub them?" The angel's wickedly seductive voice interrupted his out-of-control thoughts.

"No." Nick closed his eyes against the tempting suggestion. He was already far too aware of the woman. If she touched him...

To Nick's intense discomfort, his body instantly reacted to the idea of her hands rubbing his skin. If Candace glimpsed his lap, she would see the humiliating effect her proximity had had on him from his tented trousers. *Damn.* He was trapped until this wayward impulse subsided.

Candace shifted, adjusting the ice pack, her breath soft against the top of his head.

Nick tensed, moving his hands surreptitiously to his trouser front, shielding any bulge from her view. "That's fine. It's late. Why don't you call it a night and go to bed?"

"I want to check on Jennie first before I retire." She straightened with a rustle of fabric, and he could no longer feel her breath ruffling his hair. Her voice had taken on a different note, too. Brisk and all business. Nick missed the concern, the caring note. Then he jerked himself back to reality.

He'd been aroused by his child's nurse. It was like a bad-taste comedy. Nick didn't grope the hired help...or seduce his secretaries.

He had to get away from her.

"I'll hold the ice pack on the lump. You can let go," he said gruffly, suddenly desperate for her to leave. But even that didn't block out the heightened awareness he'd developed of Candace...where she stood...as he strained his ears trying to figure out what she was doing.

The ice pack shifted. A curl brushed against his cheek.

"Oops!" Her voice was breathless.

The ice pack slipped from her hold and landed in his lap. Nick made a grab for it and, growling with frustration, closed his eyes and prayed for control.

The sudden silence that followed stretched his nerves to breaking point.

Nick opened his eyes.

She'd moved, and now stood in front of him, staring at him, and she flushed as he caught her gaze. "I should go check on Jennie."

"Yes, you should." It came out as a low, feral growl. Wide awake now, all his weariness evaporated, he cleared his throat and held the ice pack out. "Thanks for the ice."

She reached for it the same moment that he unfolded his length from the sofa. They bumped into each other and she laughed awkwardly. Nick didn't smile. He had never felt less like laughing in his life.

"Sorry—"

"I'm sorry—"

They both broke off, her laughter coming to an abrupt end as their eyes met. Nick didn't know how it happened, but he'd taken a step forward. She didn't retreat. He couldn't have stopped what happened next if he'd tried...

Her lips were soft. Softer than any he'd ever kissed.

Hunger clawed at his belly. He fought to keep the kiss gentle, not to unleash the ferocity that lurked within him. She tasted so sweet. He pressed soft kisses along the seam of her lips, leashing the feral urge to grab her by her shoulders, yank her to him and kiss her with all the hunger that churned inside him.

Instead he concentrated on their only point of contact: their lips.

But it wasn't enough. His hands came up and cupped her jaw.

She jerked, breaking the thrall that held them both.

"No!"

Candace pulled back sharply. Nick's hands dropped away from her face. They were shaking. And he wasn't the only one affected. Her breasts were rising and falling under the snug fit of her T-shirt, the ice pack clutched between her white-knuckled hands.

Nick forced his gaze away, back to her face.

Damn. He was out of his mind. "That should not have happened."

Her eyes had gone dark. "You're right."

"It won't happen again," Nick vowed, putting the length of the sitting room between them and retreating toward the top of the stairs...then edging to the safety of his suite that lay beyond. "I wouldn't lose any sleep over it—I certainly don't intend to."

* * *

Once he'd reached his own wing of the mansion, Nick made for the luxurious bathroom, where he stripped off the travel-soiled suit pants and unbuttoned the business shirt. He was wired now. All thoughts of sleep banished.

He spread his hands on the glass vanity slab. Lowering his head, he drew in a deep breath and slowly exhaled.

In the past half hour he'd experienced swings of emotion that had badly rattled him. The vulnerability when he'd held Jennie, the realization as he fed her the night bottle that this little scrap depended on him for everything in her life. And the need to get the hell out of that nursery before the safety of his world cracked wide open.

Only to find himself over the edge of the precipice. Shuddering, he relived the torrential surge of desire that Candace had aroused. Had he walked away while he could? No, he'd acted on it.

Kissed her.

Double damn.

Bracing his weight on his arms, Nick raised his head and confronted himself in the wall of mirror above the vanity. He looked different from his usual tightly controlled, immaculately groomed self. Not outwardly—the swelling where the edge of the tin had connected didn't show. It was in his eyes where the change lay. Instead of the customary cool calculation, they were filled with turmoil.

What had unnerved him? The sudden bond he found himself forging with Jennie? Or the angelic-looking nanny who'd woken the devil in him?

Nick wasn't sure he wanted to know.

A sharp cry woke Candace.

After silencing the baby monitor, Candace sprang out of bed and ran along the carpeted landing lit by night-lights until she reached the nursery. Lifting Jennie out of the crib, she rocked the baby in her arms.

"Hush," she murmured as Jennie's head swung up and butted her chin.

The red numbers of the counter clock on the dresser glowed in the night. Two o'clock. Not yet time for a feeding. Jennie fussed in Candace's arms. Walking silenced her momentarily, then the whimpers restarted. Candace laid Jennie down on the changing surface above the dresser, and reached for the thermometer in the first-aid kit on the shelf above. Talking a stream of softly whispered nonsense to Jennie, she deftly removed the diaper and inserted the thermometer.

"Sorry, sweetheart. I know you would've preferred a tympanic thermometer, but those ears might still be tender."

A few seconds later the thermometer beeped. The reading was above normal, but far from dangerous. Quickly, Candace put on a clean diaper, then picked Jennie up and started to walk, Jennie grumbling incessantly.

Candace suppressed a sigh. "So much for not losing any sleep tonight, huh, Jennie?"

A flash of memory hit her of the wild pleasure that had pierced her when Nick Valentine had kissed her...and the flare of absolute panic that had followed.

She must've communicated her unease to the baby because Jennie let out a volley of wails.

Seconds later, the door to the nursery burst open.

Nick stood there, a dark silhouette against the shaft of light that spilled in from the landing. A rustle of movement, then a switch clicked and bright light flooded the room.

Candace blinked against the glare. Nick wore only a pair of hastily donned pants, the top button still undone. His chest was bare, his hair mussed.

He'd told her he had no intention of losing any sleep over the kiss they'd shared...and had expected her to do the same.

Yet the sight of him caused her pulse to thud.

She was a fool.

Candace looked away as Jennie wailed more loudly.

Nick advanced. "Let me see if I can settle her."

Gut instinct caused her arms to tighten.

"Give her to me," he ordered, his face closed, exhibiting no sign of the passionate man who'd kissed her with such ravenous hunger.

Candace took herself in hand. *Forget about that kiss.* This hard-eyed man was her employer. Jennie's father. Soundlessly she surrendered the baby.

Nick took Jennie with more ease than he'd shown earlier. Instantly, Jennie's cries stilled. Her eyes widened as she stared up at the man who held her. The sight of the baby bundled up against the muscled torso caused pain to splinter deep inside Candace.

When Jennie looked down from her father's face and stared at the wall of chest in front of her with a puzzled expression, Candace's throat closed. The baby reached out and touched a ridge of muscle, her puny fingers closed around a sprinkle of hair. She tugged.

Nick didn't flinch.

Jennie gave a gurgle.

And Candace wanted to cry.

It was clear that the baby hardly knew her father.

So what am I going to do about that? Candace asked herself. *Can I leave Jennie with a man who doesn't have time for his own child? A man who didn't even care enough to call home from overseas when she was sick?*

Nick Valentine needed to take responsibility for Jennie. He was her father.

"I'm going to make an appointment to take her back to the doctor tomorrow," Candace told him.

"She doesn't appear that ill." Nick was studying the baby.

He'd seen Jennie for maybe an hour after a month away and now he was an expert on her health? As much as she itched to, Candace couldn't voice that reaction—Nick Valentine was her boss. The last thing she wanted was to annoy him enough for him to dismiss her.

Besides, if she was honest, he had a point. Right now Jennie didn't look that ill. But Nick hadn't seen her flushed with fever, her body limp after being contorted with convulsions. He hadn't experienced the fear—the helplessness—that had caused his sister to sob at the hospital. When Candace had taken the baby from Alison that day, she'd been terrified by the baby's burning temperature, the spasms that had shaken her little body. Nick couldn't possibly understand.

He'd been thousands of miles away, choosing furniture and carvings for upmarket gardens, focusing on making his next million.

But blaming him, working herself up, wasn't going to help the situation. Candace pulled herself together and said with forced calm, "I don't like the way she's fretting."

"Then make a doctor's appointment in the morning." He jiggled the baby in his arms.

"What time will suit you best?"

His head jerked up. "What?"

"When will you be free?" Did he imagine she'd make an appointment without consulting him? Even she knew he was a hotshot tycoon with endless demands on his time. "Or should I ask your assistant when you're available tomorrow?"

"I can't come—I've got too much to do tomorrow."

Of course he did. Poor Jennie. "You have to come. You're her father and she's been ill."

"What exactly was the matter?"

"Chronic ear infection. Her temperature rocketed until she had convulsions. She had to be hospitalized."

And that was how she'd come into Jennie's life. Candace hadn't stopped thanking her stars for whatever twist of fate had put her on duty for the shift when Jennie arrived.

"I'd have come if—"

If it had been important enough...

Candace cut him off with a wave of her hand—she wasn't interested in his excuses. Nick had no idea what havoc she was capable of unleashing—especially driven by her own guilt, her own very personal demons. "Jennie needs you with her. And I want to make sure there's been no resurgence of the infection, that her eardrums are clear. I'd hate for Jennie to lose her hearing for life."

He gave her an unreadable look. "Arrange the appointment, and get Mr. Busby to take you. Let me know the time and I'll meet you there."

"Good—Jennie will appreciate it."

The baby might be blissfully unaware of the importance of the moment. But in the years to come, at least Candace would have the comfort of knowing she'd gotten Nick involved in taking care of his daughter.

Something about the expression on the nanny's face bothered Nick.

Nurse, he amended silently. His sister had told him Candace was a nurse...not a nanny. Frankly, Nick didn't care what Candace called herself as long as she quit having this unsettling effect on him.

He was doing everything he could to pretend her proximity was leaving him unfazed. He'd forced himself to be cool and distant, but it wasn't working. He only had to catch a whiff of her sweet, spicy perfume to want to pull her close and bury his mouth against her scented skin.

It wouldn't do.

If only he could make himself think of her as the nanny—or the nurse—rather than Candace, the woman with tousled hair and translucent silver-gray eyes who was standing a short distance away from him wearing nothing but a pair of pink-and-white candy-striped cotton pajamas. Nick's gaze fell on the monitor that poked out the breast pocket of her pajama top, and he said with more than a little desperation, "I'm glad the system works—you must've sprinted up the stairs to have got here quicker than I did."

She gave him a peculiar look. "What do you mean? I'm in the room next door."

Next door? "You're not in the nanny's quarters in the basement?"

She shook her head. "The doctor and I agreed it made sense for me to be close at hand when Jennie was ill." Her gaze was very level. "Your sister agreed. The house has so many bedrooms—all of them empty. It seemed silly for me to stay two floors away from Jennie."

"Of course."

His lukewarm response caused her to say quickly, "I'm here to look after your daughter. As long as she's happy and healthy, does it matter where I sleep?"

Nick could hardly confess that the thought of her living here—on the same floor as him, a short distance from the master suite—was going to drive him crazy.

At least, he supposed, his mind would be at peace knowing Jennie was well looked after. Even if his body was on red alert.

He suppressed a groan.

So much for getting any sleep…

Three

The next day Candace glanced at her watch for the hundredth time in the past five minutes. The minute hand had crawled to twenty minutes past noon.

Where was Nick?

On her lap, Jennie gurgled and gazed avidly at the two identically dressed boys on the opposite side of the doctor's reception room, who appeared hell-bent on stripping the florist ribbon out of a flower arrangement. Their harried-looking father kept telling them to stop, to no avail. The twins had arrived half an hour after Candace, right on the heels of a little girl with a rash on her face.

That patient had already been sent in ahead, Candace having elected to miss Jennie's scheduled appointment time and wait for Nick to arrive. Who was now forty minutes late. With every passing moment, it was becoming clearer that Nick had no intention of keeping the promise he'd made.

Candace had tried to call him several times. Only to get his voice mail. She should've expected this. He'd told her he was busy. But she'd blissfully thought this time he would put Jennie first…before work.

Had he ever intended to come? Or had he sent her on ahead with the chauffeur simply to get her out of his hair?

It didn't matter what excuse he'd make later, it wouldn't take away the ache of…of…disappointment…in Candace's heart.

She told herself the emotion she was feeling had nothing to with her ambivalent relationship with Nick…or with the desire he'd awakened within her last night. She told herself it was all about Jennie.

By not arriving for the appointment, by not even bothering to let Candace know he'd bailed, he'd irrevocably let Jennie down.

With his round face and ruddy complexion, the snowy-bearded man seated behind the heavy antique desk twiddling a pen between his fingers looked like every child's vision of Santa Claus.

Nick had been taken in by the air of jolly bonhomie when he'd first met Desmond Perry—until he'd discovered that the devil himself lurked behind that merry mask. Now he couldn't figure out how he'd failed to notice the splinters of ice in the startling blue eyes.

"The final payment is done." It had given Nick enormous satisfaction to come here, into Desmond Perry's lair, to tell him that. He glanced at his watch and pushed back the chair he'd taken because Desmond had clearly expected him to stand. He rose now to his full intimidating height. "I won't have a cup of coffee—" the older man hadn't offered "—because I have an appointment."

Desmond carefully set the pen he'd been twirling between his blunt fingers down on the leather inset of the desk. "You should know I plan to sell my stock in Valentine's," he said.

Nick said very softly, "You what?"

"I will be selling my share of your business as soon as Jilly's estate has been settled."

His share? For a moment Nick could only stare at his father-in-law in disbelief. Then reality sank in. Desmond was talking about Jilly's stocks. The stock that in terms of their prenuptial agreement Nick had given to his wife. Stock that Jilly had then bequeathed to her father in her will.

With Jilly's sudden death brought on by a virus, Desmond no longer needed to pretend any loyalty toward the son-in-law he'd bought for his daughter—but never liked. Mostly his own fault, Nick knew; he'd been unable to kowtow to the man, be the obsequious puppet Desmond had expected. For seven years he'd worked night and day to maintain the astronomical payments to repurchase the garden center Desmond had tricked Nick's mentors, Bertha and Henry Williams, into selling.

By giving Nick a job, Bertha and Henry had saved Nick from sure trouble when he'd been a teen. And though he'd gone on to establish his own business, he couldn't stand by and watch them lose the garden center they'd loved…and the home they occupied on the premises. And wily Desmond had known that.

Desmond had set him up. The price for the center had not only been an unrealistic, extortionist amount, but also marriage to Jilly. Nick had considered refusing, but Henry's heart attack and Bertha's terror had caused Nick to grit his teeth and accept the terrible terms.

But once he'd signed the contract, and taken occupation of the garden center that had once belonged to his mentors, he'd given Bertha and Henry back their home. It hadn't been the end of it.

His new father-in-law had sat back, expecting Nick to fail to meet the punishing payment schedule, which would've put the property back under his control—and allowed him to triumph over the son-in-law he detested.

But Nick had done it.

The final repayment had been made. And he'd done it without jeopardizing the financial well-being of his own company. Sure it had slowed his expansion plans down, tightened his finances, but he was still a wealthy man.

But now, as the first glimpse of freedom appeared like a fragment of sky between dark city high-rises, Desmond had dropped his next bombshell.

Nick wasn't going to roll over. "The prenup stipulated that once the full amount of the sale price was repaid to you—" and Nick had worked himself almost to death to make sure of that "—then I would have right of first refusal on the shares if Jilly ever wanted to sell them."

He'd paid dearly for Bertha and Henry's retirement dream…

"My daughter is dead. You failed to pay the price before she died—the right of first refusal died with her. In terms of her will, the stock is now mine. And I have no intention of waiting until you can raise sufficient funds for the stock," Desmond sneered. "The growth of Valentine's garden centers has not been at all what I expected. I'm selling."

Nick forced himself to keep still. Not to defend the performance of the stock. Not to reveal his shock at Desmond's revelation. Instead, raising an eyebrow, he asked, "You already have a buyer for the stock?"

"Oh, yes."

Nick allowed himself a slight, disbelieving smile at Desmond while his brain worked frantically. Alison had said she and Richard had had an offer for their shares, too. Was he sensing a conspiracy where none existed?

Nick shrugged. "Well, they'll have to wait for Jilly's estate to be finalized."

"My buyer is not in a hurry."

"Who is it? Another chain of garden centers?" Nick tried to think which of his competitors might have the liquidity in the present economic climate to force a takeover.

"Why must the buyer be a garden center? The land owned by the company is worth a fortune."

That wiped the mocking smile clean off Nick's face. "A developer?" he asked dangerously. "You're planning to sell to someone who will hunt more stock until he has enough to close all the centers and develop the land?"

Triumph glittered in Desmond's pale blue eyes. "The developer I have in mind is prepared to pay a premium rate for the stock."

The Super Center, Valentine's flagship store, was located close to Auckland city, not far from the waterfront on a sizable tract of prime real estate. It was worth a fortune, and other stores in other cities were equally well situated. A developer would love to get his hands on the company's assets.

In the back of Nick's mind, there had always been the knowledge that he could sell off some of the land to raise funds, but that would be a last resort. It was something he'd never seriously contemplated—no matter how hard Desmond rode him.

Because that would mean closing those centers. Not only would his staff lose jobs, the community where the center was located would lose, too. Each center had landscaped gardens, a café where customers could socialize, well-equipped playgrounds for children and bandstands offering musical events. A Valentine's Garden Center brought pleasure to everyone who stopped by.

To hurt him, Desmond wanted to destroy the culture Nick had built.

Desmond knew him too well…

Narrowing his gaze on his adversary, Nick challenged, "You'd sell your stock, so your crony has a chance to make a fortune out of building high-density developments?"

Desmond placed his hands behind his head and smirked. "Sounds like a good plan."

Nick rocked on his toes, tempted—not for the first time—to slam a fist in his father-in-law's corpulent stomach.

The open green space with streams and lakes that Henry had painstakingly created and lost to Desmond seven years ago would be the first site to be bulldozed and developed—Nick had no doubt about that. With it would go the craftsmanship that Valentine's stores had brought to the lifestyle market. The handmade pots. The carved garden statues. The water features that were so carefully created. The plants that were so lovingly tended.

And it wouldn't stop there. The network of suppliers would lose contracts...and as for his staff, Nick didn't want to think about the layoffs that would follow.

His anger roared into fury. Nick took a step closer to the devil behind the desk. Then he checked himself, drawing on the control that had always served him well and helped him thwart Desmond in the past.

A glance at his watch caused him to grimace inwardly. *Damn.* He'd lost all track of time. He'd been due to meet Candace at the doctor's room fifteen minutes ago. He was going to miss the chance to talk to the doctor about how well Jennie had recovered. Hurriedly, Nick stuck his hand into his pocket searching for his cell phone.

It wasn't there. Cursing silently, Nick remembered placing it in the holder between the front seats in the Ferrari before he'd left his office.

"We can discuss an alternative plan."

Distracted by his thoughts, Nick turned his head. The triumph in Desmond's expression glowed even brighter. Whatever the alternative plan was, it boded ill—Nick had no doubt about that. He had no interest in bargaining with the devil.

He wasn't going to stay a minute longer. Already he'd allowed Desmond to consume too much of his time. A twinge of shame pierced him. He'd told Candace he would be at Jennie's doctor's appointment.

She was going to be furious—and how could he blame her?

If he left now, he'd make the tail end of the appointment and be able to speak to the doctor about Jennie himself. Snatching up his suit jacket from where he'd slung it over the chair back, Nick swiveled on his heel and headed for the door.

"Nick!"

He kept walking as Desmond's voice called out from behind him, "If you don't stop right now, I'll start negotiating the stock sale."

Nick cast a glance over his shoulder. Desmond had risen to his feet, his face red with frustrated anger. It gave Nick an immense amount of satisfaction to say, "Do what you must, but you'll have to excuse me, I have something more important to deal with right now."

Nick watched frustration and rage darken Desmond's face to the color of a tomato. Quite suddenly, the other man no longer resembled Santa.

Four

Candace *was* furious with him.

It wasn't apparent from what she said, but rather from the overly cool, calm manner in which she had greeted his arrival. Nick decided he would've preferred it if she'd raged at him. Instead he was conscious of the chasm of chilly disapproval that divided them.

After leaving the doctor's rooms, Nick had given the keys to the Ferrari to Mr. Busby to take home and loaded Candace and Jennie into the more conservative Daimler, which at least provided space for Jennie's car seat. Rather ironically, Nick planned to buy Candace coffee from the café at the closest Valentine's—which had been the topic of his recent argument with Desmond.

Nick hoped the parklike surroundings and pretty gardens would pacify her—and he figured he owed her some sort of explanation.

"I'm sorry," he said finally, stopping at a crossing to allow a group of boys to wheel their bikes across.

"Sorry?" She turned her head. The eyes that clashed with his radiated silver-white heat that her cool civility couldn't cloak.

Incongruously, the heat caused desire to leap in his gut.

"I mean it." He'd never apologized to Jilly in the seven years they'd been married. Not for arriving home when dinner had congealed on the plates. Not when he'd left her standing on her own at one of the society events that were so important to her. Not even when he'd missed Jennie's birth—although that had been the one time that he'd come close.

He'd figured there was no point apologizing for anything to a woman who'd charmed her father into trapping the bridegroom she'd wanted at all costs. Saying *sorry* would've been a lie.

This was different.

"I suppose you had some life-threatening crisis at work?" she said.

Nick thought of Desmond's threat to sell Jilly's stock in Valentine's as he pulled away from the crossing. "Something like that."

"That's what I expected."

It was the weary, defeated note in Candace's voice that caused Nick to throw her a quick, sharp glance before focusing back on the road ahead. "I got there, didn't I?"

"Halfway through the deferred appointment, if that's what you mean."

He'd cursed the city traffic all the way. Now she couldn't even thank him for almost killing himself to get there. "The baby is fine. The doctor couldn't find anything wrong."

"But what if she hadn't been?"

Her tone was full of suppressed anger and disappointment and...some other emotion he couldn't name.

Why was this so important to her?

There was no point arguing. Yet a twinge of shame twisted deep within him. Nick nosed the car into a side lane and turned into the parking lot beyond. After bringing the Daimler to a halt he switched it off and changed the subject. "This is one of my centers. There's a café that overlooks a lake. Let me buy you a coffee."

She wrapped her arms around her middle and turned her head away so he couldn't read those all-too-expressive eyes. "Nick, I don't need you to buy me a coffee. I needed you to be there for Jennie."

"Maybe Jennie would like to see the ducks."

That evoked a response, though not one that he wanted to answer. "Is that the real reason we're here? Because you want to show Jennie the ducks?"

Nick searched her frozen features for sarcasm, but couldn't find any. "My first thought was that I owed you an apology." He spread his hands. "But it *is* a good place to show Jennie some ducks. I can't wait to see her face. She's going to love it."

It was the truth. To Nick's immense surprise, he was looking forward to watching Jennie's reaction.

The baby's birth had unleashed a startling realization of all that was wrong in his life. Beginning with his sham marriage to Jilly. A deal to which he should never have agreed.

"Nick…"

The uncertain note in Candace's voice captured his attention. The stiffness had left her face, although her arms were still wrapped protectively around herself. "Yes?"

"You and I need to talk."

Her expression told him that she wasn't looking forward to whatever she wanted to talk to him about. After a second's pause, Nick instinctively knew what it was about.

Damn, he should never have given in to that wild, insane urge to kiss her. God knew what she was making of his bringing her here for coffee.

Dismissively he said, "You're making too much out of the fact that I want to buy you coffee to apologize. This isn't a date…or any attempt to change the footing of our relationship to anything more personal—you don't need to worry about that."

Nick knew he was lying through his teeth. Despite his promise that there would be no more kisses, he hungered to kiss her again, and see if she tasted as good as he remembered.

But she was good for Jennie…and he needed her for Jennie's sake. He couldn't afford to screw it all up and have her leave.

He could sense her stiffening in the seat beside him, and Jennie didn't help matters by letting out a squawk from the rear seat. "I never thought this was a date," Candace told him with an edge in her voice.

"Then what do you want to talk about?"

"You and Jennie—but now is probably not a good time. Jennie wants out of the car."

Candace scrambled from the Daimler as if she couldn't wait to escape the cocoon of the car's interior, and the passenger door slammed behind her.

Nick gritted his teeth. Okay, so he'd sure got that wrong. Badly. Sex was the last thing on her mind. Whereas he couldn't think of much else. All he could think about was repeating the "mistake" they'd made the night before.

Except Nick couldn't view that kiss as a mistake. Unprofessional? Hell, yes. But a mistake? No way.

Nick had always gone after what he wanted. And right now he wanted Candace. But he didn't want to spook her and lose her. Nor could he rid himself of the wriggle of discomfort over his ruthless desire to seduce someone who worked for him. He'd never been tempted to do anything like that before.

But then again he'd never experienced anything like this.

He wanted Jennie's nanny.

And what was more, he was certain Candace desired him, too, despite her cool annoyance. The challenge lay in getting her to admit her desire—especially after all the lengths he'd gone to in order to convince her that he wasn't interested.

Yet Candace wanted to talk about him and Jennie, the last thing Nick wanted. He *never* talked about Jennie—about his suspicions that she wasn't really his daughter.

By the time Nick had gotten himself firmly back in control, Candace had already taken Jennie out of the rear car seat. Nick pressed the key fob to open the trunk, hoisted the stroller out and unfolded it.

He took Jennie from Candace and lowered her into the stroller. She let out a howl of protest and went rigid.

"Hey," he chided her, "stop that."

The objection grew more vociferous.

Nick shot Candace a helpless glance. She was watching him through narrowed eyes—okay, so he was on his own. He transferred his attention back to Jennie; he wasn't about to let a baby defeat him.

"Come on, missy, be still. Let me buckle you in."

Jennie let out a yell of objection. It was clear to Nick—and to anyone who cared to listen—that she had no intention of submitting to being strapped into the stroller. Time to change tactics.

"After we show you the ducks I'll take you up to the café. You can have a treat—an ice cream," he said craftily.

Jennie greeted his bribe with the contempt it deserved and simply shrieked more loudly.

"You little hellion," he told her softly, his admiration growing in leaps and bounds.

The noise stopped abruptly. Eyeing him assessingly, Jennie cooed and blew a raspberry.

Nick couldn't help himself—he laughed, then leaned down and planted a kiss on her plump cheek. It was soft, like a peach. A wave of emotion rushed through him.

What did it matter if she wasn't his child? No one except he would ever know that Jilly had played him for a fool.

There was no point in maintaining the distance he'd been keeping from Jennie. She didn't deserve to suffer; after all, she was the only innocent party in the entire mess.

And if he wanted, she could be his. All his.

"You *are* a hellion," he said, impressed.

She gave him a gummy smile and capitulated, allowing him to put her into the stroller.

In that moment Nick felt his heart constrict and he fell irrevocably in love.

"You're also a wicked flirt," he scolded Jennie as the clip for the restraining strap locked into place.

A movement out the corner of his eye had him lifting his head. Candace was watching them. The look in her eyes was full of yearning, but as she caught him studying her, shutters dropped into place.

It was possible that Candace was as ready as he to take their relationship to its inevitable conclusion. Yet Nick suspected that Candace would want more than simply sex. And while he could never tell her the true reason why he'd held Jennie at a distance, it might help to divulge the precarious position he was in with Valentine's. It wouldn't be easy to share that knowledge; he'd always handled his problems by himself, in his own way. He'd never been the kind of man who shared his concerns.

Maybe it was time to let a little of his tightly leashed control slip.

The idea of letting his control slip became even more attractive as Nick followed Candace through the rose-covered archway and down the pathway to the landscaped parklands by the lake. He couldn't help but notice the pert curve of her bottom under the fitted, narrow black jeans. Her long legs picked up speed when the path dipped as they approached the water's edge, causing the stroller to roll faster and faster. In the breeze her blond hair streamed like a banner over her shoulders.

When he caught up to her at the edge of the lake, she wasn't even breathing hard.

"This is a wonderful spot." She knelt down and pointed at the water. "See the ducks, Jennie?"

At last he'd done something she approved of. Nick couldn't stop the surge of pleasure.

Jennie was sitting bolt upright, starfish fingers pushing on the arms of the stroller, her eyes wide with excitement.

For the first time since leaving his office, Nick started to relax. This might work. There was still a chance for them... for him and Jennie.

More than a chance.

Resolve set in and Nick's jaw firmed. He had a responsibility to Jennie. He'd agreed to donate his seed for the baby Jilly wanted, even though he knew, almost to the day, that Jilly had changed her mind. She'd stopped talking about *their* baby... started talking about *her* baby. Initially, it hadn't sunk in that she'd found another donor...a lover. Hindsight was twenty-twenty.

Yet after Jilly's return from the fertility clinic on the Southeast Asian island of Namkhet, he'd been sure of it. It wasn't his sperm that had impregnated Jilly....

But Nick no longer cared. All that mattered was the baby leaning forward in the stroller, her eyes gleaming with delight. So vital and full of life. The child everyone believed to be his daughter. He spared a glance at the woman kneeling beside the stroller. Candace had made her opinion clear—he didn't deserve Jennie. But what did her opinion matter? Jennie could be his daughter...all he needed to do was accept her. He'd already made a start. It was proving to be much easier than he'd ever imagined—and the rewards were pure pleasure.

And little Jennie didn't know it was a lie. To Jennie he was the only father she'd known.

Nick vowed that he would *make* it work. He would prove Candace wrong. He was the only family Jennie had.

A pair of black swans glided toward them, long necks gracefully arched. Candace started to smile as Jennie beat her arms up and down and let out a squeak. Even Nick grinned at the baby's antics.

"Sorry, no food." Candace spread her hands out as the swans slowed in front of them.

"Look, there are even eels," Nick said as an inquisitive nose poked out the water. "See?" Jennie was all eyes. "Want to take a closer look?"

Not liking the sound of that, Candace said quickly, "She's fine in the stroller."

But Nick ignored her warning and unclipped the restraint. "Come on," he told Jennie. "I'll show you."

Jennie hung out of his arms as he hoisted her up, her arms flapping frantically. Little breathless puffs of baby excitement filled the air, and Candace clambered to her feet. "Nick, this isn't a good idea—"

"Don't be such a killjoy!"

Ducks crowded around, craning their necks, beady eyes fixed on him. In the water, the swans paddled in one spot. Nick laughed, shrugging aside the cautioning hand Candace placed on his arm as Jennie gurgled with unrestrained glee.

"Just look at her." With Nick reveling in the baby's amazement, Candace didn't have the heart to spoil the moment. "Next time we'll bring bread," he promised the baby.

More ducks were scrambling out of the water.

"Nick, that's probably close enough." Candace cast an anxious glance at the water's edge. "Those are geese coming— and they can be quite aggressive."

"Jennie's having the time of her life. And so am I."

There was no suitable response to that. Candace let out the breath she was holding and tried to stop hyperventilating about the way Jennie was hanging over his arm. He wouldn't drop the baby, she told herself. He really wouldn't…

So why couldn't she relax? She ought to be thrilled Nick was having such fun with Jennie, yet Candace couldn't stop fretting as she cast a wary glance along the grassy bank to the trio of advancing, honking geese.

In Nick's arms Jennie gave a squawk. The geese slowed. He chuckled. "That's my girl. Give 'em hell!"

Candace frowned, but forced herself to bite her lip and say nothing.

"Look—" Nick took a step forward and pointed "—more ducks."

Unable to stop herself, Candace hurried up beside him. "Careful, don't drop the baby!"

Nick returned his hand to Jennie's waist, anchoring her securely against him. To Candace's increasing annoyance, he ignored her and murmured to Jennie, "Those are woodland ducks. I used to feed ones just like that in the creek near my grandmother's cottage when I was a boy."

After a second, Candace's curiosity got the better of her. She knew so little about Nick, and what she'd read in the business newspapers and gossip pages mentioned nothing about a grandmother. It made him seem more human. "You lived with your grandmother?"

"Yes, she was a tough lady with a heart of gold. She never complained when I'd sneak a loaf out of the pantry to feed the ducks, even when times were tight." Hitching Jennie higher up against his shoulder, he said, "What about seeing if there's anything on the café's menu that's suitable for Jennie?"

Candace waved to the stroller where it stood surrounded by ducks. "I've got a tumbler with diluted juice she can have, and some apple slices…if the ducks haven't gotten to them. We don't need to go to the café."

"I still owe you a coffee by way of an apology."

Candace gave him a measuring look "Oh, all right then." Then realizing he might well be affronted by her lack of enthusiasm, she added, "That would be nice." And it would have the added bonus of getting them away from the water's edge where Jennie's flock of new feathered friends hovered.

She held out her arms for the baby. Nick hesitated for a fraction of a second, then surrendered Jennie. Candace stepped backward.

"Careful!"

Nick leaped forward as she stumbled. Candace teetered, grabbing at him with one hand, clinging to the baby with the other, her eyes fixing on Nick in fright.

"Jennie!" she pleaded.

For a split second Candace was aware of the solid warmth of his body, the heavy thud of his heart, before the sobs of her own panicky breath drowned it all out, and Nick's arms locked around Jennie. Jennie was safe.

To Candace's horror, Nick started to slide along the grassy bank down to the water, Jennie still clasped in his arms. He landed with a dull splash, feetfirst in knee-deep water.

The baby didn't even squeak. Instead, Jennie was hanging over his arm, reaching for the surface of the lake.

Nick was laughing. "None of that," he said as Jennie flapped her arms furiously, frantically trying to free herself from his grasp. "No swimming today."

Candace didn't think it was the least bit funny.

Yet looking down at Nick, water rippling around his suit pants, his Italian shoes totally submerged beneath the lake's reflective surface, she felt a stab of totally inappropriate desire. Jennie had almost landed in the lake, and she was lusting after Nick Valentine?

What was wrong with her?

"That was close!" she said, as her breathing slowed.

Nick chucked the little imp under her chin and Jennie gave him a toothless smile.

"She's fine."

She forgot that he'd swept the baby to safety. Anxiety and lust coalesced into anger. "It's not funny—she could've fallen in."

His smile faded. In a blink he was back to the distant, narrow-eyed businessman. "I wouldn't have you drop her."

She suppressed the flare of resentment at his suggestion that *she'd* almost dropped Jennie, when *he'd* been the one to take the baby out of the stroller in the first place. "You might not have been able to stop it."

"I would've done everything in my power."

Nick placed one foot on the bank, Jennie still squirming in his hold. "Hey, stop it, miss. You *will* end up going swimming if you carry on like that!"

"Nick!"

At her warning shriek, Nick glanced up.

"Look out!" Candace was almost incoherent with apprehension. *"The geese."*

He jerked his head around as Jennie's fingers jabbed in the direction of a goose who'd silently paddled up behind them. He swung the baby away, but it was too late. Jennie's wail rent the air.

Rushing to the water's edge, Candace blocked his way as Nick clambered back onto the bank.

Jennie was screaming, her face cherry-red with protest, her hand limp.

Candace reached for the pecked fingers. "Let me see!" Her head bent over Jennie's reddened finger. "Ouch."

"The skin's not broken."

His words set a torch to her already frayed emotions. "Don't be so callous!" Nick started to object, but she overrode him. "It's going to need cleaning. Heaven knows what might've been in that bird's beak."

"The café has a bathroom where you can clean it up, and I've got a first-aid kit with some antiseptic in the trunk of my car."

Candace glared at him. "I've got a rudimentary first-aid kit in the stroller—enough to deal with this." She drew a shuddering breath, stunned at how quickly everything had happened—and at the extent of her fear. "Jennie should not have been taken out of the stroller."

Nick stared at Candace in disbelief. "*Now it's my fault?* She wanted to get out."

"She could see perfectly well from where she was."

"You're overreacting," he said tersely.

A fresh wave of anger flooded her. "She got hurt because of *you*."

"Oh, please. That kind of thing is a normal part of growing up. It happens." He was studying her in a way that made her grow tense. "You're shaken up. I'll take Jennie and clean her up."

What was he getting at? Was he implying she was too emotional to do her job, to look after Jennie? "I'll do it! You can bring the stroller and the first-aid kit."

To Candace's distress, Jennie's wails grew louder as they stormed along the winding pathway up the rise to the café. The little body huddled against her was rigid with outrage.

As he waited for Candace to return from tending to Jennie's pecked finger, Nick couldn't stop thinking about Jennie's puckered-up little face glaring at him accusingly over Candace's shoulder as she'd been borne away.

Candace was right.

Jennie had been hurt.

And he could've—should've—avoided it.

Sometime in the past twenty-four hours he'd connected with Jennie. Nick silently promised himself that in the future he was going to make sure he spent more time with the baby so innocent of the treachery surrounding her conception. And, as little as he wanted to admit it right now, he had Candace to thank for opening his eyes to the fact that his life—what was important in it—was getting away from him.

By the time Candace and Jennie joined him at the table in the sunny sheltered spot outside the café, Jennie had stopped crying. After Candace secured her in the stroller, the baby lay back and focused intently on the Micky Mouse Band-Aid wrapped around her finger.

Nick winced. "Is it very bruised?"

"A little red. But no bruising—and no blood."

"That's a relief."

A black-skirted waitress who'd been hovering while Nick waited took their coffee order. As an afterthought, Candace added a request for biscotti.

"Jennie will enjoy chewing it—the teeth coming through have been niggling her."

Nick glanced at the baby. The stroller had been angled so the hot February sun didn't fall on Jennie's face, but her eyelids were drooping. "The biscotti might have to wait. She looks sleepy."

Candace leaned forward across him and a hint of that sexy, spicy perfume wafted over Nick. It was becoming all too familiar—and so was the intoxicating effect her closeness had on his senses. He inhaled slowly and resisted the urge to stroke back the curl that had fallen over her face.

"She's already asleep." Candace couldn't hide her astonishment. "The shock and tears must've tired her out."

Nick sensed implied accusation. "It's been a long morning for her—an outing to the doctor, the ride in the car, the fresh air and the excitement of seeing the ducks. It all added up." He fixed his gaze on Candace, challenging her to mention the mishap with the goose.

Her lips pursed and she sat up straight. "There's something you need to know."

Folding his arms behind his head, Nick rocked back on his chair and gave her a lazy smile. "What is that?"

"I haven't been completely honest with you."

His smile disappeared. "What do you mean?"

Nick thought about Candace's alarm when the goose pecked Jennie. It had hardly been the cool composure he would've expected from a nurse. Alison had sworn her references had been top rate. Was she a fraud? Not a nurse at all? Had she taken his sister in? "Don't tell me. Not only are you not a nanny, you're not a nurse, either."

"I *am* a nurse—I'm fully qualified to take care of Jennie," she said quickly.

The way his stomach dropped forced Nick to take a steadying breath. How bad could it be? "Spit it out."

"I'm Jennie's biological mother."

Nick blinked. Whatever he'd expected, it wasn't this. It took a moment for him to absorb her statement, and once he'd digested it, the tension in his belly unwound like a compressed spring uncurling and he let out a shout of laughter. "Don't be absurd!"

"I'm not being absurd. I *am* Jennie's mother."

Nick took in the set of her pink mouth, the sparkle in her eyes—and lust, wholly unwelcome, surged in his groin. Giving her a slow smile, he lowered his voice and murmured, "Do you honestly believe I would've forgotten making love to you?"

"No!" A flush stained her cheeks. "I don't mean you…" Her voice trailed away.

"Yet you claim to be Jennie's mother."

Disappointment flooded Nick. The woman might look like an angel, but she was the worst kind of fraud. A fallen angel. He didn't know what she was after yet, but Nick was sure he would find out. All it would take was patience—and he'd always possessed plenty of that. He settled down to play her for all he was worth.

"Yes, but—"

"But? You're suddenly no longer so certain?" Nick raised an eyebrow to express his disbelief. As she rushed into speech, he raised a hand to cut her off. "Before you sink yourself any further, you should know that even though I was away on a string of business trips *while Jilly was pregnant*," he emphasized, "I certainly *never* messed around during my marriage."

"I'm not implying—"

"Then what are you suggesting?" he asked silkily.

"Jilly is not the baby's mother. I am."

She spoke Jilly's name with easy familiarity. As if she'd known her...

Nick's eyes narrowed.

Was it possible that the connection between the women was his late wife's lover—Jennie's father? Was that what this whole charade of pretending to be Jennie's mother was all about? This must be what she'd been hinting at when she'd told him earlier that she wanted to talk to him about Jennie.

"So let me get this straight. Are you trying to say that Jennie was switched at birth?" Nick drawled.

"No."

"What do you mean, 'no'?"

"I agreed to be a surrogate mom."

It wasn't possible. Candace had to be lying!

Nick's initial amusement had been replaced by impatience. He knew she was going to lose this battle. The sooner he got this crazy woman out of Jennie's life the better. "Look, I don't have time for this—"

"You don't have time for your daughter's mother?"

He'd had enough. Nick rolled his eyes and rose to his feet. Taking his wallet, he drew out a fifty-dollar bill and a business card. He held them out to her. "For a cab—when you leave. But first go to my office, it's in the block at the entrance. My assistant will have a check ready by the time you get there, together with severance pay. I'll call her now to arrange it."

Candace made no move to take the card or the money. He shrugged and dropped them on the table. A downward glance revealed that Jennie was still asleep in the stroller. If luck was on his side she'd remain that way until he'd gotten her home and called an employment agency to hire a new nanny—one he'd vet himself this time. If worse came to worst, he'd call his sister.

He wheeled the stroller to the cashier inside the café, greeted her by name and asked her to call a cab. Without question she reached for the phone. Nick smiled and waved to the manager on the opposite side of the coffee shop, and pushed Jennie back out into the sunshine.

"Wait."

A hand came down on his arm. Nick brushed her off and kept walking, stroller trundling in front of him. About twenty yards down the path, Candace rushed in front of him, blocking his way, and this time she grabbed his arm with enough force to ensure he wouldn't easily shake her off.

Her eyes were intense and angry, spitting smoke. "You're firing me? For being Jennie's mother?"

Nick glared back at her. "I might not have been there at Jennie's birth, but I sure as hell saw that Jilly was pregnant! I'm firing you for being a charlatan…a liar…a fraud. Take your pick. Just count yourself lucky you hadn't raised the issue of money yet or we could've added blackmailer to the list."

He glanced pointedly down at feminine fingers spread on his arm, but what she said brought his eyes back to her face in shock.

"DNA tests don't lie."

Five

"You have a DNA test proving you are Jennie's mother?"

"Not anymore," Candace said, and felt Nick's forearm tense beneath her fingertips.

"So you are lying!"

"I don't have them—they'll be in the doctor's file. One thing I'm not is a liar." Then she tacked on, "Or a fraud."

Candace could feel the heat in her cheeks as she belatedly snatched her hand off the fine wool of Nick's suit jacket. Even through the fabric she'd been uncomfortably conscious of the warmth of his body.

She drew a second deep breath, desperately trying to calm herself down. She couldn't let him keep Jennie. He wasn't worthy of being Jennie's—any baby's—father. But it wouldn't help to get his back up.

"Okay, maybe I handled this badly," she said slowly. "You made me mad."

"*I* made *you* mad?" He was frowning down at her. "Lady, I'm not the crazy one around here."

Crazy? Candace squinted up at him. "I'm not crazy."

Nick didn't bother to answer. Instead, he wheeled the stroller—with her baby—away. Candace rushed after him. "Where are you taking Jennie?"

"Home!"

"Home? That glossy mansion that's as cold as an icicle isn't a home." Nick kept walking away from her. In desperation she said, "You're not fit to be Jennie's father!"

At that his shoulders stiffened and he slowed.

Oh, no! So much for trying not to antagonize him. Well, she had no choice now but to soldier on. "Nick, you've been away for the past month, you didn't even return home when Jennie was desperately ill and you know nothing about caring for her. What else could I think?"

He turned. There was a white line around his mouth, and his face was leached of all color. "I've had enough of this. You will never get the chance to take her away—and even if I accepted a word of your insane claim, my first question would be where the hell were you when Jennie needed a mother?"

He'd homed in on the heart of her pain—her guilt. "That's not fair—I had no choice."

Nick glared. "I still don't believe a word of this."

Candace hesitated. She'd known from that first heart-in-her-throat moment when she'd met him that her name had meant nothing to Nick. Candace wasn't a common name, yet he hadn't even done a double take when he'd said, "You must be Candace."

For one wild instant she'd thought he was pretending. Yet even when she'd revealed her surname, his expression hadn't changed. And finally she realized that Nick Valentine had never bothered to find out the identity of his baby's egg donor and surrogate mother. And now he was making out as though he knew nothing about it all…

Jilly had made it clear that he was a busy man, and Candace had slowly pieced together the image of a driven, workaholic husband who cared more for his multimillion-dollar company than his wife. Jilly had assured her that was all going to change when the baby was born.

Yet Nick Valentine had shown no interest in Candace's pregnancy—unlike Jilly, who'd traveled all the way to the exclusive Namkhet Island clinic to be there while the IVF took place, who'd kept every prenatal appointment once they'd gotten back home to New Zealand, who'd visited Candace every week and bought her treats, and loved showing her photos of the nursery she was preparing for Jennie.

Right from the outset Jilly had explained that Nick hadn't wanted to meet the surrogate…that he wanted to imagine the child as his wife's. Candace had accepted the explanation. She'd so badly wanted to be convinced that she'd done the right thing—even after the stomach-churning second thoughts had started to creep in.

Now she challenged him. "You can't walk away—this is too important. You must listen to me."

"Okay, you've got my attention…" he glanced at his watch "…for one minute."

That was better than nothing. Speaking rapidly, she said, "Jennie's a baby. She needs a parent. I gave her to you and Jilly. I *trusted* you to look after her…to love her and—"

"You *gave* her to me and Jilly?" Nick hooted with derisive laughter.

Something wasn't adding up. "You and Jilly needed a surrogate," Candace said slowly.

"Stop this!" His brows jerked together and glared at her again. "I'm not listening to any more of your crazy creations. My wife was pregnant… I witnessed her debilitating morning sickness, saw the pregnancy develop. Jilly gave birth to Jennie."

Jilly hadn't been pregnant!

Candace couldn't help herself. "*You're* crazy." She advanced on the stroller that he'd let go and grasped the handles. "I'm not leaving Jennie alone with you."

He tussled with her and the stroller jerked.

"You're going to wake Jennie," she warned.

"If you think I'm going to let some deluded woman kidnap my daughter, you can think again."

"I have no intention of kidnapping her. I'm coming with you back to your home. I'm not letting Jennie out of my sight—and if you think you can brush me off, think again. I'll walk up to every customer in this garden center and tell them I'm your baby's mother and you're trying to pay me off."

He went very still. "Don't threaten me. I'll call the police."

"You think I'm bluffing? Do you really want to stage a scene here…and get the police involved?"

"We'll finish this discussion at the house." Nick gave her a killing glare, and Candace knew she'd won a temporary reprieve.

The drive back to the Valentine mansion passed in Arctic silence.

Once the tall, imposing electronic gates swung soundlessly shut behind them, Candace started to lose her nerve. What if Nick Valentine truly was crazy? What had she done to put herself—and Jennie—at his mercy?

The Daimler came to a stop behind a Lexus parked in the circular driveway edged by clipped boxwood hedging. The evidence that someone else was at Nick's house eased Candace's apprehension.

It would be okay; they would get this sorted out, she reassured herself. But whatever happened she wasn't abandoning her baby to Nick's negligent care. He might have all the money in the world, but she'd seen firsthand what kind of parent he was. She wasn't leaving Jennie alone with him.

A glance into the backseat showed that Jennie was still

sleeping. By the time Candace had gathered up the diaper bag at her feet, Nick had the rear door open and was carefully taking the baby out of the car. Watching him, Candace had to shove aside the momentary doubt that he was the uncaring, crazy man she knew him to be. Mr. Busby, Nick's chauffeur and handyman, had arrived and taken the stroller out of the trunk, and was carrying it up the white marble stairs to the front door.

Nick followed, cradling the baby. Jennie's mouth twitched in her sleep.

Mrs. Busby was standing inside the front door. "Mrs. Timmings is in the living room."

Relief filled Candace. Alison Timmings was a sensible woman—even if her brother was crazy.

"I'll take Jennie to the nursery." Nick's stare dared Candace to argue with him. To Mrs. Busby he added, "Tell my sister I won't be long, please."

"Nick?" In the archway that opened into the living room appeared the tall brunette that Candace had first met when Jennie was admitted to hospital while Nick was away. "I heard your voice. I tried your office, but Pauline said you'd left hours ago. Where have you been?"

Without waiting for an answer, Nick's sister came toward them, her high heels tapping on the marble tiles. She smiled a greeting to Candace before making a beeline for the baby in Nick's arms. "Hello, sweetheart."

Jennie woke and smiled at Alison, holding her short arms out wide.

Her aunt swept her up in a swarm of cooing sounds. Jennie immediately clutched a handful of pearls and thrust them into her mouth.

"Looks like she's teething, Nick." Alison rescued her necklace from the baby.

"It would appear so." He moved closer. "Here, give her to me."

"I'll take her." Candace came up on the other side of his sister.

"Thank you, Candace." Alison surrendered the baby gracefully. For a moment Candace thought Nick was going to object to her having possession of the child, but then his sister was saying, "It's not like you to swan out of the office."

"Hardly swanning—although we did see some black ones after I met Candace at the doctor's office for Jennie to be checked out."

"You took her back to the doctor? Is anything wrong?" Alison asked at once, glancing to Candace for a reply.

"No, Jennie's fine," said Candace soothingly. "She was restless last night, running a bit of a temperature, so I wanted to make sure there was no resurgence of the infection."

"You're so good to her."

"Thank you." She smiled at the other woman. "I'll take Jennie upstairs so you two can talk."

"Not so fast." Nick moved to obstruct her. "I'm not letting you go anywhere until we've finished our discussion."

What he meant was *I'm not letting you out of my sight,* Candace thought rebelliously.

His sister must've thought the same thing. "Nick, you're being rude—and you're frightening Candace."

Ignoring his sister's interjection, he gave her a mean stare. "She's not frightened enough."

"Nick!"

Even as Alison objected, Candace's heart sped up. She hugged Jennie tightly. "I'm not going to back down on the truth. You don't scare me."

Alison glanced from Candace to her brother. "What truth? Anyone care to fill me in about what's going on?"

"Candace claims she's Jennie's mother."

Nick's dismissive tone set Candace's teeth on edge. She still couldn't swallow that he hadn't known. "Claims? You *know* I'm Jennie's mother! You contracted me to donate the eggs and share my womb so you and Jilly could have the child she so desperately wanted."

"Contracted?" Nick gave a snort. "Why would I want to do that?"

Candace gave him a cold stare over the baby's head. "Because you and Jilly were unable to have your own child."

He stared. His features tightened. "IVF worked successfully for Jilly and me."

Jennie shifted restlessly in her arms and Candace unsuccessfully ducked her head sideways as Jennie grabbed a handful of her hair. When she'd extracted the strands from Jennie's hands she said, "Be honest. Jilly told me all about the struggles you were having—that IVF wasn't working. That's why the two of you decided to look for an egg donor, someone who could carry the baby for her. Which, of course, is where I came in."

Now both Nick and Alison were staring at her as if she'd grown two heads.

"What?" asked Candace. "Why are you looking at me like that?"

"It's true that the IVF didn't work in the initial attempts." Nick appeared to be picking his words with care. "But then Jilly tried a new procedure at an overseas clinic."

"What my brother is trying to say," cut in Alison, "is that Jilly was pregnant." With her arms she mimed a swollen belly. "Very pregnant. She gave birth—to Jennie."

Candace gaped at them both.

A vision of Jilly clad in black leggings and a belted long cardigan floated through her mind. Jilly had been reed slim when she'd excitedly assisted the midwife at Jennie's home birth in the cottage, and bore absolutely no resemblance to the rounded belly Alison had mimed.

Hitching Jennie higher against her shoulder, Candace said slowly, "That's not possible, because Jilly was *never* pregnant."

Alison stared at Nick and raised an eyebrow.

"She's crazy." Nick shrugged. "I've been saying exactly the same thing as you, Alison, but she won't let go of her delusion that Jilly was never pregnant—that *she's* Jennie's mother."

Confusion clouded Candace's brain, making it feel wooly. Was it possible that Nick Valentine and his wife had pulled off a spectacular deception, fooling even their own families that the baby was Jilly's? Had they gone as far as to fake Jilly's pregnancy? Placed padding beneath Jilly's clothing to fool everyone—even Alison? That was crazy!

Candace struggled to put her chaotic thoughts in order.

What would be the point of such a massive deception? Nick was a wealthy man, and Jilly had made it clear that Candace could name her price for her kindness, though, of course, Candace had refused all Jilly's generous offers. It was, after all, illegal in New Zealand to be paid to be a surrogate. She'd done it because Jilly had been so desperate. As a pediatric nurse, Candace had never met a woman more deserving of a baby. Her heart had gone out to the other woman as they'd become friends.

"Perhaps Mrs. Busby could make us all a cup of tea. I'll see to it." Alison cast her brother a look that Candace couldn't interpret. "I'll also call the doctor just to check that Jennie is really going to be okay."

Had Alison decided that Candace was unhinged? Was that the reason for the secret exchange of glances, for the call to the doctor?

"Yes, by all means let's call the doctor." Candace pressed a kiss on top of Jennie's downy head, then lifted her lashes and gave Nick her most dulcet smile. "And while you're at it why don't you call Jilly's doctor to clear up once and for all the small matter of who really is Jennie's mother. Ask for a copy of the DNA report that was done once the pregnancy was confirmed."

* * *

"The DNA report?"

Nick stared at Candace in disbelief. Was she going to persist with this? Of course there was no DNA report. An urge to snatch the baby out of her arms overwhelmed him. He quashed it. To do so would reveal how deeply her mad claims were unsettling him. Far better to play it cool.

Candace's eyebrows lowered. "All I want is for you to give me a chance to prove I'm telling the truth. The doctor should have a copy of the results of the DNA tests that were done after Jennie was born as part of the terms of the surrogacy agreement—" She broke off as he rolled his eyes skyward. "You still think I'm lying!"

"I don't know anything about postbirth DNA tests or a surrogacy agreement. Don't you think that's a little strange?"

She was chewing her lip. *That mouth.* Heat popped in his groin. God!

"You're not drawing me into another debate where you clearly have no intention of conceding anything. All I want is for you to see the test results."

Was that really all Candace wanted? After all, if she'd been telling the truth, it wouldn't be an unreasonable request. Except it was a lie—it had to be. Yet she was still gnawing her lip and her eyes were troubled. She didn't look like a fraud... or a crazy. She looked worried.

And he wanted her more than ever.

Nick sucked in a deep breath. He had to get over this.

She might look like a worried angel, but how could he trust his reactions? Sure, she was lovely. And sure he desired her. Right now his priority had to be Jennie.

Still, what if Candace was telling the truth?

He tried to think sanely. Why was he so sure that everything Jilly told him was the truth and Candace's claim was pure fiction? He'd witnessed Jilly's blossoming body...that was indisputable. Yet he'd never gone with her to the doctor. Never seen her naked or touched her burgeoning belly. He'd been so certain the baby wasn't his…

In the past, Jilly had gotten what she wanted at all costs. What if…

He shied away from the thought. Jilly didn't deserve this. She was dead. Yet the distress in Candace's eyes niggled at him.

"Call the doctor," she insisted.

Nick excused himself. It took only a few minutes for him to ascertain what he'd already suspected. There was no DNA report—and Jilly's doctor had never heard of Candace. Although he did remind Nick that Jilly had used a gynecologist and midwife for the birth, and they might know more.

Nick didn't need to call them. He already knew the truth. And he took great pleasure in returning to the sitting area and confronting Candace with it. "The doctor knows nothing about a test."

"There *was* a DNA test done." She lifted her chin. "But if you want, we can redo the tests…it doesn't take long to get a result." Nick narrowed his gaze as she said, glancing down at the oversize bargain watch on her slender wrist, "Too late today, but no reason why we can't have it done on Monday."

Over his dead body were they having DNA tests done on Monday—or any other day.

There was no way that Nick was going to allow Candace to expose the real lie he'd been living. He was not Jennie's father; his wife had taken a lover.

Nick was not about to let this woman—a woman who turned his body in knots—make him the laughingstock of the city.

At the same moment as he said, "That won't be necessary," Alison—who'd come back into the room without his noticing—chimed in, "A DNA test is the perfect solution. It will answer all our questions, won't it, Nick?"

The impulse to throttle his sister, which Nick hadn't felt since adolescence, rose. "I can handle this, Alison."

She threw her hands into the air. "Of course you can. And you expect me to butt out, right?"

Nick gave her a sharp frown. He didn't have time for one of his sister's diatribes about what she considered his fear of intimacy. "I said not now, Alison."

"Don't get impatient with me." She picked her bag up and stalked toward the archway leading to the lobby. "I'm off. If you want my opinion—which you clearly don't—I think you should have that DNA test done. It's the only way you're going to know whether Candace is telling the truth or not."

Nick spared a glare for the woman who'd caused all the trouble. To his great annoyance, Jennie had snuggled up against Candace and was resting her cheek against the black T-shirt she wore. The pair looked like a modern take on Madonna and Child. Nick gnashed his teeth. "Of course Candace isn't telling the truth—and I've got Jennie's birth certificate listing me and Jilly as her parents to prove it." But Alison had already left.

"DNA doesn't lie." Candace spoke into the silence that simmered after his sister's departure. "A birth certificate can be tampered with."

Annoyance rose within Nick. "Are you accusing me of tampering with the system?"

Candace muttered something about money talking, and Nick could feel his anger growing. She was boxing him into a corner, forcing him into a place where he was going to have to agree to the test to expose her as a fraud.

Yet watching her, her head bent over the baby's, caused his anger to dissipate. Only the raw throb of betrayal remained. He wanted her...hell, he'd been growing to like her. The combination had been so seductively powerful, so consuming, he'd been ready to open himself to her...more than he ever had to any other woman.

A sense of emptiness filled him. Why had she done it? Candace didn't appear unstable. In fact, she seemed heart-wrenchingly attached to Jennie. Nick abandoned his musing. What did it matter what her motivation was?

The test would prove her a liar. Conclusively. And then he would sever all ties with no looking back.

The house was still when the darkness of midnight was broken by the silver streak of light pouring through the crack of the opening door.

Nick moved restlessly.

She came to him, floating soundlessly across the carpet like a wraith in the night. He shifted, and miraculously she was beside him, naked, eager. Her mouth covered his. Hunger rose swift and sharp. *He needed this.* And she understood.

He took her mouth, plundered it. His fingers sank into her shoulders, holding her captive. She shifted against him with one of those little catlike moves he'd seen her do, and his body went crazy.

He forgot how long it had been…

He forgot that she was a fraud he was determined to expose. He forgot everything except that he had a woman in his bed, a woman he wanted with an unfamiliar desperation.

She twisted beneath him. A silent lover, no sighs or moans split the night. Her legs tangled with his. He grasped her thighs, pushed them apart and sank between them into the moist, waiting heat of her.

His spine arched, his body driving.

Gasping, Nick opened his eyes, blind to everything except the excruciating need that pumped through him as his seed spilled.

A band of bright light fell across the bed from the open door of the en suite. Nick tensed. He reached out a hand. The bed was empty. He groped further, his fingers encountering cool, smooth sheets. Not fabric rumpled by passion.

Where the hell had she gone?

He rolled over onto his stomach, burying his face in the silk fabric, his sleep-numbed brain trying to make sense of what the hell had happened. The sheet smelled of soap and lavender; no hint of her spicy, slightly exotic fragrance lingered. The only softness a plump abandoned feather pillow, damp and crumpled.

He swore viciously.

More asleep than awake, he swung his legs out and stumbled from the bed to the bathroom. In the shower cubicle, he turned the faucets on and let the force of the cold water crash over his overheated body.

He refused to yield to the desire that still raged through him. He told himself it had all been an illusion, nothing but a cruel trick played on him by his starved libido. No woman could ever be as good as a man's desperate fantasy.

Not even Candace...

Six

His arms folded behind his head, Nick leaned back in the leather chair behind the walnut desk in the study that was his only retreat in a house Jilly had created and furnished with help from an expensive design team. It was Tuesday evening, and Candace was still living in his home.

He hadn't figured out what her motivation was for lying about being Jennie's mother—nor had she given up on her insistence that she was.

The other thing that hadn't changed was that he still craved her with a hunger that made absolutely no sense. Nick couldn't believe he was fantasizing about a woman whom he should be kicking out.

The past few days had been hell.

Every now and then a flash of that crazy dream would creep insidiously into his brain before he could banish it. *Traitor.*

First thing yesterday morning Nick had ordered Busby to drive Jennie and Candace to his doctor, where the swabs for DNA tests had been taken.

Candace had shown no surprise when he'd bowed out, inventing a meeting to attend. Yet while being thankful that she wasn't suspicious of his reasons for absenting himself, Nick couldn't help feeling that he'd given Candace more ammunition for her belief that he was an unfit father for Jennie.

But he'd been eager to avoid questions about why he wouldn't give a sample. A call to his doctor had satisfied Nick that it wasn't necessary. Buccal samples taken from Candace and Jennie by mouth swabs would be sufficient to establish with certainty that Candace wasn't, in fact, Jennie's mother. Even though his doctor had suggested that the result would be more conclusive had his DNA been available to be matched, Nick had chosen to ignore that advice.

Now, with the samples taken and the results from the diagnostic laboratory fast-tracked and due any minute, Nick had been tensing every time his cell phone beeped.

He couldn't make up his mind what he wanted more: for Candace's claim to be true, proving she hadn't lied, or for it to be false so that he could be rid of her, once and for all.

Without a shadow of a doubt, Nick knew which would be the easier solution to deal with. Getting Candace out of Jennie's life—out of his own—and returning to the even keel of his existence was what they both needed.

So why did that leave him feeling so…flat?

Nick stared sightlessly at the two antique botanical watercolors that flanked the study door. They'd belonged to Henry. Instead of selling them, the old man had insisted on gifting them to Nick. Usually the pictures gave him an immense sense of satisfaction and accomplishment.

But today all he could think of was Candace. Of how she'd disrupted his life and turned his world upside down. He wasn't going to allow her to unravel Jennie's world, too.

When he'd called his assistant yesterday morning to tell her he wouldn't be in for the day, there'd been utter silence on the other side of the line before Pauline had asked if he was ill. Only then did Nick realize that in all the years Pauline had worked for him he'd never taken a day off—the only time he didn't go in to work was when he was out of the country on business trips. Hell, he hadn't even taken time off for a honeymoon after he'd married Jilly. Much to his new bride's tearful dismay.

But there'd been no need for a honeymoon and all the trappings of romance. He'd been nothing more than his bride's bought husband—and he hadn't intended to prop up the pretense with a fake honeymoon.

Jilly's expectations had been suffocating. She'd wanted a pet. A husband who came when she crooked her finger, who mated on demand—one she could trot out and show off to her friends. Her attempts to domesticate him had had the effect of driving him away to seek his freedom in the corporate corridors she avoided and the boxing gym she despised.

Despite his romantic surname, Jilly had made a horrible mistake. He'd never been cut out to be the trophy husband she'd mistakenly believed she could groom him to be.

The phone rang.

Nick rocked forward in the chair and picked up the handset.

Within seconds his hands were clenched around the instrument in a stranglehold. "Almost a hundred percent likelihood that she is Jennie's biological mother!" he exclaimed. "How is that possible?"

The laboratory didn't have an explanation—other than the unwelcome suggestion that Candace was, in fact, Jennie's mother.

Nick wanted—needed—answers. And there was only one person alive who was able to provide them.

Grim-faced, he ended the call, rose from his desk and strode toward the door.

* * *

Candace was in the bath, when the door to the en suite flew open to reveal the tall, male frame of Nick Valentine. One look into his blazing eyes and her objections to his uninvited presence died.

Nick was in a towering rage.

His eyes were a scorching shade of black, his mouth pinched into a tight line. His fury made him look twice his normal size—which was already substantial.

Candace swallowed. Then moistened her lips nervously as his angry gaze skimmed the bits of her wet, naked body that weren't hidden by the mounds of bubbles from the baby wash she'd snitched from the nursery. One hasty downward glance, following in the wake of the burning trail his eyes had left, revealed rosy tips peaked to hard nubs. Even as she instinctively covered her breasts with her hands, she knew her last-ditch attempt at modesty was futile.

She found her voice. "Get out!"

The flags of livid, burning color high on his cheekbones told her he wasn't immune to her nakedness. Strangely enough that knowledge gave her the confidence she needed to sit upright in the bath.

If he wanted to ogle, let him damn well look.

Candace was pretty sure her body would hold no surprises that he hadn't seen before. And she would have another reason to detest him when he feasted his eyes on her.

But instead of leering, Nick retreated to the doorjamb. "Get dressed," he muttered, jerking his eyes back up to hers, his color high. "I want to talk to you."

"It will have to wait until I've finished my soak."

Two long strides across the expanse of polished black-slate tiles and he was looming over her. "This can't wait."

The bathroom that had seemed so decadently glamorous only minutes earlier was now suffocatingly intimate.

"I want you out of here." Candace hoped she didn't sound

as shaky as she felt. "You're my employer and I'm entitled to some privacy."

When Nick bent forward, Candace tensed, snapping, "Do you want me to file a suit for sexual harassment?"

Then her breath rushed out her lungs as he scooped her out of the bath. Shocked by his action, she stared up at him. He was plastered against her, the water from her body streaming down his shirt. Their gazes clashed. Beneath his anger she detected a maelstrom of other pent-up emotions—heat and turbulence and a host of indefinable nuances that were impossible to read.

Candace decided the wisest course of action right now might be silence. Nick looked fit to explode.

He stepped back, grabbed a towel and wrapped it around her, pushing the edges into her nerveless hands.

"No harassment, see?" he snarled.

His actions had paralyzed Candace. "You can't just walk in here and—"

"This is my house. I can do exactly as I please. You have ten minutes—that should give you time to dry yourself off and change." Over his shoulder he tossed, "Don't make me come and fetch you. I'll be waiting for you in my study."

Nick halted outside Candace's closed bedroom door, his head in turmoil.

His ordered existence had been turned inside out. All that he'd thought was true…wasn't. And the only person who could give him the answers he sought was naked, only one flimsy wall separating them.

God.

Nick broke into a sweat all over again as the unwanted memory of the pearlescent gleam of Candace's wet, naked flesh flashed through his mind. He'd been tempted to strip off his clothing and get naked with her. Only her timely reminder that he was her employer had stopped him.

It had been hard enough to keep his imagination reined in before; now that he'd actually seen what previously he'd only fantasized about, his body was going into overdrive.

Yet everything had been complicated by the incomprehensible discovery he'd made. Candace wasn't his daughter's nanny…nurse, he amended. Candace was Jennie's mother.

Nick didn't understand it. The situation was too surreal to absorb. How had Jilly come to have Jennie? And what had happened to the baby his wife had been carrying? The baby who had been created at the Namkhet Island clinic.

He'd watched Jilly's body changing. Every time he returned from an overseas trip sourcing products, or returned from a visit to one of the cross-country garden centers, her pregnancy had advanced. The baby had been born while he was overseas.

Had there been a switch? So where was Jilly's baby? Or had the baby died? Was there something wrong with it? Where was it? And then when had Jilly arranged for Candace to be impregnated? Or had Candace already been pregnant and sold her child?

That was the scenario he liked least of all.

But Nick was struggling to make sense of it all. His feet had carried him outside the nursery. Softly he pushed the door open and went in.

Jennie was lying in her crib, in some kind of white jumpsuit with pink ears on the hood.

Nick found himself grinning down at her, and for the first time since the unwelcome call from his doctor, the coiled tension that had him strung tighter than a bow started to unwind.

"Ears…?" He shook his head. "Who on earth designed ears for the top of a baby's head? You're not a rabbit!"

Jennie flapped her arms, and Nick could've sworn her eyes gleamed with humor. He bent close to her and whispered, "I never understood why Jilly was so desperate for a baby—" Nick broke off and gulped "—until I met you."

It was a life-changing admission.

Only now, almost too late, was he coming to realize how much Jennie meant to him. He'd resented her. She'd underlined the emptiness in his life: the wrong wife, the wrong life. It had taken the realization that he might lose the baby to realize that he wanted another chance.

Fine time for that to happen.

He gazed down at the baby. The fluffy ears atop her round head made her look incredibly cute. Her mouth moved and she blew a raspberry, then her face broke into a smile.

A wave of emotion swamped Nick. Only one thing was certain. Jennie wasn't his. He'd known it when Jilly had stopped all the talk about *their* baby. Even though he'd never called her on it, and maintained the fiction that the IVF had been successful—with his sperm. So how had he allowed this to happen? How could this little imp have crawled into the empty space in his heart?

Naturally, Candace wanted Jennie back. What mother wouldn't?

A tight chill settled over him.

Well, he wasn't going to make it easy.

For whatever reason, Candace had chosen to give Jennie up. She might regret her decision, but she'd made it, she'd signed a surrogacy agreement and he could find the document and make sure she stuck with whatever terms it entailed. He was sure Jilly would've adopted Jennie…he'd need to check whether he could've been included in the adoption without his knowledge.

But Jennie had been living with him for the past six months and Candace hadn't shown any interest in the baby during that time. No court would ignore that.

A premonition of the battle to come flashed before his eyes. He'd find out all the facts, get top legal advice. As far as he was concerned, he had as much right to the baby as Candace. More, in his mind. Then there was the fact that he'd been misled…made to believe the baby was his wife's child. Surely that would carry weight, too?

Because he wasn't about to give Jennie up. Not without a fight.

Candace would have to live with the choice she had made.

Nick's study was a surprise.

Candace hadn't been inside Nick's private domain before, and it was a total departure from the highly polished and reflective black-white-and-acid-yellow decor of the rest of the house.

This space was welcoming…

Homey.

Under normal circumstances the deep-brown leather sofas would've invited her to sink down, and the rows of books on the wooden shelves would've tempted her to browse between the covers. But now the sight of Nick standing with his back to her—arms akimbo, looking out the window into the darkness beyond—caused her stomach to knot. She was all too conscious of the huge divide between them. She was a nurse, a working woman, accustomed to long shifts; he was a millionaire, a man with a fortune at his command.

But what did it matter that he wore three-hundred-dollar jeans while hers had cost thirty dollars at Kmart? Or that his loafers were made of the finest Italian leather, whereas her slippers had come out of the supermarket bargain box? What did wealth matter when it came to love?

He swung around. His face was sterner than she'd ever seen it. "I have some questions I want answered." He gestured to the nearest sofa. "Sit down."

Candace perched on the edge and her strung-out nerves almost gave out. She pulled herself together. "I assume you wanted to see me because you have the test results and you've discovered that I was telling you the truth—and now you're ready to apologize to me."

Nick made a choking sound. *"Apologize?"*

"You've been treating me like I was some lowlife liar instead of the Good Samaritan who agreed to help you and your wife."

"Hang on a mo—"

"Jilly told me you were both undyingly grateful for a chance to have a baby." Candace flinched as the word *undyingly* hovered between them.

Before she could say *sorry* for her tactless word choice, he'd settled himself on the other end of the sofa she was on, and Candace reminded herself that Nick Valentine's own behavior in this mess was certainly less than laudable.

"Jilly was—"

"—delightful." Candace glared sideways at him. "You should've taken a leaf out your wife's book. In all the months I was pregnant you never once came to visit."

His face went blank. "Why the hell should I have come to visit you?"

"To say thank you for the enormous gift I gave you both." Her throat thickened and she felt like she was about to cry. Damned if she would. "But no, your work was too damn important."

"Wait, I didn't know—"

"How long were you married?" She wasn't interested in what he thought, didn't want to hear his justifications. When he didn't answer she repeated, "How long?"

"Seven years." Nick muttered, clearly reluctant to admit it.

"Did you love your wife?"

"That's none of your business!"

Candace held his gaze bravely. "Of course it's my business. I gave you both my baby on the assumption that Jennie was going to a loving family." Her naïveté made her want to cry. She should've taken more care…

Rather than accept Jilly's logical explanation that Nick wanted to pretend the baby was his wife's, Candace should have insisted on meeting him. Instead, she'd been satisfied by a pile of newspaper and magazine cuttings—all of which had deified him as an eco-friendly tycoon. She'd let her worries be soothed.

Dumb.

Nick rose restlessly to his feet. "I did receive a call confirming that you're Jennie's birth mother. But you must be aware by now that I didn't even know about your decision to give your baby up—you made that all by yourself."

Pain stabbed at her. Then anger flared and she gave a snort of disgust. "You're going to heap all the blame on me?"

"Don't expect me to believe you did it out of the kindness of your heart. What was in it for you?" he badgered.

Candace bent her head and studied the rich colors of the Persian rug. Why was nothing ever simple? "In terms of New Zealand law, all I was entitled to recover were the expenses I incurred."

Nick waved a dismissive hand. "I'm aware of that, but there are any number of ways around the legalities."

At the cynical note in his voice Candace glanced sharply up at him. How could he suspect? She couldn't read his expression, but his lips were curled into an unpleasant sneer.

"So what did my wife offer you for the gift of Jennie?" There was an icy inflection on the word *gift*. "What price did you put on your baby?"

It hadn't been like that. "Nothing!"

Although that wasn't strictly true. But the financial assistance had come later—once she and Jilly had become friends. That had made the arrangement acceptable, one of friendship.

It had been an unlikely friendship, but during her pregnancy

Candace had grown to feel an incredible sympathy for Nick Valentine's wife. Jilly had appeared to have everything most women dreamed of. A husband she adored. Plenty of friends. Yet she had seemed lonely, her life empty. The baby she'd wanted more than anything in the world had been an impossible dream…until Candace had come to her rescue.

"You're sure?"

"Why do you think your wife would've had to pay me for a baby?" Candace countered desperately. "Are you so devoid of human kindness that you can't believe it's possible for anyone to be selfless?"

A strange expression crossed his face.

He came closer. Candace's pulse picked up speed as he leaned forward and placed his hands on the sofa back, trapping her inside the curve of his arms. "Are you telling me you're the real deal? A true angel?"

Her breath quickened. She couldn't look away. "I'm no angel. I'm all too human."

"Are you?" His gaze dropped to her mouth.

Candace's heart thundered in her chest. She felt dazed, disoriented. "I'm just like a million other women out there," she managed breathlessly.

"I don't think so." His head came closer still. "I must've met almost a million women in my life and you're unlike anyone I've ever met."

It hurt to breathe. "A million women?" she asked skeptically.

The side of his mouth kicked up. "Maybe that's an exaggeration."

"What's so different about me?"

One hand dropped away from the sofa back to cup her cheek, his gaze intense. "I thought it was only Jennie who had skin as velvety as a Queen Anne peach."

He hadn't answered her. She didn't press him. Maybe it was for the best not to know.

"Genetics." Candace tried to laugh his intensity off. "My mother's skin is soft, too."

The back of his hand brushed down the side of her throat to the top button of the fine cotton-knit cardigan she'd donned with jeans after she'd hurriedly gotten out the bath, fearful he might make good on his threat to return.

His index finger rested on the pearly button, above the hollow between her breasts, and her breath quickened.

The button popped loose.

Candace's heart stopped.

When Nick bent forward her lips parted. There was a moment before his mouth touched hers, a time when she could've told him to stop, that she didn't want this awful complication. Candace didn't utter a sound.

Instead, her eyelids fluttered down.

His lips were unexpectedly cool as he kissed her. Heat ignited, wild and raging. The hand on her jaw pressed her closer and the angle changed. Nick let out a hiss and his touch gentled, the kiss becoming increasingly intimate. Candace burrowed against him with small, hungry movements of a cat.

The pressure of the kiss deepened for a sharp instant, then eased. Candace opened her eyes.

Nick gazed down at the woman enfolded in his arms, shaken by the emotions that stormed through him.

Beneath his fingertips the cotton of her sweater was fine and delicate. He undid the next pearl button, heard her breath catch, and glanced down. The scalloped edge with its border of embroidered pink roses was almost too feminine against his square-tipped fingers. Her still-damp hair had been pulled back from her face with a hair tie, and from this angle he could see that she wasn't wearing a smudge of makeup.

Yet she was breathtakingly beautiful—like the angel he'd imagined her to be the first time he'd seen her.

Her eyelashes fell again, shielding the misty eyes from his. The dark lashes lay against the fine-grained skin, a faint flush giving her face a warm glow that caused his breathing to falter. Swallowing, Nick undid a third button. She didn't object. The sweater fell open, revealing the curves of her breasts.

His arousal was immediate.

Pushing the cotton knit off her shoulders, he watched her face. Her eyes remained shut. When he lowered his gaze to the skin he'd bared, he saw the prickles of arousal that had broken over her rose-flushed skin.

He suppressed a moan.

Nick dropped to his knees in front of the sofa and lowered his head to carefully tongue the dainty pink tip of the breast he'd exposed.

For a split second, time froze. There wasn't a sound in the room. After a pulse beat in which Nick thought his heart might explode, Candace let out a gasp.

He licked again. Lightly. Insistently. Her head whipped back, and her hands dug into the leather of the sofa on either side of her thighs. Immediately he closed his lips over the tight nub and felt the shock of reaction that went through her. Pulling away, he pursed his lips and blew. The nipple hardened. She made a mewing sound and her hands tangled in his hair, pulling him back to her.

Nick's head rushed down, his mouth wide, and he sucked her in.

This time her spine arched. Her breathing grew rapid, becoming harsh pants in the quiet of the study. Nick's fingers were clumsy with haste as he opened the remaining buttons. Rising up, he parted the edges of the sweater. His chest seized tight as he gazed at the sleek skin, the full curves of her bare breasts.

"Ah…"

He wasn't sure who'd broken the silence—him or her. His hands came up. Slowly, reverently, he framed the full ripeness of her breasts, the peaks popping hard. He bent his head toward the breast he hadn't yet touched and laved it with long sweeps of his tongue.

She convulsed against his mouth, her body superbly responsive, even though her eyes were still screwed shut.

His breathing was harsh and erratic, loud in the cozy intimacy of the study. Releasing her breasts, Nick sat back on his heels and tore his shirt open.

Then, taking both her hands in his, he pressed them against his naked chest under his rumpled shirt.

"Touch me," he commanded as her eyes shot open. "Feel my heart pounding."

As she stroked his chest, Nick was engulfed in the endless, misty depths. He felt himself sinking…drowning.

"Candace."

She blinked. But instead of the spell breaking, she came to life. Her fingers feathered down beneath his shirt…across his stomach…until lightning forked through him. Nick swallowed, his mouth parched dry.

"I can't think," he muttered hoarsely. "All I can do is… feel."

Sensation, wave on wave, broke over him as her fingertips swept lightly across his skin. His hands closed on her hips, the denim of her well-washed cotton jeans soft under his thumbs. Rising high on his knees in front of her, he yanked her off the sofa into his arms and hauled her up against him. Hard. He hugged her to him and claimed her mouth, and kissed her deeply.

When he'd finished, he loosened his arms a little until his hands rested on her shoulders. He sat back on his heels as they both gulped in air, their breathing audible in the overheated room.

"Wow." She sounded awed.

Nick suddenly felt about thirty feet tall. He gave a husky half laugh and let his fingers caress the rounds of her shoulders where her sweater had fallen away to expose tempting creamy skin.

"Again?"

"I'm not sure I'll survive if you keep kissing me like that," she said honestly. "My knees are weak."

"So what was it like with…him?"

The eyes that met him were wide and suddenly very, very wary. "Who?"

"Jennie's father."

She tore out of his arms with a force that caught him off guard. "Stop this, Nick. It's not funny!"

Her reaction startled him. "Hey…"

Perhaps his morbid curiosity had freaked her out. But he'd wanted to know, dammit. A surge of unfamiliar possessiveness swept through him.

Hell, he couldn't stop thinking about her—and he couldn't remember when last he'd had the hots like this over a woman.

He'd certainly never felt this way about Jilly in the seven years' famine that had been their marriage.

Candace was on her feet, rebuttoning the knit top, her color high, her gaze averted.

"Tell me about him." Nick stood. "I need to know."

She raised her head. Her mouth was set, her eyes flashed. "C'mon, Mr. Valentine. Stop playing games. You must know you're Jennie's father."

Seven

Nick looked pole-axed.

"I need a Scotch," he said, and crossed over to the liquor cabinet to pour two fingers of amber liquid into a heavy crystal glass. "Can I get you one, too?"

Candace shook her head and suppressed the instinctive urge to tell him that sugar water would be better for shock. Somehow she didn't think Nick would appreciate it.

His hand closed around her wrist and he gently drew her down onto the couch beside him. "Now run that past me again."

She simply wasn't ready to confront the fact that she and this man who caused such an emotional response in her had made a child together.

A perfect, wonderful little girl.

Jennie...

A child Candace had no intention of leaving in his care, a child she wanted back...whatever it took.

But she was starting to suspect that Nick might not

surrender Jennie so easily. And Candace was delaying the inevitable moment of confrontation, thinking about the best way to address it.

"Jennie is your child." Candace's stomach churned. "Your sperm was used for the IVF. And the DNA tests after her birth confirmed that you are her father."

At the time she'd signed the surrogacy agreement, she'd been affronted by the clause requesting a DNA test before the baby was delivered to the Valentines. But she'd understood that the couple had wanted to be assured that the baby was Nick's—not the child of some stranger she'd slept with.

"Frankly, I'm stunned that you believe Jennie is my child," he finally admitted, not looking at her, "and more than a little skeptical."

He hadn't known. Her suspicion that he and Jilly had worked together to pull off the pretense of a lifetime had been off the mark. She'd been so sure he'd known that Jennie wasn't Jilly's baby, that for reasons of their own he and Jilly had wanted to keep that secret.

Now it appeared Nick really had believed Jennie was his wife's child all along.

That stunned her.

Her attention shifted back to him as he ran his hands through his hair in a distracted manner. "I told you Jilly was pregnant—and my sister confirmed it."

"But…" Candace's voice trailed away.

He raised an eyebrow. "But?"

"Jilly couldn't have children," she said slowly.

"She told you that?"

Candace nodded, miserably conscious that every word was knocking the nails further into the coffin of her hopes. Oh, heavens, what had she done? Had she ruined her chances of securing custody of Jennie? "She said that the IVF wasn't working—that her doctor had established that she'd been one of those unlucky women who undergo menopause very early."

Nick blew out a pent-up breath. "Well, clearly my wife was lying to someone. She told me that the IVF had been successful. That she was pregnant." There was a strange note in his voice. "I watched her pregnancy progress over nine months...even though I was away a lot of that time. Hell, she spent a fortune on designer maternity wear."

"And, of course, you had no reason not to believe her."

Nick shook his head. "I had my doubts, but not for the reason you think. You see, I thought Jilly had a lover." His mouth kinked. "Someone who'd obviously been more successful at impregnating her than I had been."

Nick hadn't even believed Jennie was his child?

Candace suppressed the urge to howl with frustration at the injustice of it all. If she'd said nothing about him being Jennie's father, maybe he would've been only too glad to relinquish custody of the baby to her.

It was enough to make Candace feel seriously sick with regret.

Yet it wouldn't have been right. How could she have taken Jennie under false pretenses? Nick had been lied to enough already...

She drew a deep breath and said slowly, "That must've been hard to accept."

"Somewhat."

Normally the dry retort would've amused her, but Candace couldn't bring herself to smile. Not now. Maybe not ever... if she'd destroyed her chance of getting Jennie back. Yet she couldn't stop the flood of sympathy for Nick.

"So Jilly faked her pregnancy."

"Faked her pregnancy?"

This was awkward. "Only you know for sure whether it was possible. I have heard of women who hate their bodies when they're pregnant—don't want anyone to see them naked, move into a separate room. If Jilly had been like that…" Candace could feel herself coloring. She didn't want to be privy to this man's personal life with his dead wife. The thought of him and Jilly together caused her stomach to sink.

"It's possible," he said tightly.

"Jilly flew with me to the clinic where the insemination was done."

"You went to Namkhet Island?"

Candace nodded.

"Jilly said she was planning to be inseminated there. I consented to my sperm being used—and acted out the whole fiction. I even received bills," he said. "I never knew that she'd traded places with you nor that she never intended to undergo any of the procedures there herself. In fact, I came to believe she'd taken her lover with her and replaced my sperm with his."

"I can vouch that there was no lover."

"So the bills I received for the IVF procedures were your bills, not Jilly's as I assumed?"

Candace's discomfort increased. "Yes—that was part of the arrangement."

"Of course." Nick's mouth twisted. "There was also a bill for double accommodation and shared meals at the most glamorous resort on the island. Jilly told me she needed time alone to steel herself against the very real possibility that the IVF might again not work. Once the hotel bill was forwarded to me for payment, I knew instantly that she'd lied to me."

Candace felt sick. Clearly Nick had assumed Jilly had stayed there with her lover. "That was for me—I told Jilly it wasn't necessary." She hadn't needed a luxury holiday to convince her that she was doing the right thing. She'd done it for Jilly and her husband who had no other way of getting the child they craved. "Jilly said it was important to her that she get to know me. It felt a little weird, but I told myself she wanted to make sure the surrogate she'd picked wasn't a lunatic before she went through with the final insemination. I might've done the same thing in her place."

Nick laughed without humor. "Receiving the bill was a relief. The worst of it all was I didn't care that Jilly had taken a lover. I even hoped it might finally pave the way for a divorce."

Poor Jilly.

What he'd told Candace gave her some insight into the relationship—or lack of relationship—between Jilly and Nick. It appeared they'd drifted apart...so separate they might as well have lived in different houses, on different continents. No wonder Jilly had been able to fake a pregnancy while arranging with a surrogate to create a baby her husband had known nothing about.

"That's why you didn't go to the island with her," Candace said. "Because she convinced you she wanted time alone. And once you discovered she'd lied, it was easy to convince yourself that she had no intention of having your baby."

He nodded.

Jilly had told her Nick had been too busy. She'd accepted it at the time, but now Candace found that she desperately wanted to hear Nick's own version of how events had unfolded.

"But I never confronted her with it. We'd been through IVF before—several times. Unsuccessfully. Jilly told me I didn't have to be there. That the frozen embryos and sperm would be forwarded by the specialist we'd been dealing with here in Auckland."

He met her eyes. "I questioned how reputable the institution was—hell, I even did some checking. Everything seemed fine. There'd been some breakthroughs achieved, and I could understand why Jilly wanted to give it a try—why she thought it might be her last chance." Nick rubbed the bridge of his nose. "To be honest, my first reaction was relief that she didn't appear to want me along. Jilly could be very..." he paused "...demanding."

"She only wanted what any wife would expect—your time and your love."

Dropping his hand, Nick slanted her a mocking stare. "Not quite. She wanted a baby—a totally different thing. Clearly she had already put in place an elaborate plan to switch the recipient of..."

"Your sperm," Candace added helpfully.

"Exactly."

"It's hard to believe you didn't know." Candace's head was whirling as she tried to process everything Nick had told her. "I signed contracts..." Her voice trailed away. "You must've signed them, too."

His face said it all. "If there is a signature there, I'm sure an expert would pronounce it a forgery."

"Why did she go to such lengths?" It puzzled Candace. "Did she hope you'd spend more time with her if there was a baby in the house?"

"You know nothing about what my wife expected. And she's dead now, so it's all in the past. But, believe me, our marriage should never have taken place." Nick changed the subject. "But now I have to start accepting that Jennie came from your womb. Did the egg belong to you—" Nick paused "—or was there another donor I don't know about involved?"

Candace had to feel pity as she watched him grappling with the enormity of his discovery. "The egg was mine—and I carried Jennie in my womb. That's why I am her biological mother."

"Biological mother?" Nick swore. "Your egg was fertilized by—" He broke off.

"Your sperm." Candace added the words as clinically at she could. She was a nurse. She worked with babies all the time, knew where they came from. Nothing about this was foreign to her. So why did she feel as if she stood on the edge of a whole new dimension?

This time Nick said politely but with far more force, *"Hell."* He shook his head again as if to clear it. "I still can't believe Jilly *planned* this." He paused, his face hardening. "I should be thankful, I suppose, that she bothered to use my sperm."

Beneath his anger Candace could sense his hurt and confusion. She touched his arm. "Nick, I really don't think there was a lover. Jilly told me you were soul mates. She wanted your baby. Desperately. That's why I had to undergo DNA confirmation after Jennie's birth—she wanted to be sure the baby was yours."

An indecipherable emotion flickered across Nick's face—guilt perhaps?—and then it was gone. "Jilly certainly didn't ask my permission to take a sample for DNA for matching—assuming she took one."

"Oh, she had a sample, the test confirmed you were my baby's father. It could've been your toothbrush…a hair from your brush…as long as it had your DNA on it."

"Anything Jilly wanted Jilly got—and the hell with what it cost."

There was a savage note in his voice that warned Candace this was about much more than Jilly taking tissue samples without his knowledge. Candace got the impression that Nick was a man who had been pushed to the brink of his endurance.

And that conviction only grew when he added grimly, "I'm still going to need proof before I accept that I'm Jennie's father."

The axis of Nick's world had tilted.

He was grateful for the string of meetings that kept him occupied the following morning. Yet his mind kept buzzing with questions to which he had no answers: Why hadn't Jilly told him about her infertility? How could Jilly have arranged a surrogate and fooled him so easily? And, more importantly, what was he going to do about Candace?

There was one final question that was the easiest to resolve…was Jennie his daughter? Deep in his heart he knew it didn't matter, because either way she was his. The blood tie no longer mattered.

But there was something very seductive about the idea that part of him and part of Candace had merged to produce the little girl who was fast becoming the most important person in his life.

At midday, a break in his schedule gave Nick the opportunity to visit the doctor. Within twenty-four hours he'd know for sure whether Jennie was his child or not. Once a swab had been taken and bagged, he headed the Ferrari to Valentine's Garden Center and walked down to the lake. The grassy edge was crowded with preening ducks—the ducks that had so intrigued his Jennie—while the trio of trouble-causing geese stood in the lee of a nearby willow tree.

Damn birds didn't know what they'd unleashed. Nick knew he had his work cut out to convince Candace that he was perfectly capable of caring for Jennie. That he wasn't the unfit father she'd pegged him as.

The question of what he was going to do about Candace remained unresolved.

If Nick was honest with himself, he knew precisely what he wanted to do with Candace. He wanted to take her to his bed, slake this restless need that vibrated through him—the hunger and desire that sent his thoughts winging her way at the most inopportune moments. Thoughts that had him fantasizing about pulling her to him, covering her mouth with his and…

Hell, why not call it what it was? He wanted to cover her body with his, and he hardly cared whether he got her naked or not. All he cared about was possessing her—every inch of her creamy flesh. Touching her, tasting her, making her his.

Yet if he did that, he'd be left with the biggest headache of all. Nick wasn't certain that if he took Candace in every way he dreamed, he'd be left intact. Would the burning passion consume more of his sense of self than he was willing to risk?

Then there was the impact a hot, reckless affair with Candace would have on the baby. Would it jeopardize his relationship with Jennie?

Yet this was hardly the kind of question Nick could bring himself to ask his lawyer.

The call from Apple Orchards Rest Home came just after Candace had fed Jennie her lunch in the garden on a picnic blanket overlooking the ocean.

Candace's mother had suffered a fall, the kindly rest home director explained, once she'd allayed Candace's fears of the worst. Nothing was broken—the x-ray had confirmed that. But her mother had been badly shaken.

Candace promised to come at once.

Terminating the call, Candace considered Jennie, who'd crawled to the edge of the picnic rug, her hand reaching for a cluster of tiny white daisies that had sprung up in the immaculately kept lawn.

In principle, today was Candace's day off. She hadn't taken time off because she'd wanted to stay close to Jennie in the wake of the confrontation with Nick. To be truthful, despite the confirmation that she was Jennie's biological mother, an unreasoning fear lingered that if she left the property she might not be able to gain access again.

Candace knew she was overreacting.

Yet it was impossible to forget that bone-chilling moment outside the café when Nick had told her he was taking Jennie home and she could collect her paycheck from his office.

In her mind Candace had seen the tall gates of the Valentine mansion closing to her forever. She'd known it would be impossible to get back into Jennie's world once she'd been shut out...and that primal fear lingered. Enough for her to have decided against visiting her mother today. But now her mom had taken a fall.

The guilt was hard to shake.

Candace knew Mrs. Busby was more than capable of looking after the baby for a few hours while she checked on her mom. Yet she hesitated. Mrs. Busby had her own responsibilities. Wednesday was the day she planned the week's meals and did the shopping. Candace hated the thought of throwing Mrs. Busby's schedule off. Nor did she want to arouse the housekeeper's curiosity. To raise questions Candace didn't want to be forced to answer...

The alternative course was to leave Jennie with Alison. But that was quickly ruled out when she learned that Alison had gone with her husband to an urgent meeting. Turning her attention back to the baby, now with a fistful of daisies, Candace considered Jennie. A smear of apple puree on her chin had Candace reaching for a cloth. The baby laughed as Candace wiped it, and love for Jennie swept through her.

There was no other choice. She'd take Jennie with her to check on her mother, because she had no intention of asking her baby's father for help. Ever since yesterday, she'd been plagued by unwanted images, her body prickling with unwelcome awareness of the man who was starting to consume far too much of her thoughts. He was Jennie's father, for heaven's sake. He could never be her lover...

She could not allow herself to need Nick Valentine.

Eight

"Mrs. Timmings is here to see you."

Nick glanced up at his PA. Alison had been remarkably patient—he'd been expecting to hear from her long before this. His sister had always had an overwhelming interest in his life…and the bombshell he'd dropped about Candace announcing she was Jennie's mother would've been driving Alison crazy.

He knew he should've contacted her and told her the outcome of the DNA tests. Alison would've expected it of him.

With a mental sigh he said, "I'll be with her in a minute."

His sister appeared in the doorway behind Pauline. "Too late. I'm already here."

Nick mentally braced himself for the scolding to come. "How are you, Alison?"

She settled herself in one of the four chairs arranged around a table in a sunny spot in front of the glass wall looking out over the lake and parklands beyond.

Getting up from the black leather executive chair behind his desk, Nick crossed to the table where his sister sat and pulled out the chair beside her.

"Not good. Richard has received notice from the NorthPark Mall Group that our appliance stores have to move out of all their shopping centers."

Nick gave her a sharp look, his already overloaded brain whirling with this new setback. But at least Alison wasn't asking about Candace...or Jennie.

"Have you and Richard defaulted on a payment?" he asked.

Alison hesitated. "One…"

"You should've come to me, Allie. I would've helped you." *He should've offered.* But he'd never realized his sister and brother-in-law's chain of appliance stores was in quite so precarious a financial state.

"You know how proud Richard is—he wouldn't take help. But it wasn't that we couldn't afford to pay the rent." Alison looked utterly miserable. "Oh, Nick, it was all my fault. We changed banks because we managed to get a more favorable rate on our home loan, but part of the arrangement was that Richard had to transfer the business accounts there, too."

Nick nodded. "That's pretty standard."

"But I forgot to give the bank the authority to deduct the rent to NorthPark. I only found out when I checked the bank statements the day after the payment was supposed to go through that it had bounced." She gave a helpless shrug. "No one from the bank even called to let me know before they'd bounced the check. Our old bank would've called first."

"That's the price of change—it takes time to build a relationship with a bank." Nick thought about the irony of his observation. He had better relationships with his own bank than he'd ever had with his dead wife.

But Jilly wouldn't have been his wife if he hadn't been forced into marrying her.

Too late to dwell on that. Nick focused his thoughts back on his sister's predicament. "You spoke to the NorthPark Mall Group? Paid the late rent?"

"Of course." She nodded. "And I thought it was all sorted out. Then the letter came from their lawyers. I called and they told me we'd breached the contract so the group was exercising their right to terminate. Richard checked with our lawyers and they can do it."

"Seems odd that they'd be so eager to evict you," said Nick. "It's not easy to get new tenants for the kind of floor space you occupy. Especially in this economy. Is there something else you're not telling me?"

"No—we've been model tenants in all the shopping centers NorthPark owns."

"Hmm." Nick's mind was racing.

"Richard has started looking for new space in other malls, but it's going to be hard to match the deal we had and find premises that are one hundred percent suitable. It's scary—we might actually have to shut down some of the stores. Oh, Nick, I should've been more organized!"

There was nothing he could say to make Alison feel better. Rising to his feet, Nick went around the table and gave her a clumsy hug.

She hugged him back and sniffed. "You're being so nice—you're going to make me cry."

"I'm always nice."

"Not really—you're usually distant. No, don't withdraw and ruin it all," she said hastily as he straightened up. "I just want you to know I'm so grateful you didn't tell me it's all my fault."

"How would that help?"

She made a sound that was half laugh, half sob. "Oh, Nick, that sounds more like you." She looked up at him, a small smile curving her lips. "I'm glad you're my brother—you know that?"

He shrugged.

"How are things?"

Nick looked away. "Fine."

"You're not going to tell me about Candace…about her claim that Jennie is her daughter?" His sister was quivering with curiosity.

"Will you let me rest until I do?"

"Probably not. I've left you alone all week—I didn't want to be nosy." She paused. "Nick, did you have an affair with her?"

That offended him. "No! I suppose I'm going to have to get used to that kind of reaction. You're my sister, and if you thought that, then it won't be the last time it comes up."

"If you didn't have an affair with her, then she can't possibly be Jennie's mother."

"Wrong again." He smiled wryly. "Turns out Jilly faked her pregnancy and engaged a surrogate."

"A surrogate?" Alison's eyes popped. *"Candace?"*

Nick nodded.

"So Candace was telling the truth? She *is* Jennie's mother?"

"That's the way it looks." His tests hadn't come back yet, but Candace's voice had held a persuasive conviction when she'd told him that Jilly had made sure Jennie was his. But Nick wasn't ready to concede that until he had hard proof.

His sister placed her elbows on the table. "She must've planned to get into your home."

Nick considered his sister. As much as he wanted to agree, it was unlikely that Candace could've managed to orchestrate that. Nor did he believe that she was the conniving type.

Unlike his late wife.

"I don't think that would've been possible. Not unless she could've played a role in Jennie's ear infection—and I think you'll agree that's impossible."

"But she would've recognized Jennie's name when we came into the emergency room that night."

Nick nodded. "Granted."

"And she didn't hesitate to take advantage."

He didn't want to defend Candace, but he couldn't stop himself from saying, "Perhaps she was curious."

Alison considered him. "I imagine you're right. What woman wouldn't be? Her baby... A mother would want to know that she was okay. And I made it simple for her. The boys were giving me such a hard time that afternoon..."

She sucked in her cheeks, making her look even more harried. "She was so easy to talk to, so interested in the boys... and Jennie. I told her all about Margaret leaving us high and dry. That's when she said she wouldn't be averse to working as a nanny for a while because she didn't have a full-time job. I'm so sorry, Nick."

When he didn't respond, she dropped her head into her hands. "I don't seem to be able to stop screwing up at the moment, do I?"

"Don't worry about it." Awkwardly he patted her shoulder. Staring over his sister's head into the courtyard outside, he asked with studied casualness, "Did you mention that I was overseas?"

Her head came up. "I probably did."

That would've sealed Candace's conviction that Jennie needed her. But there was no point in telling his sister the problem she had unwittingly caused.

"So what have you decided to do?" Alison asked.

Trust her to get to the crux of his problem. "I don't know." Yet.

It wasn't like him to be indecisive. Vacillation went against his character. But he had Jennie to think about—what he wanted had to be best for Jennie, too.

"It could've been worse," Alison was saying.

"Worse?" What did his sister mean? As far as Nick was concerned, it had gotten as bad as it could.

"Jilly could've picked a real loser, like the kinds of friends she picked. Candace is cool—as my sons would say." Alison rose to her feet and gathered up her bag. "I might pop in on the way home to see how she's coping with all this. Thanks for listening to my woes, Nicky—I'm feeling a lot better already."

What his sister meant was that she was going to try to build a bridge with the woman who might prove to be necessary to Jennie. Nick knew he should be thinking like that, too.

But he was still struggling with the idea of Candace as Jennie's mother. All he could think of was Candace as a woman—the one he'd held in his arms, the one he'd kissed... the one he was dying to seduce.

A sexy angel he couldn't wait to see again.

Work be damned.

"You know what?" He forced a half smile. "I don't seem to be able to concentrate today. I might come with you—blow the cobwebs from my brain."

Nick ignored the shock on his sister's face. First Pauline, now Alison. He hadn't become that much of a workaholic, had he?

Her mother was already back from the hospital, relaxing in her room at Apple Orchards Rest Home when Candace and Jennie arrived. She looked pale and tired.

"How are you feeling, Mom?"

"I've had better days." Catherine Morrison's mouth twitched into a smile and Candace wanted to applaud her mother's bravery.

"I've brought someone to meet you," she said instead. She bent over the stroller and unclipped the straps. "This is Jennie."

Catherine turned her head on the lace-edged pillow that matched the handmade quilt Candace had bought as a housewarming gift after her mother had moved into Apple Orchards five months ago. The room was cozily furnished.

Candace had bought a compact love seat covered in pretty fabric where Catherine could sit in the sun by the window on days when she felt a little stronger. The dressing table where her mother's favorite perfumes and toiletries were stored and the bed's headboard were her mother's own. So were the collection of knickknacks and photos on the bookshelf in the corner. The homey touches had transformed the institutionalized space.

"Hello, Jennie," her mother said to the granddaughter she didn't know existed.

A lump thickened at the back of Candace's throat. "I'm looking after her."

"But what about your work at the hospital, darling? I thought you were going back to a full-time post once you had me settled."

"I'll go back to that when I'm ready. I needed a break."

For the last four months of her pregnancy, Candace hadn't seen her mother. She'd established a fiction that she'd decided to travel overseas—Jilly had even generously offered her the funds to make the story a reality. It hadn't taken the needy expression in Jilly's eyes to affirm what a sacrifice she was making with the offer. Candace had known Jilly would miss visiting her, seeing Jennie grow as Candace's pregnancy progressed.

Candace had declined. She hadn't felt comfortable accepting the gift. Instead, she'd dropped out of sight, renting a cottage on the rugged West Coast, an hour's drive from Auckland, where she'd lived quietly while her family and friends assumed she was on the other side of the world.

There was a certain irony in the fact that during the time Candace had been living that deception, Jilly had been practicing her own deception with a surreal fake pregnancy.

Perhaps that was why Jilly had visited the cottage so often—sometimes even spending the night in the cramped second bedroom that was little more than a closet. It would have been the only time Jilly could break out of her lie because it was only with Candace that she wasn't pregnant. The charade must've been exhausting, waiting for someone to catch any slip...

Yet now Candace knew that those visits to the cottage, the nights away, would only have added fuel to Nick's belief that his wife was having an illicit affair.

By the time Jennie had been born, Candace had been drained. The strain of the imminent parting from her baby had taken its toll. After nine months spent caring for her unborn baby, suddenly there was a dark, black hole of loss that threatened to swallow her.

Her mother had known instantly that something was wrong. She'd assumed—wrongly—that her daughter must've fallen in love with someone across the ocean.

Of course, Candace hadn't been able to confess the enormity of what she'd done. The only way to survive was not to think about Jennie. To get back to work. It hadn't taken her long to realize her days as a pediatric nurse were over.

She couldn't bear to work with babies and children. Every time she looked into a little girl's face, Candace wondered about her baby girl. What she was doing. And, most important, if she was loved.

The decision to switch to working in the emergency room—as far away from young babies as she could get—had been inevitable.

Then her mother had almost died.

Catherine had fallen off a ladder while packing winter blankets into storage and cracked her skull. It had been touch and go—and had taken a week for her to regain consciousness. The doctors had feared she would be permanently brain-damaged.

Looking at her mother now, Candace marveled over the amazing changes time had wrought.

Her mother wasn't out of the woods yet and she still

suffered memory lapses, but with every month that passed, Catherine grew stronger. The chances of the stroke that the doctors had initially feared were lessening.

"I'd like to go sit in the garden," her mother said suddenly. "And I'm sure Jennie would like that far better than being cooped up in an old woman's room."

"You're not old," Candace said automatically, though her mother had aged since the accident. Being outside would lift her spirits and the vitamin D would be good for her, too. "Are you sure you're up to it?"

"Oh, yes. The sunshine is beautiful."

Candace helped her mother into a wheelchair and planted Jennie on her lap. Then she pushed them both out into the sunlight.

"Let's go to the rose gardens," Catherine suggested.

Halting the wheelchair in her mother's favorite spot, Candace said, "Here, let me take Jennie from you. She must be heavy."

"She's fine." Catherine gave her a faint smile. "It's been a long time since I held a baby. She smells just as I remember you did...of that special fragrance babies have. Clean skin, well-laundered clothes and something else—" she bent her head and inhaled "—lavender?"

"And tea tree."

"Lavender will help her sleep." Her mother looked startled. "I'd forgotten that."

"It has good antiseptic properties, too." Candace didn't want to look too elated at the tiny breakthrough in her mother's ability to recall information.

"But the lavender doesn't always work." Reaching out a hand, Candace touched the baby's head tenderly.

"She doesn't sleep?"

"Most of the time she's an angel." That instantly reminded her of Nick. He'd called *her* an angel...

"There's a rocker in her room that I sit in when I give Jennie her nighttime bottle. That sends her to sleep most nights."

"But what about her parents?"

Candace looked up to find her mother watching her, a frown wrinkling her forehead.

"Where are her parents?" Catherine asked again.

Drawing a deep breath, Candace said, "Her mother is dead."

"Oh, poor little tyke. What about her father?"

"He's a businessman—he owns a string of garden centers that keep him busy."

"That's a shame." Her mother's brow wrinkled. "I used to visit Valentine's Garden Centers. I loved buying plants—particularly my roses."

Candace stared at her mother. "I work for Nick Valentine," she said slowly, the air that had been so summery suddenly chilling her. She shook the eerie sensation off.

Her mother wouldn't—couldn't—know that Nick and Candace were Jennie's parents. It wasn't possible. Catherine only remembered the centers because she'd been an avid gardener before the accident.

"In fact, we recently took Jennie to one of the centers—she loved the ducks."

"There must've been swans, too."

"Oh, there were." Was her mother starting to remember? Months ago the doctors had said that her mother might never remember things from the past, so each recollection was a moment to treasure and be grateful for. "There were geese, too—one pecked Jennie." That memory was one Candace would sooner forget.

But there would be other memories to replace that. Like the sight of Jennie in her grandmother's lap. This was a moment Candace would treasure forever.

* * *

By the time Candace pulled the station wagon up in front of the Valentine mansion, the late-afternoon rays of sun had taken on a golden hue. The light warmed the stark lines of the residence, softening the hard, sculpted angles of the design.

She—and Jennie—were exhausted. But in Candace's case it was the exhaustion of deep satisfaction, the feeling of a mission accomplished.

The glow didn't dissipate when the front door opened and Nick appeared.

"So you've decided to come back," he said from the bottom of the stairs as she clambered out of the car.

A quiver of apprehension fluttered in her stomach. Nick Valentine always looked crisply immaculate, but the man who faced her appeared nowhere near as well-put-together as usual. He was wearing suit pants, his jacket had been discarded and the white striped business shirt hung out, giving him an unusually rumpled look. She noticed that the top two buttons were unbuttoned, revealing a triangle of golden skin at his throat. Candace jerked her gaze upward, and clashed with a stormy pair of navy-blue eyes.

"Where have you been?"

She couldn't have found her voice even if she'd tried.

"I've been calling you for hours," he bit out.

Oh, no! Candace scrabbled in the side pocket of her tote and extricated her phone. Switching it on, she was met by a chorus of beeps signifying missed messages.

"My phone was off." Remorse filled her. "I'm sorry, Nick. I didn't realize."

A vague memory of switching the phone off before entering her mom's room surfaced. She'd been so preoccupied she'd forgotten to turn it back on.

She could hardly blame Nick for being irate.

Though normally he would never have noticed her absence. He never left the office early—that was one of the golden rules of Nick Valentine's busy life. Everyone agreed on that. Jilly, Mrs. Busby, his chauffeur. Their schedules had all revolved around his very set hours.

Yet today that had changed…

"Was it something urgent you were calling about? Is everything okay?"

The tumble of questions was met with a short terse nod. Candace took in the way his hair stood up, as though he'd been running his fingers through the almost black strands.

"If everything's okay, then why are you home?"

As the words left her mouth, it occurred to her that those were not the words of an employee. She sounded like a wife.

Flushing uncomfortably, she muttered, "Sorry, that's none of my business."

"It is your business all right. You're the reason I came home. I canceled a meeting with a new supplier, because my sister wanted to see you."

"She wanted to see me?" Candace frowned.

Why?

"Alison's been concerned about you."

"Oh." So much had happened it seemed like a century since that awful confrontation that his sister had witnessed. "I'm sorry we were out." Candace started up the stairs, Jennie firmly clasped in her arms.

Nick's hand came down on her shoulder, halting her. "Where were you?"

With her standing two steps above him their eyes were level. Seeing the dark blue this close up was strangely intimate… and incredibly disconcerting. Candace sought a distraction. "Is your sister still here?"

"No, she left hours ago. I was about to file a missing persons report."

She hitched Jennie up higher in her arms and smiled uncertainly. "You're joking, right?"

The brooding scrutiny he subjected her to made her heart skip a beat. "Except I wasn't sure that you were missing...I thought you might have taken Jennie into hiding."

"Kidnapped her?" Astonishment caused her to blink. "I'd never do something so stupid."

His mouth relaxed imperceptibly. But all he said was, "Good."

"If I did something like that, I'd kiss goodbye to any sympathy I might get from the courts when I challenge your custody of Jennie."

Nick glanced over her shoulder, and Candace became aware of Mrs. Busby hovering in the lobby.

"I'll take the baby, shall I?" she asked.

Reluctantly, Candace surrendered Jennie to the housekeeper.

"Come into the sitting room." Nick stood back, allowing her to pass into the stark room that Candace had decided she hated.

She halted in the middle of the cold space and wished, for once, that the immense flat-screen television was on so it could break the taut silence that vibrated between her and Nick. Candace could see the tension humming in his tall lean frame.

"I'd advise you to think long and hard before deciding to drag this through the courts," he murmured. "You have everything to lose."

Instantly, she started to panic. "What do you mean?"

He came closer, and the breathless fear changed into something else...something more dangerous, rooting her to the spot.

"It would be foolish to threaten me." He spoke through his teeth. "I'm being as patient as I can. Don't push me too far."

"Or what?" Candace challenged boldly. "What will you do?"

"I might be tempted to pursue court proceedings myself

and have you prohibited from coming within a hundred feet of Jennie."

The impact of his words jolted her. Candace stared at him, stunned by his reaction. If he made good on his threat, her baby would disappear behind high walls and electronic gates. Then she'd be forced to go to court to challenge the legality of his custody of Jennie. That would take money. A great deal of money. Money that she didn't have.

A vision of a future too bleak to contemplate faced her. She'd be standing on the outside—in a world that would become a desert if she was without her baby.

"You can't do that."

"Is that a challenge?"

"No...*please*." Tears spilled out her eyes. "I couldn't bear never to see Jennie again. Please, not that."

"Oh, Christ, don't cry!"

The rough brush of his mouth against hers came as a shock. Yet instead of shoving him away Candace found herself yielding...leaning into the warmth of his body as he kissed her again. And again.

She tasted the salt of her tears, a hint of mint. Then she closed her eyes and her body slumped against him, his heat and hunger filling the empty numbness. His arms steadied her, pulling her more firmly into his embrace.

One hand stroked her hair, and he whispered, "Steady on."

She rested her head against his shirt and sniffed.

His hands cupped her nape, tipping her head back. She shut her eyes, refusing to let him see the hopelessness, the hurt flooding through her.

"Look at me, Candace."

Finally, she opened her eyes.

There was an expression on his face that caused her throat to constrict.

"I shouldn't have said that."

"You're such a bastard." She discovered she was crying in earnest now. "How could you do that to me?"

"Candace—"

"Don't touch me."

She wrenched herself away and rushed from the room before he kissed her again…and she lost what little of her heart still remained intact.

Nine

In the summery morning light that streamed into his bathroom and sparkled off the white tiles, Nick stared at a face half covered in shaving cream in the mirror.

His eyes were bloodshot from lack of sleep. Through the long hours of the night he'd been unable to shake from his mind the hurt, shocked look in Candace's eyes. Her pain had haunted his dreams last night.

He didn't much like what he saw; he wasn't proud of himself.

Without flinching, he thought about how the women in his life might have reacted if they'd been caught in the same position as Candace: Bertha Williams, his grandmother, his sister…even his devious wife. And he came to one conclusion.

Every one of them would have fought to keep her child. And every one of them would've been stunned that he could threaten to cut a woman off from the child she'd given birth to.

Even if she had agreed to give that baby up…

Nick lifted his hand and carefully brought the razor down in a long sweeping line. In minutes the white foam was gone, the shave complete. His skin glowed, clear and unsullied by stubble.

Yet Nick suspected the same wasn't true of his soul...

Once showered and dressed, Nick paused on the upstairs landing. Glancing at his watch, he saw it was already well past breakfast time.

Instead of heading for the stairs, he checked himself and went the other way. To the wing that held the nursery—and Candace's room.

Where the landing widened into a sitting area, he stopped.

Candace had pushed the glass table aside and was lying flat on her back on the carpet. A DVD showing a group of mothers doing exercises with babies was playing on the television screen that hung on a wall. Candace's arms were fully extended as she swung Jennie above her.

Both of them were laughing.

The shorts Candace wore were white and very, very brief. The ice-blue tank top fitted snugly over her curvy breasts.

Hell. The hollow in Nick's chest contracted into a tight, hard ball.

Desperately he looked away, scanning the room. The place looked—sounded—like a home. In a way that the perfectly decorated space never had before.

It even felt like a home.

He dithered on the periphery, not wanting to break the mood.

But a movement must've given him away because Candace turned her head—and saw him. Her laughter stilled. She lowered the baby and started to sit up.

"Don't stop," he said. "It looks like Jennie's having the time of her life."

Candace smiled hesitantly, and Nick felt as if the room had been flooded with more sunshine.

His cell phone chose that moment to ring.

It was his doctor confirming that he was almost certainly Jennie's father.

Nick thanked him for his help and killed the call. Staring at the woman on the mat, a heavy beat thundered in his ears.

Candace had told the truth. He hadn't believed her. Once again the sense of his soul being less than pure struck him. He shook off the thought, strode forward and sank onto the floor beside her, his legs awkwardly long in the confined space.

Jennie reached a hand toward him, and he gave her his. She grasped his thumb with a grip that was surprisingly strong.

"You'll get wool from the carpet all over your suit," Candace warned, folding slim, bare legs under her and resting Jennie in her lap, still attached to his finger.

Nick forced his eyes away from her smooth limbs.

Down, boy.

So this was how she was going to play it. As if that ugly scene between them last night had never happened.

For a split second Nick considered forcing the issue, trying to explain his confusion—what Jennie was coming to mean to him. Strangely enough, he hadn't needed the doctor's call to care about the baby. That had happened all by itself in some miraculous way.

The hesitation stretched into a pulsing pause, became overlong, and the moment passed.

Finally, he took the conversational olive branch she'd offered. "A bit of lint on my trousers hardly matters."

Everything that mattered in his life sat right in front of him. Jennie, snuggled into Candace's lap, holding on to his thumb like there was no tomorrow. Candace, her cheeks flushed with exertion, her eyes sparkling.

"Candace—"

Her eyes were bright, inquiring. "Mmm?"

"That was my doctor."

The brightness faded a little.

"And?"

"The tests are back. You were right. Jennie is my daughter."

Ominously, she didn't say that she'd told him so. She tightened her arms around the baby until Jennie objected. Her stillness was starting to concern him.

He needed them…both of them.

Jennie perched on Candace's lap looking comfortable and at ease. Both had been so utterly absorbed in each other until he'd come along and ruined it. They didn't need him at all.

That realization made his heart miss a beat.

For the first time he had some inkling of how Jilly must've felt in those long years she was married to him.

He'd behaved like a bastard, resenting the fact that Jilly had trapped him into a marriage he hadn't wanted…yet couldn't refuse. It had been a choice between the devil and the deep blue sea, and he'd been determined not to drown. So Jilly, the agent of his downfall, had borne the brunt of his anger.

Nick was starting to like himself less and less…

As if she sensed his thoughts, Jennie dropped his thumb and turned her attention to tugging at strands of blond hair that had escaped Candace's hair tie. Instead of pulling away, Candace simply laughed.

Nick cleared his throat. "Look, every year there's a carnival at the Super Center on the Sunday closest to Valentine's Day. That's this weekend. It's very festive." God, he was starting to sound desperate. With studied casualness he asked, "Would you like to come with me this year?"

"You're asking me on a date? To be your Valentine?"

Damn.

He couldn't read her expression. What the hell was he supposed to say now?

Nick forced a laugh. "No, no. Nothing like that."

"Oh…"

God, he was screwing this up badly.

"Candace—" He broke off and reached out the hand Jennie had held and covered Candace's with it. She flinched.

He withdrew swiftly and brushed a nonexistent piece of fluff from his jacket, trying to face up to the fact that he wasn't behaving with very much subtlety or grace.

"I just thought you might want to join us—spend the day with Jennie."

The joy that lit up her eyes was blinding. "Thank you. I'd love that."

So spending the day with him held no appeal, but spending it with Jennie was something else. He should've expected that. He might be driven by lust, but clearly Candace didn't reciprocate.

Ah, well. "Valentine's…growing happy families. A loving home begins at Valentine's."

"What?" Confusion clouded her eyes.

"Those slogans are part of our latest advertising campaign," he explained.

"Oh, yes." Her face had cleared. "I've seen the television ads."

She didn't think he'd lost it.

Yet.

Just as well she couldn't read his mind—she'd have run screaming from the room.

"It's a day for families," he said awkwardly. "For Jennie's sake, you should be there."

This time Candace didn't say a word.

Nick wondered if that had been overkill. Too late to wish he hadn't been quite so heavy-handed on the whole family angle. There was nothing for him to do but rise to his feet and say, "Well, I'd better get moving or I'll be late for work."

"You're the boss, what would it matter?"

"It matters," he said. "I've always believed a boss should

lead by example. And lately I've been sneaking out quite a bit."

Though what worried him most was how much he'd enjoyed playing hooky.

The temperature rose swiftly, turning into one of those glorious summer days that lingered.

With Nick at work, Candace decided to take advantage of the weather and take Jennie swimming. The water in the pool was silken and cool—and Jennie was in her element, hanging over Candace's arm, smacking the surface of the water with fat palms while Candace laughed.

All through the day she'd been kicking herself. Why hadn't she told Nick that Jennie should live with her, not him? She'd had the perfect opportunity this morning...

Instead, she'd chickened out.

Perhaps it had been the look on his face. There'd been something—a vulnerability—that had tugged at her heart. He'd looked...lonely.

Candace told herself that she was being ridiculous. Men like Nick Valentine weren't lonely. They married wealthy trophy wives, lived in glossy architect-designed mansions, owned multimillion-dollar businesses.

Except Nick's wife was dead...

He couldn't possibly be missing Jilly, Candace told herself. Hadn't Nick told her he'd suspected Jilly of having an affair? The extent of Jilly's deception over the baby signaled to Candace that theirs had not been a healthy marriage.

A footfall scraped the deck and Candace turned her head. The sight of Nick coming toward her, threading his way between the lounging chairs, caused a flutter in her belly.

This made it two days in a row that he was home early... maybe being the boss had its perks after all.

"You're early," she commented, squinting up at him as his highly polished Italian shoes halted at the pool's edge.

"I secured a contract to do the landscaping and supply the plants and garden furnishings for two coastal resorts. It's a coup. I called it a day." Nick glanced at his watch, then met her gaze and raised a quizzical eyebrow. "Half past six is not much earlier than normal."

"Half past six?" Candace squawked. "Already?"

"Time flies when you're having fun."

Candace ignored his quip. "Gosh, Jennie will turn into a prune."

"She looks fine to me." Nick squatted down on his haunches and wiggled his fingers at the baby. She gave him a delicious smile and chuckled. "I might go change into swim trunks and join you."

The notion of being trapped with a good-humored, nearly naked Nick in a pool on such a balmy summer's evening was more than Candace could handle.

"I should get Jennie out. She must be starving."

His face went wooden, and she felt suddenly small and mean. "You know, a little while longer won't kill her. You go change…we'll wait for you."

It took Nick only five minutes to change into swim trunks, grab a towel and hurry back to the pool.

Candace and Jennie were still in the water, the baby squealing with pleasure as Candace swung her back and forth, skimming the pool's surface.

After dropping his towel on the lounger, Nick launched himself into the water. Jennie's eyes popped out as he surfaced beside them. Her face puckered in distress and for a moment it looked like she might cry.

"Hey, hey," he murmured, mentally kicking himself. "It's only me…not some sea monster."

When he looked up, Candace was watching him, but she was smiling.

"She wants you."

Jennie had her arms out, and she rewarded him with a gurgle as he swam closer.

Nick's insides melted. "Come here, you."

Taking her from Candace, he scooped her to him and made little growls against her neck.

Jennie giggled, and bounced excitedly in his arms. Her fingers hooked around his hand as she bumped up and down.

"Hey, take it easy. I'll be in trouble if I drop you," he whispered. The memory of the day she'd been pecked by the goose and he'd nearly fallen in the lake still made him shudder.

That wasn't happening again…

Jennie stuck out her fingers and closed them around his. Gold glinted on his left hand in the slanting rays.

"You wear a wedding ring."

He glanced at the wedding band, then across to the woman who'd asked. Her gaze was still trained on his hand. "Yes."

"A lot of men don't wear a ring."

"Jilly bought it for me." She'd bought her own rings, too, Nick remembered with a touch of discomfort. But wearing a ring had saved him plenty of explanations at inopportune moments—not that some of Jilly's acquaintances had paid much attention to the band of gold that had marked him as her property.

"You're still wearing it."

"I hadn't thought about taking it off." There hadn't been another woman in his life so it hadn't entered his mind. Except now there was Candace…

Their eyes meshed—and held. Her pupils, so black against the misty gray eyes, expanded. Trapping him.

"Ouch!"

He gazed down at Jennie's fist clutching at the dusting of hair on his arm. "That hurt."

The baby dimpled up at him, showing a gleam of pearly white.

"She's got a tooth." He stared at Candace.

"One. Lower incisor. The next one should cut any day now…"

"Wow." Nick transferred his attention back to the wriggling bundle in his arms. "You're growing up fast. I hadn't even thought about braces yet."

"Soon she'll be dating."

But Nick didn't laugh. Instead, he squeezed his eyes shut. "Jeez, that idea really hurts. I don't want to think about it." When he cracked open one eye, he found Jennie watching him. She cooed.

It made Nick feel like the most important man in the world. Hell, he *was* the most important man in his daughter's world—at least until she turned sixteen and started dating—and he wasn't about to screw up again.

"I'll have to lock you up," he told her. "Vet all the boys who come visiting."

He peeked across at Candace, but she wasn't laughing. Instead, he was surprised by the strange expression on her face. Then she turned away and made for the pool end nearest the house and gracefully exited the water.

As he watched her pick up a white towel and dry her face, it struck Nick that Candace must be thinking about the coming years without Jennie. He would be there for their daughter. Candace would be gone. His daughter would have no mother to guide her through the minefield of teen-girl years.

Hell.

Of course he'd lean on his sister for help and, in time, Candace would have a family of her own. A husband. Babies…

Emotion flared inside him. He couldn't imagine her with some other, faceless man. It hurt to think of her with a child other than Jennie.

The intensity of his response took him by surprise. What the hell was going on?

The answer came at once.

Nick didn't need to watch Candace towel off those tantalizing legs to know he wanted to stroke her skin, kiss her lips, make love to her. He didn't want some other man sharing the moments he dared not even admit to fantasizing about.

Jennie chose that moment to protest and look around, an expression of bewildered panic on her face.

"You want Mommy?" Bending his head, Nick whispered against her ear, "Me, too. But that's our secret, 'kay? Because it's an impossible fantasy."

Jennie grumbled.

Nick knew exactly how the baby felt. For now he could be generous. "It's all right, I'll take you to her."

With the baby in his arms, Nick waded over to the steps. When he reached the top step, Candace was waiting. Jennie almost leaped out of Nick's arms and Candace swaddled her in the thick towel.

The bond wasn't all on Candace's side—Jennie was equally drawn to her biological mother.

The gold rays of the sun caught her face as she gazed at the baby in her arms, her expression content and happy. "I'd better get her some supper. She'll be hungry after that swim."

"Why don't you feed her out here?" suggested Nick. "It's such a beautiful summer evening—no point wasting it by being closeted inside."

Candace hesitated only for a second. "Okay. I'll take her upstairs to whip her swimsuit off and put a dry diaper on, then bring her dinner out."

Nick watched her saunter to the glass doors, her hips swaying, the content, gurgling baby in her arms. Everything worked so well now. Yet Nick knew Candace's time with

Jennie was limited. And, for him, becoming involved with Candace was an impossible fantasy.

Because of their daughter.

Nor could Candace continue to live with them. It would only cause heartache for Jennie in the long term. The longer it lingered, the greater the hurt would be. Nick knew the situation could only end in tears.

Candace was going to have to leave. Sooner would be better for Jennie; and the woman who had him tied up in sexual knots was going to hate him even more when he suggested it.

Candace had been right, Nick realized twenty minutes later. Jennie was hungry, and it didn't take long for the baby to devour her dinner.

Sitting across the table from Candace, with Jennie in a high chair between them as the sun's sloping rays reflected off the mirrored surface of the water, the mood felt almost domestic.

Nick watched Jennie's eyelids droop. He'd opened a bottle of crisp Sauvignon Blanc and poured both himself and Candace a glass, but hers was still full.

Candace followed his gaze. "She's almost asleep."

"Why don't you put little madam to bed and come back and finish your wine? I'll see what Mrs. Busby has planned for dinner."

Nick suspected that he was playing with fire and Candace looked as though she might object. But she surprised him by saying, "A sandwich would suit me fine. I shouldn't be long."

Adrenaline rushed through Nick's veins as he smiled at her. "Don't be."

He told himself nothing was going to happen.

He and Candace were going to share a glass of wine together, have a light meal…and that would be the end of it. He was capable of controlling his emotions…his desires. After all, he'd been doing it for years.

True to her word, Candace was back within fifteen minutes. To Nick's everlasting regret, she'd donned a pair of navy sweats and a white T-shirt. No sign of the aqua one-piece swimsuit remained. Pity…

But very much safer.

"Good timing," said Nick. Mrs. Busby had just left after placing a tray of sandwiches on the table.

"Jennie is exhausted." Candace set the baby monitor on the table and sank into the chair opposite, then pulled a plate toward her.

"It's the water. She should sleep well."

"Until two o'clock." Candace grimaced. "That's the drill."

"She wakes up every night?" He hadn't known.

"Like clockwork." Peeling back the protective food wrap that covered the platter of sandwiches, she said, "These look delicious."

"Smoked chicken and avocado on this side. The others are Swiss cheese and salad."

"Yum." Candace helped herself. It didn't take long for them to demolish the contents of the tray, eating in companionable silence. When the platter was empty, Candace raised her wineglass. "To Mrs. Busby. She's a wonder."

Leaning forward, Nick clinked his glass against hers. "I'll drink to that."

Tilting her head to one side, Candace studied him. "She tells me she's worked for you for ten years."

Had it already been a decade? Nick thought about it. He'd been married to Jilly for seven years, and Mrs. Busby had been with him for several years before Jilly had had this house designed, built and decorated. "It's possible. I first employed her when I lived over on the North Shore. I owned a drafty old Victorian house with an enormous garden."

Jilly had hated the house as much as he'd loved it. It had been the first casualty of their marriage.

"Mrs. Busby told me about it—she said it had been built by one of the pioneers of the city. She misses it."

"I never knew that."

"She told me about the gardens—about the ferns you planted behind the house. She said it was like a secret world—she thought that Jennie would've loved playing in there, that it was the kind of place where a child could imagine fairies and elves."

"Goblins, too." Nick couldn't suppress the tide of nostalgia that the memory of the house brought.

"Don't you miss it?"

Candace's question brought him back to the present. He dismissed the momentary sense of loss, and his customary mantle of control dropped into place. He lived in the present, not the past. What happened now he could control. The past had already happened; nothing could change it.

"No." To soften the brusque reply, he shrugged and said, "It was time to move on."

Candace glanced up at the white structure behind them. "You moved on to something a lot more modern. This house is a completely different proposition."

"It's a good investment—it's everything the market wants. Great architectural style. Location." He gestured to the sea shimmering in the setting sun. "The value has more than doubled."

There was no point saying it had been Jilly's house, not his. It had never felt like home.

Candace brushed a strand of hair behind her ear. "You want me to believe that you sold the Victorian house to upgrade to something that needed less restoration and was a better monetary investment?"

He met her gaze levelly. "What other reason could there be?"

She made an impatient sound in her throat. "Mrs. Busby thought you lived here because Jilly loved it."

After a pause, Nick said, "Sounds like Mrs. Busby and you had a real heart-to-heart chat."

Leaning forward, Candace touched his arm. Lightning forked along his skin. "She wasn't gossiping," she said earnestly. "She's very fond of you."

"That surprised you?"

She looked startled by his question. Finally, she said, "Truthfully?"

"By all means be truthful."

Nick braced himself, and hoped she wouldn't be too truthful.

"Yes, it did surprise me. You come across as being very distant and remote. Not the kind of man who would be easy to work for. Yet she's adamant that you're the best employer she's ever had—even though she seems to have found Jilly..." Candace hesitated "...trying sometimes. Not that she said it in so many words. It was more in what she *didn't* say—and how much she raved about you."

"Mrs. Busby deserves a raise—for loyalty at the very least. Because Jilly *could* be trying." And demanding. And insecure. And like the house she adored, with its plethora of glass and mirrors that needed constant shining, she'd been high-maintenance.

"Do you miss her terribly?"

Nick didn't hesitate. "No."

Candace's eyes widened and her mouth formed an *O*.

"Did you want me to lie to you?"

"My impression was that you were everything she'd ever wanted."

Nick looked away. He fumbled and drew the gold wedding band off his finger. "It's long past time to take this off. What Jilly and I had could hardly be called a marriage."

The sound of Candace's sharply drawn breath filled the sudden silence.

"Nick—"

He didn't look at her. "Jilly is dead. I don't want to conduct a postmortem over a marriage that never even got off the ground."

Her hand stroked along his arm. "I never meant to—"

Man, she was killing him. The worst of it was she had no clue. Finally, he looked at her. "I should never have married Jilly."

Her eyes were so soft he could've sworn she understood what he felt. The confusion. The guilt. The frustration at the lost years.

The yearning for a woman like her.

Her hand released him, and he felt the loss. Picking up her wineglass, Candace took a deep sip.

Nick knew how she felt. Except she had no idea how bad he had it—the whole damn bottle of wine wouldn't ease the desire that heated him, it would only inflame it. And Nick had no intention of losing sight of the most important aspect of his existence—his control.

However much he wanted Candace.

He knew the time had come to retreat. Before he lost his head and did something he might later regret. Rising to his feet, he said, "I have a long day tomorrow. I think I'll turn in."

"Nick…"

He paused, his pulse thudding. "What is it?"

Candace shook her head. "Don't worry about it."

"Tell me," he insisted.

She hesitated, then said, "Do you still want me to come with you and Jennie to the carnival on Sunday?"

Nick was sure that wasn't what she'd planned to say, but he didn't challenge her. "Of course." The coward in him added,

"Alison and her husband, Richard, and her boys will no doubt be there too. It's a great day out."

Nick didn't want Candace guessing how pleased he was that she'd agreed to go.

Ten

A welcoming banner festooned with hearts fluttered over the arched entrance to Valentine's Garden Super Center.

"How did you manage to arrange for so many roses to be in bloom for today's carnival?" Candace asked Nick as he pushed Jennie's stroller under the arch covered in cascades of red, pink and white.

Nick's mouth slanted. "Good planning—I leave nothing to chance."

Candace gave him a narrow-eyed glance. Before she could react, a cloud of red, heart-shaped balloons floated toward them. A teenager wearing a T-shirt proclaiming *Valentine's... Gardens of Love* emerged from behind the bunch and held a balloon out to Candace.

"Thank you." Candace smiled and accepted the red heart. Bending forward, she tied it to the stroller. Jennie's eyes lit up and her hand reached out. At her touch the balloon bobbed away, and Jennie squealed with pleasure.

Nick laughed. Straightening, Candace met his dancing

eyes. There was a moment of pure, joyous accord, before she came to her senses and walked away quickly, leaving Nick to follow with the stroller.

She couldn't allow herself to forget that Nick had wanted to get her out of her daughter's life. Candace knew the battle wasn't over yet. Nick was a hard-nosed businessman; he'd simply be choosing his time to regroup and attack again. She dared not let her guard down.

Inside the garden center, a lively sight met her eyes. The area around the coffee shop had been transformed, with extra tables and chairs arranged on the cobbles, and red-and-white petunias cascading out of planter boxes. On the wooden adventure playground children swarmed down rope ladders and over wooden battlements, and beyond the playground red, blue, and yellow canvas booths had been set up. In the nearest booth three young women were painting toddlers' faces, while the booths beyond housed hook-the-fish, a skittle lane, a balloon twister and an assortment of other festive activities.

"Goodness, it *is* a carnival."

"Close enough." Taking one hand from the stroller, Nick placed it under Candace's elbow and guided her through the crowd while deftly maneuvering the stroller with his other hand. Instantly, shivers skittered across the bare skin where his hand rested. Candace forced herself to pretend she hadn't noticed.

In the farthest corner a table had been cleared, and a waitress descended on them, brandishing menus. Nick's hand released Candace, and he drew out a chair for her and then parked the stroller with a suddenly heavy-eyed Jennie in the corner beside them.

"There are pony rides and more booths down by the lake—even a kissing booth," said Nick.

Candace sat, determined not be drawn into a discussion about kissing. The lingering sizzle from where his hand had rested was more than enough. She didn't need any mention of kissing to heighten the constant warmth that enveloped her whenever Nick was nearby. So she changed the subject. "It's all too much for Jennie to take in. Look, all the excitement, and she's almost asleep!"

Nick laughed, then greeted the waitress by name, took the menus and passed one to Candace. "What would you like? I recommend the berry smoothies."

"A smoothie sounds lovely." Candace was relieved that Nick hadn't pursued the topic of kissing booths.

The waitress gathered up the menus and departed. Candace glanced around. A little way off, an old-fashioned gazebo swayed with a trio of musicians. Plenty of older customers— and some younger couples—sat on the benches scattered throughout the carnival scene, enjoying the music. Her mother would've loved this...

But the days for this kind of pleasure were past for Catherine Morrison. "You've catered to everyone—all ages," she said, trying not to let regret take hold at the thought of what her mother had lost.

Nick nodded. "Our Valentine's Sunday carnival is part of the annual social calendar for many of our customers. Some have been coming for years. Old couples. Young families. At the heart of it all, everyone wants love...a family...and a home."

She liked him in this gentler mood. It wasn't the controlled—and controlling—Nick Valentine he usually presented to the world. This was a different Nick—nothing like the uncaring businessman she'd pegged him to be.

A much more likable Nick.

Fixing her attention on his face, she said, "You sound like you believe in that, too."

"Of course I do. Our centers provide a chance for people to build fantastic gardens they and their families can enjoy— irrespective of age...or of how many people are in their families."

The passion Nick was talking about was absent from the soulless perfection of the sculpted pool deck, flat lawns and clipped boxwood hedging of his own home. Candace couldn't keep from saying, "But what about your own garden?"

"What do you mea—"

"Nick! I almost didn't spot you hiding back there in the corner." A stooping, angular woman with salt-and-pepper hair and a weather-beaten face stopped beside their table.

He got to his feet and gave her a great bear hug. "Bertha."

Once Nick had pulled away from her embrace, the old lady's sharp green eyes inspected Candace, then dropped to Jennie sleeping in the stroller. "This is that newborn baby I came to your house to see?"

"This is Jennie."

Could that be pride in Nick's voice?

"My, but she's grown." The woman fixed an accusing stare on Nick. "I can't even pick her up because that would waken her. I keep telling you to bring her to work so I can see her."

"I'm sorry."

Nick Valentine actually sounded humble. Who was this woman?

Candace realized she was attracting equal interest. "I'm Candace." She hesitated, then added, "Jennie's nanny."

Not the whole truth, but a version she could live with.

For now.

"Candace, meet Bertha Williams."

"This young man used to mow my lawns."

"Bertha and Henry gave me a job in their garden center and taught me to grow vegetables, generate cuttings. They ignited my love of gardening and then convinced me that my dream to enroll in a landscaping course at night school could be turned into reality."

"We owned it for forty years, before losing it. Nick had to wrest the center away from the businessman who was ready to build houses on the property. Henry and I might have been

fine gardeners but we couldn't keep the money straight."
Bertha's brutally honest account made no apologies for their
shortcomings. "Nick set it right." The old woman gave him a
fond smile. "So after Nick moved us back into the manager's
house seven years ago, I insisted that he hire me."

Nick grinned at her. "It was a good investment."

"Good for us, too. Since you took over the business it's
given Henry and I time together. Even despite his heart attack,
freed from the strain of running the business, the years have
been wonderful."

For once Candace couldn't believe that Nick's decision to
employ Bertha had been driven solely by profit. Even though
her eyes were bright with life, Bertha's hands were crippled
with arthritis, her back hunched. Seven years ago she would've
already been over sixty. Nick must really care about the old
woman.

Yet he hadn't brought Jennie to visit her...

Because he hadn't believed that Jennie was his child?

Before she could speculate further, Bertha said, "Giving
Nick a summer job all those years ago was the best business
decision we ever made."

"Flattery gets you everywhere," Nick told Bertha, lifting his
napkin as the waitress delivered the smoothies to the table.

Candace smiled her thanks to the waitress, placed her straw
in the deep pink drink and sipped. Despite being so driven,
it appeared Nick did have some redeeming qualities. Bertha
clearly thought he was wonderful. Mrs. Busby had extolled
his virtues as an employer and now Bertha was implying that
he'd single-handedly saved their garden center. Would taking
Jennie from her father be the best thing for the child?

Candace found herself wavering.

Then she forced herself to take stock. Jennie's well-being
came first. She gazed at the man who had thrown her into
such confusion. Could Nick Valentine match the kind of love
she could give her daughter?

"Would you like to join us for a cup of tea, Bertha?" Nick was asking as he picked up his own smoothie.

Bertha glanced from Nick to Candace. A crafty expression crept across her time-wrinkled face. "I think I've kept you young people long enough." Patting Candace's shoulder, she added, "Nick works too hard, my dear. Do an old lady a favor and make sure he takes it easy today…and has some fun."

Satisfaction settled over Nick.

Down near the lake the carnival was in full swing. Two black ponies led by a woman with long braids plodded along the path beside the lake, their young riders clutching at the reins.

Things were finally going better, he decided as Candace slowed the stroller, in which Jennie was still sleeping, and brought it to a halt.

Changing Candace's belief that he was a poor parent hadn't been as easy as he'd thought it would be. For one thing, Nick found it difficult to talk about himself. For another, while he'd vowed to spend more time with Jennie and to behave more like her father, that meant changing habits of a lifetime. He would do it. He'd already made great strides in spending more time at home. Hell, even Pauline and his sister had noticed. Nick had every intention of honoring the promise he'd made to Jennie the day she'd almost ended up in the lake—except he'd never been the kind of man who wore his heart on his sleeve.

Fortunately, his plan of inviting Candace to see firsthand the family-friendly empire he'd built had been nicely jump-started with Bertha's zealous endorsement. He could've kissed the woman who'd played such an important role in his life.

How could Candace not reconsider her low opinion of him?

A little way down the rolling bank, he caught sight of his sister waving frantically. "There's Alison," he told

Candace. "Come on, if Jennie wakes up she can play with her cousins."

They reached the lake, and he introduced Candace to his sister's husband, Richard, while their two sons crowded around—the four- and six-year-old both talking at once.

"Can we go see Princess Piggy?"

Nick shuddered theatrically.

"Scoot," their father ordered.

"Can we have money to get some cotton candy?"

Alison rolled her eyes. "I'm sure your dad will give you money…be back in ten minutes."

"I might go with them," said Richard. "Just to make sure they don't get into trouble."

As the boys and their father disappeared around the bend in the path, Alison turned to Candace and shook her head. "Kids! You're lucky you don't have any."

As Nick glared at his sister, Alison immediately realized her mistake. "Oh, I'm so sorry, Candace, that was tactless, I wasn't thinking."

"Who's Princess Piggy?" asked Candace in what Nick was sure was a brave attempt to distract his sister.

Alison brightened up. "Haven't you seen the kissing booth? You ought to get Nick to take you—it's his favorite booth." Alison grinned.

Candace shot Nick a wary glance. Nick could've rung his sister's neck. "That's not very nice."

Alison hooked her arms through his and Candace's and bore them both along with her. "See? There's Princess Piggy."

Inside a fully enclosed booth was a pink pig sporting a strapped-on glitzy rhinestone crown and a passion-pink satin sash. Nick grimaced and his sister giggled.

"Look at Nick's face," she whispered to Candace loudly enough for Nick to hear.

He watched as Candace glanced up at him and her gray eyes started to smile. Nick fought to keep his face impassive and not give away the effect she had on him. "The funds we raise today will be donated to charity," Nick explained. "Princess Piggy's stall is often one of the most successful."

"People pay to kiss a pig?" The doubtful look Candace cast the Kiss-the-Princess banner above the stall told Nick what she thought of the idea.

Nick pointed to a row of glass jars with names written on the front in black marker, each containing money. "See those jars? People pay for someone else to kiss the pig. Around midday the contents are tallied up, and the person with the most monetary 'votes' in his jar is tracked down and forced to kiss the Princess." Nick gave the porker a sour look.

"I take it you've had to do that in years past?"

"My staff seem to think it's extremely amusing."

"The proceeds go to charity and Nick's a good sport." Alison pointed at the first jar. "I think I see your name there again this year."

Nick groaned.

Beside him he heard Candace laugh, which almost made the prospect of kissing Princess palatable today.

"And here I imagined everyone was queuing up to kiss the prettiest woman at the fair." Amusement lingered in Candace's voice.

Had she been jealous? Nick found the notion curiously heartening. But Candace bent forward over the railing, preventing him from reading the expression on her face.

"Princess Piggy's quite cute," said Candace.

"Sure," said Nick unenthusiastically. "Alison certainly thinks so." He gave his sister a mock frown.

"Hey," said Alison. "To make up for the fact that I'm certain you'll have to kiss the darling again today, I'll babysit for you tonight…if you want to take Candace out for dinner?"

Nick's heart flipped. But Candace was flushing as she said quickly, "No, no, that's not—"

Before she could turn down the offer, Nick cut in. "That's a great idea. Thanks, Ally." He touched Candace's arm. "Don't forget, Bertha told us to have fun."

Candace's bottom lip jutted out endearingly, causing Nick to fight the impulse to kiss it.

"I'm sure you'll both enjoy some time out," said Alison, looking around her. "Speaking of which, I've been left alone far too long. I'd better go and check where those boys of mine have gotten to."

Before Nick could ask his sister to wait so they could finalize Jennie's sleepover arrangements for the night, he spied a familiar snowy head in the approaching throng.

Putting an arm around Candace, he braced himself for the inevitable clash of wills with his father-in-law. "I didn't expect to see you here, Desmond."

"As a future stockholder in Valentine's, I wanted to investigate my investment. What better time than today?" The grim smile didn't light up his glacial eyes. "Aren't you going to introduce me to your woman?"

Nick felt Candace tense.

Resisting what was rapidly becoming a familiar urge to land his fist in Desmond's stomach, he said, "This is my father-in-law. Desmond, this is Jennie's nanny, Candace." He chose the explanation she'd offered Bertha, and thankfully Candace didn't contradict him.

"I see."

Without sparing the sleeping baby in the stroller a glance, Desmond looked Candace up and down, making his opinion of what he saw very clear. Nick resisted the urge to let his hand fall from where he'd rested it protectively in the small of her back.

"I doubt it," said Nick levelly.

"I see a pretty woman living in your home—"

Candace tensed under Nick's touch.

"A woman *my sister* employed while I was overseas on

business." Nick spoke from between gritted teeth, furious with his father-in-law's implication, and even more furious because he couldn't in clear conscience tell Desmond to get his mind out the gutter.

Because the irrefutable truth was that Nick was lusting after Candace. The spark of attraction that had flared that first night had raged out of control. Now that he'd discovered they'd created a daughter together, Nick couldn't get the picture of making love to Candace—the real, passionate way, not the clinical IVF way—out of his mind. It was driving him crazy. *She* was driving him crazy.

Even now he caught the scent of her perfume as the wind lifted tendrils of her hair off her nape. He was intensely conscious that only one layer of cotton fabric separated the fingers resting on her back from her bare flesh beneath. And the idea that Desmond had spotted what Nick was so determined to conceal turned his stomach.

He dropped his hand from where it rested.

"Was that your sister who rushed past me?" asked Desmond.

Nick's hackles rose. He was sure that Desmond knew it had been Alison. "Why? Did you want an update on how her husband is progressing on finding new premises?"

It was a shot in the dark. But the slight widening of Desmond's eyes gave him away even before he blustered, "I have no idea what you're talking about."

"I'm sure you do." Nick lowered his voice. "Leave Alison and Richard out of it. This is our fight."

Desmond glanced away, then back. "I see someone I need to talk to—I'm sure you'd agree with me that people would line up to buy an apartment on the lake's edge."

"It's not going to happen," Nick said, "and that's a promise."

Desmond glared at him, and the rush of anger that his father-in-law so often provoked rose fast and hard in Nick. He stepped forward.

"Nick," said Candace, "let's move on. I'd like to wheel Jennie around to keep her from waking."

Nick suspected that Candace's timely concern had more to do with stopping him from flattening Desmond than from worry about Jennie's waking. His initial surge of annoyance ebbed to be replaced by a more complicated emotion as he glanced across to Candace.

An unspoken connection leaped between them.

"I found my boys," Alison said from behind them, bringing Nick abruptly back to earth, and then she added, "Oh, hello Desmond."

Muttering a greeting, Desmond gave Nick an ugly look and stalked away.

"What did I just interrupt?" Alison let go of her sons' hands.

For a moment Nick thought his sister had spotted that instant of electric intensity between him and Candace. How could he explain something he didn't understand himself?

Then Alison grabbed her younger son as he drifted away. "Don't you disappear again. Your dad is coming any minute." She rolled her eyes as both boys grumbled and she shot Candace an apologetic smile. "They're little rogues." Turning to Nick, she asked, "Now, what's Desmond doing here?"

Relief filled Nick. Alison's sharp eyes had missed that moment of secret connection he'd shared with Candace. "I suspect he's responsible for much of the misery you and Richard are experiencing at present."

"But why?" asked Alison.

From the corner of his eye Nick caught the flicker of shock on Candace's face. "He wants to hurt me—and hurting you is a very good way of accomplishing that."

"You know what?" Alison stuck her hands on her hips. "I'm going to drum up support to have that jerk be the one to have to kiss Princess Piggy today. I'm going to get a jar with Desmond's name in big bold black letters started."

Alison's vehemence was enough to assure Nick that today Desmond would be the one kissing the pig.

"Don't do anything foolish," he warned. "We're going to win this battle against Desmond." Then, turning to Candace, he said ruefully, "Sorry we're dragging you into something you don't deserve to be part of. But take note that my sister may be the most dangerous woman in the whole world."

Then he realized that was totally true. It had been Alison who had engineered his date with Candace tonight—and, given the connection that was growing between them, that was going to be a truly risky occasion.

Eleven

The restaurant Nick chose for dinner was located in Auckland's highly fashionable Viaduct Basin.

A valet had taken the Ferrari away to park it. And, despite the restaurant's being heavily booked, the manager had found them a table on the edge of the terrace outside, overlooking the water where the reflection of the evening sun shimmered in shades of rose, orange and gold between berthed luxury yachts.

The beauty of the scene tugged at Candace's heart. "This is glorious."

"Isn't it?"

Nick pulled his chair up around so that he could sit beside her and they both could look out over the water. Instantly, Candace's senses started to sing with subtle tension. He was so big, so overpowering in a black long-sleeved shirt and black trousers. To distract herself from the effect he was having on her, she smoothed the simple ivory cotton sundress that was the only thing in her wardrobe remotely suitable for tonight's outing.

"Bertha will be pleased that I've taken her advice," said Nick leaning toward her. "Go enjoy yourselves. That might as well have been her and Henry's life motto."

Conscious of Nick's shoulder only inches from her own, Candace murmured, "It sounds like they were happy together—they had each other."

"Yes, they have each other."

Nick shifted, stretching his legs out, and Candace couldn't help but notice the way the fabric of his dark trousers rippled as his thigh muscles bunched. She looked away quickly, feeling her cheeks warm. At least with Nick sitting next to her, thankfully he wouldn't notice.

He gave a contented sigh. "This is the life. From now on, I'm going to listen more to Bertha. I haven't done enough enjoying—or living—in the past dozen years."

"In those years you built up a successful business, married a woman who loved you, fathered a baby. Isn't that life?"

Nick didn't answer. Instead, after a long pause, he slung his arm around the back of her chair, and said, "So what do you do to enjoy yourself?"

Now it was her turn to fall silent.

"My sister told me that you'd recently come back from traveling abroad when she met you at the hospital."

There was a certain irony that she'd been caught in a lie by his sister. The convenient catchphrase to explain away the months of absence while her pregnancy came to term. Now that easy fiction had come back to haunt her.

"I wasn't traveling," she said at last. To her relief, just then a waitress arrived with pen and pad to take their orders. Nick's hand slid off the chair back, and rested on Candace's shoulder. She was very conscious of the warm weight against her skin. The shoestring shoulder strap of the ivory sundress offered no protection from his touch as his fingers played idly, brushing against her, causing shivers of desire to ripple.

After the waitress left with their orders, Candace changed the subject. "Bertha seems very fond of you."

"She's known me a long time. Henry, her husband, employed me when I landed in trouble as a teenager for playing hooky from school."

"I got the impression you lived nearby?"

His fingers stilled, and Candace breathed a sigh of relief.

"Yes," he said with clear reluctance. "I lived with my grandmother—she had a vegetable garden and used to send me to buy seed from the center."

Getting personal information out of Nick was like trying to get blood from a stone. "And your parents?"

He shrugged. "They moved to live in Kenya when I was ten years old. They took Alison with them because she was only a baby. My grandmother thought it would be better for me to stay with her and get an education. It might've been better if I'd gone with my parents—I would certainly have gotten into a lot less trouble. Henry's offer of a summer job probably saved my grandmother from shipping me off to Africa to avoid expulsion from school."

He must've missed his parents. Candace's heart ached for him. "Did you see them often?"

"No, they've never been back to New Zealand—they still live in Kenya," he added as she started to ask. "But Alison came back for my grandmother's funeral, and she chose to stay on."

Candace wasn't letting him off the hook. She wanted to know more about what made Nick Valentine tick. "You're very close to Alison."

Lifting one shoulder, he let it fall. "She's my sister."

No confessions of endless devotion. But what had she expected? Yet she'd seen the way they teased each other and the clear bond of affection between them.

"Nick, why do you always want me to think the worst of you?"

A flush crawled along the side of his neck.

There was a long pause before he replied huskily, "Perhaps it's safer that way." He dropped his arm off the back of her chair, moved his chair around until he sat opposite her, then added, "Here come our appetizers."

"That's right, change the subject," she muttered, incredibly annoyed for some reason that she couldn't fathom.

The waitress set down their orders, then moved an ice bucket beside their table and placed the bottle of wine in the ice. Candace refused the offer of wine, and dug silently into the bowl of chowder she'd ordered.

When she'd finished, she set down her spoon and asked, "Do you ever talk about important stuff?"

"What important stuff?"

Candace gave an impatient sigh. "You're a master at this, aren't you?"

"I don't know what you're talking about."

But the wariness in the indigo gaze told her Nick knew precisely what she meant and he was equally determined to avoid the issue.

"You know, I might have thought you were a bad father—"

"Hey, wait a min—"

"—but I never had you tagged for a coward."

Anger flared, turning his eyes that blacker shade of midnight and his head went back. "A coward?"

"Yes, a coward. You're afraid of talking about anything that matters."

"You've been gossiping with my sister," he said tonelessly.

"No, I haven't. But how interesting that we agree." Candace drew a deep, steadying breath. Ah, well, she'd started this; there was no turning back now. "You're afraid of intimacy."

"You know nothing about me!"

"Because you don't allow anyone to get close?"

His face had tightened into an expressionless mask. "You don't know what you're talking about."

"Your wife loved you—you didn't let even her inside."

Nick bent forward and spoke in a soft, forceful voice. "My wife never loved me. She wanted to own me, possess my every waking thought, my soul. That's not love."

For the first time, the facade had cracked and she'd glimpsed anger and a ferocious passion that caused the tiny hairs on her arms to prickle.

"Nick…" She placed a hand on his arm.

"Don't touch me." His tone was dark and raw. "Unless you're prepared to reap the consequences."

Excitement licked at her, taking Candace by surprise. She'd never been reckless. The spreading desire warned her that was about to change. She forced herself not to be distracted. To focus. She wanted to know what kind of man Nick Valentine was.

"So tell me, *make* me understand."

The look he gave her was hostile. "Okay, you want to hear the story of what you consider great love? I'll tell you."

Candace was no longer so sure she wanted to hear whatever he was about to tell her. Lifting her hand from his arm, she said, "Nick—"

"You accused me of being a coward. You can damn well listen, *then* you can judge."

Nick took the wine out of the ice bucket. Before he could pour any into her glass, Candace shook her head. She suspected that she needed to be one hundred percent sober for the coming conversation.

Instead of pouring himself wine, Nick placed the wine back in the bucket. "My wife was a photographer. She took photos of flowers and had them blown up onto canvases—"

"Yes, I know. They're very popular. I bought one of her

works at a gallery exhibition." For her mother's birthday—the last one they'd celebrated before the accident. The photograph had been expensive, but it had been worth every cent. Her mother still loved it. "That's how we met."

Then they'd met again when Jilly had bumped into her at the hospital visiting a friend's premature baby. That was the first time Candace had glimpsed the other woman's yearning for a baby. They'd bumped into each other several times after that and Candace had been touched by Jilly's concern for her friend's baby.

"Well, we have that in common. It's how I met her, too. I was contracted to landscape her father's garden—I'd already built up a successful string of garden centers. Jilly was taking photos of some of the flowers when I came to check the landscaper's plans for the garden. She started to talk to me, and before I knew it I was being invited to lavish parties at the Perry residence with promises of securing more lucrative landscaping work, and somehow I became her regular date."

Candace could visualize the scene. Nick, strong, handsome, so full of drive and energy. "She fell in love with you."

He shook his head. "You're making romantic assumptions. She fell in love with the vision of what she thought she could mold me into."

Mold Nick? He must be joking! Anyone could see that this was a man who knew his own mind. This man was no one's toy.

"She couldn't get what she wanted, so like a spoiled little girl she told her father I'd seduced her and refused to marry her. Desmond and I had an angry stand-off and I told him that he, and his daughter, could go to hell. He told me that he would make sure I would marry his Jilly."

The white line around Nick's mouth warned her there was more. "What happened?"

"Bertha and Henry's bank loan was called in. Desmond

stepped in and bought the center. Then Henry discovered that Desmond, the bank manager and a developer had cooked up a scheme to establish a high-density housing development on the land. He and Bertha were devastated."

She stared at him aghast. "You're joking!"

"I wish I were. He'd found my Achilles' heel. Desmond is a very wealthy man. The banker involved was an old friend of his who held all Desmond's bank accounts."

"You could've reported the banker."

"For what? Bertha and Henry were too old to still be in debt for such a large amount, even though the value of the land more than covered the debt. But it could be argued that it was a sound business decision."

"It was immoral."

"Sure."

He smiled at her, and a chill settled in Candace's stomach. "There's more to the story, isn't there?"

"Bertha and Henry were evicted from the house on the property. The shock caused Henry to have a heart attack. I went to see Desmond full of sound and fury. Desmond told me that I could stop it all."

"How?"

"By marrying his daughter. But he didn't intend to make it easy for me—he wanted me to pay for not marrying her earlier. In return for agreeing to marry Jilly, he would sell Bertha and Henry's garden center to me at a ridiculously inflated price. He resented me. He made it quite clear that things would only get worse for Bertha and Henry if I didn't accept his deal. They would lose not only the garden center, but also the home where they'd lived for forty years. Desmond also intended to humiliate the old couple by having them declared bankrupt. The center would be sold and developed—" Nick stopped, an agonized expression on his face "—God, he's so predictable."

"Oh, Nick…" Candace could see it all. Jilly desperate for

the man of her dreams, Desmond wanting to get his way at all costs, and Nick wanting the best for the elderly couple who had given him a chance in life. "How tragic."

"I had no choice... I couldn't risk Bertha's happiness and Henry's health. It brought Henry and Bertha a future together. It was worth it. Now she has her job in the garden center—which she loves." He shrugged. "So I married Jilly. Part of the deal, in addition to a brutal repayment schedule, was that I gifted stock in Valentine's to Jilly in our prenuptial contract—a tangible hold over me for good behavior." His mouth slanted. "I had right of first refusal on buying those shares back once the full price for the Williamses' business was paid or Jilly and I had a baby—whichever came first. But she died before I made the final payment."

"But you had Jennie..."

Was that why Jilly had been so desperate to have a baby? To secure for the husband she'd trapped into a marriage he'd never wanted some degree of freedom? Candace wanted to believe Jilly had regretted the way events had played out.

Nick was shaking his head. "That is no help because, remember, I was sure Jennie wasn't mine—and now I've discovered Jennie is not Jilly's biological baby. She's yours."

"But Jilly adopted her," Candace argued. "Jennie is very much Jilly's baby. That stock is yours."

Nick shrugged. "I have a team of lawyers looking into that right now."

"What did you do after you accepted the deal?"

"I started to work like a dog so that I could repay Desmond."

"And you employed Bertha?"

"At first I tried to get her and Henry to stay in the house on the property. She's a proud old woman, and she wouldn't accept what she regarded as charity. Now I owned the garden center that had been hers and Henry's. So I offered Bertha a job and in return she and Henry got to stay in the house while working for me for four mornings a week. The rest of the time she spends with Henry."

"No wonder Bertha adores you."

"She doesn't know the half of it—" he gave her a warning glance "—and I trust she never will."

"I won't say a word."

It wasn't surprising that he didn't trust love. It was clear that he'd never loved poor, needy Jilly. In her desperation, Jilly had driven him away before any relationship between them had gotten off the ground.

"Given the state of your relationship, why the decision to start a family?"

"Jilly had always wanted a baby." Nick looked away. "She'd made that clear from the moment I placed a wedding band on her finger. I wasn't spending a lot of time home…I think she was lonely."

At the mention of their wedding Candace felt an unexpected stab of jealousy. Yet their union hadn't yielded a child. Maybe that was never meant to be. But the flip side of that coin was equally hard to accept: she and Nick couldn't possibly be meant to be, either.

Or could they?

"But something changed." Nick interrupted her thoughts. "When Jilly stopped talking about *our* baby, I became convinced she had a lover, someone she preferred to father her baby."

"Maybe she stopped thinking of the baby as *hers,*" said Candace slowly. "After all, the eggs and womb were mine. It had nothing to do with your role at all."

"That would make sense." Nick shook his head. "God, what a mess. I drew the wrong conclusion. But I didn't care enough to confront her. I was relieved—all I could think about was paying Desmond back. In the back of my mind I knew I would eventually divorce Jilly. It suited me that her child wasn't mine. It was an easy way out for me."

She touched his hand where it lay on the table. "I'm sorry, Nick."

He held her gaze. "It's not a very nice story."

"No. But you must've felt terribly trapped."

"Like my back was against the wall," he admitted.

"Yet you never took it out on Jennie."

"I wouldn't be truthful if I didn't confess that I did resent her a little—I believed she was another man's baby. But it didn't take me long to figure out she's the innocent in all this—and it's not hard to love her. She's very special."

Her fingers were still resting on his hand. It was a masculine hand with scrapes and calluses. A strong, capable hand. His fingers closed around hers. Her gaze flicked to his, only to be snared in the blazing heat.

After that, Candace couldn't have said what she ate when the main course arrived. The intensity of Nick's gaze, the way her stomach bottomed out every time their eyes met—all left her with an edgy feeling of expectation that grew as the evening wore on. She couldn't help thinking that Nick had depths she'd never expected. He'd suffered so much, worked so hard…and proven himself to be a man of honor.

A man worthy of being a father to Jennie.

Once back home, Nick followed Candace up the marble stairway.

She paused on the landing where it widened into a sitting area. "Thank you for dinner—it was lovely to get out."

There was a moment of awkward silence, then Nick muttered, "The hell with it." He stepped closer, gave her a brief chance to escape.

Candace murmured huskily, "I'll go to my room now."

Yet she didn't move.

The silence between them stretched out. Two beats. Then three. At last, when Nick was quite sure she'd had all the time in the world to make her decision, he reached for her. Candace never hesitated. She flew into his arms.

It wasn't a gentle kiss—Nick was far too aroused for that. The tension that had been rising in him for days had reached a breaking point. By the time it ended, he was breathing heavily.

Their eyes met. Something shifted, subtle, impossible to recognize.

Nick's hands came up to tangle in her silky hair, holding her so that when he lowered his head a second time his mouth slanted across hers, creating the perfect kiss.

Candace didn't object. She kissed him back with enough eager intensity for him to know that the blazing attraction was mutual.

Hunger twisted inside him, hot and wild.

When the kiss ended this time, Nick had to battle for control as tremors of anticipation quaked through him.

Slowly...

He'd thought he could leash the power, but Candace quickly proved him wrong. It didn't take much. Her hands crept up, along his shirtfront...up...until they rested on his shoulders. Rising on her toes, her tongue tip tantalized his bottom lip, shredding what little restraint he still possessed.

His hands shaking, Nick unfastened the frustratingly small buttons of the chemise-style front of her dress. The edges parted, and his fingers found the soft skin of her breasts. She wore no bra. Heat exploded in him.

Nick groaned.

"I don't know how much of this I can take," he muttered hoarsely, his hands closing over the curves.

She leaned closer, her body pressing up against his. Nick released the soft flesh, and his arms slid around her. He let his hands wander down her back, over the cotton jersey that fell in soft folds over her hips. He clasped her hips, pulled her close to him, so she could feel his body's hard response.

Candace moved in little restless circles against him. Nick's erection leaped, straining to be free.

This was more woman than he'd ever held...even in his dreams. Nick groaned again.

She nibbled his bottom lip. Nick yanked her closer so that she was plastered up against him, her softness yielding to him. The shoestring straps of her dress slid down her shoulders. He bent his head and pressed openmouthed kisses along the crest of her shoulders tasting her...inhaling the hauntingly familiar sweet, spicy scent of her until Candace shuddered in his arms.

Nick's heart pumped furiously, the blood pounding in his head.

He became aware of the chandelier blazing above them, of the backdrop of arched windows illuminating them to the deserted garden outside.

Scooping her off her feet, he headed past the closed doors of Jilly's rooms to his suite beyond. He kicked the door shut, and four long strides took him to the king-size bed with its pile of casually arranged pillows. Muted light pooled from the two bedside lamps, warming the dull gold cover. He let her slide down his torso onto the bed with excruciating slowness, tormenting him, prolonging the pleasure. By now he was shaking inside, the desire he'd been suppressing spilling over.

"God, but you're beautiful."

With the straps already half-down her arms, and the bodice open, Nick pushed the dress over her hips. Underneath she wore tiny lace panties. Those went next. Grabbing the collar of his shirt, he yanked it—still buttoned—hurriedly over his head. Undoing his belt, then his pants, he shucked them off. They landed in a heap on the carpet.

Then he followed her down onto the bed among the mountain of dull gold and black cushions.

Her skin was pale and creamy. *Luscious.* He touched her

with a trembling hand. So soft. So warm. Impatience clawed at him. He stroked her, his fingertips exploring the rise of her breasts, the valley between, the flat plain of her stomach. Driven by increasing desperation, he sought out the sweetest, most responsive spots.

By the time his hand found the moist skin between her inner thighs, she was damp and superbly responsive. He slid two fingers into the moist channel. Her hips came off the bed, and Nick almost came apart.

He couldn't do this. He couldn't wait...

There was a moment when he thought about the new pack of condoms in his bedside drawer, then he abandoned it. What did it matter if he impregnated her? He was going to marry her. Nick wasn't conscious of making the decision—he simply knew that it was the right one.

"I'm sorry," he whispered, drawing his fingers out. She shuddered, her hips undulating. "I can't wait."

Nick shifted over her, covering her.

"Are you okay? I'm not too heavy?" He caught a glimpse of her incandescent silver eyes as she shook her head forcefully, her hair whipping around her face.

Then her legs tangled with his for a moment before they parted, granting him the access he'd only fantasized about before. He pressed into the space, his heart thundering.

She'd borne his child.

"Take me," she murmured.

All thought dissolved as her hands slid into the tight space between them and closed around the length of him.

Nick gritted his teeth. "I can't hold back."

Surging forward, the blunt length of him pushed into her readied softness. Nick fought against the strength of the sensations that shook him as her heat swallowed him; he fought to hold on, to give her time to catch up.

"I've never been this hot," he whispered, and licked the soft skin behind her ear.

She arched up beneath him and gasped.

Nick clutched her buttocks and drove deeper. Pleasure ripped through him.

One. Two. Three thrusts.

Candace gasped again and flung her head back.

It was enough to send Nick spinning into oblivion. He shot deep inside her womb, where his child had lain, and then the passion and heat consumed them both.

Nothing had ever felt more right to Nick.

Candace opened her eyes—and the sight of the dark gold bedcover caused her to freeze. She didn't need the shafts of sunbeams or the sinking sensation in her stomach to tell her she'd fallen asleep in Nick Valentine's bed.

She jerked fully awake.

Jennie…did Jennie need her?

Then she remembered. Jennie was spending the night with Nick's sister. She rolled over, and gazed straight into Nick's lazy eyes.

"Hello," he said softly.

His hand came up and brushed a strand of hair off her cheek. She managed not to flinch as heat arced through her. Shifting, her legs brushed against his naked ones beneath the sheets.

A fiery tide of embarrassment swept over her. Candace swallowed and anchored the silk sheet under her arms so that it wouldn't shift. "This is so awkward."

"Why?" His lips curved up. "Don't feel that away. After all, we have a daughter—this should've happened a long time ago. We've done things the wrong way around."

Oh, help!

A tender, teasing Nick Valentine was more than she could handle. How could she ever have thought those beautiful indigo eyes remote and inscrutable? The warmth and fire and emotion that filled them now tore at her heart.

She remembered how his passion had grown to a strange, very moving desperation last night.

He'd made her feel so special.

But now in the light of the morning after, it felt…wrong.

His fingers trailed down her cheek and came to a rest in the hollow of her throat. He caressed the sensitized, bare skin, and Candace was conscious of his square-tipped fingers touching her…slipping closer to the edge of the sheet trapped above her breasts.

And under the sheets his body was naked.

So was hers…

What had she done? All she could think of was that it was going to be impossible to keep working in Nick's home. How could she have jeopardized everything? Her relationship with her daughter, her position in Nick's house? Stupid. Stupid. Stupid.

And for what?

One night of desperate passion? That was forever going to lurk between them; they would never be able to put it to rest. She was going to have to leave. Leave Jennie.

Her heart clenched in pain.

And leave Nick.

The cold ache that numbed her chest was as unexpected as it was unwelcome.

No.

It couldn't possibly hurt to think of leaving Nick…

No. No. *No.* He meant nothing to her.

Yet the denial did nothing to ease the ache as she remembered how he'd listened to Bertha yesterday, how he'd laughed when his sister had tormented him about having to kiss Princess Piggy, how he'd ripped her heart out when he'd told her about his hollow marriage at dinner last night.

She couldn't possibly have—

No, she didn't want to think about it. Falling in love with Nick would be the stupidest thing she'd ever done.

"Come here." He pulled her into his arms.

For a split second, Candace resisted, then she let herself be drawn up against him. Shivers of delight raced through her as his bare skin brushed hers. He kissed her. Her mouth blossomed beneath his, opening, taking him into her, drawing him deep.

With a shock she realized how easy it would be to succumb.

Candace tore out of his arms, putting the length of the bed between them.

"Nick—no." Her breathing was ragged. She paused for a moment. "I don't want to make love again."

"You don't mean that—"

"I do," she said with a firmness she was far from feeling. "It's not going to happen again. This was the one and only time."

The soft light went out of his eyes. "Don't dismiss something you might regret losing later."

"Believe me, I won't regret this. We can't be lovers. It won't work." She said it with a finality that she hoped was convincing. And prayed he wouldn't recognize the undertone of desperation in her voice.

Twelve

The throaty roar of the Ferrari coming up the driveway caused the tension that had been lurking in the pit of Candace's stomach since Nick had made love to her two days ago to tighten another notch.

Run. Hide.

The anxiety that had been gnawing at her resurfaced. *You're not in love with him.* Candace sharply pulled herself together. There was no need to run, and she wasn't retreating to hide in the nursery. She was going to stay seated right where she was—on the carpet of the upstairs sitting room, playing with Jennie.

"You're losing it," she admonished herself. "Nick's home. So what?"

The memory of the time he'd kissed her here in this very place after she'd held the ice pack to his head flashed through her mind. Oh, God. Nowhere was safe from him, from the emotions he aroused in her.

Then Jennie gurgled, and, as always, Candace's heart warmed.

The baby's smile put everything in perspective.

She'd done nothing wrong. So she'd slept with Nick Valentine—a foolish mistake. Hardly the love of a lifetime. She had to keep telling herself that. Despite the starbursts of intense pleasure the experience had released, despite the sense of inevitability about what had happened, it was an error of judgment she bitterly regretted.

But there was no reason for it to cause her this much distress.

Except if there were consequences…

Candace told herself there wouldn't be. It was the wrong time of month. But she'd been reckless. *Stupid.* It was time to come to terms with what had happened, take the necessary steps to deal with any unfortunate circumstances and move on. She couldn't allow every thought of Nick to keep causing her heart palpitations.

The only problem was that Nick was making it incredibly difficult to put that night behind her.

Every look, every comment, seemed to be calculated to throw her into a state of confusion, where desire warred with good sense.

Even now, the sound of his footsteps coming up the marble stairway made her pulse go wild.

Nick was coming!

For one panicky moment Candace wished she'd retreated to the nursery when she'd had the opportunity. Then she steadied herself.

Get over it.

But the sight of his grim face knocked her off the frivolous emotional seesaw of her own dilemma.

"What's wrong?"

Something terrible had clearly happened.

Nick crossed the carpet, tossed a large envelope on the coffee table, and reached for Jennie.

"Nick…" The cold, set expression on his face as he lifted the baby into his arms unnerved her. "What's *happened?*"

He turned his head and gazed at her over the baby's head. There was a blank opacity in his eyes that made her heart stop. "Talk to me," she said. "You're scaring me."

"Desmond—" He broke off, burying his face in Jennie's neck.

"What about him?" What could his father-in-law have done to evoke this kind of reaction?

"He wants Jennie."

"What do you mean?" Chills goosed over her skin. "What's going on?"

"He's launched legal action." Nick raised his head and nodded toward the envelope he'd cast onto the table. "He wants custody of Jennie."

Candace covered her face with her hands. "Oh, my God." Spreading her fingers, she raised her head and stared helplessly at Nick. "Will he get it?"

"Not while I breathe." Determination turned his voice to steel. "He has money and power, but so do I. And this time I'm going to fight him."

"Why is he doing this?"

Nick hesitated, then said reluctantly, "He claims that I am a womanizer, that Jennie is neglected. It appears it was sparked by seeing you with me at the carnival—perhaps he thought I'd defiled his daughter's memory. That I'd already replaced her…with you."

That only made her feel so much worse. Because Desmond hadn't been wrong. By the end of the day she had been in Nick's bed. Jilly's bed. Oh, darn…

How sordid.

So much for putting it all behind her. It was proving to be impossible.

"Surely he won't have a case? He'd have to prove you grossly neglected Jennie." Anyone could see that wasn't true. Jennie was exploring the buttons of his chest, so at home in his arms that it brought a lump to Candace's throat.

Nick's mouth slanted up. "Even you thought that was true at one time."

"But not anymore." And that was true.

"He'll call Jilly's friends as witnesses to say I never cared for her, that I ignored her while we were married. Emotional abuse, they'll call it."

"But it was understandable," Candace defended him. "And it doesn't relate to Jennie."

"The same people will say that I wasn't interested in Jilly's pregnancy, that I wasn't even present for the baby's birth, that I went away for long periods for work and didn't even return when my child was ill—and it's all true."

He sounded so wretched that Candace's heart went out to him.

Nick settled down on the carpet beside her. Jennie stretched her hands out to the toys scattered around Candace, and he set her down. Both of them watched the baby as she tried to crawl toward the nearest blocks.

"How could I ever have known that she would wrap herself around my heart?" His gaze met Candace's. "I won't lose her. Desmond doesn't realize what he's started. I've already instructed my lawyers to oppose it. I think his suit is based on a pack of lies, but I'm not prepared to risk losing." Nick shifted closer. "Candace, we're going to make it clear he has no claim to Jennie—no biological tie exists between Jennie and Desmond."

"But Jilly adopted Jennie."

"I'm still waiting for proof that the adoption went through. You and I are Jennie's biological parents—and we both love her." His hand settled on hers where it pressed into the carpet.

"I don't think this is about Jennie—I think this is about clinging on to Jilly. He can't accept that she's gone."

Candace shifted her weight to enable her to turn her hand palm up, and laced her fingers with his, drawing immeasurable comfort from his touch. She'd been so careful to stay out of Nick's reach for the past couple of days in case she gave away her newly discovered feelings to him. The tender emotions were so precious, she had to shelter them from the bruising and battering that were inevitable.

But this time his touch wasn't about sex. It was about so much more.

"It must be hard for Desmond to have lost his daughter." Watching Jennie playing, she couldn't stop a twinge of sympathy for Jilly's father from stirring within her. How terrible to lose a child. "Poor man."

"Don't waste too much sympathy on him. I'm sure he only came up with this idea after seeing you with me on Sunday."

"You don't suppose—" She broke off, not wanting to voice the unkind thought.

"I don't suppose...what?"

"You spoke about Desmond trying to hurt you through Alison on Sunday. You don't suppose he's only doing this to hurt you again? That it's not about Jennie at all?"

Nick didn't respond, but the grip of his fingers grew tighter. Jennie was gnawing at a block. Her gums had been swollen, the next tooth would be through very soon.

"Such an overreaction would be insane," she said finally, hoping her response wasn't misplaced.

"Not for Desmond," said Nick slowly. "He's more than capable of that kind of malice. I simply hadn't considered that he might want to hurt me that much."

She turned her head and met his gaze. "Why would he want to do such a thing?"

"It's a power thing...he couldn't get me to bend to his will. Perhaps he thinks Jennie would be my breaking point."

"And would she be?"

Candace held her breath as she waited for his answer. This was crucially important, far more important than the throwaway tone of the question suggested.

There was a flash of something...vulnerability?...in the navy depths of his eyes. "It would kill me to lose Jennie."

The simple intensity of his response rocked her to the foundations of her existence. *He cared.* Candace wasn't sure why it mattered so much, only that it did.

He loved Jennie.

She placed her other hand over his, cradling his hand between both of hers. Her love for him flowed through her fingers, and she hoped it would give him the strength he needed to do what was right.

Without taking his eyes from her, he raised her hands and placed a kiss very carefully, first on the back of one hand, then on the other.

A rush of emotion overtook her.

Currents electrified the space between them. A compelling need to defuse the sudden tension vibrating between them made her say with forced lightness, "Boy, you certainly picked the family to marry into."

Nick shook his head. "They did the picking."

She remembered what he'd told her about how Jilly and her father had all but blackmailed him into marriage, and his suppressed frustration became totally understandable.

At last she said, "What are we going to do?"

We?

Nick stared at the woman sitting, legs outstretched, on the floor beside him, while their baby inched forward half crawling, half sliding as she tried to reach for a brightly colored ball. The firm hold of Candace's hand warmed him.

"It's not your problem," he said automatically.

Her eyes sparkled. "Of course it's my problem. I'm Jennie's mother. You're not going to leave me out in the cold on this."

"It would weaken Desmond's crazy suit to announce that Jennie is not Jilly's child—she's yours." It was a dangerous move. And it would give Candace an advantage that he would never be able to regain. Still, it might be a risk worth taking. "That way Desmond can claim no biological tie with the baby."

"It will cause a scandal."

"I don't care." But he hadn't thought about how it would affect her, and he discovered that he didn't have any desire to see her hurt or humiliated. "Will it matter to you if I announce it to the world?"

"Of course not!" A luminosity lit her gray eyes that made her more beautiful than ever. "I can think of nothing more wonderful than being publicly branded as Jennie's mother."

The moment of truth had come—if he announced that she was Jennie's mother, there would be no going back, there'd be no more talk of her leaving...

When she'd first told him that she was Jennie's mother, he'd wanted her out of the baby's life at all costs. But she'd called to something deep and dark and primitive in him, something he didn't fully comprehend.

All Nick knew was that he wasn't going to let her go.

The decision he'd come to the night he'd lost his senses returned from where he'd buried it at the back of his consciousness...it was a plan. A plan that might even work.

Thinking about it, he realized it was a team solution. *We.* He was starting to like the sound of that.

"Then marry me," he said simply.

"What?"

Her eyes darkened with disbelief.

"If you marry me, then as her biological parents we will be

able to show any judge that living with us is the best solution for Jennie. Together we will refute any evidence that Desmond might choose to present that Jennie is neglected. She has a father and mother who love her, and a safe and secure home. What more could any child need?"

And best of all, not only would he get to keep Jennie... Candace would never be able to leave.

"It's the best solution for Jennie," said Nick.

The best solution for Jennie? If she married him, Candace knew she would get hurt. Marrying a man she was falling in love with, living with him day by day, but never loved by him in return...

It sounded like hell on earth.

In her shock she couldn't think of anything logical to say, so she stated the obvious. "I'm not the kind of woman a man like you marries."

"What is the kind of woman a man like me marries?" One dark eyebrow arched up. "Someone like Jilly?"

Help.

"She'd be better suited to be your wife than me."

"I have to disagree." One of his hands let hers go and he cupped her face, his thumb stroking her jawline. "I don't think anyone would make a better mother for Jennie than you would."

Her insides melted.

"You might even already be pregnant with a sister or brother to Jennie. I didn't use protection the other night—or are you on the pill?"

Unfair.

"No, I'm not. But it's highly unlikely...I've already worked it out. So don't feel you have to marry me for that reason."

"I don't have to do anything. But marrying me will be the best thing to do."

Why was he suggesting this? Nick had spent seven years

in a loveless union. Last time he'd been trapped into it. This time he was volunteering it of his own accord. What was he thinking by proposing such an arrangement?

The answer came to her at once.

He was doing it for Jennie.

Nick was prepared to sacrifice himself. Out of his love for his daughter.

For Jennie.

Candace glanced down at the baby playing obliviously with blocks…and her heart ached. Tears pricked at the back of her throat. She'd come here to work as Jennie's nanny because she'd been convinced that Nick was neglecting her baby. She'd known he didn't love Jennie with the same depth of emotion that she did. She'd been ready to take Jennie away.

Now he'd just proved conclusively how much he loved their daughter.

Drawing a deep shaky breath, Candace returned her attention to the man who had turned all her assumptions about him upside down. "But what about you?" It was a cry from her heart. She didn't want him to give up so much for his daughter. "It's certainly not the best solution for you—you'll be trapped in a marriage you don't want all over again."

"This time it will be different."

Her heart leaped. Was it possible that he was starting to feel the same way about her as she felt about him?

Candace was almost afraid to ask. Her heart was beating so hard she was sure he must hear it, sitting so close to her. "How will it be different?"

She tensed, wired, every nerve ending expectant as she waited for his answer.

One finger trailed down her cheek, leaving a trail of fire in its wake. "This time I will have a lover."

So he hadn't said he loved her. But *lover* was good, wasn't it? Candace wavered. No, she decided, she wanted more; she needed him to tell her he loved her. Choosing her words carefully, she asked, "But how will this be different? Jilly was your lover, too."

The teasing finger stilled. "I never made love to Jilly."

Was he saying that he'd only had sex with his dead wife, that he'd never loved her? Did that mean he loved her, Candace?

"I know you didn't love her."

"I didn't love her, nor did I *make* love to her."

"What do you mean…?" Voice trailing away, she waited. Was Nick saying something else altogether…something she could hardly believe was true?

"You've seen my bedroom. It was mine alone. Jilly had her own suite, her own bed. I never shared it. We never slept together." His mouth compressed at her incredulous look. "There was no sex. Not for seven long years."

"You once told me there were no other women—" Candace broke off unable to finish.

"That's right."

My God.

No wonder he'd been so…*desperate*. Now he was telling her that he expected their marriage to have sex. Yet he'd never said he loved her.

Stupid! He wasn't marrying her because he loved her. He was marrying her to gain Jennie a set of biological parents—a set of parents who loved their daughter and would make it clear to any court.

Nick was making the same mistake of going into a loveless marriage with the best intentions for the wrong reasons all over again. Except this time, instead of saving Bertha and Henry, he was trying to save Jennie. And this time sex would be part of the deal.

The pain below her heart grew more intense.

Nick Valentine deserved to find a woman he could really love. For all his life. Candace wished that woman were her. But it wouldn't be her. Even though he was the father of her baby…and the man she loved.

Nick would never be hers.

Shaking her head, she said slowly, "I'm sorry Nick, I can't marry you."

Not even for Jennie.

Nick had retreated to the sanctuary of his study, where he'd poured himself one measure of single-malt Scotch, then collapsed onto the burgundy love seat.

He'd been so certain she would say yes.

If Candace married him, it would've been a tidy solution, and Jennie would've been safe. He couldn't fathom why she'd refused the most sensible course of action under the circumstances.

There'd been flashes of time over the past few days when he could've sworn she desired him almost as much as he craved her. It had been there in the way her gaze flicked to him, then quickly away, in the soft flush of color that followed, in the slight stutter she developed when he stood too close.

But she'd turned him down flat.

Well, he supposed it served him right for being so sure of her.

He raised the heavy crystal glass to his lips and took a sip, savoring the smoky flavor.

It wasn't over yet. Nick was determined to escalate that reciprocal passion he'd sensed in her. He was convinced he could change her *no* to a *yes*.

He knew he didn't have a lot of time. He'd have to move fast if he wanted a marriage to thwart the thorn in his side that Desmond had become. He had to move now.

If he wanted to keep Candace.

Thirteen

Nick had rarely entered Jilly's suite of rooms during their marriage.

Now as he crossed the threshold he noticed that it smelled… empty…like a hotel room long deserted. The curtains were drawn, dimming the room. He flicked the light switch, picked up a remote and activated it. The curtains opened and sunlight filtered in through the lacy blinds beneath.

The bedcover in Jilly's signature gray and white and lime lay smooth and uncreased. Two crystal perfume bottles stood on the dresser, and a Lalique vase stuffed with silk tulips occupied a writing desk beside the windows.

Feeling like an intruder, Nick crossed to where a dressing room opened off Jilly's en suite. Her clothes had already been packed up and given to charity. The wall safe was empty. Nick had placed Jilly's jewels in a bank deposit box in trust for Jennie, the day after the funeral.

Any hope that he might discover secrets that had not died with Jilly was fading rapidly. The bathroom cupboards held only unopened toiletries, clean towels and a hairdryer. Impersonal items waiting for the next occupant. The personal items Jilly had used were long gone.

Back in her bedroom he checked the dresser drawers, her bedside table…all empty…as he'd expected. He'd gone through them himself. Nick moved on to her writing desk, already knowing what he'd find.

The first drawer revealed her wallet, a checkbook, an expired passport and a folder of canceled credit cards. The next drawer down contained Jilly's lime-green laptop and an iPhone. The final drawer held a box of Jilly's gold embossed stationery, envelopes, her address book…exactly as she'd left them. He lifted the stationery box out and opened it. Letterheads with *Jilly Valentine* surrounded by tiny pink hearts. He smiled. How Jilly. There were thank-you notes, too. He put the box back and started to close the drawer, then paused.

Taking out the stationery box again, he lifted the large black address book, and pulled out a second black volume. Jilly's appointment book. Next he opened the drawer above and extracted her laptop with its power cable.

Seating himself on the padded desk chair, Nick flipped open the cover of the five-year appointment book. Finally he booted the laptop up. In less time than expected he'd found a file labeled *Journal*. Opening it, Nick started to read.

The following morning, Nick strode past an unsuspecting receptionist and, at the end of the corridor, entered the corner office unannounced.

Desmond Perry sat behind his desk, puffed up as an angry toad. Red-faced, he demanded, "What's the meaning of bursting into my office like this?"

Nick took a seat in one of the two chairs in front of the desk, and leaned back. "If you prefer, I can arrange to see you another time with my lawyer in attendance. Or you can listen to what I have to say now."

Desmond stopped blustering. "What do you want?"

"I want you to stop harassing my sister and brother-in-law and tell your crony at NorthPark to withdraw his eviction notice." Nick paused, while Desmond stared at him. "I want you to forget about trying to acquire enough of a stake in Valentine's to force a takeover—yes, I know about your plan to develop the land, not for high-density apartments, but for a shopping mall in partnership with NorthPark."

"How did—"

Nick held up a hand. "And you're going to halt all legal action to get custody of Jennie."

"Why should I do anything you want?"

Nick started with what was most important to him first. *Jennie*. "Jennie isn't Jilly's daughter."

"I know that."

It appeared that Candace was right; Desmond was only trying to hurt him though his daughter, enough to make him pursue a frivolous legal suit purely to frustrate Nick. But did he know who her real mother was?

"Then you know you have no right to her."

The older man picked up a pen and tapped it against the wooden edge of the desk. "My daughter adopted her—she's my grandchild."

Nick's first reaction was to lean over the desk and punch Desmond, as he'd been dying to do for weeks. Instead, he said, "I intend to challenge that adoption. I don't want my daughter growing up like Jilly did, with a guardian whose only way of showing his love is to buy her whatever she wants."

Desmond blinked, and Nick regretted his hotheaded reply. The man had lost a daughter. Then he remembered the pain that had poured out in Jilly's diary. It was no wonder that the only way she knew to respond to being in love was to try to buy the loved one.

It had been a disastrous course of action; but spoiled, emotionally starved Jilly had been too insecure to know any other way.

Nick held his father-in-law's gaze, until Desmond looked away first.

"I found the journal Jilly kept. It made for very interesting reading." That jerked Desmond's attention back to him, Nick noticed with satisfaction. "She poured everything into it— even the reason why the IVF was done offshore—she knew she would never get her harebrained scheme past the ethics committee that approves surrogate arrangements in New Zealand. When I gave the necessary signature for my sperm to be transferred offshore, I had no knowledge that it wouldn't be used to impregnate my wife, but rather the surrogate she had chosen."

Jilly had written of her overriding need for a baby to fill the emptiness of her life. That had caused Nick a pang of guilt. He'd been so busy resenting Jilly for forcing him into an untenable situation that he'd never tried to figure out what had been behind her desire for a child. Jilly had also written about her craving to experience pregnancy firsthand. Nick could only assume that longing had triggered the fake pregnancy she'd enacted—together with the desperation for Jennie to be seen as *her* child.

Watching Desmond carefully, Nick added, "New Zealand law requires the baby's real mother to be listed on the birth certificate. Jilly bribed the midwife who tended to the baby's birth to state that Jilly was the baby's mother." When Candace had first claimed to be Jennie's mother, Nick had known it was impossible. According to the birth certificate, Jilly was Jennie's mother. Jilly's journal had solved another piece of the puzzle.

Heaven knew what else Jilly had done.

It was time to play his hand. "The baby's birth certificate will be corrected." He hoped to attend to the change quietly.

Jennie's status as Candace's daughter was something he intended to handle as tactfully as he could. "Do you want your daughter's fraud to be made public? The fact that she lied to me, her husband, about being pregnant while forging my consent to a surrogacy arrangement? About bribing medical practitioners to go along with fertilizing another woman's egg and implanting it offshore into that woman without my knowledge and consent? About paying off a midwife to falsify a birth certificate? Do you want people to know how mentally frail she was? How your years of emotional neglect affected her?"

Desmond started to object, then he stopped.

"You've worked to build a media image as a philanthropist, a devoted father to Jilly. Desmond, do you want that tainted?" Nick pressed on. "Do you want the real story of your troubled relationship with your daughter made public? The facts of how she manipulated the surrogate system exposed, along with how she bribed medical officials?"

Holding his breath, Nick waited. Would it be enough to persuade Desmond to back down?

"No," Desmond conceded at last. He tossed aside the pen he'd been fiddling with, and spat out, "I'd rather she was remembered as the beautiful, happy woman she was before she married you."

Nick nodded. "I was not the right man for her—there can be no doubt about that." He regretted the years he and Jilly had both wasted. From Jilly's journal he'd learned that in her way she did love him, and she'd come to realize her mistake in forcing him into a union he didn't want. That had been one of the motivations for a baby. To bring them closer together. She'd thought that Nick needed a child—she'd viewed him as a great prospective father. That had deeply touched Nick, giving him a way forward to remember Jilly in a kinder way.

And Jilly had done more…

"Inside Jilly's journal, I also discovered a codicil Jilly

added to her will, leaving her stock in Valentine's to me." The codicil was dated shortly before Jennie was born. Nick was grateful she'd taken time to create it.

Desmond picked up the pen again. "My lawyer told me Jilly had instructed him to draw up a codicil, but he didn't have the signed document. We decided she'd had second thoughts."

"She signed it. And it's witnessed. It's valid. I've sent it to my lawyer," Nick said. "He'll communicate with the lawyer handling Jilly's estate."

After a long moment, Desmond gave a sigh. He looked less arrogant—and much older—than when Nick had first entered the large corner office. "It looks like there's not much for me to say."

"You'll drop the suit for custody?"

Desmond gave a terse nod.

"You will agree to speak to NorthPark about having Alison and Richard's eviction notice revoked?" Again a nod. "And you will stop pursuing Valentine stock?"

"I'll do what you want." There was still anger on the older man's face.

Nick reminded himself that Desmond had lost his daughter tragically, unexpectedly, and whatever their convoluted father-daughter relationship, he'd loved Jilly in his own way.

Although Nick wanted as little as possible to do with Desmond in the future, he didn't want the man to be an enemy, forever scheming how to hurt him. There'd been a moment earlier when he'd itched to hit Desmond; he was relieved that he hadn't.

It would've made him less of a man in his own eyes—and he knew that Candace would've hated to hear that he'd used violence against a father who must still be grieving.

Bottom line: he wanted the feud with Jilly's father to be over. To that end he said, "I plan to build a children's playground at the flagship Valentine's in Jilly's memory."

Desmond studied him warily. "I'd like you to open it—I'll make sure the event has plenty of publicity."

"Jilly would've appreciated that. Thank you." The anger started to fade from Desmond's face. "Perhaps you could build a bench somewhere with a plaque dedicating it to her. She loved flowers."

"I could do that. There's a rose garden where Jilly often took photographs, with a sundial in the center. A bench would fit in perfectly. Many people could sit and enjoy the surroundings."

Desmond nodded slowly. "I might come and sit there myself."

"Good." He could tolerate that, Nick decided, rising to his feet. He held out his hand. "I'm glad we've resolved our differences." He only hoped the coming confrontation with Candace was going to proceed as smoothly.

Nick knew Desmond Perry would no longer present a threat to his family.

Candace was reclining on a lounger in the shade under the poolside umbrella, rubbing the fluff that was Jennie's hair dry after a lunchtime swim in the pool, when she heard the scrape of the sliding doors and looked up.

Her pulse picked up as Nick emerged from the house. He'd left early for work this morning, and Candace discovered that she'd missed him. She'd gotten used to the three of them—Nick, Jennie and her—sharing breakfast on the deck on the sunny early mornings but he'd kept himself away since she'd turned down his proposal.

It had left her feeling restless.

Sitting up, she set down the towel and pulled the T-shirt Jennie wore straight, then checked to see that the sarong she'd donned over her own damp swimsuit hadn't parted to reveal her tummy or legs. Since she'd made love with Nick, she'd taken great care not to allow any opportunity for those burning moments of awareness to arise.

"She's a real water baby," she remarked, stroking Jennie's head before glancing back up to Nick.

"The signs were always there," said Nick. He barely glanced at Candace's scantily clad body as he pulled up a chair from the table arrangement where they ate in the morning. "I need to talk to you."

His face was stern.

"Yes?"

"Desmond has agreed to withdraw the application for custody of Jennie."

She couldn't stop the huge grin that lit up her face. "That's fabulous news. Nick, I'm so relieved. When?"

"As we speak. My lawyers are talking to his."

"Oh, I could hug you." Then she wished she hadn't added they last bit as his face remained set. Nick didn't even joke in response. Something was wrong. "There's more isn't there?"

"I found Jilly's journal and I've been reading her appointment book."

He paused.

Candace waited, feeling puzzled at the withdrawal she sensed in him. On her lap, Jennie grew restless.

"Do you know that you're not named as Jennie's mother on the birth certificate?"

She frowned at the switch in subject. "You said that when I first told you I was Jennie's mother. I thought you'd simply never seen it." It had seemed typical of the remote, uninvolved father she'd pegged him to be. "That can't be right."

She didn't like the way he was watching her, like a dark panther waiting to pounce on the first slip she made. She swung her legs to the ground so that she was perched on the edge of the lounger. Spreading the biggest towel on the deck in front of the lounger, she placed Jennie on it and handed her a teething ring. Immediately, Jennie started to chew.

"You had a midwife at the birth."

"Yes—Jilly wanted the home experience, she thought it would give you and her a better chance to bond with the baby than a hospital birth, where your involvement would be minimal." Candace paused. "She even said you'd decided not to be present because you would be overseas. Thinking about it now, you wouldn't even have known about the birth, right?"

He shook his head. "I didn't. Jilly told me she was three weeks off her due date, that it would be a good time to take a trip to meet three new suppliers…and on the way home I attended a gardeners' conference. I thought there was still plenty of time."

"Oh." It put paid to another assumption she'd made. "It was fortunate for Jilly the timing worked out."

"Yes." He was still watching her, but the flat line of his mouth had softened.

Candace found she was breathing easier. "When you failed to turn up at Jennie's birth, I started to grow truly worried about what kind of father you would be. I told Jilly I wished I hadn't signed away my right to stay in contact with the baby after the birth. Jilly was quick to point out that she'd always made it clear that you didn't really want to know about the surrogate, that you wanted to pretend the baby was Jilly's. But I couldn't understand how any father would want to miss such a momentous occasion."

"It certainly wasn't part of Jilly's plan for you to stay in the picture. I discovered from my reading that Jilly bribed the midwife to list her as the mother on the birth certificate."

"I never knew that." Candace thought about it as she watched Jennie toss the ring down, then pick it up again and shove it back in her mouth. "But it makes sense. That's why she wanted a home birth with a midwife?" Sadness swept her.

"I would've been happier at the hospital, given that Jennie was my first child and anything could've gone wrong. But it was so important to her that I gave in."

"Is there anything else you want to tell me?"

Even over the two yards separating them, she could sense his tension.

It was hardly a good time to confess the one aspect of her behavior she wasn't proud of. It would be better to wait for a time when Nick was more open to discussion. Candace knew she was putting it off. When would there ever be an easy time?

She drew a deep breath and squarely met Nick's indigo gaze. "Yes. Jilly gave me money."

Nick's almost black gaze bored into her. "You lied to me. You told me you weren't paid for being a surrogate."

"I wasn't," she said automatically. "You—I mean Jilly—paid for the medical expenses and she covered my other expenses. The one thing she did pay for that I didn't want was the stay in the resort when the IVF was done. And she spoiled me with gifts when she visited during the pregnancy…I didn't have the heart to refuse because it gave her such pleasure. But this payment was different."

"How?" He gave a snort.

"It was a large sum."

"Okay." He nodded. "So when did she give you money? Did you call her?"

"No! I wasn't ever supposed to make contact again." Candace glanced down at Jennie again, remembering how the despair in the empty days after Jennie's birth had sapped her. "After I'd given Jennie up, she called to see how I was."

Then she lifted her gaze to Nick's, hoping he couldn't sense her inner shaking or recognize the fear and vulnerability. "I was a mess. Jilly came around to see me—she didn't bring Jennie. When I first heard her car pull up, I hoped with a desperate yearning I can't even begin to describe to you that she'd reconsidered, that she was prepared to relax the noncontact clause in the surrogate contract. But she was alone. I told her that my mother was in the hospital after falling off a ladder in the pantry. She was unconscious, and brain damage was suspected. I started to cry. I couldn't stop. I didn't know what I was going to do. You probably won't believe me, but Jilly gave me comfort."

"I do believe you. Jilly liked to be needed. Too many of the people in her life didn't need her at all," Nick said slowly. "It may be part of the reason she was so eager for a baby."

"When it became clear that my mother was going to need care, Jilly offered to pay for her place at Apple Orchards."

"So in the end you did accept payment for Jennie."

Candace shook her head frantically. "*No*. It was never meant to be like that! How could you think that I'd accept a womb-for-hire arrangement?" It hurt that he'd assumed the worst. "I kept saying no, but Jilly insisted. I gave in, because it made my life, and Mom's, easier."

Nick didn't say anything. He just stared at her with a blank expression, the muscle high on his cheek pulsing furiously.

"You know what?" The shaking had taken over her whole body. "I'll tell you something I haven't even admitted to myself. I felt so guilty later. Because deep down I feel like I traded Jennie for my mother's comfort. And even telling Jilly I would try to pay her back didn't help ease the guilt. We both knew it was far beyond my means."

"I'm sorry." Nick rose to his feet and settled himself beside her on the lounger, and groped awkwardly for her hand. "I found reference to the payment she'd made—and I jumped to the conclusion you'd taken money in exchange for Jennie. Jilly liked you," he added after a small silence. "There was an entry after one of the times she'd spoken to you at the hospital, saying how sympathetic you were. She worked hard to become friendly with you."

Candace gripped his hand, and the trembling started to

subside. "I liked her, too. But I felt a little sorry for her…she was so desperate for the child she couldn't have."

"She sensed that she could manipulate you…I suspect she might have helped your mother because she felt remorse about it."

"How awful."

"Not that awful." Nick tipped his head in the direction of the baby sitting on the towel in front of them. "It gave us both Jennie."

The distance she'd sensed between them when he first came out had gone.

"And I met you." Nick gave her a bittersweet smile. "That would never have happened if not for Jilly."

Before Candace could respond, he'd risen to his feet.

"I'd better get back to work. I have several appointments this afternoon about the company's expansion into the South Island and the sooner I get them over, the sooner I can be home again." He paused, and then said, "Perhaps we can go and see your mother on the weekend. I'd like to meet her."

Fourteen

"Oh, you've brought Jennie back for a visit." Catherine Morrison stood in the open doorway of her large sunny bedroom. "Come, bring her stroller in."

The first thought Nick had on meeting Candace's mother was that Jennie had been here before. The second was that he could see where Candace had gotten her lovely gray eyes. And that led him to realize that Jennie would, in all probability, be blessed with a pair of angel eyes, too.

His final realization was that Catherine had no idea Jennie was her granddaughter.

"Jennie fell asleep in the car, and we managed to get her into the stroller without her waking. Mom, this is Nick Valentine," said Candace.

Catherine inspected him curiously, and then smiled, a lovely gentle smile that reminded him immeasurably of Candace. "I'm pleased to meet you."

"Sit by the window, Nick." Candace pointed to a sofa covered with roses. "Mom can sit next to you. I'll sit on the bed."

"We could go down to the lounge," suggested her mother. "There's a lot more space down there."

Candace wrinkled her nose.

"The lounge was full of people playing bingo." Nick grinned conspiratorially at Catherine. "It will be too noisy to talk."

Catherine nodded slowly. "I'd forgotten about the bingo."

"We'll take a walk down to the roses a bit later." Candace perched herself on the bed, Jennie's stroller beside her.

"You like roses," Nick said to the older woman.

Her eyes lit up. "Oh, yes…but you could've guessed that from my room."

Glancing around, Nick took in the design of the sofa, the creamy white roses in the vase on the dresser and the photo of a pale pink, old-fashioned damask rose printed onto a canvas block that hung above the bed. Jilly's work. He studied it. The photograph revealed all the best sides of Jilly. Her femininity. Her passion for beauty. He could see why Candace had chosen it for her mother.

"That was my birthday present. Candace chose it for me."

"Yes, I know."

"Do you know Candace well?"

"Mom—"

"Are you…" Catherine's voice trailed away and she glanced at Candace. "What does one call it these days? He's too sophisticated to be called a boyfriend."

Candace had gone bright red, and Nick started to smile. Then he took pity on her. "You can tell your mom if you want."

"He *is* your boyfriend." Catherine looked delighted. "You were so sad when you came back from your trip, I thought you'd had your heart broken." She clapped her hand over her mouth. "Sorry."

Nick quickly reassured her. "I didn't break her heart."

"Mom—" Candace got up from the bed and crossed over

to perch herself on the arm of the sofa beside her mother. "I have to apologize to you. I've been keeping a secret from you. There was no trip. I agreed to help a woman—have a baby. I agreed to donate my eggs and carry the baby for her. Part of the agreement was that I'd keep it a secret. I should've told you."

Catherine made the connection immediately; she glanced at the stroller and back to Candace. "Jennie is your daughter."

She touched Candace's hand, and Nick's throat closed at the tender empathy in the gesture. How different Jilly's life could've been with a mother like Catherine.

"It must've hurt terribly to give her up," she was saying.

Candace's eyes glimmered with unshed tears. "It did. But she had parents who wanted her."

Nick thanked her silently for that.

"But you're looking after her...is that a good idea, darling?"

"Her mom died. She needs me."

The simple words rang out in the room.

Nick faced the truth of them. Jennie needed Candace. So did Catherine. And so did he. Candace brought light and sunshine into all their lives.

He loved her.

The knowledge settled over him without any sense of shock. In his heart he'd known it all along. The special qualities she possessed—her loyalty, her patience, her generosity—made her easy to love.

But he'd been too afraid to face up to it and admit it. So he'd hidden behind emotions he'd called desire and passion, want and even lust...

But he loved her. And that admission freed him.

Catherine was watching him with gentle understanding in her eyes. "You will make sure Candace doesn't get hurt?"

"Mom!"

"Of course," Nick assured Catherine, ignoring Candace's horrified expression.

"You will take care of her if anything happens to me?"

For a split second, Nick glimpsed stark fear in the eyes so like Candace's. "I'll take care of her—and Jennie. But be assured nothing's going to happen to you. Not for a very long time."

"Thank you." The smile was sweet. Then Catherine looked down at the baby in the pram. "Look, Jennie's waking up—"

A cross gurgle of complaint made them all laugh.

"I think the time has come for that walk in the garden," said Nick.

They'd gotten back to the house—Candace didn't think it could ever be called a home—and she'd bathed and fed Jennie. Nick walked into the nursery as she was putting a sleepy Jennie into the crib.

Restlessness seized Candace. Excusing herself on a pretext, she'd gone downstairs to make herself a cup of chamomile tea and had just settled down in the upstairs sitting room with the hot drink and a magazine when Nick came out of the nursery.

"She's fast asleep." He sat down on the love seat opposite her and stretched back, folding his arms behind his head.

She shifted, aware of him watching her, conscious that night was falling and that the two of them were alone with so much unspoken between them.

"I liked your mother," he said at last.

Candace set the magazine down on a lamp table beside her cooling tea. "Thank you."

"But I will admit that I was surprised today," he added.

"Why?"

"Your mother had met Jennie before."

"Once. She had a fall and the staff called me to come and see her because she was badly shaken." She looked at him through her lashes. "It was the day you thought I'd kidnapped Jennie—and you almost filed a missing persons report."

"Ah, that day."

"I didn't want to call you for help...so I took her with me. I'm sorry, Nick, I should've told you."

"But then you would've had to explain about your mother."

Nodding, she agreed, "Exactly."

There was a long pause.

"You're going to marry me," he said with such a lack of fanfare that for a second Candace thought she'd misheard. But the leap of her heart, coupled with the determined resolve in his eyes, told her that she'd heard right.

"Nick..." She sat forward on the edge of the love seat, and searched for the right words.

This was exactly what she didn't need. She might love Nick until it hurt. But she wasn't marrying him, because she wasn't prepared to confine him in a trap he would come to resent.

Sex would never be enough...

If there was one thing Candace was certain of by now, it was that Nick had an overdeveloped sense of responsibility. He'd done everything in his power to save Henry and Bertha's garden center because they'd offered a young rebel a job; he'd been prepared to do everything in his power to help Jilly have the baby she desperately desired, even though he'd never loved her.

Now Candace couldn't rid herself of the memory of the expression on Nick's face when he'd all but promised her mother he would take care of her, too.

"You can't just say things like that," she said at last.

"I'm not just saying it...we're getting married."

"Why? So that you can take care of me?"

His eyes grew slumberous. "Among other things."

"I don't need you to take care of me!"

Candace wasn't going to allow him to distract her. Sex would never be enough. Not without love. And she wasn't about to fool herself that her love would be enough for both of them. Nick had been down that road once before, and it had brought nothing but unhappiness to everyone concerned.

Finally, she had no choice but to tell him the truth. "I have no intention of trapping you into a loveless marriage."

"You're not Jilly." Nick got to his feet and came around the glass coffee table to sit beside her. "You wouldn't be trapping me. I want to marry you. Trust me to know the difference."

He was too close.

Help!

If she said yes, all her problems would be solved. It would be so easy to throw herself into his arms and accept his proposal. She'd be able to live with her daughter; she'd have Nick at her side, her partner by day, her lover by night.

It was too tempting.

Fear that he'd talk her into a marriage she wanted so badly made her say, "You're only doing this because my mother said I needed to be taken care of."

He took her hand.

"Not true." Nick tugged her toward him. "I've already asked you to marry me once, so I certainly didn't need Catherine to come up with the idea."

She let him draw her closer, inch by breathtaking inch. "I hadn't forgotten. But last time you asked me for Jennie's sake…because you love your daughter."

"Clearly I've been doing it all wrong." Nick had maneuvered her right next to him, now he bent his head and kissed her. Her lips parted. But instead of deepening the kiss, he murmured, "What I should have been saying was that you need to marry me for *my* sake."

Candace was too scared to breathe. "What do you mean?"

Then he kissed her. This time it was deep and dark and sexy, none of the light butterfly wings that he'd been tormenting her with for the past few seconds.

When he'd finished, he raised his head and his eyes met hers. "Haven't you figured it out yet?"

His expression was gentle, and Candace could feel her throat tightening with emotion.

But she didn't dare hope...so she waited.

"I love you."

It felt like her birthday and Christmas had come at the same time. Candace closed her eyes and offered a prayer of thanks.

When she opened them again, he was still gazing down at her, his expression quizzical. "If you marry me, we would be a family. You, me and Jennie. Then there's Catherine and my sister and her family." He smiled at her. "That's more family than I ever dreamed of having."

"Oh, Nick. I love you, too."

"So you will marry me?" Uncertainty flickered in his eyes, and then it was gone. "I'm not going to allow you to say no again."

"I have no intention of saying no." Candace found herself smiling. "All those noes...it sounds ridiculous. So I'll just have to say yes."

He punched the air. "Yes!"

That made Candace burst out laughing, but she stopped abruptly as he kissed her again. Her arms crept up around his neck, and she leaned into him.

"Let's go to bed." Nick's heart was thudding against her chest.

She pulled away and gave him a demure smile. "Why not?"

Rising swiftly, Nick helped her to her feet. Then, arm in arm, they made their way to his suite.

This time they made love with slow intensity. Every touch counted. Every kiss brought a burst of new emotion. By the time Nick finally pulled her over him and they united, both of them were ready for the hot glow that waited. The heat built and built until the world spun.

Afterward, Nick pulled her into his arms, and pressed a kiss on her forehead. "That was fantastic."

"I'd have to agree," she said.

"One more thing." Nick shifted the pillows before leaning back, and arranging her into the crook of his arm. "There's a house that's come up for sale that I want to show you."

She turned her head, and looked up at him. "Oh, good, does this mean you're going to sell the marble mausoleum?" A weight she didn't know existed lifted.

"Mausoleum?" he sounded affronted.

"It's not a home," said Candace. "It's too cold."

"Cold? The heating system is spectacular."

"I don't mean the temperature—it doesn't have a heart."

Nick gave her a secret smile. "Wait until you see what I have to show you. I think you'll want to call it home."

"You might have to consider trading the Ferrari in for a family model," Candace told Nick as he throttled the Ferrari back and slowed down. They'd left Jennie with Alison and her sons while Nick took her to see the secret house he'd been so tantalizingly closemouthed about.

A Realtor's For Sale sign leaned drunkenly against a large pohutukawa tree.

"Is this it?" she asked.

Nick swung the sports car into an overgrown tree-lined driveway. "It's a jungle in here," he commented. "Let's see what state the house is in."

Puzzled, Candace turned her head to look at him, and her heart constricted at the sight of his beloved profile. He would forever have this effect on her. She must be the most fortunate woman in the world. She pulled her thoughts together and tried to remember what she'd wanted to ask. It came to her. "I thought you'd already seen the house."

"A long time ago. Seven years ago to be exact."

And then she knew. She placed her hand on his thigh, and dug her fingers in. "Nick!"

Laughing, he trod on the brake. The car came to a stop. "Careful where you grab me, woman."

"I don't care what state the house is in, this is where I want to live."

"Hang on, we need to take a look first. The house might no longer be a good investment."

Candace said a rude word. "I don't care if it's a bad investment, if you still love this place we're living here."

His eyes softened. "You'd make that great a sacrifice?"

"Nothing compared to the sacrifice I thought you were willing to make." Candace shot him a cheeky grin. "At least I know you love me—a house can be fixed."

"Okay, let's go see."

The Ferrari nosed through the trees, and Candace's breath caught as she glimpsed the grand old structure rising ahead. This was the house Mrs. Busby had told her he'd loved and sold when he'd married Jilly. "Oh, it's beautiful."

"It needs painting for starters."

"What's a little paint?" When Nick pulled up outside the homestead, she jumped out. "Hurry up…and don't forget the keys."

It took them half an hour to wander through the place, Nick showing her nooks and crannies she would not otherwise have found.

"It was built back in the 1880s when trading ships used to stop off not far away. The floors are made of kauri wood."

"I can see why you love it. It reeks of heritage. I think I've fallen in love." She slanted him a glance as she slipped her hand into his. "Again."

* * * * *

A sneaky peek at next month...

Desire

PASSIONATE AND DRAMATIC LOVE STORIES

2 stories in each book - only **£5.30!**

My wish list for next month's titles...

In stores from 20th January 2012:

- ☐ Caught in the Billionaire's Embrace – Elizabeth Bevarly
- & The Tycoon's Temporary Baby – Emily McKay
- ☐ The Proposal – Brenda Jackson
- & To Tempt a Sheikh – Olivia Gates
- ☐ Reunited...with Child – Katherine Garbera
- & One Month with the Magnate – Michelle Celmer
- ☐ A Lone Star Love Affair – Sara Orwig
- & Falling for the Princess – Sandra Hyatt

Available at WHSmith, Tesco, Asda, Eason, Amazon and Apple

Just can't wait?

Don't miss Pink Tuesday
One day. 10 hours. 10 deals.

PINK TUESDAY
IS COMING!

10 hours...10 unmissable deals!

This Valentine's Day we will be bringing
you fantastic offers across a range of
our titles—each hour, on the hour!

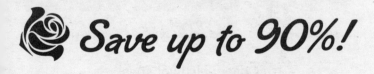

Pink Tuesday starts
9am Tuesday 14th February

Find out how to grab a Pink Tuesday deal—
register online at **www.millsandboon.co.uk**

*Visit us
Online*

0212/PM/MB362

Have Your Say

You've just finished your book.
So what did you think?

We'd love to hear your thoughts on our 'Have your say' online panel
www.millsandboon.co.uk/haveyoursay

- 🌹 Easy to use
- 🌹 Short questionnaire
- 🌹 Chance to win Mills & Boon® goodies